Praise for international bestseller Karin Slaughter

From magazines

'Another brilliantly chilling tale from Slaughter'
heat

'Beautifully paced, appropriately grisly, and terrifyingly plausible'
Time Out

'An explosive thriller with plenty of twists – this is
criminally spectacular!'
OK!

'Unsparing, exciting, genuinely alarming . . . excellent
handling of densely woven plot, rich in interactions,
well characterised and as subtle as it is shrewd'
Literary Review

'Bone-chilling . . . Expertly shifting back and forth in
both time and point of view, Slaughter builds the suspense
to a perfect crescendo'
Publishers Weekly

'Gripping, gruesome and definitely not for the faint-hearted'
Woman & Home

'It's not easy to transcend a model like Patricia Cornwell,
but Slaughter does so in a thriller whose breakneck plotting
and not-for-the-squeamish forensics provide grim
manifestations of a deeper evil her mystery trumpets
without ever quite containing'
Kirkus Reviews

Praise for international bestseller Karin Slaughter

From bestselling authors

'A great read . . . This is crime fiction at its finest'
MICHAEL CONNELLY

'Karin Slaughter is a fearless writer. She takes us to the deep, dark places other novelists don't dare to go . . . will cement her reputation as one of the boldest thriller writers working today'
TESS GERRITSEN

'With *Blindsighted*, Karin Slaughter left a great many mystery writers looking anxiously over their shoulders. With *Kisscut*, she leaves most of them behind'
JOHN CONNOLLY

'Slaughter has created a ferociously taut and terrifying story which is, at the same time, compassionate and real. I defy anyone to read it in more than three sittings'
DENISE MINA

'If you're looking for an unflinching suspense thriller with an emphasis on character, this is the one'
GEORGE P. PELECANOS

'A shockingly good novel'
LAURA LIPPMAN

'Taut, mean, nasty and bloody well written. She conveys a sense of time and place with clarity and definite menace – the finely tuned juxtaposition of sleepy Southern town and urgent, gut-wrenching terror'
STELLA DUFFY

Also by Karin Slaughter

Kisscut
A Faint Cold Fear
Indelible
Faithless
Triptych
Skin Privilege
Fractured
Martin Misunderstood
Genesis
Broken
Fallen

Like a Charm (Ed.)

KARIN SLAUGHTER

blindsighted

arrow books

Published by Arrow Books 2011

Copyright © Karin Slaughter 2001

First published in Great Britain in 2001 by
Century
Random House, 20 Vauxhall Bridge Road,
London SW1V 2SA

www.randomhouse.co.uk

Addresses for companies within The Random House Group Limited can be
found at: www.randomhouse.co.uk/offices.htm

The Random House Group Limited Reg. No. 954009

A CIP catalogue record for this book is available from the British Library

Penguin Random House is committed to a sustainable future for
our business, our readers and our planet. This book is made from
Forest Stewardship Council® certified paper.

MIX
Paper from
responsible sources
FSC® C018179

Printed and bound in Great Britain by Clays Ltd, Elcograf S.p.A.

Typeset by Deltatype Limited, Birkenhead, Merseyside

For my daddy, who taught me to love the South, and for Billie Bennett, who encouraged me to write about it

blindsighted

MONDAY

ONE

Sara Linton leaned back in her chair, mumbling a soft 'Yes, Mama' into the telephone. She wondered briefly if there would ever come a point in time when she would be too old to be taken over her mother's knee.

'Yes, Mama,' Sara repeated, tapping her pen on the desk. She felt heat coming off her cheeks, and an overwhelming sense of embarrassment took hold.

A soft knock came at the office door, followed by a tentative 'Dr. Linton?'

Sara suppressed her relief. 'I need to go,' she said to her mother, who shot off one last admonishment before hanging up the phone.

Nelly Morgan slid open the door, giving Sara a hard look. As office manager for the Heartsdale Children's Clinic, Nelly was the closest thing Sara had to a secretary. Nelly had been running the place for as long as Sara could remember, even as far back as when Sara was herself a patient here.

Nelly said, 'Your cheeks are on fire.'

'I just got yelled at by my mother.'

Nelly raised an eyebrow. 'I assume with good reason.'

'Well,' Sara said, hoping that would end it.

'The labs on Jimmy Powell came in,' Nelly said, still eyeing Sara. 'And the mail,' she added, dropping a stack of letters on top of the inbasket. The plastic bowed under the added weight.

Sara sighed as she read over the fax. On a good day, she diagnosed earaches and sore throats. Today, she would have to tell the parents of a twelve-year-old boy that he had acute myeloblastic leukemia.

'Not good,' Nelly guessed. She had worked at the clinic long enough to know how to read a lab report.

'No,' Sara agreed, rubbing her eyes. 'Not good at all.' She sat back in her chair, asking, 'The Powells are at Disney World, right?'

'For his birthday,' Nelly said. 'They should be back tonight.'

Sara felt a sadness come over her. She had never gotten used to delivering this kind of news.

Nelly offered, 'I can schedule them for first thing in the morning.'

'Thanks,' Sara answered, tucking the report into Jimmy Powell's chart. She glanced at the clock on the wall as she did this and let out an audible gasp. 'Is that right?' she asked, checking the time against her watch. 'I was supposed to meet Tessa at lunch fifteen minutes ago.'

Nelly checked her own watch. 'This late in the day? It's closer to suppertime.'

'It was the only time I could make it,' Sara said, gathering charts together. She bumped the in-box and papers fell onto the floor in a heap, cracking the plastic tray.

'Crap,' Sara hissed.

Nelly started to help, but Sara stopped her. Aside from the fact that Sara did not like other people cleaning up her messes, if Nelly somehow managed to get down on her knees, it was doubtful she would be able to get back up without considerable assistance.

4

'I've got it,' Sara told her, scooping up the whole pile and dropping it on her desk. 'Was there anything else?'

Nelly flashed a smile. 'Chief Tolliver's holding on line three.'

Sara sat back on her heels, a feeling of dread washing over her. She did double duty as the town's pediatrician and coroner. Jeffrey Tolliver, her ex-husband, was the chief of police. There were only two reasons for him to be calling Sara in the middle of the day, neither of them particularly pleasant.

Sara stood and picked up the phone, giving him the benefit of the doubt. 'Somebody better be dead.'

Jeffrey's voice was garbled, and she assumed he was using his cellular phone. 'Sorry to disappoint you,' he said, then, 'I've been on hold for ten minutes. What if this had been an emergency?'

Sara started shoving papers into her briefcase. It was an unwritten clinic policy to make Jeffrey jump through hoops of fire before he could speak to Sara on the telephone. She was actually surprised that Nelly remembered to tell Sara he was on the phone.

She glanced at the door, mumbling, 'I knew I should've just left.'

'What?' he asked, his voice echoing slightly on the cellular.

'I said you always send someone if it's an emergency,' she lied. 'Where are you?'

'At the college,' he answered. 'I'm waiting for the deputy dogs.'

He was using their term for the campus security at Grant Tech, the state university at the center of town.

She asked, 'What is it?'

'I just wanted to see how you were doing.'

'Fine,' she snapped, pulling the papers back out of her briefcase, wondering why she had put them there in the

5

first place. She flipped through some charts, shoving them into the side pocket.

She said, 'I'm late for lunch with Tess. What did you need?'

He seemed taken aback by her curt tone. 'You just looked distracted yesterday,' he said. 'In church.'

'I wasn't distracted,' she mumbled, flipping through the mail. She stopped at the sight of a postcard, her whole body going rigid. The front of the card showed a picture of Emory University in Atlanta, Sara's alma mater. Neatly typed on the back beside her address at the children's clinic were the words, 'Why hast thou forsaken me?'

'Sara?'

A cold sweat came over her. 'I need to go.'

'Sara, I –'

She hung up the phone before Jeffrey could finish his sentence, shoving three more charts into her briefcase along with the postcard. She slipped out the side door without anyone seeing her.

Sunlight beamed down on Sara as she walked into the street. There was a chill in the air that had not been there this morning, and the dark clouds promised rain later on tonight.

A red Thunderbird passed, a small arm hanging out the window.

'Hey, Dr. Linton,' a child called.

Sara waved, calling 'Hey' back as she crossed the street. Sara switched the briefcase from one hand to the other as she cut across the lawn in front of the college. She took a right onto the sidewalk, heading toward Main Street, and was at the diner in less than five minutes.

Tessa was sitting in a booth on the far wall of the

empty diner, eating a hamburger. She did not look pleased.

'Sorry I'm late,' Sara offered, walking toward her sister. She tried a smile, but Tessa did not respond in kind.

'You said two. It's nearly two-thirty.'

'I had paperwork,' Sara explained, tucking her briefcase into the booth. Tessa was a plumber, like their father. While clogged drains were no laughing matter, very seldom did Linton and Daughters get the kind of emergency phone calls that Sara did on a daily basis. Her family could not grasp what a busy day was like for Sara and were constantly irritated by her lateness.

'I called the morgue at two,' Tessa informed her, nibbling a french fry. 'You weren't there.'

Sara sat down with a groan, running her fingers through her hair. 'I dropped back by the clinic and Mama called and the time got away from me.' She stopped, saying what she always said. 'I'm sorry. I should have called.' When Tessa did not respond, Sara continued, 'You can keep being mad at me for the rest of lunch or you can drop it and I'll buy you a slice of chocolate cream pie.'

'Red velvet,' Tessa countered.

'Deal,' Sara returned, feeling an inordinate sense of relief. It was bad enough having her mother mad at her.

'Speaking of calls,' Tessa began, and Sara knew where she was going even before she asked the question. 'Hear from Jeffrey?'

Sara raised up, tucking her hand into her front pocket. She pulled out two five-dollar bills. 'He called before I left the clinic.'

Tessa barked a laugh that filled the restaurant. 'What did he say?'

'I cut him off before he could say anything,' Sara answered, handing her sister the money.

Tessa tucked the fives into the back pocket of her blue jeans. 'So, Mama called? She was pretty pissed at you.'

'I'm pretty pissed at me, too,' Sara said. After being divorced for two years, she still could not let go of her ex-husband. Sara vacillated between hating Jeffrey Tolliver and hating herself because of this. She wanted just one day to go by without thinking about him, without having him in her life. Yesterday, much like today, had not been that day.

Easter Sunday was important to her mother. While Sara was not particularly religious, putting on panty hose one Sunday out of the year was a small price to pay for Cathy Linton's happiness. Sara had not planned on Jeffrey being at church. She had caught him out of the corner of her eye just after the first hymn. He was sitting three rows behind and to the right of her, and they seemed to notice each other at the same time. Sara had forced herself to look away first.

Sitting there in church, staring at the preacher without hearing a word the man was saying, Sara had felt Jeffrey's gaze on the back of her neck. There was a heat from the intensity of his stare that caused a warm flush to come over her. Despite the fact that she was sitting in church with her mother on one side of her and Tessa and her father on the other, Sara had felt her body responding to the look Jeffrey had given her. There was something about this time of year that turned her into a completely different person.

She was actually fidgeting in her seat, thinking about Jeffrey touching her, the way his hands felt on her skin, when Cathy Linton jabbed her elbow into Sara's ribs. Her mother's expression said she knew exactly what was going through Sara's mind at that moment and did not like it one bit. Cathy had crossed her arms angrily, her posture indicating she was resigning herself to the fact that Sara would go to hell for thinking about sex at the Primitive Baptist on Easter Sunday.

There was a prayer, then another hymn. After what seemed like an appropriate amount of time, Sara glanced over her shoulder to find Jeffrey again, only to see him with his head bent down to his chest as he slept. This was the problem with Jeffrey Tolliver, the idea of him was much better than the reality.

Tessa tapped her fingers on the table for Sara's attention. 'Sara?'

Sara put her hand to her chest, conscious that her heart was pounding the same way it had yesterday morning in church. 'What?'

Tessa gave her a knowing look, but thankfully did not pursue it. 'What did Jeb say?'

'What do you mean?'

'I saw you talking to him after the service,' Tessa said. 'What did he say?'

Sara debated whether or not to lie. Finally, she answered, 'He asked me out for lunch today, but I told him I was seeing you.'

'You could've cancelled.'

Sara shrugged. 'We're going out Wednesday night.'

Tessa did everything but clap her hands together.

'God,' Sara groaned. 'What was I thinking?'

'Not about Jeffrey for a change,' Tessa answered. 'Right?'

Sara took the menu from behind the napkin holder, though she hardly needed to look at it. She or some member of her family had eaten at the Grant Filling Station at least once a week since Sara was three years old, and the only change to the menu in all that time had been when Pete Wayne, the owner, had added

9

peanut brittle to the dessert menu in honor of then president Jimmy Carter.

Tessa reached across the table, gently pushing down the menu. 'You okay?'

'It's that time of year again,' Sara said, rummaging around in her briefcase. She found the postcard and held it up.

Tessa did not take the card, so Sara read aloud from the back, 'Why hast thou forsaken me?' She put the card down on the table between them, waiting for Tessa's response.

'From the Bible?' Tessa asked, though surely she knew.

Sara looked out the window, trying to compose herself. Suddenly, she stood up from the table, saying, 'I need to go wash my hands.'

'Sara?'

She waved off Tessa's concern, walking to the back of the diner, trying to hold herself together until she reached the bathroom. The door to the women's room had stuck in the frame since the beginning of time, so Sara gave the handle a hard yank. Inside, the small black-and-white tiled bathroom was cool and almost comforting. She leaned back against the wall, hands to her face, trying to wipe out the last few hours of her day. Jimmy Powell's lab results still haunted her. Twelve years ago, while working her medical internship at Atlanta's Grady Hospital, Sara had grown familiar with, if not accustomed to, death. Grady had the best ER in the Southeast, and Sara had seen her share of difficult traumas, from a kid who had swallowed a pack of razor blades to a teenage girl who had been given a clothes hanger abortion. These were horrible cases, but not altogether unexpected in such a large city.

Cases like Jimmy Powell's coming through the children's clinic hit Sara with the force of a wrecking ball. This would be one of the rare cases when Sara's two jobs would converge. Jimmy Powell, who liked to watch college basketball and held one of the largest collections of Hot Wheels Sara had personally ever seen, would more than likely be dead within the next year.

Sara clipped her hair back into a loose ponytail as she waited for the sink to fill with cold water. She leaned over the sink, pausing at the sickly sweet smell coming from the basin. Pete had probably dumped vinegar down the drain to keep it from smelling sour. It was an old plumber's trick, but Sara hated the smell of vinegar.

She held her breath as she leaned back over, splashing her face with water, trying to wake up. A glance back at the mirror showed nothing had improved, but a wet spot from the water was just below the neckline of her shirt.

'Great,' Sara mumbled.

She dried her hands on her pants as she walked toward the stalls. After seeing the contents of the toilet, she moved to the next stall, the handicap stall, and opened the door.

'Oh,' Sara breathed, stepping back quickly, only stopping when the sink basin pressed against the back of her legs. She put her hands behind her, bracing herself on the counter. A metallic taste came to her mouth, and Sara forced herself to take in gulps of air so that she wouldn't pass out. She dropped her head down, closing her eyes, counting out a full five seconds before she looked up again.

Sibyl Adams, a professor at the college, sat on the toilet. Her head was tilted back against the tiled wall, her eyes closed. Her pants were pulled down around her ankles, legs splayed wide open. She had been stabbed in the abdomen. Blood filled the toilet between her legs, dripping onto the tiled floor.

Sara forced herself to move into the stall, crouching in front of the young woman. Sibyl's shirt was pulled up, and Sara could see a large vertical cut down her abdomen, bisecting her navel and stopping at the pubic bone. Another cut, much deeper, slashed horizontally under her breasts. This was the source of most of the blood, and it still dripped in a steady stream down the body. Sara put her hand to the wound, trying to halt the bleeding, but blood seeped between her fingers as if she were squeezing a sponge.

Sara wiped her hands on the front of her shirt, then tilted Sibyl's head forward. A small moan escaped from the woman's lips, but Sara could not tell if this was a simple release of air from a corpse or the plea of a living woman. 'Sibyl?' Sara whispered, barely able to manage the word. Fear sat in the back of her throat like a summer cold.

'Sibyl?' she repeated, using her thumb to press open Sibyl's eyelid. The woman's skin was hot to the touch, as if she had been out in the sun too long. A large bruise covered the right side of her face. Sara could see the impression of a fist under the eye. Bone moved under Sara's hand when she touched the bruise, clicking like two marbles rubbing together.

Sara's hand shook as she pressed her fingers against Sibyl's carotid artery. A fluttering rose against her fingertips, but Sara wasn't sure if it was the tremor in her own hands or life that she was feeling. Sara closed her eyes, concentrating, trying to separate the two sensations.

Without warning, the body jerked violently, pitching forward and slamming Sara onto the floor. Blood spread out around both of them, and Sara instinctively clawed to get out from under the convulsing woman. With her feet and hands she groped for some kind of purchase on the slick bathroom floor. Finally, Sara managed to slide out from underneath her. She turned Sibyl over, cradling her head, trying to help her through the convulsions. Suddenly, the jerking stopped. Sara put her ear to Sibyl's mouth, trying to make out breathing sounds. There were none.

Sitting up on her knees, Sara started compressions, trying to push life back into Sibyl's heart. Sara pinched the younger woman's nose, breathing air into her mouth. Sibyl's chest rose briefly, but nothing more. Sara tried again, gagging as blood coughed up into her mouth. She spat several times to clear her mouth, prepared to continue, but she could tell it was too late. Sibyl's eyes rolled back into her head and her breath hissed out with a low shudder. A trickle of urine came from between her legs.

She was dead.

TWO

Grant County was named for the good Grant, not Ulysses, but Lemuel Pratt Grant, a railroad builder who in the mid-1800s extended the Atlanta line deep into South Georgia and to the sea. It was on Grant's rails that trains carted cotton and other commodities all across Georgia. This rail line had put cities like Heartsdale, Madison, and Avondale on the map, and there were more than a few Georgia towns named after the man. At the start of the Civil War, Colonel Grant also developed a defense plan should Atlanta ever come under siege; unfortunately, he was better with railroad lines than front lines.

During the Depression, the citizens of Avondale, Heartsdale, and Madison decided to combine their police and fire departments as well as their schools. This helped economize on much needed services and helped persuade the railroads to keep the Grant line open; the county was much larger as a whole than as individual cities. In 1928, an army base was built in Madison, bringing families from all over the nation to tiny Grant County. A few years later, Avondale became a stopping point for railroad maintenance on the Atlanta-Savannah line. A few more years passed, and Grant College sprang up in Heartsdale. For nearly sixty years, the county prospered, until base closings, consolidations, and Reaganomics trickled down, crushing the economies of Madison and Avondale within three years of each other. But for the college, which in 1946 became a technological university specializing in agri-business, Heartsdale would have followed the same downward trend as its sister cities.

As it was, the college was the lifeblood of the city, and police chief Jeffrey Tolliver's first directive from Heartsdale's mayor was to keep the college happy if he wanted to keep his job. Jeffrey was doing just that, meeting with the campus police, discussing a plan of action for a recent outbreak of bicycle thefts, when his cell phone rang. At first, he did not recognize Sara's voice and thought the call was some kind of prank. In the eight years he had known her, Sara had never sounded so desperate. Her voice trembled as she said three words he had never expected to come from her mouth: I need you.

Jeffrey took a left outside the college gates and drove his Lincoln Town Car up Main Street toward the diner. Spring was very early this year, and already the dogwood trees lining the street were blooming, weaving a white curtain over the road. The women from the garden club had planted tulips in little planters lining the sidewalks, and a couple of kids from the high school were out sweeping the street instead of spending a week in afterschool detention. The owner of the dress shop had put a rack of clothes on the sidewalk, and the hardware store had set up an outdoor gazebo display complete with porch swing. Jeffrey knew the scene would be a sharp contrast to the one waiting for him at the diner.

He rolled down the window, letting fresh air into the stuffy car. His tie felt tight against his throat, and he found himself taking it off without thinking. In his mind, he kept playing Sara's phone call over and over in his head, trying to get more from it than the obvious facts. Sibyl Adams had been stabbed and killed at the diner.

Twenty years as a cop had not prepared Jeffrey for this kind of news. Half of his career had been spent in Birmingham, Alabama, where murder seldom surprised. Not a week went by when he wasn't called out to investigate at least one homicide, usually a product of Birmingham's extreme poverty: drug transactions gone wrong, domestic disputes where guns were too readily available. If Sara's call had come from Madison or even Avondale, Jeffrey would not have been surprised. Drugs and gang violence were fast becoming a problem in the outlying towns. Heartsdale was the jewel of the three cities. In ten years, the only suspicious fatality in Heartsdale involved an old woman who had a heart attack when she caught her grandson stealing her television.

'Chief?'

Jeffrey reached down, picking up his radio. 'Yeah?'

Marla Simms, the receptionist at the station house, said, 'I've taken care of that thing you wanted.'

'Good,' he answered, then, 'Radio silence until further notice.'

Marla was quiet, not asking the obvious question. Grant was still a small town, and even in the station house there were people who would talk. Jeffrey wanted to keep a lid on this as long as possible.

'Copy?' Jeffrey asked.

Finally, she answered, 'Yes, sir.'

Jeffrey tucked his cell phone into his coat pocket as he got out of the car. Frank Wallace, his senior detective on the squad, was already standing sentry outside the diner.

'Anyone in or out?' Jeffrey asked.

He shook his head. 'Brad's on the back door,' he said. 'The alarm's disconnected. I gotta think the perp used it for his in and out.'

Jeffrey looked back at the street. Betty Reynolds, the owner of the five-and-dime, was out sweeping the sidewalk, casting suspicious glances at the diner. People would start walking over soon, if not out of curiosity, then for supper.

Jeffrey turned back to Frank. 'Nobody saw anything?'

'Not a thing,' Frank confirmed. 'She walked here from her house. Pete says she comes here every Monday after the lunch rush.'

Jeffrey managed a tight nod, walking into the diner. The Grant Filling Station was central to Main Street. With its big red booths and speckled white countertops, chrome rails and straw dispensers, it looked much as it probably had the day Pete's dad opened for business. Even the solid white linoleum tiles on the floor, so worn in spots the black adhesive showed through, were original to the restaurant. Jeffrey had eaten lunch here almost every day for the last ten years. The diner had been a source of comfort, something familiar after working with the dregs of humanity. He looked around the open room, knowing it would never be the same for him again.

Tessa Linton sat at the counter, her head in her hands. Pete Wayne sat opposite her, staring blindly out the window. Except for the day the space shuttle *Challenger* had exploded, this was the first time Jeffrey had ever seen him not wearing his paper hat inside the diner. Still, Pete's hair was bunched up into a point at the top, making his face look longer than it already was.

'Tess?' Jeffrey asked, putting his hand on her shoulder. She leaned into him, crying. Jeffrey smoothed her hair, giving Pete a nod.

Pete Wayne was normally a cheerful man, but his expression today was one of absolute shock. He barely acknowledged Jeffrey, continuing to stare out the windows lining the front of the restaurant, his lips moving slightly, no sound coming out.

A few moments of silence passed, then Tessa sat up. She fumbled with the napkin dispenser until Jeffrey offered his handkerchief. He waited until she had blown her nose to ask, 'Where's Sara?'

Tessa folded the handkerchief. 'She's still in the bathroom. I don't know –' Tessa's voice caught. 'There was so much blood. She wouldn't let me go in.'

He nodded, stroking her hair back off her face. Sara was very protective of her little sister, and this instinct had transferred to Jeffrey during their marriage. Even after the divorce, Jeffrey still felt in some way that Tessa and the Lintons were his family.

'You okay?' he asked.

She nodded. 'Go ahead. She needs you.'

Jeffrey tried not to react to this. If not for the fact that Sara was the county coroner, he would never see her. It said a lot about their relationship that somebody had to die in order for her to be in the same room with him.

Walking to the back of the diner, Jeffrey felt a sense of dread overcome him. He knew that something violent had happened. He knew that Sibyl Adams had been killed. Other than that, he had no idea what to expect when he tugged open the door to the women's bathroom. What he saw literally took his breath away.

Sara sat in the middle of the room, Sibyl Adams's head in her lap. Blood was everywhere, covering the body, covering Sara, whose shirt and pants were soaked

18

down the front, as if someone had taken a hose and sprayed her. Bloody shoe and hand prints marked the floor as if a great struggle had occurred.

Jeffrey stood in the doorway, taking all this in, trying to catch his breath.

'Shut the door,' Sara whispered, her hand resting on Sibyl's forehead. He did as he was told, walking around the periphery of the room. His mouth opened, but nothing would come out. There were the obvious questions to ask, but part of Jeffrey did not want to know the answers. Part of him wanted to take Sara out of this room, put her in his car, and drive until neither one of them could remember the way this tiny bathroom looked and smelled. There was the taste of violence in the air, morbid and sticky in the back of his throat. He felt dirty just standing there.

'She looks like Lena,' he finally said, referring to Sibyl Adams's twin sister, a detective on his force. 'For just a second I thought . . .' He shook his head, unable to continue.

'Lena's hair is longer.'

'Yeah,' he said, unable to take his eyes off the victim. Jeffrey had seen a lot of horrible things in his time, but he had never personally known a victim of violent crime. Not that he knew Sibyl Adams well, but in a town as small as Heartsdale, everyone was your neighbor.

Sara cleared her throat. 'Did you tell Lena yet?'

Her question fell on him like an anvil. Two weeks into his job as police chief, he had hired Lena Adams out of the academy in Macon. Those early years, she was like Jeffrey, an outsider. Eight years later he had promoted her to detective. At thirty-three, she was the youngest detective and only woman on the senior squad. And now her sister had been murdered in their own backyard, little more than two hundred yards from the police station. He felt a sense of personal responsibility that was almost suffocating.

'Jeffrey?'

Jeffrey took a deep breath, letting it go slowly. 'She's taking some evidence to Macon,' he finally answered. 'I called the highway patrol and asked them to bring her back here.'

Sara was looking at him. Her eyes were rimmed with red, but she hadn't been crying. Jeffrey was glad of this one thing, because he had never seen Sara cry. He thought if he saw her crying that something in him would give.

'Did you know she was blind?' she asked.

Jeffrey leaned against the wall. He had somehow forgotten that detail.

'She didn't even see it coming,' Sara whispered. She bent her head down, looking at Sibyl. As usual, Jeffrey couldn't imagine what Sara was thinking. He decided to wait for her to talk. Obviously, she needed a few moments to collect her thoughts.

He tucked his hands into his pockets, taking in the space. There were two stalls with wooden doors across from a sink that was so old the fixtures for hot and cold were on opposite sides of the basin. Over this was a gold speckled mirror that was worn through at the edges. All told, the room was not more than twenty feet square, but the tiny black and white tiles on the floor made it seem even smaller. The dark blood pooling around the body didn't help matters. Claustrophobia had never been a problem for Jeffrey, but Sara's silence was like a fourth presence in the room. He looked up at the white ceiling, trying to get some distance.

Finally Sara spoke. Her voice was stronger, more confident. 'She was on the toilet when I found her.'

For lack of anything better to do, Jeffrey took out a small spiralbound notebook. He grabbed a pen from his breast pocket and started to write as Sara narrated the events that had led up to this moment. Her voice became monotone as she described Sibyl's death in clinical detail.

'Then I asked Tess to bring my cell phone.' Sara stopped speaking, and Jeffrey answered her question before she could get it out.

'She's okay,' he provided. 'I called Eddie on the way here.'

'Did you tell him what happened?'

Jeffrey tried to smile. Sara's father was not one of his biggest fans. 'I was lucky he didn't hang up on me.'

Sara did not so much as smile, but her eyes finally met Jeffrey's. There was a softness there that he had not seen in ages. 'I need to do the prelim, then we can take her to the morgue.'

Jeffrey tucked the pad into his coat pocket as Sara gently slid Sibyl's head to the floor. She sat back on her heels, wiping her hands on the back of her pants.

She said, 'I want to have her cleaned up before Lena sees her.'

Jeffrey nodded. 'She's at least two hours away. That should give us time to process the scene.' He indicated the stall door. The lock was busted off. 'Was the lock that way when you found her?'

'The lock's been that way since I was seven,' Sara said, pointing to her briefcase beside the door. 'Hand me a pair of gloves.'

Jeffrey opened the case, trying not to touch the blood on the handles. He pulled out a pair of latex gloves from an inside pocket. When he turned around, Sara was standing at the foot of the body. Her expression had changed, and despite the blood staining the front of her clothes, she seemed to be back in control.

Still, he had to ask, 'Are you sure you want to do this? We can call somebody from Atlanta.'

Sara shook her head as she slipped on the gloves with practiced efficiency. 'I don't want a stranger touching her.'

Jeffrey understood what she meant. This was a county matter. County people would take care of her.

Sara tucked her hands into her hips as she walked around the body. He knew she was trying to get some perspective on the scene, to take herself out of the equation. Jeffrey found himself studying his ex-wife as she did this. Sara was a tall woman, an inch shy of six feet, with deep green eyes and dark red hair. He was letting his mind wander, remembering how good it felt to be with her, when the sharp tone of her voice brought him back to reality.

'Jeffrey?' Sara snapped, giving him a hard look.

He stared back at her, aware that his mind had wandered off to what seemed like a safer place.

She held his gaze a second longer, then turned toward the stall. Jeffrey took another pair of gloves out of her briefcase and slipped them on as she talked.

'Like I said,' Sara began, 'she was on the toilet when I found her. We struggled to the floor, I rolled her on her back.'

Sara lifted Sibyl's hands, checking under her fingernails. 'There's nothing here. I imagine she was taken by surprise, didn't know what was going on until it was too late.'

'You think it was quick?'

'Not too quick. Whatever he did, it looks planned to me. The scene was very clean until I came along. She would've bled out on the toilet if I hadn't had to use the rest room.' Sara looked away. 'Or maybe not, if I hadn't been late getting here.'

Jeffrey tried to comfort her. 'You can't know that.'

She shrugged this off. 'There's some bruising on her wrists where her arms hit the handicap bars. Also' – she opened Sibyl's legs slightly – 'see here on her legs?'

Jeffrey followed her directions. The skin on the inside of both knees was scratched away. 'What's that?' he asked.

'The toilet seat,' she said. 'The bottom edge is pretty sharp. I imagine she squeezed her legs together as she struggled. You can see some of the skin caught on the seat.'

Jeffrey glanced at the toilet, then looked back at Sara. 'Think he pushed her back on the toilet, then stabbed her?'

Sara didn't answer him. Instead, she pointed to Sibyl's bare torso. 'The incision isn't deep until the middle of the cross,' she explained, pressing into the abdomen, opening up the wound so that he could see. 'I'd guess it was a double-edged blade. You can see the Y shape on either side of the puncture.' Sara easily slipped her index finger inside the wound. The skin made a sucking noise as she did this, and Jeffrey gritted his teeth, looking away. When he turned back, Sara was giving him a questioning look.

She asked, 'Are you okay?'

He nodded, afraid to open his mouth.

She moved her finger around inside the hole in Sibyl Adams's chest. Blood seeped out from the wound. 'I'd say it's at least a four-inch blade,' she concluded, keeping her eyes on him. 'Is this bothering you?'

He shook his head, even though the sound was making his stomach turn.

Sara slipped her finger out, continuing, 'It was a very

sharp blade. There's no hesitation around the incision, so like I said, he knew what he was doing when he started.'

'What was he doing?'

Her tone was very matter-of-fact. 'He was carving her stomach. His strokes were very assured, one down, one across, then a thrust into the upper torso. That was the death blow, I would imagine. Cause will probably be exsanguination.'

'She bled to death?'

Sara shrugged. 'Best guess right now, yeah. She bled to death. It probably took about ten minutes. The convulsions were from shock.'

Jeffrey couldn't suppress the shudder that came. He indicated the wound. 'It's a cross, right?'

Sara studied the cuts. 'I'd say so. I mean, it can't really be anything else, can it?'

'Do you think this is some kind of religious statement?'

'Who can tell with rape?' she said, stopping at the look on his face. 'What?'

'She was raped?' he said, glancing at Sibyl Adams, checking for obvious signs of damage. There was no bruising on her thighs or scrapes around the pelvic area. 'Did you find anything?'

Sara was quiet. Finally she said, 'No. I mean, I don't know.'

'What did you find?'

'Nothing.' She snapped off her gloves. 'Just what I told you. I can finish this back at the morgue.'

'I don't –'

'I'll call Carlos to come get her,' she said, referring to her assistant at the morgue. 'Meet me back there when you're finished here, okay?' When he didn't answer, she

24

said, 'I don't know about the rape, Jeff. Really. It was just a guess.'

Jeffrey didn't know what to say. One thing he knew about his ex-wife was she did not make guesses in the field. 'Sara?' he asked. Then, 'Are you all right?'

Sara gave a mirthless laugh. 'Am I all right?' she repeated. 'Jesus, Jeffrey, what a stupid question.' She walked over to the door, but didn't open it. When she spoke, her words came out clear and succinct. 'You have to find the person who did this,' she said.

'I know.'

'No, Jeffrey.' Sara turned around, giving him a piercing look. 'This is a ritualistic attack, not a one-off. Look at her body. Look at the way she was left here.' Sara paused, then continued, 'Whoever killed Sibyl Adams planned it out carefully. He knew where to find her. He followed her into the bathroom. This is a methodical murder by someone who wants to make a statement.'

He felt light-headed as he realized that what she was saying was the truth. He had seen this kind of murder before. He knew exactly what she was talking about. This was not the work of an amateur. Whoever had done this was probably working his way up to something much more dramatic at this very moment.

Sara still did not seem to think he understood. 'Do you think he'll stop with one?'

Jeffrey did not hesitate this time. 'No.'

THREE

Lena Adams frowned, flashing her headlights at the blue Honda Civic in front of her. The posted speed limit on this particular stretch of Georgia I-20 was sixty-five, but like most rural Georgians, Lena saw the signs as little more than a suggestion for tourists on their way to and from Florida. Case in point, the Civic's tags were from Ohio.

'Come on,' she groaned, checking her speedometer. She was boxed in by an eighteen-wheeler on her right and the Civic-driving Yankee in front, who was obviously determined to keep her just above the speed limit. For a second, Lena wished she had taken one of Grant County's cruisers. Not only was it a smoother ride than her Celica, there was the added pleasure of scaring the crap out of speeders.

Miraculously, the eighteen-wheeler slowed, letting the Civic pull over. Lena gave a cheery wave as the driver flipped her off. She hoped he had learned his lesson. Driving through the South was Darwinism at its best.

The Celica climbed up to eighty-five as she sped out of the Macon city limits. Lena took a cassette tape out of its case. Sibyl had made her some driving music for the trip back. Lena slid the tape into the radio and smiled when the music started, recognizing the opening to Joan Jett's 'Bad Reputation.' The song had been the sisters' anthem during high school, and they had spent many a night speeding through back roads, singing 'I don't give a damn about my bad reputation' at the top of their lungs. Thanks to an errant uncle, the girls were considered trash without the benefit of being particularly poor or, courtesy of their half Spanish mother, all that white.

Running evidence up to the GBI lab in Macon was little more than courier work in the big scheme of things, but Lena was glad to have the assignment. Jeffrey had said she could take the day to cool down, his euphemism for getting her temper under control. Frank Wallace and Lena were butting heads over the same problem that had haunted their partnership from the beginning. At fifty-eight years old, Frank wasn't thrilled to have women on the force, let alone one as a partner. He was constantly leaving Lena out of investigations, while she was constantly trying to force herself back in. Something would have to give. As Frank was two years from retirement, Lena knew she would not be the one to bend first.

In truth, Frank was not a bad guy. Other than suffering from the kind of crankiness brought on by old age, he seemed to make an effort. On a good day, she could understand that his overbearing attitude came from a deeper place than his ego. He was the kind of man who opened doors for women and took his hat off indoors. Frank was even a Mason at the local lodge. He was not the kind of guy who would let his female partner lead an interrogation, let alone take point on a house raid. On a bad day, Lena wanted to lock him in his garage with the car running.

Jeffrey was right about the trip cooling her down. Lena made good time to Macon, shaving a full thirty minutes off the drive courtesy of the Celica's V-6. She liked her boss, who was the exact opposite of Frank Wallace. Frank was all gut instinct, while Jeffrey was more cerebral. Jeffrey was also the kind of man who was comfortable around women and did not mind when they voiced their opinions. The fact that he had from day one groomed Lena for her job as detective was not lost on her. Jeffrey did not promote her to meet some county quota or make himself look better than his predecessor; this was Grant County, after all, a town that had not even been on the maps until fifty years ago. Jeffrey had given Lena the job because he respected her work and her mind. The fact that she was a woman had nothing to do with it.

'Shit,' Lena hissed, catching the flash of blue lights behind her. She slowed the car, pulling over as the Civic passed her. The Yankee beeped his horn and waved. It was Lena's turn to give the Ohioan a one-finger salute.

The Georgia highway patrolman took his time getting out of his car. Lena turned to her purse in the backseat, rummaging around for her badge. When she turned back around, she was surprised to see the cop standing just to the rear of her vehicle. His hand was on his weapon, and she kicked herself for not waiting for him to come to the car. He probably thought she was looking for a gun.

Lena dropped the badge in her lap and held her hands in the air, offering, 'Sorry,' out the open window.

The cop took a tentative step forward, his square jaw working as he came up to the car. He took off his sunglasses and gave her a close look.

'Listen,' she said, hands still raised. 'I'm on the job.'

He interrupted her. 'Are you Detective Salena Adams?'

She lowered her hands, giving the patrolman a questioning look. He was kind of short, but his upper body was muscled in that way short men have of overcompensating for what they lacked in height. His arms were so thick they wouldn't rest flat to his sides. The buttons of his uniform were pulled tight against his chest.

'It's Lena,' she offered, glancing at his name tag. 'Do I know you?'

'No, ma'am,' he returned, slipping on his sunglasses. 'We got a call from your chief. I'm supposed to escort you back to Grant County.'

'I'm sorry?' Lena asked, sure she hadn't heard correctly. 'My chief? Jeffrey Tolliver?'

He gave a curt nod. 'Yes, ma'am.' Before she could ask him any further questions, he was walking back to his car. Lena waited for the patrolman to pull back onto the road, then started off after him. He sped up quickly, edging up to ninety within minutes. They passed the blue Civic, but Lena did not pay much attention. All she could think was, What did I do this time?

FOUR

Though the Heartsdale Medical Center anchored the end of Main Street, it was not capable of looking nearly as important as its name would imply. Just two stories tall, the small hospital was equipped to do little more than handle whatever scrapes and upset stomachs couldn't wait for doctors' hours. There was a larger hospital about thirty minutes away in Augusta that handled the serious cases. If not for the county morgue being housed in the basement, the medical center would have been torn down to make way for student housing a long time ago.

Like the rest of the town, the hospital had been built during the town's upswing in the 1930s. The main floors had been renovated since then, but the morgue was obviously not important to the hospital board. The walls were lined with light blue tile that was so old it was coming back into style. The floors were a mixed check pattern of green and tan linoleum. The ceiling overhead had seen its share of water damage, but most of it had been patched. The equipment was dated but functional.

Sara's office was in the back, separated from the rest of the morgue by a large glass window. She sat behind her desk, looking out the window, trying to collect her thoughts. She concentrated on the white noise of the morgue: the air compressor on the freezer, the swish-

swish of the water hose as Carlos washed down the floor. Since they were below ground, the walls of the morgue absorbed rather than deflected the sounds, and Sara felt oddly comforted by the familiar hums and swishes. The shrill ring of the phone interrupted the silence.

'Sara Linton,' she said, expecting Jeffrey. Instead, it was her father.

'Hey, baby.'

Sara smiled, feeling a lightness overcome her at the sound of Eddie Linton's voice. 'Hey, Daddy.'

'I've got a joke for you.'

'Yeah?' She tried to keep her tone light, knowing humor was her father's way of dealing with stress. 'What's that?'

'A pediatrician, a lawyer, and a priest were on the *Titanic* when it started to go down,' he began. 'The pediatrician says, 'Save the children.' The lawyer says, 'Fuck the children!' And the priest says, 'Do we have time?''

Sara laughed, more for her father's benefit than anything else. He was quiet, waiting for her to talk. She asked, 'How's Tessie?'

'Taking a nap,' he reported. 'How about you?'

'Oh, I'm okay.' Sara started drawing circles on her desk calendar. She wasn't normally a doodler, but she needed something to do with her hands. Part of her wanted to check her briefcase, to see if Tessa had thought to put the postcard in there. Part of her did not want to know where it was.

Eddie interrupted her thoughts. 'Mom says you have to come to breakfast tomorrow.'

'Yeah?' Sara asked, drawing squares over the circles.

His voice took on a singsong quality. 'Waffles and grits and toast and bacon.'

'Hey,' Jeffrey said.

Sara jerked her head up, dropping the pen. 'You scared me,' she said, then, to her father, 'Daddy, Jeffrey's here –'

Eddie Linton made a series of unintelligible noises. In his opinion, there was nothing wrong with Jeffrey Tolliver that a solid brick to the head would not fix.

'All right,' Sara said into the phone, giving Jeffrey a tight smile. He was looking at the etched sign on the glass, where her father had slapped a piece of masking tape over the last name TOLLIVER and written in LINTON with a black marker. Since Jeffrey had cheated on Sara with the only sign maker in town, it was doubtful that the lettering would be more professionally fixed anytime soon.

'Daddy,' Sara interrupted, 'I'll see you in the morning.' She hung up the phone before he could get another word in.

Jeffrey asked, 'Let me guess, he sends his love.'

Sara ignored the question, not wanting to get into a personal conversation with Jeffrey. This was how he sucked her back in, making her think that he was a normal person capable of being honest and supportive when in actuality the minute Jeffrey felt like he was back in Sara's good graces he'd probably run for cover. Or, under the covers, to be more exact.

He said, 'How's Tessa doing?'

'Fine,' Sara said, taking her glasses out of their case. She slid them on, asking, 'Where's Lena?'

He glanced at the clock on the wall. 'About an hour away. Frank's going to page me when she's ten minutes out.'

Sara stood, adjusting the waist of her scrubs. She had showered in the hospital lounge, storing her bloodied clothes in an evidence bag in case they were needed for trial.

She asked, 'Have you thought about what you're going to tell her?'

He shook his head no. 'I'm hoping we can get something concrete before I talk to her. Lena's a cop. She's going to want answers.'

Sara leaned over the desk, knocking on the glass. Carlos looked up. 'You can go now,' she said. Then, explaining to Jeffrey, 'He's going to run blood and urine up to the crime lab. They're going to put it through tonight.'

'Good.'

Sara sat back in her chair. 'Did you get anything from the bathroom?'

'We found her cane and glasses behind the toilet. They were wiped clean.'

'What about the stall door?'

'Nothing,' he said. 'I mean, not nothing, but every woman in town's been in and out of that place. Last count Matt had over fifty different prints.' He took some Polaroids out of his pocket and tossed them onto the desk. There were close-ups of the body lying on the floor alongside pictures of Sara's bloody shoe and hand prints.

Sara picked up one of these, saying, 'I guess it didn't help matters that I contaminated the scene.'

'It's not like you had a choice.'

She kept her thoughts to herself, putting the pictures in logical sequence.

He repeated her earlier evaluation. 'Whoever did this knew what he was doing. He knew she would go to the restaurant alone. He knew she couldn't see. He knew the place would be deserted that time of day.'

'You think he was waiting for her?'

Jeffrey gave a shrug. 'Seems that way. He probably came in and out the back door. Pete had disconnected the alarm so they could leave it open to air the place out.'

'Yeah,' she said, remembering the back door to the diner was propped open more times than not.

'So, we're looking for someone who knew her activities, right? Somebody who was familiar with the layout of the diner.'

Sara did not want to answer this question, which implied that the killer was someone living in Grant, someone who knew the people and places the way only a resident could. Instead, she stood and walked back to the metal filing cabinet on the other side of her desk. She took out a fresh lab coat and slipped it on, saying, 'I've already taken X rays and checked her clothing. Other than that, she's ready.'

Jeffrey turned, staring out at the table in the center of the morgue. Sara looked, too, thinking that Sibyl Adams was a lot smaller in death than she seemed in life. Even Sara couldn't get used to the way death reduced people.

Jeffrey asked, 'Did you know her well?'

Sara mulled over his question. Finally she said, 'I guess. We both did career day at the middle school last year. Then, you know, I ran into her at the library sometimes.'

'The library?' Jeffrey asked. 'I thought she was blind.'

'They have books on tape there, I guess.' She stopped in front of him, crossing her arms. 'Listen, I have to tell you this. Lena and I kind of had a fight a few weeks back.'

Obviously, he was surprised. Sara was surprised, too. There were not a lot of people in town she did not get along with. But Lena Adams was certainly one of them.

Sara explained, 'She called Nick Shelton at the GBI asking for a tox report on a case.'

Jeffrey shook his head side to side, not understanding. 'Why?'

Sara shrugged. She still didn't know why Lena had tried to go over her head, especially considering it was well known that Sara had a very good working relationship with Nick Shelton, the Georgia Bureau of Investigation's field agent for Grant County.

'And?' Jeffrey prompted.

'I don't know what Lena thought she could accomplish by calling Nick directly. We had it out. No blood was shed, but I wouldn't say we parted on friendly terms.'

Jeffrey shrugged, as if to say, What can you do? Lena had made a career out of ticking people off. Back when Sara and Jeffrey were married, Jeffrey had often voiced his concern over Lena's impetuous behavior.

'If she was' – he stopped, then – 'if she was raped, Sara. I don't know.'

'Let's get started,' Sara answered quickly, walking past him into the morgue. She stood in front of the supply cabinet, looking for a surgical gown. She paused, her hands on the doors as she played back their conversation in her mind, wondering how it had turned from a forensic evaluation into a discussion about Jeffrey's potential outrage had Sibyl Adams not just been killed but raped as well.

'Sara?' he asked. 'What's wrong?'

Sara felt her anger spark at his stupid question. 'What's wrong?' She found the gown and slammed the doors shut. The metal frame rattled from the force. Sara turned, ripping the sterile pack open. 'What's wrong is I'm tired of you asking me what's wrong when it's pretty damn obvious what's wrong.' She paused, snapping out the gown. 'Think about it, Jeffrey. A woman literally died in my arms today. Not just a stranger, someone I knew. I should be at home right now taking a long shower or walking the dogs and instead I've got to go in there and cut her up, worse than she already is, so I can tell you whether or not you need to start pulling in all the perverts in town.'

Her hands shook with anger as she tried to get into the gown. The sleeve was just out of her reach, and she was turning to get a better angle when Jeffrey moved to help her.

Her tone was nasty when she snapped, 'I've got it.'

He held his hands up, palms toward her as if in surrender. 'Sorry.'

Sara fumbled with the ties on the gown, ending up knotting the strings together. 'Shit,' she hissed, trying to work them back out.

Jeffrey offered, 'I could get Brad to go walk the dogs.'

Sara dropped her hands, giving up. 'That's not the point, Jeffrey.'

'I know it's not,' he returned, approaching her the way he might a rabid dog. He took the strings and she looked down, watching him work out the knot. Sara let her gaze travel to the top of his head, noting a few grey strands in with the black. She wanted to will into him the ability to comfort her instead of trying to make a joke of everything. She wanted for him to magically develop the capacity for empathy. After ten years, she should have known better.

He loosened the knot with a smile, as if with this simple act he had just made everything better. He said, 'There.'

Sara took over, tying the strings together in a bow.

He put his hand under her chin. 'You're okay,' he said, not a question this time.

'Yeah,' she agreed, stepping away. 'I'm okay.' She pulled out a pair of latex gloves, turning to the task at hand. 'Let's just get the prelim over with before Lena gets back.'

Sara walked over to the porcelain autopsy table bolted to the floor in the middle of the room. Curved with high sides, the white table hugged Sibyl's small body. Carlos had placed her head on a black rubber block and draped a white sheet over her. Except for the black bruise over her eye, she could be sleeping.

'Lord,' Sara muttered as she folded back the sheet. Taking the body out of the kill zone had intensified the damage. Under the bright lights of the morgue, every aspect of the wound stood out. The incisions were long and sharp across the abdomen, forming an almost perfect cross. The skin puckered in places, drawing her attention away from the deep gouge at the intersection of the cross. Postmortem, wounds took on a dark, almost black, appearance. The rifts in Sibyl Adams's skin gaped open like tiny wet mouths.

'She didn't have a lot of body fat,' Sara explained. She indicated the belly, where the incision opened wider just above the navel. The cut there was deeper, and the skin was pulled apart like a tight shirt that had popped a button. 'There's fecal matter in the lower abdomen where the intestines were breached by the blade. I don't know if it was this deep on purpose or if the depth was accidental. It looks stretched.'

She indicated the edges of the wound. 'You can see the striation here at the tip of the wound. Maybe he moved the knife around. Twisted it. Also . . . ' She paused, figuring things out as she went along. 'There are traces of excrement on her hands as well as the bars in the stall, so I have to think she was cut, she put her hands to her belly, then she wrapped her hands around the bars for some reason.'

She looked up at Jeffrey to see how he was holding up. He seemed rooted to the floor, transfixed by Sibyl's body. Sara knew from her own experience that the mind could play tricks, smoothing out the sharp lines of violence. Even for Sara, seeing Sibyl again was perhaps worse than seeing her the first time.

Sara put her hands on the body, surprised that it was still warm. The temperature in the morgue was always low, even during the summer, because the room was underground. Sibyl should have been a lot cooler by now.

'Sara?' Jeffrey asked.

'Nothing,' she answered, not prepared to make guesses. She pressed around the wound in the center of the cross. 'It was a double-edged knife,' she began. 'Which helps you out some. Most stabbings are serrated hunting knives, right?'

'Yeah.'

She pointed to a tan-looking mark around the center wound. Cleaning the body, Sara had been able to see a lot more than her initial exam in the bathroom had revealed. 'This is from the cross guard, so he put it all the way in. I imagine I'll see some chipping on the spine when I open her up. I felt some irregularities when I put my finger in. There's probably some chipped bone still in there.'

Jeffrey nodded for her to continue.

'If we're lucky, we'll get some kind of impression from the blade. If not that, then maybe something from the cross guard bruising. I can remove and fix the skin after Lena sees her.'

She pointed to the puncture wound at the center of

the cross. 'This was a hard stab, so I would imagine the killer did it from a superior position. See the way the wound is angled at about a forty-five?' She studied the incision, trying to make sense of it. 'I would almost say that the belly stab is different from the chest wound. It doesn't make sense.'

'Why is that?'

'The punctures have a different pattern.'

'Like how?'

'I can't tell,' she answered truthfully. She let this drop for the moment, concentrating on the stab wound at the center of the cross. 'So he's probably standing in front of her, legs bent at the knee, and he takes the knife back to his side' – she demonstrated, pulling her hand back – 'then rams it into her chest.'

'He uses two knives to do this?'

'I can't tell,' Sara admitted, going back to the belly wound. Something wasn't adding up.

Jeffrey scratched his chin, looking at the chest wound. He asked, 'Why not stab her in the heart?'

'Well, for one, the heart isn't at the center of the chest, which is where you would have to stab in order to hit the center of the cross. So, there's an aesthetic quality to his choice. For another, there's rib and cartilage surrounding the heart. He would have to stab her repeatedly to break through. That would mess up the appearance of the cross, right?' Sara paused. 'There would be a great amount of blood if the heart was punctured. It would come out at a considerable velocity. Maybe he wanted to avoid that.' She shrugged, looking up at Jeffrey. 'I suppose he could have gone under the rib cage and up if he wanted to get to the heart, but that would have been a crapshoot at best.'

'You're saying the attacker had some kind of medical knowledge?'

Sara asked, 'Do you know where the heart is?'

He put his hand over the left side of his chest.

'Right. You also know your ribs don't meet all the way in the center.'

He tapped his hand against the center of his chest. 'What's this?'

'Sternum,' she answered. 'The cut's lower, though. It's in the xiphoid process. I can't say if that's blind luck or calculated.'

'Meaning?'

'Meaning, if you're hell-bent on carving a cross on somebody's abdomen and putting a knife through the center, this is the best place to stab somebody if you want the knife to go through. There are three parts to the sternum,' she said, using her own chest to illustrate. 'The manubrium, which is the upper part, the body, which is the main part, then the xiphoid process. Of those three, the xiphoid is the softest. Especially in someone this age. She's what, early thirties?'

'Thirty-three.'

'Tessa's age,' Sara mumbled, and for a second she flashed on her sister. She shook this from her mind, focusing back on the body. 'The xiphoid process calcifies as you age. The cartilage gets harder. So, if I was going to stab someone in the chest, this is where I'd make my X.'

'Maybe he didn't want to cut her breasts?'

Sara considered this. 'This seems more personal than that.' She tried to find the words. 'I don't know, I would think that he would want to cut her breasts. Know what I mean?'

'Especially if it's sexually motivated,' he offered. 'I mean, rape is generally about power, right? It's about being angry at women, wanting to control them. Why would he cut her there instead of in a place that makes her a woman?'

'Rape is also about penetration,' Sara countered. 'This certainly qualifies. It's a strong cut, nearly clean through. I don't think –' She stopped, staring at the wound, a new idea forming in her mind. 'Jesus,' she mumbled.

'What is it?' Jeffrey asked.

She could not speak for a few seconds. Her throat felt as if it was closing in on her.

'Sara?'

A beeping filled the morgue. Jeffrey checked his pager. 'That can't be Lena,' he said. 'Mind if I use the phone?'

'Sure.' Sara crossed her arms, feeling the need to protect herself from her own thoughts. She waited until Jeffrey was sitting behind her desk before she continued the examination.

Sara reached above her head, turning the light so that she could get a better look at the pelvic area. Adjusting the metal speculum, she mumbled a prayer to herself, to God, to anybody who would listen, to no avail. By the time Jeffrey returned, she was sure.

'Well?' he asked.

Sara's hands shook as she peeled off her gloves. 'She was sexually assaulted early on in the attack.' She paused, dropping the soiled gloves on the table, imagining in her mind Sibyl Adams sitting on the toilet, putting her hands to the open wound in her abdomen, then bracing herself against the bars on either side of the stall, completely blind to what was happening to her.

He waited a few beats before prompting, 'And?'

Sara put her hands on the edges of the table. 'There was fecal matter in her vagina.'

Jeffrey did not seem to follow. 'She was sodomized first?'

'There's no sign of anal penetration.'

'But you found fecal matter,' he said, still not getting it.

'Deep in her vagina,' Sara said, not wanting to spell it out, knowing she would have to. She heard an uncharacteristic waver in her voice when she said, 'The incision in her belly was deep on purpose, Jeffrey.' She stopped, searching for words to describe the horror she had found.

'He raped her,' Jeffrey said, not a question. 'There was vaginal penetration.'

'Yes,' Sara answered, still searching for a way to clarify. Finally she said, 'There was vaginal penetration after he raped the wound.'

FIVE

Night had come quickly, the temperature dropping along with the sun. Jeffrey was crossing the street just as Lena pulled into the parking lot of the station house. She was out of her car before he reached her.

'What's going on?' she demanded, but he could tell she already knew something was wrong. 'Is it my uncle?' she asked, rubbing her arms to fight the chill. She was wearing a thin T-shirt and jeans, not her usual work attire, but the trip to Macon was a casual one.

Jeffrey took off his jacket, giving it to her. The weight of what Sara had told him sat on his chest like a heavy stone. If Jeffrey had anything to do with it, Lena would never know exactly what had happened to Sibyl Adams. She would never know what that animal had done to her sister.

'Let's go inside,' he said, putting his hand under her elbow.

'I don't want to go inside,' she answered, jerking her arm away. His coat fell between them.

Jeffrey leaned down, retrieving his jacket. When he looked up, Lena had her hands on her hips. As long as he had known her, Lena Adams had sported a chip on her shoulder the size of Everest. Somewhere in the back of his mind, Jeffrey had been thinking she would need a shoulder to cry on or words of comfort. He could not accept that there wasn't a soft side to Lena, maybe because she was a woman. Maybe because just a few minutes earlier he had seen her sister lying ripped apart in the morgue. He should have remembered that Lena Adams was harder than that. He should have anticipated the anger.

Jeffrey slipped his jacket back on. 'I don't want to do this outside.'

'What are you going to say?' she demanded. 'You're going to say he was driving, right? And that he swerved off the road, right?' She ticked off the progression on her fingertips, giving him nearly verbatim the police handbook procedure for informing someone that a family member had died. Build up to it, the manual said. Don't spring it on them suddenly. Let the family member/loved one get used to the idea.

Lena counted it off, her voice getting louder with each sentence. 'Was he hit by another car? Huh? And they took him to the hospital? And they tried to save him, but they couldn't. They did everything they could, huh?'

'Lena –'

She walked back toward her car, then turned around. 'Where's my sister? Did you already tell her?'

Jeffrey took a breath, releasing it slowly.

'Look at that,' Lena hissed, turning toward the station house, waving her hand in the air. Marla Simms was looking out one of the front windows. 'Come on out, Marla,' Lena yelled.

'Come on,' Jeffrey said, trying to stop her.

She stepped away from him. 'Where is my sister?'

His mouth did not want to move. Through sheer force of will, he managed, 'She was in the diner.'

Lena turned, walking down the street toward the diner.

Jeffrey continued, 'She went to the bathroom.'

Lena stopped in her tracks.

'There was someone in there. He stabbed her in the chest.' Jeffrey waited for her to turn around, but she still did not. Lena's shoulders were straight, her posture a study in stillness. He continued, 'Dr. Linton was having lunch with her sister. She went into the bathroom and found her.'

Lena turned slowly, her lips slightly parted.

'Sara tried to save her.'

Lena looked him straight in the eye. He forced himself not to look away.

'She's dead.'

The words hung in the air like moths around a streetlamp.

Lena's hand went to her mouth. She walked in an almost drunken half circle, then turned back to Jeffrey. Her eyes bored into his, a question there. Was this some kind of joke? Was he capable of being this cruel?

'She's dead,' he repeated.

Her breathing came in short staccatos. He could almost see her mind kicking into action as she absorbed the information. Lena walked toward the station house, then stopped. She turned to Jeffrey, mouth open, but said nothing. Without warning, she took off toward the diner.

'Lena!' Jeffrey called, running after her. She was fast for her size, and his dress shoes were no match for her sneakers pounding down the pavement. He tucked his arms in, pumping, pushing himself to catch her before she reached the diner.

He called her name again as she neared the diner, but she blew past it, taking a right turn toward the medical center.

'No,' Jeffrey groaned, pushing himself harder. She was going to the morgue. He called her name again, but

45

Lena did not look back as she crossed onto the hospital's drive. She slammed her body into the sliding doors, popping them out of their frames, sounding the emergency alarm.

Jeffrey was seconds behind her. He rounded the corner to the stairs, hearing Lena's tennis shoes slapping against the rubber treads. A boom echoed up the narrow stairwell as she opened the door to the morgue.

Jeffrey stopped on the fourth step from the bottom. He heard Sara's surprised 'Lena' followed by a pained groan.

He forced himself to take the last few steps down, made himself walk into the morgue.

Lena was bent over her sister, holding her hand. Sara had obviously tried to cover the worst of the damage with the sheet, but most of Sibyl's upper torso still showed.

Lena stood beside her sister, her breath coming in short pants, her whole body shaking as if from some bone-chilling cold.

Sara cut Jeffrey in two with a look. All he could do was hold his hands out. He had tried to stop her.

'What time was it?' Lena asked through chattering teeth. 'What time did she die?'

'Around two-thirty,' Sara answered. Blood was on her gloves, and she tucked them under her arms as if to hide it.

'She feels so warm.'

'I know.'

Lena lowered her voice. 'I was in Macon, Sibby,' she told her sister, stroking back her hair. Jeffrey was glad to see Sara had taken the time to comb some of the blood out.

Silence filled the morgue. It was eerie seeing Lena standing beside the dead woman. Sibyl was her identical twin, alike in every way. They were both petite women, about five four and little more than one hundred twenty pounds. Their skin had the same olive tone. Lena's dark brown hair was longer than her sister's, Sibyl's curlier. The sisters' faces were a study in contrast, one flat and emotionless, the other filled with grief.

Sara turned slightly to the side, removing her gloves. She suggested, 'Let's go upstairs, okay?'

'You were there,' Lena said, her voice low. 'What did you do to help her?'

Sara looked down at her hands. 'I did what I could do.'

Lena stroked the side of her sister's face, her tone a little sharper when she asked, 'What exactly was it that you could do?'

Jeffrey stepped forward, but Sara gave him a sharp look to stop him, as if to say his time to help the situation had come and gone about ten minutes ago.

'It was very fast,' Sara told Lena, obviously with some reluctance. 'She started to go into convulsions.'

Lena laid Sibyl's hand down on the table. She pulled the sheet up, tucking it under her sister's chin as she spoke. 'You're a pediatrician, right? What exactly did you do to help my sister?' She locked eyes with Sara. 'Why didn't you call a real doctor?'

Sara gave a short incredulous laugh. She inhaled deeply before answering, 'Lena, I think you should let Jeffrey take you home now.'

'I don't want to go home,' Lena answered, her tone calm, almost conversational. 'Did you call an ambulance? Did you call your boyfriend?' A tilt of her head indicated Jeffrey.

Sara's hands went behind her back. She seemed to be physically restraining herself. 'We're not going to have this conversation now. You're too upset.'

'I'm too upset,' Lena repeated, clenching her hands. 'You think I'm upset?' she said, her voice louder this time. 'You think I'm too fucking upset to talk to you about why you fucking couldn't help my sister?'

As quickly as she had taken off in the parking lot, Lena was in Sara's face.

'You're a doctor!' Lena screamed. 'How can she die with a fucking doctor in the room?'

Sara did not answer. She looked off to the side.

'You can't even look at me,' Lena said. 'Can you?'

Sara's focus did not change.

'You let my sister die and you can't even fucking look at me.'

'Lena,' Jeffrey said, finally stepping in. He put his hand on her arm, trying to get her to back off.

'Let me go,' she screamed, punching him with her fists. She started to pummel his chest, but he grabbed her hands, holding them tight. She still fought him, screaming, spitting, kicking. Holding her hands was like grabbing a live wire. He kept a firm hand, taking the abuse, letting her get it all out until she crumpled into a ball on the floor. Jeffrey sat beside her, holding her while she sobbed. When he thought to look, Sara was nowhere to be found.

Jeffrey pulled a handkerchief out of his desk with one hand, holding the phone to his ear with the other. He put the cloth to his mouth, dabbing at the blood as a metallic version of Sara's voice asked him to wait for the beep.

'Hey,' he said, taking away the cloth. 'You there?' He waited a few seconds. 'I want to make sure you're okay, Sara.' More seconds passed. 'If you don't pick up, I'm going to come over.' He expected to get a response to this, but nothing came. He heard the machine run out and hung up the phone.

Frank knocked on his office door. 'The kid's in the bathroom,' he said, meaning Lena. Jeffrey knew Lena hated to be called a kid, but this was the only way Frank Wallace could think to show his partner that he cared.

Frank said, 'She's got a mean right, huh?'

'Yeah.' Jeffrey folded the handkerchief for a fresh corner. 'She know I'm waiting for her?'

Frank offered, 'I'll make sure she doesn't make any detours.'

'Good,' Jeffrey said, then, 'Thanks.'

He saw Lena walking through the squad room, her chin tilted up defiantly. When she got to his office, she took her time shutting the door, then slumped into one of the two chairs across from him. She had the look of a teenager who had been called into the principal's office.

'I'm sorry I hit you,' she mumbled.

'Yeah,' Jeffrey returned, holding up the handkerchief. 'I got worse at the Auburn-Alabama game.' She did not respond, so he added, 'And I was in the stands at the time.'

Lena propped her elbow on the armrest and leaned her head into her hand. 'What leads do you have?' she asked. 'Any suspects?'

'We're running the computer right now,' he said. 'We should have a list in the morning.'

She put her hand over her eyes. He folded the handkerchief, waiting for her to speak.

She whispered, 'She was raped?'

'Yes.'

'How badly?'

'I don't know.'

'She was cut,' Lena said. 'This is some Jesus freak?'

49

His answer was the tnuth. 'I don't know.'

'You don't seem to know a hell of a lot,' she finally said.

'You're right,' he agreed. 'I need to ask you some questions.'

Lena did not look up, but he saw her give a slight nod.

'Was she seeing anybody?'

Finally she looked up. 'No.'

'Any old boyfriends?'

Something flickered in her eyes, and her answer didn't come as quickly as the last. 'No.'

'You sure about that?'

'Yes, I'm sure.'

'Not even somebody from a few years back? Sibyl moved here, what, about six years ago?'

'That's right,' Lena said, her voice hostile again. 'She took a job at the college so she could be near me.'

'Was she living with someone?'

'What does that mean?'

Jeffrey dropped the handkerchief. 'It means what it means, Lena. She was blind. I'm assuming she needed help getting around. Was she living with someone?'

Lena pursed her lips, as if debating whether or not to answer. 'She was sharing a house on Cooper with Nan Thomas.'

'The librarian?' This would explain why Sara had seen her at the library.

Lena mumbled, 'I guess I have to tell Nan about this, too.'

Jeffrey assumed Nan Thomas already knew. Secrets did not stay kept for very long in Grant. Still, he offered, 'I can tell her.'

'No,' she said, giving him a scathing look. 'I think it would be better coming from someone who knows her.'

The implication was clear to Jeffrey, but he chose not to confront her. Lena was looking for another fight, that much was obvious. 'I'm sure she's probably already heard something. She won't know the details.'

'She won't know about the rape, you mean?' Lena's leg bobbed up and down in a nervous twitch. 'I guess I shouldn't tell her about the cross?'

'Probably not,' he answered. 'We need to keep some of the details close in case somebody confesses.'

'I'd like to handle a false confession,' Lena mumbled, her leg still shaking.

'You shouldn't be alone tonight,' he told her. 'You want me to call your uncle?' He reached for the phone, but she stopped him with a no.

'I'm fine,' she said, standing. 'I guess I'll see you tomorrow.'

Jeffrey stood, too, glad to conclude this. 'I'll call you as soon as we have something.'

She gave him a funny look. 'What time's the briefing?'

He saw where she was going with this. 'I'm not going to let you work on this case, Lena. You have to know that.'

'You don't understand,' she said. 'If you don't let me work on this, then you're going to have another stiff for your girlfriend down at the morgue.'

SIX

Lena banged her fist on the front door of her sister's house. She was about to go back to her car and get her spare set of keys when Nan Thomas opened the door.

Nan was shorter than Lena and about ten pounds heavier. Her short mousy brown hair and thick glasses made her resemble the prototypical librarian that she was.

Nan's eyes were swollen and puffy, fresh tears still streaking down her cheeks. She held a balled-up piece of tissue in her hand.

Lena said, 'I guess you heard.'

Nan turned, walking back into the house, leaving the door open for Lena. The two women had never gotten along. Except for the fact that Nan Thomas was Sibyl's lover, Lena would not have said two words to her.

The house was a bungalow built in the 1920s. Much of the original architecture had been left in place, from the hardwood floors to the simple molding lining the doorways. The front door opened into a large living room with a fireplace at one end and the dining room at the other. Off this was the kitchen. Two small bedrooms and a bath finished the simple plan.

Lena walked purposefully down the hallway. She opened the first door on the right, entering the bedroom that had been turned into Sibyl's study. The room was neat and orderly, mostly by necessity. Sibyl was blind, things had to be put in their place or she would not be able to find them. Braille books were stacked neatly on the shelves. Magazines, also in Braille, were lined up on the coffee table in front of an old futon. A computer sat on the desk lining the far wall. Lena was turning it on when Nan walked into the room.

'What do you think you're doing?'

'I need to go through her things.'

'Why?' Nan asked, going over to the desk. She put her hand over the keyboard, as if she could stop Lena.

'I need to see if anything was strange, if anyone was following her.'

'You think you'll find it in here?' Nan demanded, picking up the keyboard. 'She only used this for school. You don't even understand the voice recognition software.'

Lena grabbed the keyboard back. 'I'll figure it out.'

'No, you won't,' Nan countered. 'This is my house, too.'

Lena put her hands on her hips, walking toward the center of the room. She spotted a stack of papers beside an old Braille typewriter. Lena picked them up, turning to Nan. 'What's this?'

Nan ran over, grabbing the papers. 'It's her diary.'

'Can you read it?'

'It's her personal diary,' Nan repeated, aghast. 'These are her private thoughts.'

Lena chewed her bottom lip, trying for a softer tactic. That she had never liked Nan Thomas was not exactly a secret in this house. 'You can read Braille, right?'

'Some.'

'You need to tell me what this says, Nan. Somebody killed her.' Lena tapped the pages. 'Maybe she was being followed. Maybe she was scared of something and didn't want to tell us.'

Nan turned away, her head tilted down toward the pages. She ran her fingers along the top line of dots, but Lena could tell she wasn't reading it. For some reason, Lena got the impression she was touching the pages because Sibyl had, as if she could absorb some sense of Sibyl rather than just words.

Nan said, 'She always went to the diner on Mondays. It was her time out to do something on her own.'

'I know.'

'We were supposed to make burritos tonight.' Nan stacked the papers against the desk. 'Do what you need to do,' she said. 'I'll be in the living room.'

Lena waited for her to leave, then continued the task at hand. Nan was right about the computer. Lena did not know how to use the software, and Sibyl had only used it for school. Sibyl dictated into the computer what she needed, and her teaching assistant made sure copies were made.

The second bedroom was slightly larger than the first. Lena stood in the doorway, taking in the neatly made bed. A stuffed Pooh bear was tucked between the pillows. Pooh was old, balding in places. Sibyl had rarely been without him throughout her childhood, and throwing him away had seemed like heresy. Lena leaned against the door, getting a mental flash of Sibyl as a child, standing with the Pooh bear. Lena closed her eyes, letting the memory overwhelm her. There wasn't much Lena wanted to remember about her childhood, but a particular day stuck out. A few months after the accident that had blinded Sibyl, they were in the backyard, Lena pushing her sister on the swing. Sibyl held Pooh tight to her chest, her head thrown back as she felt the breeze, a huge smile on her face as she relished this simple pleasure. There was such a trust there, Sibyl getting on the swing, trusting Lena not to push her too hard or too high. Lena had felt a responsibility. Her chest swelled from it, and she kept pushing Sibyl until her arms had ached.

Lena rubbed her eyes, shutting the bedroom door. She went into the bathroom and opened the medicine cabinet. Other than Sibyl's usual vitamins and herbs, the cabinet was empty. Lena opened the closet, rummaging past the toilet paper and tampons, hair gel and hand towels. What she was looking for, Lena did not know. Sibyl didn't hide things. She would be the last person to be able to find them if she did.

'Sibby,' Lena breathed, turning back to the mirror on the medicine cabinet. Seeing Sibyl, not herself. Lena spoke to her reflection, whispering, 'Tell me something. Please.'

She closed her eyes, trying to navigate the space as Sibyl would. The room was small, and Lena could touch both walls with her hands as she stood in the center. She opened her eyes with a weary sigh. There was nothing there.

Back in the living room, Nan Thomas sat on the couch. She held Sibyl's diary in her lap, not looking up when Lena came in. 'I read the last few days' worth of stuff,' she said, her tone flat. 'Nothing out of place. She was worried about a kid at school who was flunking.'

'A guy?'

Nan shook her head. 'Female. A freshman.'

Lena leaned her hand against the wall. 'Did you have any workmen in or out in the last month?'

'No.'

'Same mailman delivering to the house? No UPS or FedEx?'

'Nobody new. This is Grant County, Lee.'

Lena bristled at the familiar name. She tried to bite

back her anger. 'She didn't say she felt like she was being followed or anything?'

'No, not at all. She was perfectly normal.' Nan clutched the papers to her chest. 'Her classes were fine. We were fine.' A slight smile came to her lips. 'We were supposed to take a day trip to Eufalla this weekend.'

Lena took her car keys out of her pocket. 'Right,' she quipped. 'I guess if anything comes up you should call me.'

'Lee –'

Lena held up her hand. 'Don't.'

Nan acknowledged the warning with a frown. 'I'll call you if I think of anything.'

By midnight, Lena was finishing off her third bottle of Rolling Rock, driving across the Grant County line outside of Madison. She contemplated throwing the empty out the car window but stopped herself at the last minute. She laughed at her twisted sense of morality; she would drive under the influence but she would not litter. The line had to be drawn somewhere.

Angela Norton, Lena's mother, grew up watching her brother Hank dig himself deeper and deeper into a bottomless pit of alcohol and drug abuse. Hank had told Lena that her mother had been adamantly against alcohol. When Angela married Calvin Adams, her only rule of the house was that he not go out drinking with his fellow policemen. Cal was known to slip out now and then, but for the most part, he honored his wife's wishes. Three months into his marriage, he was making a routine traffic stop along a dirt road outside of Reece, Georgia, when the driver pulled a gun on him. Shot twice in the head, Calvin Adams died before his body hit the ground.

At twenty-three, Angela was hardly prepared to be a

widow. When she passed out at her husband's funeral, her family chalked it up to nerves. Four weeks of morning sickness later, a doctor finally gave her the diagnosis. She was pregnant.

As her condition progressed, Angela became more despondent. She wasn't a happy woman to begin with. Life in Reece was not easy, and the Norton family had seen its share of hardship. Hank Norton was known for his volatile temper and was considered to be the kind of mean chunk you didn't want to run into in a dark alley. At her older brother's knee, Angela had learned not to put up much of a fight. Two weeks after giving birth to twin baby girls, Angela Adams succumbed to an infection. She was twenty-four years old. Hank Norton was the only relative willing to take in her two girls.

To hear Hank tell the story, Sibyl and Lena had turned his life around. The day he took them home was the day he stopped abusing his body. He claimed to have found God through their presence and to this day said he could recall minute by minute what it was like to hold Lena and Sibyl for the first time.

In truth, Hank only stopped shooting up speed when the girls came to live with him. He did not stop drinking until much later. The girls were eight when it happened. A bad day at work had sent Hank on a binge. When he ran out of liquor, he decided to drive instead of walk to the store. His car didn't even make it to the street. Sibyl and Lena were playing ball out in the front yard. Lena still didn't know what had been going through Sibyl's mind as she chased the ball into the driveway. The car had struck her from the side, the steel bumper slamming into her temple as she bent to retrieve the ball.

County services had been called in, but nothing came of the investigation. The closest hospital was a forty-minute drive from Reece. Hank had plenty of time to sober up and give a convincing story. Lena could still recall being in the car with him, watching his mouth work as he figured out the story in his mind. At the time, eight-year-old Lena was not quite sure what had happened, and when the police interviewed her she had supported Hank's story.

Sometimes Lena still had dreams about the accident, and in these dreams Sibyl's body bounced against the ground much as the ball had. That Hank had allegedly not touched another drop of alcohol since then was of no consequence to Lena. The damage had been done.

Lena opened another bottle of beer, removing both hands from the wheel to twist off the cap. She took a long pull, grimacing at the taste. Alcohol had never appealed to her. Lena hated being out of control, hated the dizzy sensation and the numbness. Getting drunk was something for the weak, a crutch for people who were not strong enough to live their own lives, to stand on their own two feet. Drinking was running away from something. Lena took another swig of beer, thinking there was no better time than the present for all of these things.

The Celica fishtailed as she took the turn off the exit too hard. Lena corrected the wheel with one hand, holding tight to the bottle with the other. A hard right at the top of the exit took her to the Reece Stop 'n' Save. The store inside was dark. Like most businesses in town, the gas station closed at ten. Though, if memory served, a walk around the building would reveal a group of teenagers drinking, smoking cigarettes, and doing things their parents did not want to know about. Lena and Sibyl had walked to this store many a dark night, sneaking out of the house under Hank's none-too-watchful eye.

Scooping up the empty bottles, Lena got out of the

car. She stumbled, her foot catching on the door. A bottle slipped out of her hands and busted on the concrete. Cursing, she kicked the shards away from her tires, walking toward the trash can. Lena stared at her reflection in the store's plate glass windows as she tossed her empties. For a second, it was like looking at Sibyl. She reached over to the glass, touching her lips, her eyes.

'Jesus.' Lena sighed. This was one of the many reasons she did not like to drink. She was turning into a basket case.

Music blared from the bar across the street. Hank considered it a test of will that he owned a bar but never imbibed. The Hut looked like its name, with a southern twist. The roof was thatched only until it mattered, then a rusted tin lined the pitched surface. Tiki torches with orange and red lightbulbs instead of flames stood on either side of the entrance, and the door was painted to look like it had been fashioned from grass. Paint peeled from the walls, but for the most part you could still make out the bamboo design.

Drunk as she was, Lena had the sense to look both ways before she crossed the street. Her feet were about ten seconds behind her body, and she held her hands out to her sides for balance as she walked across the gravel parking lot. Of the fifty or so vehicles in the lot, about forty were pickup trucks. This being the new South, instead of gun racks they sported chrome runners and gold striping along their sides. The other cars were Jeeps and four-wheel drives. Nascar numbers were painted onto the back windshields. Hank's cream-colored L983 Mercedes was the only sedan in the lot.

The Hut reeked of cigarette smoke, and Lena had to take a few shallow breaths so she wouldn't choke. Her eyes burned as she walked over to the bar. Not much had changed in the last twenty or so years. The floor was still sticky from beer and crunchy from peanut shells. To the left were booths that probably had more DNA material in them than the FBI lab at Quantico. To the right was a long bar fashioned from fifty-gallon barrels and heart of pine. A stage was on the far wall, the rest rooms for men and women on either side. In the middle of the bar was what Hank called a dance floor. Most nights, it was packed back to front with men and women in various stages of drunken arousal. The Hut was a two-thirty bar, meaning everybody looked good at two-thirty in the morning.

Hank was nowhere to be seen, but Lena knew he wouldn't be far on amateur night. Every other Monday, patrons of the Hut were invited to stand onstage and embarrass themselves in front of the rest of the town. Lena shuddered as she thought about it. Reece made Heartsdale look like a bustling metropolis. Except for the tire factory, most of the men in this room would have left a long time ago. As it was, they were content to drink themselves to death and pretend they were happy.

Lena slid onto the first vacant stool she could find. The country song on the jukebox had a pounding bass, and she leaned her elbows on the bar, cupping her hands over her ears so that she could hear herself think.

She felt a bump on her arm and looked up in time to see *Websters* definition of a hick sitting down beside her. His face was sunburned from his neck to about an inch from his hairline where he had obviously been working outside wearing a baseball hat. His shirt was starched within an inch of its life, and the cuffs were tight around his thick wrists. The jukebox stopped abruptly, and Lena worked her jaw, trying to make her ears pop so she didn't feel like she was in a tunnel.

Her gentleman neighbor bumped her arm again, smiling, saying, 'Hey, lady.'

Lena rolled her eyes, catching the bartender's eye. 'JD on the rocks,' she ordered.

'That'n's on me,' the man said, slapping down a ten-dollar bill. When he spoke, his words slurred together like a wrecked train, and Lena realized he was a lot drunker than she planned ever to be.

The man gave her a sloppy smile. 'You know, sugar, I'd love to get biblical with you.'

She leaned over, close to his ear. 'If I ever find out you have, I'll cut your balls off with my car keys.'

He opened his mouth to reply but was jerked off the barstool before he could get a word out. Hank stood there with the man's shirt collar in his hand, then shoved him into the crowd. The look he fixed Lena with was just as hard as the one she imagined was on her own face.

Lena had never liked her uncle. Unlike Sibyl, she wasn't the forgiving type. Even when Lena drove Sibyl to Reece for visits, Lena spent most of her time in the car or sitting on the front porch steps, keys in her hand, ready to go as soon as Sibyl walked out the front door.

Despite the fact that Hank Norton had injected speed into his veins for the better part of his twenties and thirties, he was not an idiot. Lena showing up on Hank's proverbial doorstep in the middle of the night could only mean one thing.

Their eyes were still locked as music started to blare again, shaking the walls, sending a vibration from the floor up the barstool. She saw rather than heard what Hank was asking when he said, 'Where's Sibyl?'

Tucked behind the bar, more like an outhouse than a place of business, Hank's office was a small wooden box with a tin roof. A lightbulb hung from a frayed electrical wire that had probably been installed by the WPA. Posters from beer and liquor companies served as wallpaper. White cartons filled with liquor were stacked against the back wall, leaving about ten square feet for a desk with two chairs on either side. Surrounding these were piles of boxes stuffed with receipts that Hank had accumulated from running the bar over the years. A stream running behind the shack kept mold and moisture in the air. Lena imagined Hank liked working in this dark, dank place, passing his days in an environment more suitable for a tongue.

'I see you've redecorated,' Lena said, setting her glass on top of one of the boxes. She could not tell if she wasn't drunk anymore or if she was too drunk to notice.

Hank gave the glass a cursory glance, then looked back at Lena. 'You don't drink.'

She held up the glass in a toast. 'To the late bloomer.'

Hank sat back in his office chair, his hands clasped in front of his stomach. He was tall and skinny, with skin that tended to flake in the winter. Despite the fact that his father was Spanish, Hank's appearance more closely resembled his mother's, a pasty woman who was as sour as her complexion. In her mind, Lena had always thought it appropriate that Hank bore a close resemblance to an albino snake.

He asked, 'What brings you to these parts?'

'Just dropping by,' she managed around the glass. The whiskey was bitter in her mouth. She kept an eye on Hank as she finished the drink and banged the empty glass back down on the box. Lena did not know what was stopping her. For years she had waited to get the upper hand with Hank Norton. This was her time to hurt him as much as he had hurt Sibyl.

'You started snortin' coke, too, or have you been crying?'

Lena wiped her mouth with the back of her hand. 'What do you think?'

Hank stared at her, working his hands back and forth. This was more than a nervous habit, Lena knew. Speed injected into the veins of his hands had given Hank arthritis at an early age. Since most of the veins in his arms had calcified from the powdered additive used to cut the drug, there wasn't much circulation there, either. His hands were cold as ice most days and a constant source of pain.

The rubbing stopped abruptly. 'Let's get it over with, Lee. I've got the show to put on.'

Lena tried to open her mouth, but nothing came out. Part of her was angered by his flippant attitude, which had marked their relationship from the very beginning. Part of her did not know how to tell him. As much as Lena hated her uncle, he was a human being. Hank had doted on Sibyl. In high school, Lena could not take her sister everywhere, and Sibyl had spent a lot of time home with Hank. There was an undeniable bond there, and as much as Lena wanted to hurt her uncle, she felt herself holding back. Lena had loved Sibyl, Sibyl had loved Hank.

Hank picked up a ballpoint pen, turning it head over end on the desk several times before he finally asked, 'What's wrong, Lee? Need some money?'

If only it were that simple, Lena thought.

'Car broke down?'

She shook her head slowly side to side.

'It's Sibyl,' he stated, his voice catching in his throat.

When Lena did not answer, he nodded slowly to himself, putting his hands together, as if to pray. 'She's sick?' he asked, his voice indicating he expected the worst. With this one sentence, he showed more emotion than Lena had ever seen him express in a lifetime of knowing her uncle. She looked at him closely as if for the first time. His pale skin was blotched with those red dots pasty men get on their faces as they age. His hair, silver for as long as she could recall, was dulled with yellow under the sixty-watt bulb. His Hawaiian shirt was rumpled, which was not his style, and his hands tremored slightly as he fidgeted with them.

Lena did it the same way Jeffrey Tolliver had. 'She went to the diner in the middle of town,' she began. 'You know the one across from the dress shop?'

A slight nod was all he gave.

'She walked there from the house,' Lena continued. 'She did it every week, just to be able to do something on her own.'

Hank clasped his hands together in front of his face, touching the sides of his index fingers to his forehead.

'So, uhm.' Lena picked up the glass, needing something to do. She sucked what little liquor was left off the ice cubes, then continued. 'She went to the bathroom, and somebody killed her.'

There was little sound in the tiny office. Grasshoppers chirped outside. Gurgling came from the stream. A distant throbbing came from the bar.

Without preamble, Hank turned around, picking through the boxes, asking, 'What've you had to drink tonight?'

Lena was surprised by his question, though she shouldn't have been. Despite his AA brainwashing, Hank Norton was a master at avoiding the unpleasant. His need to escape was what had brought Hank to drugs and alcohol in the first place. 'Beer in the car,' she said, playing along, glad for once that he did not want the gory details. 'JD here.'

He paused, his hand around a bottle of Jack Daniel's. 'Beer before liquor, never sicker,' he warned, his voice catching on the last part.

Lena held out her glass, rattling the ice for attention. She watched Hank as he poured the drink, not surprised when he licked his lips.

'How's work treating you?' Hank asked, his voice tinny in the shack. His lower lip trembled slightly. His expression was one of total grief, in direct opposition to the words coming from his mouth. He said, 'Doing okay?'

Lena nodded. She felt as if she was smack in the middle of a car accident. She finally understood the meaning of the word *surreal*. Nothing seemed concrete in this tiny space. The glass in her hand felt dull. Hank was miles away. She was in a dream.

Lena tried to snap herself out of it, downing her drink quickly. The alcohol hit the back of her throat like fire, burning and solid, as if she had swallowed hot asphalt.

Hank watched the glass, not Lena, as she did this.

This was all she needed. She said, 'Sibyl's dead, Hank.'

Tears came to his eyes without warning, and all that Lena could think was that he looked so very, very old. It was like watching a flower wilt. He took out his handkerchief and wiped his nose.

Lena repeated the words much as Jeffrey Tolliver had earlier this evening. 'She's dead.'

His voice wavered as he asked, 'Are you sure?'

Lena nodded quickly up and down. 'I saw her.' Then, 'Somebody cut her up pretty bad.'

His mouth opened and closed like a fish's. He kept his eyes even with Lena's the way he used to do when he was trying to catch her in a lie. He finally looked away, mumbling, 'That doesn't make sense.'

She could have reached out and patted his old hand, maybe tried to comfort him, but she didn't. Lena felt frozen in her chair. Instead of thinking of Sibyl, which had been her mind's initial reaction, she concentrated on Hank, on his wet lips, his eyes, the hairs growing out of his nose.

'Oh, Sibby.' He sighed, wiping his eyes. Lena watched his Adam's apple bob as he swallowed. He reached for the bottle, resting his hand on the neck. Without asking, he unscrewed the cap and poured Lena another drink. This time, the dark liquid nearly touched the rim.

More time passed, then Hank blew his nose loudly, patting at his eyes with the handkerchief. 'I can't see anyone trying to kill her.' His hands shook even more as he folded the handkerchief over and over. 'Doesn't make sense,' he mumbled. 'You, I could understand.'

'Thanks a lot.'

This was sufficient enough to spark Hank's irritation. 'I mean because of the job you do. Now get that damn chip off your shoulder.'

Lena did not comment. This was a familiar order.

He put his palms down on the desk, fixing Lena with a stare. 'Where were you when this happened?'

Lena tossed back the drink, not feeling the burn so much this time. When she returned the glass to the desk, Hank was still staring at her.

She mumbled, 'Macon.'

'Was it some sort of hate crime, then?'

Lena reached over, picking up the bottle. 'I don't know. Maybe.' The whiskey gurgled in the bottle as she poured. 'Maybe he picked her because she was gay. Maybe he picked her because she was blind.' Lena gave a sideways glance, catching his pained reaction to this. She decided to expound upon her speculation. 'Rapists tend to pick women they think they can control, Hank. She was an easy target.'

'So, this all comes back to me?'

'I didn't say that.'

He grabbed the bottle. 'Right,' he snapped, dropping the half empty bottle back into its box. His tone was angry now, back to the nuts and bolts. Like Lena, Hank was never comfortable with the emotional side of things. Sibyl had often said the main reason Hank and Lena never got along was that they were too much alike. Sitting there with Hank, absorbing his grief and anger as it filled the tiny shed, Lena realized that Sibyl was right. She was looking at herself in twenty years, and there was nothing she could do to stop it.

Hank asked, 'Have you talked to Nan?'

'Yeah.'

'We've got to plan the service,' he said, picking up the pen and drawing a box on his desk calendar. At the top he wrote the word FUNERAL in all caps. 'Is there somebody in Grant you think would do a good job?' He waited for her response, then added, 'I mean, most of her friends were there.'

'What?' Lena asked, the glass paused at her lips. 'What are you talking about?'

'Lee, we've got to make arrangements. We've got to take care of Sibby.'

Lena finished the drink. When she looked at Hank, his features were blurred. As a matter of fact, the whole room was blurred. She had the sensation of being on a roller coaster, and her stomach reacted accordingly. Lena put her hand to her mouth, fighting the urge to be sick.

Hank had probably seen her expression many times before, most likely in the mirror. He was beside her, holding a trash can under her chin, just as she lost the battle.

TUESDAY

SEVEN

Sara leaned over the kitchen sink in her parents' house, using her father's wrench to loosen the faucet. She had spent most of the evening in the morgue performing Sibyl Adams's autopsy. Going back to a dark house, sleeping alone, had not been something she wanted to do. Add to that Jeffrey's last threat on her answering machine to come by her house, and Sara did not really have a choice as to where she slept last night. Except for sneaking in to pick up the dogs, she had not even bothered to change out of her scrubs.

She wiped sweat from her forehead, glancing at the clock on the coffeemaker. It was six-thirty in the morning and she had slept all of two hours. Every time she closed her eyes, she thought of Sibyl Adams sitting on the toilet, blind to what was happening to her, feeling everything her attacker was doing.

On the plus side, short of some type of family catastrophe, there was no way in hell today could possibly be as bad as yesterday.

Cathy Linton walked into the kitchen, opened a cabinet, and took down a coffee cup before she noticed her oldest daughter standing beside her. 'What are you doing?'

Sara slid a new washer over the threaded bolt. 'The faucet was leaking.'

'Two plumbers in the family,' Cathy complained,

pouring herself a cup of coffee, 'and my daughter the doctor ends up fixing the leaky faucet.'

Sara smiled, putting her shoulder behind the wrench. The Lintons were a plumbing family, and Sara had spent most of her summers during school working alongside her father, snaking drains and welding pipe. Sometimes she thought the only reason she had finished high school a year early and worked through summers getting her undergrad degree was so she would not have to poke around spider-infested crawl spaces with her father. Not that she didn't love her father, but, unlike Tessa, Sara's fear of spiders could not be overcome.

Cathy slid onto the kitchen stool. 'Did you sleep here last night?'

'Yeah,' Sara answered, washing her hands. She turned off the faucet, smiling when it didn't leak. The sense of accomplishment lifted some of the weight off her shoulders.

Cathy smiled her approval. 'If that medical thing doesn't work out, at least you'll have plumbing to fall back on.'

'You know, that's what Daddy told me when he drove me to college the first day.'

'I know,' Cathy said. 'I could have killed him.' She took a sip of coffee, eyeing Sara over the rim of the cup. 'Why didn't you go home?'

'I worked late and I just wanted to come here. Is that okay?'

'Of course it's okay,' Cathy said, tossing Sara a towel. 'Don't be ridiculous.'

Sara dried her hands. 'I hope I didn't wake you up when I came in.'

'Not me,' Cathy answered. 'Why didn't you sleep with Tess?'

Sara made herself busy straightening the towel on the

rack. Tessa lived in a two-bedroom apartment over the garage. In the last few years, there had been nights when Sara had not wanted to sleep alone in her own house. She generally stayed with her sister rather than risk waking her father, who invariably wanted to discuss at great length what was troubling her.

Sara answered, 'I didn't want to bother her.'

'Oh, bullshit.' Cathy laughed. 'Good Lord, Sara, nearly a quarter of a million dollars to that college and they didn't teach you to lie better than that?'

Sara took down her favorite mug and poured herself some coffee. 'Maybe you should've sent me to law school instead.'

Cathy crossed her legs, frowning. She was a small woman who kept herself trim by doing yoga. Her blond hair and blue eyes had skipped over Sara and been passed on to Tessa. Except for their matching temperaments, anyone would be hard-pressed to tell that Cathy and Sara were mother and daughter.

'Well?' Cathy prompted.

Sara couldn't keep the smile off of her lips. 'Let's just say Tess was a little busy when I walked in and leave it at that.'

'Busy by herself?'

'No.' Sara barked an uncomfortable laugh, feeling her cheeks turn red. 'God, Mother.'

After a few moments, Cathy lowered her voice, asking, 'Was it Devon Lockwood?'

'Devon?' Sara was surprised by the name. She hadn't been able to see exactly who Tessa was wrangling around with in bed, but Devon Lockwood, the new plumber's helper Eddie Linton had hired two weeks ago, was the last name she was expecting to come up.

Cathy shushed her. 'Your father will hear.'

'Hear what?' Eddie asked, shuffling into the kitchen.

His eyes lit up when he saw Sara. 'There's my baby,' he said, kissing her cheek with a loud smack. 'Was that you I heard coming in this morning?'

'That was me,' Sara confessed.

'I got some paint chips in the garage,' he offered. 'Maybe we can go look at them after we eat, pick a pretty color for your room.'

Sara sipped her coffee. 'I'm not moving back in, Dad.'

He jabbed a finger at the cup. 'That'll stunt your growth.'

'I should be so lucky,' Sara grumbled. Since the ninth grade, she had been the tallest member of her immediate family, just inching past her father by a hair.

Sara slid onto the stool her mother vacated. She watched her parents as they went through their morning routine, her father walking around the kitchen, getting in her mother's way until Cathy pushed him into a chair. Her father smoothed his hair back as he leaned over the morning paper. His salt-and-pepper hair stuck out in three different directions, much like his eyebrows. The T-shirt he was wearing was so old and worn holes were breaking through over his shoulder blades. The pattern on his pajama pants had faded out over five years ago, and his bedroom slippers were falling apart at the heels. That she had inherited her mother's cynicism and her father's sense of dress was something Sara would never forgive them for.

Eddie said, 'I see the *Observer's* milking this thing for every penny.'

Sara glanced at the headline of Grant's local paper. It read: 'College Professor Slain in Grisly Attack.'

'What's it say?' Sara asked before she could stop herself.

He traced his finger down the page as he read. ' "Sibyl Adams, a professor at GIT, was savagely beaten to death yesterday at the Grant Filling Station. Local police are baffled. Police Chief Jeffrey Tolliver" ' – Eddie stopped, muttering, 'the bastard' under his breath – ' "reports they are exploring every possible lead in order to bring the young professor's murderer to justice." '

'She wasn't beaten to death,' Sara said, knowing that the punch to Sibyl Adams's face had not killed her. Sara gave an involuntary shudder as she recalled the physical findings during the autopsy.

Eddie seemed to notice her reaction. He said, 'Was anything else done to her?'

Sara was surprised her father had asked this. Normally, her family went out of their way not to ask questions about that side of Sara's life. She had felt from the beginning that they were all more than a little uncomfortable with her part-time job.

Sara asked, 'Like what?' before she got her father's meaning. Cathy looked up from mixing the pancake batter, a look of trepidation on her face.

Tessa burst into the kitchen, popping the swinging door on its hinge, obviously expecting to find Sara alone. Her mouth opened in a perfect o.

Cathy, standing at the stove making pancakes, tossed over her shoulder, 'Good morning, sunshine.'

Tessa kept her head down, making a beeline for the coffee.

'Sleep well?' Eddie asked.

'Like a baby,' Tessa returned, kissing the top of his head.

Cathy waved her spatula in Sara's direction. 'You could learn from your sister.'

Tessa had the common sense to ignore this comment. She opened the French door leading to the deck and jerked her head outside, indicating Sara should follow.

Sara did as she was told, holding her breath until the door was closed firmly behind her. She whispered, 'Devon Lockwood?'

'I still haven't told them about your date with Jeb,' Tessa countered.

Sara pressed her lips together, silently agreeing to the truce.

Tessa tucked one of her legs underneath her as she sat on the porch swing. 'What were you doing out so late?'

'I was at the morgue,' Sara answered, sitting beside her sister. She rubbed her arms, fighting the early morning chill. Sara was still in her scrubs and a thin white T-shirt, hardly enough for the temperature. 'I needed to check some things. Lena –' She stopped herself, not sure she could tell Tessa what had happened with Lena Adams in the morgue last night. The accusations still stung, even though Sara knew it was Lena's grief talking.

She said, 'I wanted to get it over with, you know?'

All mirth had left Tessa's features. 'Did you find anything?'

'I faxed a report to Jeffrey. I think it's going to help him get some solid leads.' She stopped, making sure she had Tessa's attention. 'Listen, Tessie. Be careful, okay? I mean, keep the doors locked. Don't go out alone. That kind of thing.'

'Yeah.' Tessa squeezed her hand. 'Okay. Sure.'

'I mean –' Sara stopped, not wanting to terrify her sister, but not wanting to put her in danger either. 'You're both the same age. You and Sibyl. Do you see what I'm getting at?'

'Yeah,' Tessa answered, but it was obvious she did not want to talk about it. Sara couldn't blame her sister. Knowing in intimate detail what had happened to Sibyl Adams, Sara was finding it hard to get through the day.

'I put the postcard –' Tessa began, but Sara stopped her.

'I found it in my briefcase,' she said. 'Thanks.'

'Yeah,' Tessa said, a stillness to her voice.

Sara stared out at the lake, not thinking about the postcard, not thinking about Sibyl Adams or Jeffrey or anything. There was something so peaceful about the water that for the first time in weeks, Sara felt herself relax. If she squinted her eyes, she could see the dock at the back of her own house. It had a covered boathouse, a small floating barnlike structure, like most of the docks on the lake.

She imagined herself sitting in one of the deck chairs, sipping a margarita, reading a trashy novel. Why she pictured herself doing this, Sara did not know. She seldom had time to sit lately, she did not like the taste of alcohol, and at the end of the day she was nearly cross-eyed from reading patient charts, pediatric journals, and forensic field manuals.

Tessa interrupted her thoughts. 'I guess you didn't get much sleep last night?'

Sara shook her head as she leaned against her sister's shoulder.

'How was it being around Jeffrey yesterday?'

'I wish I could take a pill and forget all about him.'

Tessa raised her arm, putting it around Sara's shoulders. 'Is that why you couldn't sleep?'

Sara sighed, closing her eyes. 'I don't know. I was just thinking about Sibyl. About Jeffrey.'

'Two years is a long time to carry a torch for somebody,' Tessa said. 'If you really want to get over him, then you need to start dating.' She stopped Sara's protest. 'I mean real dates, where you don't drop the guy as soon as he gets close.'

Sara sat up, pulling her knees to her chest. She knew

what her sister was suggesting. 'I'm not like you. I can't just sleep around.' Tessa didn't take offense at this. Sara had not expected her to. That Tessa Linton enjoyed an active sex life was pretty much known to everyone in town but their father.

'I was just sixteen when Steve and I got together,' Sara began, referring to her first serious boyfriend. 'Then, well, you know what happened in Atlanta.' Tessa nodded. 'Jeffrey made me like sex. I mean, for the first time in my life, I felt like a complete person.' She clenched her fists, as if she could hold on to that feeling. 'You have no idea what that meant to me, to be suddenly awake after all those years of focusing on school and work and not seeing anybody or having any kind of life.'

Tessa was quiet, letting Sara talk.

'I remember our first date,' she continued. 'He was driving me back to the house in the rain and he stopped the car all of a sudden. I thought it was a joke, because we'd both been talking about how much we liked to walk in the rain just a few minutes earlier. But he left the lights on and he got out of the car.' Sara closed her eyes, seeing Jeffrey standing in the rain, his coat collar turned up to the cold. 'There was a cat in the road. It had been hit, and it was obviously dead.'

Tessa was silent, waiting. 'And?' she prompted.

'And he picked it up and moved it out of the road so that no one else would hit it.'

Tessa couldn't hide her shock. 'He picked it up?'

'Yeah.' Sara smiled fondly at the memory. 'He didn't want anyone else to hit it.'

'He touched a dead cat?'

Sara laughed at her reaction. 'I never told you that before?'

'I think I'd remember.'

Sara sat back in the swing, using her foot to keep it steady. 'The thing was, at dinner he told me how much he hates cats. And here he was, stopping in the middle of the road in the dark, in the rain, to move the cat out of the road so that no one else would hit it.'

Tessa could not mask her distaste. 'Then he got back in the car with dead-cat hands?'

'I drove, because he didn't want to touch anything.'

Tessa wrinkled her nose. 'Is this the part where it gets romantic, because I'm feeling slightly sick to my stomach.'

Sara gave her a sideways glance. 'I drove him back to the house, and of course he had to come in to wash his hands.' Sara laughed. 'His hair was all wet from the rain and he kept his hands up like he was a surgeon who didn't want to mess up his scrub.' Sara held her arms in the air, palms facing back, to illustrate.

'And?'

'And I took him into the kitchen to wash his hands because that's where the antibacterial soap is, and he couldn't squeeze the bottle without contaminating it, so I squeezed it for him.' She sighed heavily. 'And he was leaning over the sink washing his hands, then I was lathering up his hands for him, and they felt so strong and warm and he's always so goddamn sure of himself that he just looked up and kissed me right on the lips, without any hesitation, like he knew all along that while I was touching his hands all I could think about was how it would feel to have his hands on me, touching me.'

Tessa waited until she was finished, then said, 'Except for the dead cat part, that's the most romantic story I've ever heard.'

'Well.' Sara stood, walking over to the deck railing.

'I'm sure he makes all his girlfriends feel special. That's one thing he's very good at, I guess.'

'Sara, you'll never understand that sex is different for some people. Sometimes it's just fucking.' She paused. 'Sometimes it's just a way to get some attention.'

'He certainly got my attention.'

'He still loves you.'

Sara turned, sitting on the railing. 'He only wants me back because he lost me.'

'If you were really serious about getting him out of your life,' Tessa began, 'then you would quit your job with the county.'

Sara opened her mouth to respond, but she could not think of how to tell her sister that some days her county work was the only thing that kept her sane. There were only so many sore throats and earaches Sara could take before her mind started to go numb. To give up her job as coroner would be giving up a part of her life that she really enjoyed, despite the macabre aspects.

Knowing Tessa could never understand this, Sara said, 'I don't know what I'm going to do.'

There was no response. Tessa was looking back at the house. Sara followed her gaze through the kitchen window. Jeffrey Tolliver was standing by the stove, talking to her mother.

The Linton home was a split level that had been constantly renovated throughout its forty-year life. When Cathy took an interest in painting, a studio with a half bath was added on to the back. When Sara became obsessed with school, a study with a half bath was built into the attic. When Tessa became interested in boys, the basement was renovated in such a way that Eddie could get from anywhere in the house to the basement in three seconds flat. A stairway was at either end of the room and the closest bathroom was one floor up.

The basement had not changed much since Tessa moved away for college. The carpet was avocado green and the sectional sofa a dark rust. A combination Ping-Pong/pool table dominated the center of the room. Sara had broken her hand once, diving for a Ping-Pong ball and slamming into the console television instead.

Sara's two dogs, Billy and Bob, were on the couch when Sara and Jeffrey walked down the stairs. She clapped her hands, trying to get them to move. The greyhounds did not budge until Jeffrey gave a low whistle. Their tails wagged as he walked over to pet them.

Jeffrey didn't mince words as he scratched Bob's belly. 'I tried to call you all night. Where were you?'

Sara didn't feel he was entitled to that kind of information. She asked, 'Did you get anything on Sibyl yet?'

He shook his head. 'According to Lena, she wasn't seeing anybody. That rules out an angry boyfriend.'

'Anybody in her past?'

'Nobody,' he answered. 'I guess I'll ask her roommate some questions today. She was living with Nan Thomas. You know, the librarian?'

'Yeah,' Sara said, feeling things starting to click in her head. 'Did you get my report yet?'

He shook his head, not understanding. 'What?'

'That's where I was last night, doing the autopsy.'

'What?' he repeated. 'You can't do an autopsy without someone present.'

'I know that, Jeffrey,' Sara snapped back, crossing her arms. One person questioning her competency in the last twelve hours was quite enough. She said, 'That's why I called Brad Stephens.'

'Brad Stephens?' He turned his back to her, muttering something under his breath as he stroked underneath Billy's chin.

'What did you say?'

'I said you're acting strange lately.' He turned, facing her. 'You performed the autopsy in the middle of the night?'

'I'm sorry you find that strange, but I have two jobs to do, not just what I do for you.' He tried to stop her but she continued. 'In case you've forgotten, I have a full patient load at the clinic in addition to what I do at the morgue. Patients, by the way' – she checked her watch, not really noting the time – 'that I have to start seeing in a few minutes.' She tucked her hands into her hips. 'Was there a reason you came by?'

'To check on you,' he said. 'Obviously you're all right. I guess that should come as no surprise to me. You're always all right.'

'That's right.'

'Sara Linton, stronger than steel.'

Sara gave what she hoped was a condescending look. They had played out this scene so many times around the time of their divorce that she could recite both sides of the argument by heart. Sara was too independent. Jeffrey was too demanding.

She said, 'I have to go.'

'Wait a minute,' he said. 'The report?'

'I faxed it to you.'

It was his turn to put his hands on his hips. 'Yeah, I got that. You think you found something?'

'Yes,' she answered, then, 'No.' She crossed her arms defensively. She hated when he downshifted from an argument into something to do with work. It was a cheap trick, and it always caught her off guard. She recovered somewhat, saying, 'I need to hear back on the blood this morning. Nick Shelton is supposed to call me at nine, then I can tell you something.' She added, 'I wrote this on the cover page for my report.'

'Why did you rush the blood?' he asked.

'Gut feeling,' Sara answered. That was all she was prepared to give him at this moment. Sara did not like to go on half pieces of information. She was a doctor, not a fortune-teller. Jeffrey knew this.

'Take me through it,' he said.

Sara folded her arms, not wanting to do this. She glanced back up the stairs to make sure no one was listening. 'You read the report,' she said.

'Please,' he said. 'I want to hear it from you.'

Sara leaned against the wall. She closed her eyes for a brief second, not to help her recall the facts, but to give herself some distance from what she knew.

She began, 'She was attacked on the toilet. She was probably easily subdued because of her blindness and the surprise element. I think he cut her early on, lifting her shirt, making the cross with his knife. The cut to her belly came early. It's not deep enough for full penetration. I think he inserted his penis more to defile her than anything else. He then raped her vaginally, which would explain the excrement I found there. I'm not sure if he climaxed. I don't imagine climax would be the issue for him.'

'You think it's more about defiling her?'

She shrugged. Many rapists had some sort of sexual dysfunction. She didn't see why it would be any different with this one. The gut rape practically pointed it out.

She said, 'Maybe it's the thrill of doing it in a semipublic place. Even though the lunch rush was over, someone could have come in and caught him.'

He scratched his chin, obviously letting himself absorb this.

'Anything else?'

'Can you clear some time to come by?' he asked. 'I can set up a briefing at nine-thirty.'

'A full briefing?'

He shook his head. 'I don't want anybody to know about that,' he ordered, and for the first time in a long while, she was in complete agreement with him.

She said, 'That's fine.'

'Can you come in around nine-thirty?' he repeated.

Sara ran through her morning. Jimmy Powell's parents would be in her office at eight. Going from one horrible meeting to another would probably make her day easier. What's more, she knew that the sooner she briefed the detectives on Sibyl Adams's autopsy results, the sooner they could go out and find the man who had killed her.

'Yeah,' she said, walking toward the stairs. 'I'll be there.'

'Wait a minute,' he said. 'Lena's going to be there, too.'

Sara turned around, shaking her head. 'No way. I'm not going to give a blow-by-blow of Sibyl's death in front of her sister.'

'She has to be there, Sara. Trust me on this.' He must have gathered her thoughts from the look she gave him. He said, 'She wants the details. It's how she deals with things. She's a cop.'

'It's not going to be good for her.'

'She's made her decision,' he repeated. 'She'll get the facts one way or another, Sara. It's better she gets the truth from us than read whatever lies they put in the paper.' He paused, probably seeing he still had not changed her mind. 'If it was Tessa, you would want to know what happened.'

'Jeffrey,' Sara said, feeling herself relent despite her better judgment. 'She doesn't need to remember her sister this way.'

He shrugged. 'Maybe she does.'

At a quarter till eight in the morning, Grant County was just waking up. A sudden overnight rain had washed the pollen out of the streets, and though it was still cool out, Sara drove her BMW Z3 with the top down. The car had been purchased during a post-divorce crisis when Sara had needed something to make herself feel better. It had worked for about two weeks, then the stares and the comments about the flashy car had made her feel a bit ridiculous. This was not the kind of car to drive in a small town, especially since Sara was a doctor, and not just a doctor but a pediatrician. Had she not been born and raised in Grant, Sara suspected she would have been forced to sell the car or lose half her patients at the clinic. As it was, she had to put up with the constant comments from her mother about how ridiculous it was for a person who barely managed to coordinate her wardrobe to drive a flashy sports car.

Sara tossed a wave to Steve Mann, the owner of the hardware store, as she drove toward the clinic. He waved back, a surprised smile on his face. Steve was married with three kids now, but Sara knew he still had a crush on her in that way that first loves tend to hold on. As her first real boyfriend, Sara had a fondness for him, but nothing more than that. She remembered those awkward moments she spent as a teenager, being groped in the back of Steve's car. How she was too embarrassed to look him in the eye the day after they had first had sex.

Steve was the kind of guy who was happy to set his roots down in Grant, who cheerfully went from being the star quarterback at Robert E. Lee High School to working with his father in the hardware store. At that age, Sara had wanted nothing more than to get out of Grant, to go to Atlanta and live a life that was more exciting, more challenging, than what her home town could offer. How she ended up back here was as much a mystery to Sara as anyone else.

She kept her eyes straight ahead as she passed the diner, not wanting to be reminded of yesterday afternoon. She was so intent on avoiding that side of the street that she nearly ran into Jeb McGuire as he walked in front of the pharmacy.

Sara pulled alongside him, apologizing, 'I'm sorry.'

Jeb laughed good-naturedly as he jogged over to her car. 'Trying to get out of our date tomorrow?'

'Of course not,' Sara managed, forcing a smile onto her face. With all that had happened yesterday, she had completely forgotten about agreeing to go out with him. She had dated Jeb off and on when he first moved to Grant eleven years ago and bought the town's pharmacy. Nothing serious had ever developed between them, and things had pretty much cooled between them by the time Jeffrey came along. Why she had agreed to start dating him again after all this time, Sara could not say.

Jeb pushed his hair back off his forehead. He was a lanky man with a runner's build. Tessa had once compared his body to Sara's greyhounds. He was good-looking, though, and certainly did not have to look far to find a woman who would go out with him.

He leaned on Sara's car, asking, 'Have you thought about what you want for dinner?'

Sara gave a shrug. 'I can't decide,' she lied. 'Surprise me.'

Jeb raised an eyebrow. Cathy Linton was right. She was a horrible liar.

'I know you got caught up in all that yesterday,' he began, waving toward the diner. 'I totally understand if you want to cancel.'

Sara felt her heart flip at the offer. Jeb McGuire was a nice man. As the town's pharmacist, he engendered a certain amount of trust and respect from the people he served. On top of that, he was pretty good-looking. The only problem was he was too nice, too agreeable. They had never argued because he was too laid back to care. If anything, this made Sara think of him more as she would a brother rather than a potential lover.

'I don't want to cancel,' she said, and oddly enough, she didn't. Maybe it would be good for her to get out more. Maybe Tessa was right. Maybe it was time.

Jeb's face lit up. 'If it's not too cool, I can bring my boat and take you out on the lake.'

She gave him a teasing look. 'I thought you weren't going to get one until next year?'

'Patience has never been a strong suit,' he answered, though the fact that he was talking to Sara proved that point to the contrary. He jabbed his thumb toward the pharmacy, indicating he needed to go. 'I'll see you around six, okay?'

'Six,' Sara confirmed, feeling some of his excitement rub off on her. She put the car in gear as he trotted over to the pharmacy. Marty Ringo, the woman who did checkout at the pharmacy, was standing at the entrance, and he put his arm around her shoulder as he unlocked the door.

Sara coasted into the clinic's parking lot. The Heartsdale Children's Clinic was rectangular in shape with an octagonal room made of glass brick swelling out at the front. This was the waiting area for patients. Fortunately, Dr. Barney, who had designed the building himself, was a better doctor than he was an architect. The front room had a southern exposure, and the glass bricks turned the place into an oven in the summer and a freezer in the winter. Patients had been known to have their fevers break while waiting to see a doctor.

The waiting room was cool and empty when Sara opened the door. She looked around the dark room, thinking not for the first time that she should redecorate. Chairs that could hardly be called anything but utilitarian were set out for patients and their parents. Sara and Tessa had spent many a day sitting in those chairs, Cathy beside them, waiting for their names to be called. In the corner was a play area with three tables so children who felt like it could draw or read while they waited. Issues of *Highlights* sat beside *People* magazine and *House & Garden*. Crayons were stacked neatly in their trays, paper beside them.

Looking back, Sara wondered if she had decided in this room to become a doctor. Unlike Tessa, the prospect of going to Dr. Barney never frightened Sara, probably because Sara was rarely sick as a child. She liked the part when they were called back and got to go into the places that only the doctors were allowed to go. In seventh grade, when Sara had shown an interest in science, Eddie had found a biology professor at the college who needed his main water line replaced. The professor tutored Sara in exchange for the work. Two years later, a chemistry professor needed his whole house replumbed, and Sara was performing experiments along████████ ██ege students.

The lights came on and Sara blinked to adjust her

eyes. Nelly opened the door separating the exam rooms from the waiting room.

'Good morning, Dr. Linton,' Nelly said, handing Sara a stack of pink messages, taking Sara's briefcase. 'I got your message this morning about the meeting at the station. I've already moved around your appointments. You don't mind working a little late?'

Sara shook her head, going through the messages.

'The Powells will be here in about five minutes, and there's a fax on your desk.'

Sara looked up to thank her, but she was already off, probably running down Elliot Felteau's schedule. Sara had hired Elliot straight out of his residency at Augusta Hospital. He was eager to learn what he could and eventually buy a partnership in the practice. While Sara wasn't sure how she felt about having a partner, she also knew Elliot was at least ten years away from being in a position to make an offer.

Molly Stoddard, Sara's nurse, met her in the hallway. 'Ninety-five percent blast on the Powell kid,' she said, citing the lab results.

Sara nodded. 'They'll be here any minute.'

Molly offered Sara a smile that said she did not envy Sara the task ahead of her. The Powells were good people. They had divorced a couple of years ago but shown surprising solidarity where their children were concerned.

Sara said, 'Can you pull a phone number for me? I want to send them to a man I know at Emory. He's doing some interesting trials with early stage AML.'

Sara gave the name as she slid open her office door. Nelly had put Sara's briefcase by her chair and a cup of coffee on her desk. Beside this was the fax she had mentioned. It was the GBI report on S— The Hems's blood work. Nick had scribbled an apology at the top, saying he would be in meetings most of the day and knew Sara would want to know the results as soon as possible. Sara read the report twice, feeling a cold ache in her stomach as she digested it.

She sat back in her chair, looking around her office. Her first month on the job had been hectic, but nothing like Grady. Maybe three months passed before Sara got used to the slower pace. Earaches and sore throats were plentiful, but not many kids came in with critical cases. Those went to the hospital over in Augusta.

Darryl Harp's mother was the first parent to give Sara a picture of her child. More parents followed suit, and pretty soon she started taping them to the walls of her office. Twelve years had passed since that first picture, and photographs of kids wallpapered her office wall and spilled into the bathroom. She could glance at any one of them and remember the kid's name and most of the time his or her medical history. Already she was seeing them come back to the clinic as young adults, telling them at nineteen years old they should probably consider seeing a general practitioner. Some of them actually cried. Sara had gotten choked up on a couple of occasions. Since she wasn't able to have children, she often found she developed strong attachments to her patients.

Sara opened her briefcase to find a chart, stopping at the sight of the postcard she had gotten in the mail. She stared at the photograph of Emory University's entrance gates. Sara remembered the day the acceptance letter had come from Emory. She had been offered scholarships to schools up north with more recognizable names, but Emory had always been a dream of hers. Real medicine took place there, and Sara could not imagine herself living anywhere else but the South.

She flipped the card over, tracing her finger along the

neatly typed address. Every year since Sara had left Atlanta, around the middle of April, she got a postcard like this one. Last year's had been from The World of Coke, the message stating, 'He's got the whole world in His hands.'

She started when Nelly's voice came through the speaker on the phone.

'Dr. Linton?' Nelly said. 'The Powells are here.'

Sara let her finger rest just above the red reply button. She dropped the card back in her briefcase, saying, 'I'll be right out to get them.'

EIGHT

When Sibyl and Lena were in the seventh grade, an older boy named Boyd Little thought it was funny to sneak up on Sibyl and snap his fingers in her ear. Lena followed him off the school bus one day and jumped on his back. Lena was small and quick, but Boyd was one year older and about fifty pounds heavier. He beat her to a pulp before the bus driver could break them up.

Keeping this episode in mind, Lena Adams could honestly say that she had never felt so physically ravaged as she did the morning after her sister's death. She finally understood why they called it 'hung over' because her entire body felt hung over her bones, and it took a good half hour under a hot shower before she could stand up straight. Her head felt ready to crack open from the stress in her brain. No amount of toothpaste could take the horrendous taste out of her mouth, and her stomach felt as if someone had wrapped it tightly into a ball and tied a couple of strings of dental floss around it.

She sat at the back of the briefing room of the station house, willing herself not to throw up again. Not that there was much left she could vomit. Her insides felt so vacant that her stomach was actually concave.

Jeffrey walked over to her, offering a cup of coffee. 'Drink some of this,' he ordered.

She didn't argue. At the house this morning, Hank

had told her the same thing. She had been too embarrassed to take anything from him, let alone advice, so she had suggested a different place for him to put the coffee.

As soon as she put the cup down, Jeffrey said, 'It's not too late, Lena.'

'I want to be here,' she countered. 'I have to know.'

He held her gaze for what seemed like an eternity. Despite the fact that any source of light was like needles in her eyes, she was not the first to break contact. Lena waited until he had left the room to sit back in her chair. She leaned the bottom of the cup on her knee as she closed her eyes.

Lena did not remember how she got home last night. The thirtyminute trip from Reece was still a blur. She did know that Hank had driven her car, because when she got into it this morning to drive to the station, the seat was pushed all the way back and the mirror was adjusted at an odd angle. The last thing Lena remembered was looking at her reflection in the plate glass window of the Stop 'n' Save. The next memory was the blaring ring of the telephone when Jeffrey had called to tell her about the briefing, practically begging her not to come. Everything else was lost to her.

Getting dressed this morning had been the hardest part. After the long shower, Lena wanted nothing more than to crawl back into bed, tucked into a ball. She would have been perfectly happy doing this for the rest of the day, but she couldn't give in to that weakness. Last night had been a mistake, but a necessary one. Obviously, she had needed to let herself go, to grieve as much as she could without falling apart.

This morning was a different story. Lena had forced herself to put on slacks and a nice jacket, the kind of outfit she wore every day on the job. Strapping on her holster, checking her gun, Lena had felt herself slipping back into being a cop instead of the victim's sister. Still, her head ached and her thoughts seemed to be stuck like glue on the inside of her brain. With an unprecedented sympathy, she understood how alcoholics got started. Somewhere in the back of her mind, she couldn't help thinking that a stiff drink would do her a world of good.

The door to the briefing room squeaked open, and Lena looked up in time to see Sara Linton standing in the hallway, her back to Lena. Sara was saying something to Jeffrey, and it did not look polite. Lena felt a pang of guilt for the way she treated Sara the night before. Despite what Lena had said, she knew that Sara was a good doctor. From all accounts, Linton had given up a very promising career in Atlanta to come back to Grant. She was owed an apology, something Lena did not even want to think about at this point in time. If records had been kept on the matter, Lena's outburst-to-apology ratio would be heavily weighted in the outburst department.

'Lena,' Sara said. 'Come on back with me.'

Lena blinked, wondering when Sara had crossed the room. She was standing at the door to the supply closet.

Lena scooted up in her chair to stand, forgetting about the coffee. Some of it spilled on her pants, but she didn't care. She set the cup on the floor and followed Sara's orders. The supply closet was large enough to be called a room, but the sign on the door had given it this designation years ago, and nobody had bothered to make a clarification. Among other things stored here were evidence, dummies for the CPR classes the police gave in the fall, and the emergency supply kit.

'Here,' Sara said, pulling up a chair. 'Sit.'

Again, Lena did as she was told. She watched as Sara rolled out a tank of oxygen.

Sara hooked up a mask to the tank, saying, 'Your head is hurting because the alcohol depletes oxygen in your blood.' She flexed the rubber band around the mask, holding it out to Lena. 'Take slow, deep breaths and it should start to feel better.'

Lena took the mask, not actually trusting Sara, but at this point she would have sucked the ass end of a skunk if someone had told her it would make her head stop pounding.

After a few more breaths, Sara asked, 'Better?'

Lena nodded, because it was better. She wasn't feeling up to her usual self, but at least she could open her eyes all the way.

'Lena,' Sara said, taking the mask back. 'I wanted to ask you about something I found.'

'Yeah?' Lena said, feeling put on her guard. She was expecting Sara to try to talk her out of being here during the briefing, so when the other woman spoke, Lena was surprised.

'When I was examining Sibyl,' Sara began, storing the tank back against the wall, 'I found some physical evidence that I wasn't exactly expecting.'

'Like what?' Lena asked, her mind starting to work again.

'I don't think it has a bearing on the case, but I have to tell Jeffrey what I found. It's not up to me to make that kind of decision.'

Despite the fact that Sara had helped her headache, Lena did not have patience for her games. 'What are you talking about?'

'I'm talking about the fact that your sister's hymen was intact up until the rape.'

Lena felt her stomach drop. She should have thought

of this, but too much had happened in the last twenty-four hours for Lena to come to logical conclusions. Now the whole world would know her sister was gay.

'I don't care, Lena,' Sara said. 'Really. However she wanted to live her life is fine with me.'

'What the hell does that mean?'

'It means what it means,' Sara answered, obviously thinking that was enough. When Lena did not respond, she added, 'Lena, I know about Nan Thomas. I put two and two together.'

Lena leaned her head back against the wall, closing her eyes. 'I guess you're giving me a heads up, huh? For telling everybody else my sister was gay?'

Sara was quiet, then, 'I hadn't planned on putting that in my briefing.'

'I'll tell him,' Lena decided, opening her eyes. 'Can you give me a minute?'

'Sure.'

Lena waited until Sara had left the room, then put her head into her hands. She wanted to cry, but no tears would come. Her body was so dehydrated she was amazed she still had spit in her mouth. She took a deep breath to brace herself and stood.

Frank Wallace and Matt Hogan were in the briefing room when she came out of the supply closet. Frank gave her a nod, but Matt made himself busy putting cream in his coffee. Both detectives were in their fifties, both from a very different time than the one Lena had grown up in. Like the rest of the detectives on the senior squad, they operated by the old rules of the police fraternity, where justice at any cost was right. The force was their family, and anything that happened to one of their officers affected them as it would a brother. If Grant was a close-knit community, the detectives were even closer. As a matter of fact, Lena knew that every one of her fellow detectives were members at the local lodge. Except for the simple matter of her not having a penis, she imagined she would have been invited to join a long time ago, if not out of respect, then obligation.

She wondered what these two old men would think knowing they were working a case to find out who had raped a lesbian. Once, a long time ago, Lena had actually heard Matt start a sentence with the words, 'Back when the Klan was doing some good . . . ' Would they be as vigilant if they knew about Sibyl, or would their anger dissipate? Lena did not want to find out the hard way.

Jeffrey was reading a report when she knocked on his open office door.

'Sara get you straightened out?' he asked.

She did not like the way he phrased his question, but Lena said yes anyway as she closed the door.

Jeffrey was obviously surprised to see her close the door. He set aside the report and waited for her to sit down before asking, 'What's up?'

Lena felt the best thing to do was blurt it out. 'My sister was a lesbian.'

Her words hung in the air over their heads like cartoons. Lena fought the urge to give a nervous laugh. She had never spoken them out loud before. Sibyl's sexuality was something Lena was not comfortable talking about, even with her sister. When Sibyl moved in with Nan Thomas a short year after moving to Grant, Lena had not pushed for details. She honestly had not wanted to know them.

'Well,' Jeffrey said, his voice indicating surprise, 'thank you for telling me that.'

'Do you think it impacts the investigation?' Lena asked, wondering if this was all for nothing.

'I don't know,' he answered, and she felt he was

telling the truth. 'Has anyone been sending her threatening mail? Making disparaging remarks?'

Lena wondered about this, too. Nan had said nothing new had happened in the last few weeks, but she also knew Lena was not open to discussing anything that might bring up the fact that Nan was fucking her sister. 'I guess you should talk to Nan.'

'Nan Thomas?'

'Yeah,' Lena said. 'They lived together. The address is on Cooper. Maybe we could go after the briefing?'

'Later today,' he said. 'Around four?'

Lena nodded her agreement. She couldn't stop herself from asking, 'Are you going to tell the guys?'

He seemed surprised by her question. After giving her a long look, he said, 'I don't think it's necessary at this stage. We'll talk to Nan tonight and go from there.'

Lena felt an inordinate amount of relief.

Jeffrey glanced at his watch. 'We'd better get to the briefing.'

NINE

Jeffrey stood at the front of the briefing room, waiting for Lena to come out of the bathroom. After their discussion, she had asked for a few minutes. He hoped she took the time to get herself together. Despite her temper, Lena Adams was a smart woman and a good cop. He hated to see her going through this alone. Jeffrey also knew that she would not have it any other way.

Sara sat in the front row, her legs crossed. She was wearing an olive-colored linen dress that fell to just above her ankles. Two slits came up either side of her legs, stopping just below her knees. Her red hair was pulled up into a ponytail behind her neck, like she had worn it to church on Sunday. Jeffrey remembered the expression on her face when she had noticed him sitting in the pew behind her and wondered if there would ever be a time in his life again when Sara was actually pleased to see him. He had stared at his hands the entire service, biding his time until he could slip out without causing too much commotion.

Sara Linton was what Jeffrey's father liked to call a tall drink of water. Jeffrey had been attracted to Sara because of her strong will, her fierce independence. He liked her aloofness and the way she talked down to his football buddies. He liked the way her mind worked and the fact that he could talk about every aspect of his job and know she would understand. He liked that she couldn't cook and that she could sleep through a hurricane. He liked that she was a horrible house cleaner and that her feet were so big she could wear his shoes. What he really liked was that she knew all these things about herself and was actually proud of them.

Of course, her independence had a downside. Even after six years of marriage, he wasn't sure he knew one damn thing about her. Sara was so good at projecting a strong facade that after a while he wondered if she even needed him. Between her family, the clinic, and the morgue, there did not seem to be a whole lot of time left for Jeffrey.

While he knew cheating on Sara was not the best way to go about changing things, he did know that at that point in time, something had to give in their marriage. He wanted to see her hurt. He wanted to see her fight for him and their relationship. That the first would happen and not the latter still kept his mind spinning. At times, Jeffrey was almost angry with Sara that something so meaningless, something so stupid as a mindless sexual indiscretion, had broken up their marriage.

Jeffrey leaned against the podium, his hands clasped in front of him. He pushed Sara from his mind and concentrated on the task at hand. On the card table beside him was a sixteen-page list of names and addresses. All convicted sexual offenders living in or moving to the state of Georgia were required to register their name and address with the Georgia Bureau of Investigation's Crime Information Center. Jeffrey had spent last night and most of the morning compiling this information on the sixty-seven Grant residents who had registered since the law was passed in 1996. Going through their crimes was a daunting task, not least of all because he knew that sexual predators were like cockroaches. For every one you saw, there were twenty more hiding behind the walls.

He did not let his mind dwell on this as he waited to start the meeting. The briefing room was hardly filled to capacity. Frank Wallace, Matt Hogan, and five other detectives were part of the senior squad. Jeffrey and Lena rounded out this number to nine. Of the nine, only Jeffrey and Frank had worked in municipalities larger than Grant. Sibyl Adams's killer certainly seemed to have better odds.

Brad Stephens, a junior patrolman who despite his youth and lack of rank knew how to keep his mouth shut, stood just beside the door in case anyone tried to come in. Brad was a kind of mascot around the squad, and the fact that he still had most of his baby fat gave him a round, cartoonish appearance. His thin blond hair always looked as if someone had just rubbed a balloon against it. His mother often brought his lunch to the station. He was a good kid, though. Brad had still been in high school when he contacted Jeffrey about being on the force. Like most of his younger cops, he came from Grant; his people were here. He had a vested interest in keeping the streets safe.

Jeffrey cleared his throat for attention as Brad opened the door for Lena. If anyone was surprised to see her there, they didn't say. She took a chair in the back, her arms crossed over her chest, her eyes still red either from her recent binge or from crying or from both.

'Thank you for coming on such short notice,' Jeffrey began. He gave Brad a nod, indicating that he should start circulating the five packets Jeffrey had put together earlier.

'Let me preface this by saying anything said in this room today should be treated as highly confidential information. What you hear today is not for general consumption and any leaks could greatly impede our case.' He waited as Brad finished his rounds.

'I'm sure all of you know by now that Sibyl Adams was killed yesterday at the Filling Station.' Nods came from the men who were not going through the copies. What he said next made them all look up. 'She was raped before she was killed.'

There seemed to be a rise in the temperature of the room as he let this set in. These men were from different times. Women were as mysterious to them as the origins of the planet. Sibyl's rape would galvanize them into action like nothing else.

Jeffrey held up his copy of the list as Brad passed out the packets according to the names Jeffrey had written on the outside. Jeffrey said, 'I pulled this list of offenders off the computer this morning. I've sectioned them off to the usual teams, with the exception of Frank and Lena.' He saw her mouth open to complain, but continued. 'Brad will be working with you, Lena. Frank is with me.'

Lena sat back in a defiant posture. Brad was hardly on her level, and her look said she knew exactly what he was doing. She would also realize as soon as she interviewed the third or fourth man on her list that Jeffrey was keeping her on a tight leash. Rapists tended to attack women in their own ethnic and age group. Lena and Brad would be interviewing every minority over the age of fifty with a sexual assault on his record.

'Dr. Linton will give you the rundown on the specifics.' He paused, then, 'My first guess would be that the attacker has some kind of religious leaning, maybe a fanatic. I don't want that to be the focus of your questioning, but keep it in the back of your mind.' He stacked the papers on the podium. 'If somebody comes up that we should look at, I want a call on my radio. I don't want any suspect falling down in custody or accidentally getting his head blown off.'

Jeffrey studiously avoided meeting Sara's eyes as he said this last part. Jeffrey was a cop, he knew how things worked in the street. He knew that every man in this room had something to prove where Sibyl Adams was concerned. He also knew how easy it was to slip over that line between legal justice and human justice when you were out in the field, facing down the kind of animal who could rape a blind woman and carve a cross onto her abdomen.

'That clear?' he asked, not expecting an answer and not getting one. 'I'll turn this over to Dr. Linton, then.'

He walked to the back of the room, standing behind and to the right of Lena as Sara took the podium. She walked over to the chalkboard, reached up, and pulled down the white projection screen. Most of the men in this room had seen her in diapers, and the fact that they all had their notebooks out said volumes about Sara's professional abilities.

She gave Brad Stephens a nod and the room went dark.

The green opaque projector whirred to life, sending a flash of bright light onto the screen. Sara moved a photograph onto the bed and slid it under the glass.

'Sibyl Adams was found by me in the women's bathroom of the Filling Station around two-thirty yesterday afternoon,' she said, focusing the projector's lens.

There was movement in the room as a Polaroid of Sibyl Adams lying partially nude on the bathroom floor came into view. Jeffrey found himself staring at the hole in her chest, wondering what kind of man could do the things that had been done to that poor young woman.

He did not want to think about Sibyl Adams, blind, sitting on that toilet while her attacker slit her open for his own sick reasons. He did not want to think about what was going through her mind as her abdomen was being raped.

Sara continued. 'She was sitting on the toilet when I opened the door.

'Her arms and legs were splayed open and the cut you see here' – she indicated the screen – 'was bleeding profusely.'

Jeffrey leaned over slightly, trying to see what Lena's reaction to this was. She stood stock still, her spine a perfect right angle to the floor. He understood why she needed to do this, but he could not grasp how she was doing it. If someone in his family had gone through this, if Sara had been ravaged like this, Jeffrey knew in his heart that he would not want to know. He could not know.

Sara stood at the front of the room, her arms crossed over her chest. 'She started to seize shortly after I established that she had a pulse. We fell to the ground. I tried to control the seizures, but she expired several seconds later.'

Sara jerked the projector's drawer out to replace the photo with another. The machine was a dinosaur, borrowed from the high school. It wasn't as if Sara could send the crime photos down to the Jiffy Photo for enlargements.

The next picture that came on-screen was a close up of Sibyl Adams's head and neck. 'The bruise under her eye came from a superior position, probably early on in the assault to discourage a struggle. A knife was held at her throat, very sharp, measuring about six inches. I'd say this was a boning knife, probably common to any kitchen. You can see a slight cut here.' She traced her finger on the screen, along the middle of Sibyl's neck. 'It didn't draw blood, but enough pressure was used to score the skin.' She looked up, catching Jeffrey's eye. 'I would imagine the knife was used to keep her from calling out while he raped her.'

She continued. 'There is a small bite mark on her left shoulder.' The picture of this came up. 'Bite marks are common with rape. This one shows the impression of the upper teeth only. I found nothing distinctive in the pattern, but I've sent the . . . ' Sara paused, probably remembering Lena was in the room. 'The impression was sent to the FBI lab for cross matching. If a known offender on file matches the impression, then we could assume that he's the perpetrator in this crime. However,' she warned, 'as we all know, the FBI won't consider this a high-priority case, so I don't think we can hang our hats on this piece of evidence. A more likely scenario would be to use the impression as validation after the fact. That is to say, find a solid suspect and nail him with the dental impression.'

Next, the screen showed a photograph of the inner sides of Sibyl's legs. 'You can see scrapes here at the knee where she gripped her legs around the toilet bowl during the assault.' Another picture came, this one of Sibyl's bottom. 'There are irregular bruises and scrapes on the buttocks, again from friction against the toilet seat.

'Her wrists,' Sara said, putting in another photo, 'show bruising from the handicap bars on the stall. Two fingernails were broken in the process of gripping the bars, probably to lift herself up and away from her assailant.'

Sara slid in the next photograph. 'This is a close-up of the incisions to her abdomen,' she narrated. 'The first cut was made from just below the collarbone all the way to the pelvic bone. The second cut was made from right to left.' She paused. 'I would guess from the irregular depth of the second cut that this was a backhanded movement by a lefthanded assailant. The cut is deeper as it moves to her right side.'

The next Polaroid was a close-up of Sibyl's chest. Sara was quiet for a few beats, probably thinking the same thing Jeffrey was thinking. Up close, he could see where the puncture wound had been stretched. Not for the first time, he felt his stomach roll at the thought of what was done to this poor woman. He hoped to God she had not been conscious of what was happening to her.

Sara said, 'This is the final cut. It's a puncture wound through the sternum. It goes straight through to her spine. I would guess this was the source of most of the blood.' Sara turned to Brad. 'Lights?'

She walked toward her briefcase, saying, 'The symbol on her chest seems to be a cross. The assailant used a condom during the rape, which as we know is pretty common with the advent of DNA testing. Black lighting revealed no sperm or fluids. Blood on the scene appears to be only from the victim.' She took a sheet of paper out of her briefcase. 'Our friends at the Georgia Bureau of Investigation were nice enough to pull some strings last night. They worked up the blood analysis for me.'

She put on her copper-rimmed glasses and began reading, 'High concentrations of hyoscyamine, atrosin and belladonnine as well as traces of scopolamine were found in her central blood and urine.' She looked up. 'This would suggest that Sibyl Adams ingested a lethal dose of belladonna, which belongs in the deadly nightshade plant family.'

Jeffrey glanced at Lena. She remained quiet, her eyes on Sara.

'An overdose of belladonna can mimic a complete shutdown of the parasympathetic nervous system. Sibyl Adams was blind, but her pupils were dilated from the drug. The bronchioles in her lungs were swollen. Her core body temperature was still high, which is what made me wonder about her blood in the first place.' She turned to Jeffrey, answering the question he had asked this morning. 'During the post, her skin was still warm to the touch. There were no environmental factors that would cause this. I knew it had to be something in the blood.'

She continued. 'Belladonna can be broken down for medical applications, but it's also used as a recreational drug.'

'You think the perp gave it to her?' Jeffrey asked. 'Or is this the kind of thing she would take on her own?'

Sara seemed to consider this. 'Sibyl Adams was a chemist. She certainly wouldn't take such a volatile drug, then run out for lunch. This is a very strong hallucinogen. It affects the heart, breathing, and circulation.'

'Nightshade grows all over town,' Frank pointed out.

'It's pretty common,' Sara agreed, looking back at her notes. 'The plant isn't easy to process. Ingestion is going to be the key component here. According to Nick, the easiest and most popular way to take belladonna is to soak the seeds in hot water. Just this morning I found three recipes on the Internet for preparing belladonna as a tea.'

Lena offered, 'She liked to drink hot tea.'

'There you go,' Sara said. 'The seeds are highly soluble. I imagine within minutes of drinking it she would have started experiencing elevated blood pressure, heart palpitations, dry mouth, and extreme nervousness. I would also guess this led her to the bathroom, where her rapist was waiting for her.'

Frank turned to Jeffrey. 'We need to talk to Pete Wayne. He served her lunch. He gave her the tea.'

'No way,' Matt countered. 'Pete's lived in town all his life. This isn't the kind of thing he'd do.' Then, as if this was the most important thing in Pete's favor, Matt added, 'He's in the lodge.'

Murmurs came from the other men. Someone, Jeffrey wasn't sure who, said, 'What about Pete's colored man?'

Jeffrey felt a trickle of sweat run down his back. He could see where this was going already. He held his hands up for silence. 'Frank and I will talk to Pete. You guys have your assignment. I want reports back at the end of the day.'

Matt seemed about to say something, but Jeffrey stopped him. 'We're not helping Sibyl Adams by sitting in this room pulling theories out of our asses.' He paused, then indicated the packets Brad had handed out. 'Knock on every goddamn door in town if you have to, but I want an accounting for every man on those lists.'

As Jeffrey and Frank walked to the diner, the words 'Frank's colored man' sat in the back of Jeffrey's mind like a piece of hot coal. The vernacular was familiar from his childhood, but he had not heard it used in at least thirty years. It amazed Jeffrey to see that such overt racism still existed. It also scared him that he had heard it in his own squad room. Jeffrey had worked in Grant for ten years, but he was still an outsider. Even his southern roots didn't pay his dues into the good old boy club. Coming from Alabama didn't help matters. A typical prayer among southern states was 'Thank God for Alabama,' meaning, thank God we're not as bad off as they are. This was part of the reason he was keeping Frank Wallace close at hand. Frank was a part of these men. He was in the club.

Frank shucked off his coat, folding it across his arm as he walked. He was tall and thin like a reed with a face rendered unreadable from years of being a cop.

Frank said, 'This black guy, Will Harris. I got called in a few years back on a domestic dispute. He popped his wife.'

Jeffrey stopped. 'Yeah?'

Frank stopped alongside him. 'Yeah,' he said. 'Beat her pretty bad. Busted her lip. When I got there, she was on the floor. She was wearing this cotton bag-looking kind of dress.' He shrugged. 'Anyway, it was torn.'

'You think he raped her?'

Frank shrugged. 'She wouldn't press charges.'

Jeffrey started walking again. 'Anybody else know about this?'

'Matt,' Frank said. 'He was my partner then.'

Jeffrey felt a sense of dread as he opened the door to the diner.

'We're closed,' Pete called from the back.

Jeffrey said, 'It's Jeffrey, Pete.'

He came out of the storeroom, wiping his hands on his apron. 'Hey, Jeffrey,' he said, nodding. Then, 'Frank.'

'We should be finished up in here this afternoon, Pete,' Jeffrey said. 'You'll be able to open tomorrow.'

'Closing for the rest of the week,' Pete said as he retied his apron strings. 'Don't seem right to be open what with Sibyl and all.' He indicated the row of stools in front of the bar. 'Get y'all some coffee?'

'That'd be great,' Jeffrey said, taking the first stool. Frank followed suit, sitting down beside him.

Jeffrey watched Pete walk around the counter and take out three thick ceramic mugs. The coffee steamed as he poured it into the cups.

Pete asked, 'You got anything yet?'

Jeffrey took one of the mugs. 'Can you run through what happened yesterday? I mean, from the point Sibyl Adams came into the restaurant?'

Pete leaned back against the grill. 'I guess she came in about one-thirty,' he said. 'She always came in after the lunch rush. I guess she didn't want to be poking around with her cane in front of all those people. I mean, we knew she was blind, sure, but she didn't like drawing attention to it. You could see that. She was kind of nervous in crowds.'

Jeffrey took out his notebook, though he didn't really need to take notes. What he did know was that Pete seemed to know a lot about Sibyl Adams. 'She come in here a lot?'

'Every Monday like clockwork.' He squinted his eyes, thinking. 'I guess for the last five years or so. She came in sometimes late at night with other teachers or Nan from the library. I think they rented a house over on Cooper.'

Jeffrey nodded.

'But that was only occasionally. Mostly it was Mondays, always by herself. She walked here, ordered her lunch, then was out by around two usually.' He rubbed his chin, a sad look coming over his face. 'She always left a nice tip. I didn't think anything about it when I saw her table empty. I guess I just thought she had gone while I wasn't looking.'

Jeffrey asked, 'What'd she order?'

'Same thing as always,' Pete said. 'The number three.'

Jeffrey knew this was the waffle platter with eggs, bacon, and a side of grits.

'Only,' Pete clarified, 'she didn't eat meat, so I always left off the bacon. And she didn't drink coffee, so I gave her some hot tea.'

Jeffrey wrote this down. 'What kind of tea?'

He rooted around behind the counter and pulled out a box of generic brand tea bags. 'I picked it up for her at the grocery store. She didn't drink caffeine.' He gave a small laugh. 'I liked to make her comfortable, you know? She didn't get out much. She used to say to me that she liked coming here, that she felt comfortable.' He fiddled with the box of tea.

'What about the cup she used?' Jeffrey asked.

'I don't know about that. They all look the same.' He walked to the end of the counter and pulled out a large metal drawer. Jeffrey leaned over to look inside. The drawer was actually a large dishwasher filled with cups and plates.

Jeffrey asked, 'Those from yesterday?'

Pete nodded. 'I can't begin to guess which one was hers. I started the washer before she was –' He stopped, looking down at his hands. 'My dad, he always told me to take care of the customers and they'd take care of you.' He looked up, tears in his eyes. 'She was a nice girl, you know? Why would anybody want to hurt her?'

'I don't know, Pete,' Jeffrey said. 'Mind if we take this?' He pointed to the box of tea.

Pete shrugged. 'Sure, nobody else drank it.' The laugh came again. 'I tried it once just to see. Tasted like brown water.'

Frank pulled a tea bag out of the box. Each bag was wrapped and sealed in a paper envelope. He asked, 'Was old Will working here yesterday?'

Pete seemed taken aback by the question. 'Sure, he's

worked lunch every day for the last fifty years. Comes in about eleven, leaves by two or so.' He studied Jeffrey. 'He does odd jobs for people around town after he leaves here. Mostly yard work, some light carpentry.'

'He buses tables here?' Jeffrey asked, though he had eaten enough lunches in the diner to know what Will Harris did.

'Sure,' Pete said. 'Buses tables, mops the floors, takes people their food.' He gave Jeffrey a curious look. 'Why?'

'No reason,' Jeffrey answered. Leaning over, he shook the man's hand, saying, 'Thanks, Pete. We'll let you know if we need anything else.'

TEN

Lena traced her finger along the street map in her lap. 'Left here,' she told Brad.

He did as he was told, steering the cruiser onto Baker Street. Brad was okay, but he tended to take people at face value, which is why back at the station when Lena said she had to go to the bathroom, then headed the exact opposite direction of the women's room, he hadn't said anything. A joke around the station house was to hide Brad's patrolman's hat from him. At Christmas, they had stuck it on top of one of the reindeer on display in front of city hall. A month ago, Lena had spotted the hat on top of the statue of Robert E. Lee in front of the high school.

Lena knew Jeffrey partnering her with Brad Stephens was his way of keeping her at the periphery of the investigation. If she had to guess, she would say that every man on their list was either dead or too old to stand up without help.

'The next right,' she said, folding the map. She had sneaked into Marla's office and looked up Will Harris's address in the phone book during her alleged trip to the bathroom. Jeffrey would interview Pete first. Lena wanted a crack at Will Harris before her chief could get to him.

'Right here,' Lena said, indicating he could pull over. 'You can stay here.'

Brad slowed the car, putting his fingers to his mouth. 'What's the address?'

'Four-thirty-one,' she said, spotting the mailbox. She slipped off her seat belt and opened her door before the car came to a complete stop. She was walking up the driveway by the time Brad caught up with her.

'What are you doing?' he asked, trotting alongside her like a puppy. 'Lena?'

She stopped, putting her hand in her pocket. 'Listen, Brad, just go back to the car.' She was two ranks above him. Technically, Brad was supposed to follow her orders. This thought seemed to cross his mind, but he shook his head no.

He said, 'This is Will Harris's place, isn't it?'

Lena turned her back to him, continuing up the driveway.

Will Harris's house was small, probably little more than two rooms and a bath. The clapboard was painted bright white and the lawn was neatly tended. There was a well-tended look to the place that set Lena on edge. She could not think that the person who lived in this house could do such a thing to her sister.

Lena knocked on the screen door. She could hear a television inside, and distant movement. Through the screen mesh, she could see a man struggling to get out of his chair. He was wearing a white undershirt and white pajama pants. A puzzled expression was on his face.

Unlike most people who worked in town, Lena wasn't a regular at the diner. Somewhere in the back of her mind Lena had considered the diner Sibyl's territory and hadn't wanted to intrude. Lena had never really met Will Harris. She had been expecting someone younger. Someone more menacing. Will Harris was an old man.

When he finally reached the door and saw Lena, his lips parted in surprise. Neither spoke for a moment, then Will finally said, 'You must be her sister.'

Lena stared at the old man. She knew in her gut that Will Harris had not killed her sister, but there was still the possibility that he knew who had.

She said, 'Yes, sir. Do you mind if I come in?'

The hinge on the screen door screeched as it opened. He stepped aside, holding the door open for Lena.

'You gotta excuse my appearance,' he said, indicating his pajamas. 'I wasn't exactly expecting visitors.'

'That's okay,' Lena offered, glancing around the small room. The living room and kitchen space were blended, a couch delineating the two. There was a square hallway off the left through which Lena could see a bathroom. She guessed the bedroom was on the other side of the wall. Like the outside of the house, everything was neat and tidy, well cared for despite its age. A television dominated the living room. Surrounding the set were wall-to-wall bookcases packed with videos.

'I like to watch a lot of movies,' Will said.

Lena smiled. 'Obviously.'

'Mostly, I like the old black and white ones,' the old man started, then turned his head toward the large picture window lining the front of the room. 'Lord a'mighty,' he mumbled. 'I seem to be real popular today.'

Lena suppressed a groan as Jeffrey Tolliver walked up the driveway. Either Brad had told on her or Pete Wayne had fingered Will.

'Morning, sir,' Will said, opening the screen door for Jeffrey.

Jeffrey gave him a nod, then shot Lena the kind of look that made her palms sweat.

Will seemed to sense the tension in the room. 'I can go in the back if you need.'

Jeffrey turned to the old man and shook his hand. 'No need, Will,' he said. 'I just need to ask you a few questions.'

Will indicated the couch with a sweep of his hand. 'Mind if I get me some more coffee?'

'No, sir,' Jeffrey answered, walking past Lena toward the couch. He fixed her with the same hard look, but Lena sat beside him anyway.

Will shuffled back to his chair, groaning as he sat. His knees popped and he smiled apologetically, explaining, 'Spend most of my days on my knees in the yard.'

Jeffrey took out his notebook. Lena could almost feel the anger coming off of him. 'Will, I've got to ask you some questions.'

'Yes, sir?'

'You know what happened at the diner yesterday?'

Will placed his coffee cup down on a small side table. 'That girl never hurt nobody,' he said. 'What was done to her –' He stopped, looking at Lena. 'My heart goes out to you and your family, sweetheart. It really does.'

Lena cleared her throat. 'Thank you.'

Jeffrey had obviously been expecting a different response from her. His look changed, but she couldn't make out what he was thinking. He turned back to Will. 'You were at the diner until what time yesterday?'

'Oh, around one-thirty or a little before two, I think. I saw your sister,' he told Lena, 'just as I was leaving.'

Jeffrey waited a few beats, then said, 'You're sure about that?'

'Oh, yes, sir,' Will returned. 'I had to go pick up my auntie at the church. They get out of choir practice at two-fifteen sharp. She don't like to wait.'

Lena asked, 'Where does she sing?'

'The AME over in Madison,' he answered. 'You ever been there?'

She shook her head, doing the math in her head. Even if Will Harris had been a viable suspect, there was no way he could have killed Sibyl, then made it to Madison in time to pick up his aunt. A quick phone call would give Will Harris an airtight alibi.

'Will,' Jeffrey began, 'I hate to ask you about this, but my man Frank says there was some problem a while back.'

Will's face dropped. He had been looking at Lena up until this point, but now he stared at the carpet. 'Yes, sir, that's right.' He looked over Jeffrey's shoulder as he spoke. 'My wife, Eileen. I used to go at her something bad. I guess it was before your time we got into a scuffle. Maybe eighteen, nineteen years ago.' He shrugged. 'She left me after that. I guess I let the drink lead me down the wrong path, but I'm a good Christian man now. I don't go in for all that. I don't see my son much, but I see my daughter often as I can. She lives in Savannah now.' His smile came back. 'I got two grandbabies.'

Jeffrey tapped his pen on the notebook. Lena could see over his shoulder that he had not written anything. He asked, 'Did you ever take Sibyl her meals? In the diner, I mean.'

If he was surprised by the question, Will didn't let it register. 'I guess I did. Most days I help Pete out with things like that. His daddy kept a woman around to wait tables when he was running the place, but Pete,' he said, chuckling, 'old Pete, he can hold on to a dollar.' Will waved his hand, dismissing the trouble. 'It don't hurt me none to fetch some ketchup or make sure somebody gets their coffee.'

Jeffrey asked, 'Did you serve Sibyl tea?'

'Sometimes. Is there a problem?'

Jeffrey closed his notebook. 'Not at all,' he said. 'Did you see anyone suspicious hanging around the diner yesterday?'

'Lord God,' Will breathed. 'I surely would've told you by now. It was just me and Pete there, and all the regulars for lunch.'

'Thank you for your time.' Jeffrey stood and Lena followed suit. Will shook first Jeffrey's, then Lena's hand.

He held on to hers a little longer, saying, 'God bless you, girl. You take care now.'

'Goddammit, Lena,' Jeffrey cursed, slamming his notebook into the dashboard of the car. The pages fluttered out, and Lena held her hands up in front of her to keep from getting whacked in the head. 'What the hell were you thinking?'

Lena picked up the notebook off the floor. 'I wasn't thinking,' she answered.

'No fucking joke,' he snapped, grabbing the notebook.

His jaw was a tight line as he backed the car out of Will Harris's driveway. Frank had gone back to the station with Brad while Lena had been practically thrown into Jeffrey's car. He bumped the gear on the steering wheel column and the car jerked into drive.

'Why can't I trust you?' he demanded. 'Why can't I trust you to do one thing I tell you to do?' He did not wait for her answer. 'I sent you out with Brad to do something, Lena. I gave you a job on this investigation because you asked me, not because I thought you were in any position to do it. And what's my reward for this? I've got Frank and Brad seeing you go behind my back like some teenager sneaking out of the house. Are you a fucking cop or are you a fucking kid?' He slammed on the brakes, and Lena felt her seat belt cutting into her chest. They were stopped in the middle of the road, but Jeffrey did not seem to notice.

'Look at me,' he said, turning to her. Lena did as she was told, trying to keep the fear out of her eyes. Jeffrey had been mad at her plenty of times, but never like this. If she had been right about Will Harris, Lena might have a leg to stand on; as it was, she was screwed.

'You have got to get your head on straight. Do you hear me?'

She gave a sharp nod.

'I can't have you going around behind my back. What if he had done something to you?' He let that sink in. 'What if Will Harris is the man who killed your sister? What if he opened his door, saw you, and freaked out?' Jeffrey slammed his fist into the steering wheel, hissing another curse. 'You have got to do what I say, Lena. Is that clear? From now on.' He jabbed his finger in her face. 'If I tell you to interview every ant on the playground, you bring me back signed depositions on each one. Is that clear?'

She managed to nod again. 'Yeah.'

Jeffrey wasn't satisfied. 'Is that clear, Detective?'

'Yes, sir,' Lena repeated.

Jeffrey put the car back into gear. The tires caught as he accelerated, leaving a good deal of rubber on the road. Both hands gripped the wheel so hard that his knuckles were white. Lena kept quiet, hoping his anger would pass. He had every right to be pissed, but she did not know what to say. An apology seemed as useless as treating a toothache with honey.

Jeffrey rolled his window down, loosening his tie. Suddenly, he said, 'I don't think Will did it.'

Lena nodded her head up and down, afraid to open her mouth.

'Even if he did have this episode in his past,' Jeffrey began, anger coming back into his voice, 'Frank failed to mention that this thing with his wife was twenty years ago.'

Lena was silent.

'Anyway' – Jeffrey waved this off – 'even if he had it in him, he's at least sixty, maybe seventy years old. He couldn't even get into his chair, let alone overpower a healthy thirty-three-year-old woman.'

Jeffrey continued, 'So that leaves us with Pete in the diner, right?' He didn't wait for her answer; he was obviously just thinking aloud. 'Only I called Tessa on the way over here. She got there a little before two o'clock. Will was gone, and Pete was the only one there. She said Pete stayed behind the cash register until she placed her order, then he grilled her burger.' Jeffrey shook his head. 'He might've slipped into the back, but when? When did he have time? That'd take, what? Ten, fifteen minutes? Plus the planning. How did he know it would work out?' Again these questions seemed rhetorical. 'And we all know Pete. I mean, Jesus, this isn't the kind of thing a first timer would pull.'

He was silent, obviously still thinking, and Lena left him alone. She stared out the window, processing what Jeffrey had said about Pete Wayne and Will Harris. An hour ago these two men had looked like good suspects to her. Now there was nobody. Jeffrey was right to be angry at her. She could have been out with Brad, tracking down the men on their list, maybe finding the man who had killed Sibyl.

Lena's eyes focused on the houses they were driving by. At the turn, she checked the street sign, noting that they were on Cooper.

Jeffrey asked, 'You think Nan will be home?'

Lena shrugged.

The smile he gave her said he was trying. 'You can talk now, you know.'

Her lips came up, but she couldn't quite return the smile. 'Thanks.' Then, 'I'm sorry about –'

He held up his hand to stop her. 'You're a good cop, Lena. You're a damn good cop.' He pulled the car to the curb in front of Nan and Sibyl's house. 'You just need to start listening.'

'I know.'

'No, you don't,' he said, but he did not seem angry anymore. 'Your whole life has turned upside down and you don't even know it yet.'

She started to speak then stopped.

Jeffrey said, 'I understand needing to work on this, needing to keep your mind occupied, but you've got to trust me on this, Lena. If you ever cross that line with me again, I will bust you so low you'll be fetching coffee for Brad Stephens. Is that clear?'

She managed to nod her head.

'Okay,' he said, opening the car door. 'Let's go.'

Lena took her time taking off her seat belt. She got out of the car, adjusting her gun and holster as she walked toward the house. By the time she reached the front door, Nan had already let Jeffrey in.

'Hey,' Lena offered.

'Hey,' Nan resumed. She was holding a ball of tissue in her hand, the same as she had been last night. Her eyes were puffy and her nose was bright red.

'Hey,' Hank said.

Lena stopped. 'What are you doing here?'

Hank shrugged, rubbing his hands together. He was wearing a sleeveless T-shirt, and the needle tracks up his arms were on full display. Lena felt a rush of embarrassment. She had only seen Hank in Reece, where everybody knew about his past. She had seen the scars so many times that she had almost blocked them out. Now she was seeing them through Jeffrey's eyes for the first time, and she wanted to run from the room.

Hank seemed to be waiting for Lena to say something. She stumbled, managing an introduction. 'This is Hank Norton, my uncle,' she said. 'Jeffrey Tolliver, chief of police.'

Hank held out his hand, and Lena cringed to see the raised scars on his forearms. Some of them were half an inch long in places where he had jabbed the needle into his skin, looking for a good vein.

Hank said, 'How d'you do, sir.'

Jeffrey took the offered hand, giving it a firm shake. 'I'm sorry we had to meet under these circumstances.'

Hank clasped his hands in front of him. 'Thank you for that.'

They were all silent, then Jeffrey said, 'I guess you know why we're here.'

'About Sibyl,' Nan answered, her voice a few octaves lower, probably from crying all night.

'Right,' Jeffrey said, indicating the sofa. He waited for Nan to sit, then took the space beside her. Lena was surprised when he took Nan's hand and said, 'I'm so sorry for your loss, Nan.'

Tears welled into Nan's eyes. She actually smiled. 'Thank you.'

'We're doing everything we can to find out who did this,' he continued. 'I want you to know if there's anything else you need we're here for you.'

She whispered another thank-you, looking down, picking at a string on her sweat pants.

Jeffrey asked, 'Was anybody angry at you or Sibyl, do you know?'

'No,' Nan answered. 'I told Lena last night. Everything's been the same as usual lately.'

'I know that Sibyl and you chose to live kind of quietly,' Jeffrey said.

Lena got his meaning. He was being a lot more subtle than she had been last night.

'Yeah,' Nan agreed. 'We like it here. We're both small-town people.'

Jeffrey asked, 'You can't think of anybody who might have figured something out?'

Nan shook her head. She looked down, her lips trembling. There was nothing else she could tell him.

'Okay,' he said, standing. He put his hand on Nan's shoulder, indicating she should stay seated. 'I'll let myself out.' He reached into his pocket and brought out a card. Lena watched as he cupped it in one hand and wrote on the back. 'This is my home number,' he said. 'Call me if you think of anything.'

'Thank you,' Nan said, taking the card.

Jeffrey turned to Hank. 'Do you mind giving Lena a ride home?'

Lena felt dumbstruck. She couldn't stay here.

Hank was obviously taken aback as well. 'No,' he mumbled. 'That's fine.'

'Good.' He patted Nan on the shoulder, then said to Lena, 'You and Nan can take tonight to put together a list of the people Sibyl worked with.' Jeffrey gave Lena a knowing smile. 'Be at the station at seven tomorrow morning. We'll go over to the college before classes start.'

Lena didn't understand. 'Am I back with Brad?'

He shook his head. 'You're with me.'

WEDNESDAY

ELEVEN

Ben Walker, the chief of police before Jeffrey, had kept his office in the back of the station, just off the briefing room. A desk the size of an upended commercial refrigerator was in the center of the room with a row of uncomfortable chairs in front of it. Every morning, the men on the senior squad were called into Ben's office to hear their assignments for the day, then they left and the chief shut his door. What Ben did from this time until five o'clock, when he could be seen scooting down the street to the diner for his supper, was a mystery.

Jeffrey's first task when he took over Ben's job was to move his office to the front of the squad room. Using a skill saw, Jeffrey cut a hole in the Sheetrock and installed a glass picture window so that he could sit at his desk and see his men and, more important, so that his men could see him. There were blinds on the window, but he never closed them, and for the most part, his office door was always open.

Two days after Sibyl Adams's body had been found, Jeffrey sat in his office, reading a report that Marla had just handed him. Nick Shelton at the GBI had been kind enough to rush through the analysis on the box of tea. Results: it was tea.

Jeffrey scratched his chin, looking around his office. It was a small room, but he had built a set of bookshelves into one of the walls in order to keep things neat. Field manuals and statistical reports were stacked alongside marksman trophies he had won at the Birmingham competitions and a signed team football from when he had played at Auburn. Not that he really played. Jeffrey had spent most of his time on the bench, watching the other players build careers for themselves.

A photograph of his mother was tucked into the far corner of the shelf. She was wearing a pink blouse and holding a small wrist corsage in her hands. The photo was taken at Jeffrey's high school graduation. He had caught his mother giving one of her rare smiles in front of the camera. Her eyes were lit up, probably with the possibilities she saw in front of her son. That he had dropped out of Auburn a year from graduation and taken a job on the Birmingham police force was something she still had not forgiven her only child for.

Marla tapped on his office door, holding a cup of coffee in one hand and a doughnut in the other. On Jeffrey's first day, she told him that she had never fetched coffee for Ben Walker and she wasn't about to fetch it for him. Jeffrey had laughed; the thought had never occurred to him. Marla had been bringing him his coffee ever since.

'The doughnut's for me,' she said, handing him the paper cup. 'Nick Shelton's on line three.'

'Thank you,' he said, waiting for her to leave. Jeffrey sat back in his chair as he picked up the phone. 'Nick?'

Nick's southern drawl came across the line. 'How are you?'

'Not so great,' Jeffrey answered.

'I hear you,' Nick returned. Then, 'Got my report?'

'On the tea?' Jeffrey picked up the sheet of paper, looking over the analysis. For such a simple beverage, a lot of chemicals went into processing tea. 'It's just cheap store-bought tea, right?'

'You got it,' Nick said. 'Listen, I tried to call Sara this morning, but I couldn't find her.'

'That so?'

Nick gave a low chuckle. 'You're never gonna forgive me for asking her out that time, are you, buddy?'

Jeffrey smiled. 'Nope.'

'One of my drug people here at the lab is hot on this belladonna. Not many cases come in, and he volunteered to give you guys a face-to-face rundown.'

'That'd be an awfully big help,' Jeffrey said. He saw Lena through the glass window and waved her in.

'Sara talking to you this week?' Nick didn't wait for an answer. 'My guy is gonna want to talk to her about how the victim presented.'

Jeffrey bit back the cutting remark that wanted to come, forcing some cheerfulness into his voice as he said, 'How about around ten?'

Jeffrey was noting the meeting on his calendar when Lena walked in. As soon as he looked up, she began speaking.

'He doesn't do drugs anymore.'

'What?'

'At least I don't think so.'

Jeffrey shook his head, not understanding. 'What are you talking about?'

She lowered her voice, saying, 'My uncle Hank.' She held her forearms out to him.

'Oh.' Jeffrey finally got it. He had not been sure if Hank Norton was a past drug addict or had been in a disfiguring fire, his arms were so scarred. 'Yeah, I saw they were old.'

She said, 'He was a speed freak, okay?'

Her tone was hostile. Jeffrey gathered she had been stewing on this since he had left her at Nan Thomas's house. So, this made two things she was ashamed of, her sister's homosexuality and her uncle's past drug problem. Jeffrey wondered if there was anything in Lena's life other than her job that gave Lena pleasure.

'What?' Lena demanded.

'Nothing,' Jeffrey said, standing. He took his suit coat off the peg behind his door and ushered Lena out of the office. 'You got the list?'

She seemed irritated that he did not want to chastise her for her uncle's old drug habit.

She handed him a sheet of notebook paper. 'This is what Nan and I came up with last night. It's a list of people who worked with Sibyl, who might have talked to her before she . . . ' Lena did not finish the sentence.

Jeffrey glanced down. There were six names. One had a star drawn beside it. Lena seemed to anticipate his question.

She said, 'Richard Carter is her GTA. Graduate teaching assistant. She had a nine o'clock class at the school. Other than Pete, he's probably the last person who saw her alive.'

'That name sounds familiar for some reason,' Jeffrey said, slipping on his coat. 'He's the only student on the list?'

'Yes,' Lena answered. 'Plus, he's kind of weird.'

'Meaning?'

'I don't know.' She shrugged. 'I've never liked him.'

Jeffrey held his tongue, thinking that Lena did not like a lot of people. That was hardly a good reason to look at someone for murder.

He said, 'Let's start with Carter first, then we'll talk to the dean.' At the entrance, he held the door open for her. 'The mayor will have a heart attack if we don't go through the proper protocols with the professors. Students are fair game.'

The Grant Institute of Technology's campus consisted of a student center, four classroom buildings, the administrative building, and an agricultural wing that had been donated by a very grateful seed manufacturer. Lush grounds surrounded the university on one side, with the lake backing up to the other. Student housing was within walking distance of all the buildings, and bicycles were the most common mode of campus transportation.

Jeffrey followed Lena to the third floor of the science classroom building. She had obviously met her sister's assistant before, because Richard Carter's face soured when he recognized Lena at the door. He was a short, balding man who wore heavy black glasses and an ill-fitting lab coat over a bright yellow dress shirt. He had that anal-retentive air about him that most of the college people had. The Grant Institute of Technology was a school for geeks, plain and simple. English classes were mandatory but not exactly difficult. The school was geared more toward turning out patents than socially evolved men and women. That was the biggest problem Jeffrey had with the school. Most of the professors and all of the students had their heads so far up their asses they couldn't see the world in front of them.

'Sibyl was a brilliant scientist,' Richard said, leaning over a microscope. He mumbled something, then looked back up, directing his words to Lena. 'She had an amazing memory.'

'She had to,' Lena said, taking out her notebook. Jeffrey wondered not for the first time if he should let Lena ride along with him. More than anything, he wanted her underfoot. After yesterday, he did not know if he could trust her to do what he told her to do. It was better to keep her close by and safe than let her go off on her own.

'Her work,' Richard began. 'I can't describe how meticulous she was, how exacting. It's very rare to see such a high standard of attention in this field anymore. She was my mentor.'

'Right,' Lena said.

Richard gave her a sour, disapproving look, asking, 'When's the funeral?'

Lena seemed taken aback by the question. 'She's being cremated,' she said. 'That's what she wanted.'

Richard clasped his hands in front of his belly. The same disapproving look was on his face. It was almost condescending, but not quite. For just a moment, Jeffrey caught something behind his expression. Richard turned, though, and Jeffrey was not sure if he had been reading too much into things.

Lena began, 'There's a wake, I guess you'd call it, tonight.' She scribbled on her pad, then ripped the sheet off. 'It's at Brock's Funeral Home on King Street at five.'

Richard glanced down his nose at the paper before folding it neatly in two, then again, then tucking it into the pocket of his lab coat. He sniffed, using the back of his hand to wipe his nose. Jeffrey could not tell if he had a cold or was trying not to cry.

Lena asked, 'So, was there anyone strange hanging around the lab or Sibyl's office?'

Richard shook his head. 'Just the usual weirdos.' He laughed, then stopped abruptly. 'I guess that's not altogether appropriate.'

'No,' Lena said. 'It's not.'

Jeffrey cleared his throat, getting the young man's attention. 'When was the last time you saw her, Richard?'

'After her morning class,' he said. 'She wasn't feeling well. I think I caught her cold.' He took out a tissue as if to support this. 'She was such a wonderful person. I really can't tell you how lucky I was that she took me under her wing.'

'What did you do after she left school?' Jeffrey asked.

He shrugged. 'Probably went to the library.'

'Probably?' Jeffrey asked, not liking his casual tone.

Richard seemed to pick up on Jeffrey's irritation. 'I was at the library,' he amended. 'Sibyl asked me to look up some references.'

Lena took over, asking, 'Was there anyone acting strange around her? Maybe dropping by more than usual?'

Richard shook his head side to side again, his lips pursed. 'Not really. We're more than halfway through the term. Sibyl teaches upper level classes, so most of her students have been here for a couple of years at least.'

'No new faces in the crowd?' Jeffrey asked.

Again Richard shook his head. He reminded Jeffrey of one of those bobbing dogs some people put on their dashboards.

Richard said, 'We're a small community here. Somebody acting strange would stick out.'

Jeffrey was about to ask another question when Kevin Blake, the dean of the college, walked into the room. He did not look happy.

'Chief Tolliver,' Blake said. 'I assume you're here about the missing student.'

Julia Matthews was a twenty-three-year-old junior majoring in physical science. She had been missing for two days, according to her dorm mate.

Jeffrey walked around the young women's dorm

room. There were posters on the wall with encouraging statements about success and victory. On the bedside table was a photograph of the missing girl standing beside a man and a woman who were obviously her parents. Julia Matthews was an attractive girl in a plain, wholesome way. In the photograph, her dark hair was pulled into pigtails on either side of her head. She had a snaggled front tooth, but other than that, she looked like the perfect girl next door. As a matter of fact, she looked very much like Sibyl Adams.

'They're out of town,' Jenny Price, the missing girl's dorm mate, supplied. She stood in the doorway wringing her hands as she watched Jeffrey and Lena search the room.

She continued. 'It's their twentieth wedding anniversary. They went on a cruise to the Bahamas.'

'She's very pretty,' Lena said, obviously trying to calm the girl. Jeffrey wondered if Lena noticed the similarity between Julia Matthews and her sister. They both had olive-colored skin and dark hair. They both looked to be about the same age, though Sibyl was in fact ten years older. Jeffrey felt uncomfortable and set the picture down as he realized that both women resembled Lena as well.

Lena turned her attention to Jenny, asking, 'When did you first notice she was missing?'

'When I got back from class yesterday, I guess,' Jenny answered. A slight redness came to her cheeks. 'She's been gone overnight before, right?'

'Sure,' Lena supplied.

'I thought maybe she was out with Ryan. That's her old boyfriend?' She paused. 'They broke up about a month ago. I saw them at the library together a couple of days ago, around nine o'clock at night. That was the last time I saw her.'

Lena picked up on the boyfriend, saying, 'It's pretty stressful trying to have a relationship when you've got classes and work to do.'

Jenny gave her a weak smile. 'Yeah. Ryan's in the agricultural school. His workload isn't nearly as heavy as Julia's.' She rolled her eyes. 'As long as his plants don't die, he gets an A. Meanwhile we're studying all night, trying to get lab time.'

'I remember what it was like,' Lena said, though she had never been to college. The easy way lies came to her both alarmed and impressed Jeffrey. She was one of the best interviewers he had ever seen.

Jenny smiled and her shoulders relaxed. Lena's lie had done the trick. 'You know how it is, then. It's hard to make time to breathe, let alone have a boyfriend.'

Lena asked, 'They broke up because she didn't have enough time for him?'

Jenny nodded. 'He's her first boyfriend ever. Julia was really upset.' She gave Jeffrey a nervous glance. 'She really fell hard for him, you know? She was sick, like, with grief, when they broke up. She wouldn't even get out of bed.'

Lena lowered her voice, as if to leave Jeffrey out. 'I guess when you saw them in the library, they weren't exactly studying.'

Jenny glanced at Jeffrey. 'No.' She laughed nervously.

Lena walked over, blocking his view of the girl. Jeffrey took the hint. He turned his back to the two women, pretending to take an interest in the contents of Julia's desk.

Lena's voice dropped to a conversational tone. 'What do you think about Ryan?'

'You mean, do I like him?'

'Yeah,' Lena answered. 'I mean, not like like him. I mean, does he seem like a nice guy?'

The girl was quiet for a while. Jeffrey picked up a science book and thumbed through the pages.

Finally, Jenny said, 'Well, he was kind of selfish, you know? And he didn't like it when she couldn't see him.'

'Kind of controlling?'

'Yeah, I guess,' the girl answered. 'She's from the sticks, okay? Ryan kind of takes advantage of that. Julia doesn't know a lot about the world. She thinks he does.'

'Does he?'

'God, no.' Jenny laughed. 'I mean, he's not a bad guy –'

'Of course not.'

'He's just . . . ' She paused. 'He doesn't like for her to talk to other people, okay? He's, like, scared that she'll see there are better guys out there. At least, that's what I think. Julia's kind of been sheltered all her life. She doesn't know to look out for guys like that.' Again she paused. 'He's not a bad guy, he's just needy, you know? He has to know where she's going, who she'll be with, when she'll be back. He doesn't like for her to have any time to herself at all.'

Lena's voice was still low. 'He never hit her, did he?'

'No, not like that.' Again the girl was silent. Then, 'He just yelled at her a lot. Sometimes when I would come back from study group, I would listen at the door, you know?'

'Yeah,' Lena said. 'To make sure.'

'Right,' Jenny agreed, a nervous giggle escaping. 'Well, one time, I heard him in here and he was being so mean to her. Just saying nasty things.'

'Nasty like what?'

'Like that she was bad,' Jenny said. 'Like that she was going to hell for being so bad.'

Lena took her time asking the next question. 'He's a religious guy?'

Jenny made a derisive sound. 'When it's convenient. He knows that Julia is. She's really into church and all. I mean, she was back home. She doesn't go much here, but she's always talking about being in the choir and being a good Christian and that kind of thing.'

'But Ryan's not religious?'

'Only when he thinks he can work her with something. Like he says he's real religious, but he's got all kinds of body piercings, and he's always wearing black and he –' She stopped speaking.

Lena lowered her voice. 'What?' she asked then, even lower. 'I won't tell anybody.'

Jenny whispered something, but Jeffrey couldn't make out what she was saying.

'Oh,' Lena said as if she had heard it all. 'Guys are so stupid.'

Jenny laughed. 'She believed him.'

Lena chuckled with her, then asked, 'What did Julia do that was so bad, do you think? I mean, to get Ryan upset at her like that?'

'Nothing,' Jenny answered vehemently. 'That's what I asked her later. She wouldn't tell me. She just lay in bed all day, not saying anything.'

'This was around the time they broke up?'

'Yeah,' Jenny confirmed. 'Last month, like I said.' There was worry in her voice when she asked, 'You don't think he has anything to do with her being missing, do you?'

'No,' Lena said. 'I wouldn't worry about that.'

Jeffrey turned around, asking, 'What's Ryan's last name?'

'Gordon,' the girl supplied. 'Do you think Julia's in trouble?'

Jeffrey considered her question. He could tell her not to worry, but that might give the girl a false sense of security. He settled for, 'I don't know, Jenny. We'll do everything we can to find her.'

A quick visit to the registrar's office revealed that Ryan Gordon was study hall monitor this time of day. The agricultural wing was on the outskirts of the campus, and Jeffrey felt his anxiety build with every step they took across the campus. He sensed the tension coming from Lena as well. Two days had passed with no solid leads. They could very well be about to meet the man who had killed Sibyl Adams.

Granted, Jeffrey was not prepared to be Ryan Gordon's best friend, but there was something about the kid that set Jeffrey against him the minute they met. He had his eyebrow and both ears pierced as well as a ring hanging out from the septum in the middle of his nose. The ring looked black and crusty, more like something you would put in an ox rather than in a human nose. Jenny's description of Ryan Gordon had not been kind, but in retrospect, Jeffrey thought she had been generous. Ryan looked filthy. His face was an oily mix of acne and healing scabs. His hair looked like it had not been washed in days. His black jeans and shirt were rumpled. There was an odd odor coming off him.

Julia Matthews was, by all accounts, a very attractive young woman. How someone like Ryan Gordon had managed to snag her was a mystery to Jeffrey. This said a lot about the type of kid Gordon was, if he could manage to control someone who could quite clearly do a hell of a lot better than him.

Jeffrey noticed the kind part of Lena that had earlier worked Jenny Price was long gone by the time they reached the study hall classroom. She walked purposefully into the room, ignoring the curious glances coming from the other students, mostly male, as she made a beeline for the kid sitting behind the desk in front of the class.

'Ryan Gordon?' she asked, leaning over the desk. Her jacket pulled back, and Jeffrey saw the kid's eyes gave her gun a sharp glance. His lips stayed pressed into a tight, surly line, though, and when he answered, Jeffrey felt the urge to smack him.

Gordon said, 'What's it to you, bitch?'

Jeffrey grabbed the kid up by his collar and duck-walked him out of the room. Even as he did this, Jeffrey was certain there would be an angry message from the mayor before he got back to the office.

Outside the study room, he pushed Gordon into the wall. Jeffrey took out his handkerchief, wiping the grease off his hand. 'They got showers in your dorm?' he asked.

Gordon's voice was just as whiny as Jeffrey had expected. 'This is police brutality.'

To Jeffrey's surprise, Lena gave Gordon an open-palmed slap.

Gordon rubbed his cheek, his mouth turned down at the corners. He seemed to size Lena up. Jeffrey found the look he gave her almost comical. Ryan Gordon was thin as a rail, about Lena's height if not her weight. She had attitude on him in spades. Jeffrey had no doubt that Lena would rip his throat open with her bare teeth if Gordon tried to push her.

Gordon seemed to understand this. He took on a passive posture, his voice a nasally whine, perhaps from the ring in his nose, which bobbed when he spoke. 'What do you want from me, man?'

He held his arms up defensively as Lena's hand reached out to his chest.

She said, 'Put your hands down, you pussy.' She

reached down into his shirt and pulled up the cross hanging on a chain around his neck.

'Nice necklace,' she said.

Jeffrey asked, 'Where were you Monday afternoon?'

Gordon looked from Lena to Jeffrey. 'What?'

'Where were you Monday afternoon?' Jeffrey repeated.

'I don't know, man,' he whined. 'Sleeping, probably.' He sniffed, rubbing his nose. Jeffrey fought the urge to cringe as the ring in his nose moved back and forth.

'Up against the wall,' Lena ordered, pushing him around. Gordon started to protest, but a look from Lena stopped him. He spread his arms and legs out, assuming the position.

Lena patted him down, asking, 'I'm not going to find any needles, am I? Nothing that would hurt me?'

Gordon groaned, 'No,' as she reached into his front pocket.

Lena smiled, pulling out a bag of white powder. 'This isn't sugar, is it?' she asked Jeffrey.

He took the bag, surprised that she had found it. This would certainly explain Gordon's appearance. Drug addicts weren't the most conscientious groomers in the world. For the first time that morning, Jeffrey was glad to have Lena around. He would never have thought to frisk the boy.

Gordon glanced over his shoulder, looking at the bag. 'These aren't my pants.'

'Right,' Lena snapped. Spinning Gordon around, she asked, 'When was the last time you saw Julia Matthews?'

Gordon's face registered his thoughts. He obviously knew where this was leading. The powder was the least of his problems. 'We broke up a month ago.'

'That doesn't answer the question,' Lena said. She

repeated, 'When was the last time you saw Julia Matthews?'

Gordon crossed his arms in front of his chest. Jeffrey realized instantly that he had mishandled this whole thing. Nerves and excitement had gotten the better of him. In his mind, Jeffrey said the words that Gordon spoke aloud.

'I want to talk to a lawyer.'

Jeffrey propped his feet on the table in front of his chair. They were in the interview room, waiting for Ryan Gordon to be processed. Unfortunately, Gordon had kept his mouth closed tighter than a steel trap from the minute Lena read him his rights. Luckily, Gordon's roommate at the dorms had been more than happy to allow a search. This had yielded nothing more suspicious than a pack of rolling papers and a mirror with a razor blade lying on top of it. Jeffrey wasn't sure, but judging from the roommate, the drug paraphernalia could have belonged to either boy. A search of the lab where Gordon worked did not add any additional clues to the pot. The best-case scenario was Julia Matthews had realized what an asshole her boyfriend was and split.

'We fucked up,' Jeffrey said, resting his hand on a copy of the *Grant County Observer*.

Lena nodded. 'Yeah.'

He took a deep breath and let it go. 'I suppose a kid like that would've lawyered up anyway.'

'I don't know,' Lena answered. 'Maybe he watches too much TV.'

Jeffrey should have expected this. Any idiot with a television knew to ask for a lawyer when the cops showed up at your door.

'I could have been a little softer,' she countered.

'Obviously, if he's our guy, he wouldn't exactly be happy to have a woman pushing him around.' She gave a humorless laugh. 'Especially me, looking just like her.'

'Maybe that'll work some in our favor,' he offered. 'What about I leave you two alone here while we wait for Buddy Conford?'

'He got Buddy?' Lena asked, her tone indicating her displeasure. There were a handful of lawyers in Grant who took on public defender work for a reduced fee. Of them all, Buddy Conford was the most tenacious.

'He's on the rotation this month,' Jeffrey said. 'You think Gordon's stupid enough to talk?'

'He's never been arrested before. He doesn't strike me as particularly savvy.'

Jeffrey was silent, waiting for her to continue.

'He's probably pretty pissed at me for slapping him,' she said, and he could see her working out an approach in her mind. 'Why don't you help me set it up? Tell me not to talk to him.'

Jeffrey nodded. 'It might work.'

'Couldn't hurt.'

Jeffrey was silent, staring at the table. Finally he tapped his finger on the front page of the paper. A picture of Sibyl Adams took up most of the space above the fold. 'I guess you saw this?'

She nodded, not looking at the photo.

Jeffrey turned the paper over. 'It doesn't say she was raped, but they hint at it. I told them she was beaten, but she wasn't.'

'I know,' she mumbled. 'I read it.'

'Frank and the guys,' Jeffrey began, 'they haven't found anything solid from the known offender list. There were a couple Frank wanted to look at seriously, but nothing panned out. They both had alibis.'

Lena stared at her hands.

Jeffrey said, 'You can leave after this. I know you probably need to get some things together for tonight.'

Her acquiescence surprised him. 'Thank you.'

A knock came at the door, then Brad Stephens poked his head in. 'I've got your guy out here.'

Jeffrey stood, saying, 'Bring him in.'

Ryan Gordon looked even more puny in the orange jailhouse jumper than he had in his black jeans and shirt. His feet shuffled in the matching orange slippers, and his hair was still wet from the hosing down Jeffrey had ordered. Gordon's hands were cuffed behind his back, and Brad handed Jeffrey the key before leaving.

'Where's my lawyer?' Gordon demanded.

'He should be here in about fifteen minutes,' Jeffrey answered, pushing the kid down into a chair. He unlocked the handcuffs, but before Gordon could move his arms he had cuffed him back through the rungs of the chair.

'That's too tight,' Gordon whined, pushing his chest out to exaggerate his discomfort. He pulled at the chair, but his hands stayed tight behind him.

'Live with it,' Jeffrey muttered, then said to Lena, 'I'm going to leave you in here with him. Don't let him say anything off-the-record, do you hear me?'

Lena cast her eyes down. 'Yes, sir.'

'I mean it, Detective.' He gave her what he hoped was a stern look, then walked out of the room. Jeffrey took the next door down, entering the observation room. He stood with his arms crossed, watching Gordon and Lena through the one-way glass.

The interview room was relatively small with painted cement blocks for walls. A table was bolted to the center of the floor with three chairs spread around it. Two on one side, one on the other. Jeffrey watched Lena pick up the newspaper. She propped her feet up on the table, leaning the chair back a little as she opened the *Grant County Observer* to an inside page. Jeffrey heard the speaker next to him crackle as she folded the paper along the seam.

Gordon said, 'I want some water.'

'Don't talk,' Lena ordered, her voice so low Jeffrey had to turn up the speaker on the wall to hear her.

'Why? You gonna get in trouble?'

Lena kept her nose in the paper.

'You should get in trouble,' Gordon said, leaning over as much as he could in the chair. 'I'm gonna tell my lawyer you slapped me.'

Lena snorted a laugh. 'What do you weigh, one fifty? You're about five six?' She put the paper down, giving him a soft, innocent expression. Her voice was high-pitched and girlish. 'I would never hit a suspect in custody, Your Honor. He's so big and strong, I'd be afraid for my life.'

Gordon's eyes narrowed to slits. 'You think you're pretty funny.'

'Yeah,' Lena said, returning to the paper. 'I really do.'

Gordon took a minute or two to refigure his approach. He pointed to the newspaper. 'You're that dyke's sister.'

Lena's voice was still light, though Jeffrey knew she must have wanted to climb over the table and kill him. She said, 'That's right.'

'She got killed,' he said. 'Everybody on campus knew she was a dyke.'

'She certainly was.'

Gordon licked his lips. 'Fucking dyke.'

'Yep.' Lena turned the page, looking as if she was bored.

'Dyke,' he repeated. 'Fucking clit licker.' He paused,

waiting for a reaction, obviously irritated that there was none. He said, 'Gash grinder.'

Lena gave a bored sigh. 'Bushwhacker, eats at the Y, dials O on her friend's little pink telephone.' She paused, looking at him over the paper, asking, 'Leaving any out?'

While Jeffrey felt an appreciation for Lena's technique, he said a small prayer of thanks that she had not chosen a life of crime.

Gordon said, 'That's what you've got me in here for, right? You think I raped her?'

Lena kept the paper up, but Jeffrey knew her heartbeat was probably going as fast as his. Gordon could be guessing, or he could be looking for a way to confess.

Lena asked, 'Did you rape her?'

'Maybe,' Gordon said. He started rocking the chair back and forth, like a little boy craving attention. 'Maybe I fucked her. You wanna know about it?'

'Sure,' Lena said. She put the paper down, crossing her arms. 'Why don't you tell me all about it?'

Gordon leaned toward her. 'She was in the bathroom, right?'

'You tell me.'

'She was washing her hands, and I went in and fucked her up the ass. She liked it so much she died on the spot.'

Lena gave a heavy sigh. 'That's the best you can do?'

He seemed insulted. 'No.'

'Why don't you tell me what you did to Julia Matthews?'

He sat back in the chair, leaning on his hands. 'I didn't do anything to her.'

'Where is she then?'

He shrugged. 'Probably dead.'

'Why do you say that?'

He leaned forward, his chest pressed into the table. 'She's tried to kill herself before.'

Lena did not skip a beat. 'Yeah, I know. Slit her wrists.'

'That's right.' Gordon nodded, though Jeffrey could see the surprise in his face. Jeffrey was surprised, too, though it made perfect sense. Women were far more likely to choose slitting their wrists over the many other methods of suicide. Lena had made a calculated guess.

Lena summarized, 'She slit her wrists last month.'

He cocked his head, giving her a strange look. 'How'd you know that?'

Lena sighed again, picking the paper back up. She opened it with a snap, then started to read.

Gordon started rocking his chair back and forth again.

Lena did not look up from the paper. 'Where is she, Ryan?'

'I don't know.'

'Did you rape her?'

'I didn't have to rape her. She was a damn lapdog.'

'You let her go down on you?'

'That's right.'

'That the only way you could get it up, Ryan?'

'Shit.' He dropped the chair. 'You're not supposed to be talking to me anyway.'

'Why?'

' 'Cause this is off-the-record. I can say anything I want and it doesn't matter.'

'What do you want to say?'

His lips twitched. He leaned over further. From Jeffrey's perspective, he thought that with Gordon's hands cuffed behind him, the kid almost looked hog-tied.

Gordon whispered, 'Maybe I want to talk about your sister some more.'

Lena ignored him.

'Maybe I wanna talk about how I beat her to death.'

'You don't look like the type of guy who knows how to use a hammer.'

He seemed taken aback by this. 'I am,' he assured her. 'I beat her in the head, then I fucked her with the hammer.'

Lena folded the paper to a new page. 'Where'd you leave the hammer?'

He looked smug. 'Wouldn't you like to know?'

'What was Julia up to, Ryan?' Lena asked casually. 'She screwing around on you? Maybe she found a real man.'

'Fuck that, bitch,' Gordon snapped. 'I am a real man.'

'Right.'

'Take off these cuffs and I'll show you.'

'I bet you will,' Lena said, her tone indicating she was not in the least bit threatened. 'Why did she run around on you?'

'She didn't,' he said. 'That bitch Jenny Price tell you that? She doesn't know anything about it.'

'About how Julia wanted to leave you? About how you followed her around all the time, wouldn't leave her alone?'

'Is that what this is about?' Gordon asked. 'That why you got me freaking chained up?'

'We've got you chained up for the coke in your pocket.'

He snorted. 'It wasn't mine.'

'Not your pants, right?'

He slammed his chest into the table, his face a mask of anger. 'Listen, bitch –'

Lena stood in front of him, leaning over the table, her face in his. 'Where is she?'

Spit came from his mouth. 'Fuck you.'

In one quick motion, Lena grabbed the ring hanging down from his nose.

'Ow, shit,' Gordon screamed as he leaned over, his chest slamming into the table, his arms sticking up behind his back. 'Help!' he screamed. The glass in front of Jeffrey shook from the noise.

Lena whispered, 'Where is she?'

'I saw her a couple of days ago,' he managed through gritted teeth. 'Jesus, please let go.'

'Where is she?'

'I don't know,' he yelled. 'Please, I don't know! You're gonna pull it out.'

Lena released the ring, wiping her hand on her pants. 'You stupid little twit.'

Ryan wiggled his nose, probably making sure it was still there. 'You hurt me,' he whined. 'That hurt.'

'You want me to hurt you some more?' Lena offered, resting her hand on her gun.

Gordon tucked his head into his chest, mumbling, 'She tried to kill herself because I left her. She loved me that much.'

'I think she didn't have a clue,' Lena countered. 'I think she was pretty much fresh off the truck and you took advantage of her.' She stood up, leaning halfway over the table. 'What's more, I don't think you have the balls to kill a fly, let alone a living person, and if I ever' – Lena slammed her hands into the table, her anger bursting like a grenade, 'if I ever hear you say anything else about my sister, Ryan, anything at all, I will kill you. Trust me on this, I know I have it in me. I don't doubt that for a second.'

Gordon's mouth moved wordlessly.

Jeffrey was so engrossed in the interview that he didn't notice the knock at the door.

'Jeffrey?' Marla said, poking her head into the observation room. 'We got a situation at Will Harris's place.'

'Will Harris?' Jeffrey asked, thinking that was the last name he had expected to hear today. 'What happened?'

Marla stepped into the room, lowering her voice. 'Somebody threw a rock in the front window of his house.'

Frank Wallace and Matt Hogan were standing on Will Harris's front lawn when Jeffrey pulled up. He wondered how long they had been there. Wondered, too, if they knew who had done this. Matt Hogan did not have qualms about hiding his prejudices. Frank, on the other hand, Jeffrey was not sure about. What he did know was Frank had been in on the interview of Pete Wayne yesterday. Jeffrey felt his tension build as he parked the car. He did not like being in a position where he could not trust his own men.

'What the hell happened?' Jeffrey asked, getting out of the car. 'Who did this?'

Frank said, 'He got home about half an hour ago. Said he was working at old Miss Betty's house, aerating her yard. Came home and saw this.'

'It was a rock?'

'Brick, actually,' Frank said. 'Same kind you see everywhere. Had a note around it.'

'What'd it say?'

Frank looked down at the ground, then back up. 'Will's got it.'

Jeffrey looked at the picture window, which had a large hole in it. The two windows on either side were untouched, but the glass in the center would cost a small fortune to replace. 'Where is he?' Jeffrey asked.

Matt nodded toward the front door. He had the same smug look Jeffrey had seen on Ryan Gordon a few minutes ago.

Matt said, 'In the house.'

Jeffrey started toward the door, then stopped himself. He reached into his wallet and pulled out a twenty. 'Go buy some plywood,' he said. 'Bring it back here as soon as possible.'

Matt's jaw set, but Jeffrey levered him with a hard stare. 'You got something you want to say to me, Matt?'

Frank interjected, 'We'll see if we can get some glass on order while we're there.'

'Yeah,' Matt grumbled, walking toward the car.

Frank started to follow, but Jeffrey stopped him. He asked, 'You got any idea who might have done this?'

Frank stared down at his feet for a few seconds. 'Matt was with me all morning, if that's what you're getting at.'

'It was.'

Frank looked back up. 'I'll tell you what, Chief, I find out who did, I'll take care of it.'

He did not wait around for Jeffrey's opinion on this. He turned, walking back toward Matt's car. Jeffrey waited for them to drive off before walking up the drive to Will Harris's house.

Jeffrey gave the screen door a gentle knock before letting himself in. Will Harris was sitting in his chair, a glass of iced tea beside him. He stood when Jeffrey entered the room.

'I didn't mean to bring you out here,' Will said. 'I was just reporting it. My neighbor got me kind of scared.'

'Which one?' Jeffrey asked.

'Mrs. Barr across the way.' He pointed out the window. 'She's an older woman, scares real easy. She said she didn't see anything. Your people already asked her.' He walked back to his chair and picked up a piece of white paper, which he offered to Jeffrey. 'I got kind of scared, too, when I saw this.'

Jeffrey took the paper, tasting bile in the back of his throat as he read the threatening words typed onto the white sheet of paper. The note said: 'Watch your back, nigger.'

Jeffrey folded the paper, tucking it into his pocket. He put his hands on his hips, looking around the room. 'Nice place you got here.'

'Thank you,' Will returned.

Jeffrey turned toward the front windows. He did not have a good feeling about this. Will Harris's life was in danger simply because Jeffrey had talked to him the other day. He asked, 'You mind if I sleep on your couch tonight?'

Will seemed surprised. 'You think that's necessary?'

Jeffrey shrugged. 'Better safe than sorry, don't you think?'

TWELVE

Lena sat at the kitchen table in her house, staring at the salt and pepper shakers. She tried to get her head around what had happened today. She was certain that Ryan Gordon's only crime was being an asshole. If Julia Matthews was smart, she had headed back home or was lying low for a while, probably trying to get away from her boyfriend. This left the reason Jeffrey and Lena had gone to the college wide open. There were still no suspects for her sister's murder.

With each minute that passed, with each hour that went by with no solid lead toward finding the man who had killed her sister, Lena felt herself getting more and more angry. Sibyl had always warned Lena that anger was a dangerous thing, that she should allow other emotions to come through. Right now, Lena could not imagine herself ever being happy again, or even sad. She was numbed by the loss, and anger was the only thing that made her feel like she was still alive. She was embracing her anger, letting it grow inside of her like a cancer, so that she would not break down into a powerless child. She needed her anger to get her through this. After Sibyl's killer was caught, after Julia Matthews was found, Lena would let herself grieve.

'Sibby.' Lena sighed, putting her hands over her eyes. Even during the interview with Gordon, images of Sibyl had started to seep into Lena's mind. The harder she fought them off, the stronger they were.

They came in flashes, these memories. One minute, she was sitting across from Gordon, listening to his pathetic posturing, the next she was twelve years old, at the beach, leading Sibyl down to the ocean so they could play in the water. Early on after the accident that had blinded Sibyl, Lena had become her sister's eyes; through Lena, Sibyl was sighted again. To this day, Lena thought this trick was what made her a good detective. She paid attention to detail. She listened to her gut instinct. Right now, her gut was telling her any more time focusing on Gordon was wasted.

'Hey there,' Hank said, taking a Coke out of the refrigerator. He held up a bottle for Lena, but she shook her head.

Lena asked, 'Where did those come from?'

'I went to the store,' he said. 'How'd it go today?'

Lena didn't answer his question. 'Why did you go to the store?'

'You didn't have anything to eat,' he said. 'I'm surprised you haven't wasted away.'

'I don't need you to go to the store for me,' Lena countered. 'When are you going back to Reece?'

He seemed pained by her question. 'In a couple of days, I guess. I can stay with Nan if you don't want me here.'

'You can stay here.'

'It's no trouble, Lee. She's already offered her sofa.'

'You don't need to stay with her,' Lena snapped. 'Okay? Just drop it. If it's only a few days, that's fine.'

'I could stay in a hotel.'

'Hank,' Lena said, aware her voice was louder than it needed to be. 'Just drop it, okay? I've had a really hard day.'

Hank fiddled with his bottle of Coke. 'Wanna talk about it?'

Lena bit back the 'Not with you' that was on the tip of her tongue. 'No,' she said.

He took a swig of Coke, staring somewhere over her shoulder.

'There are no leads,' Lena said. 'Other than the list.' Hank look puzzled, and she explained, 'We've got this list of everybody who moved to Grant in the last six years who's a sexual predator.'

'They keep a list of that?'

'Thank God they do,' Lena said, heading off any civil liberties arguments he wanted to start. As an ex-addict, Hank tended to side with personal privacy over common sense. Lena was in no mood for a discussion about how ex-cons had paid their dues.

'So,' Hank said, 'you've got this list?'

'We've all got lists,' Lena clarified. 'We're knocking on doors, trying to see if anybody matches up.'

'To?'

She stared at him, trying to decide whether or not to go on. 'Someone with a violent sexual assault in their background. Someone who's white, between the ages of twenty-eight and thirty-five. Someone who thinks of himself as a religious person. Someone who might have seen Sibyl around. Whoever attacked her knew her routines, so this person had to be someone who knew her by sight or in passing.'

'That sounds like a pretty narrow margin.'

'There are nearly a hundred people on the list.'

He gave a low whistle. 'In Grant?' He shook his head side to side, not quite buying this.

'That's just the last six years, Hank. I guess if we go through these without finding anyone, we'll go back even further. Maybe ten or fifteen years.'

Hank pushed his hair back off his forehead, giving Lena a good look at his forearms. She pointed to his bare arms. 'I want you to keep your coat on tonight.'

Hank looked down at the old track marks. 'If you want me to, okay.'

'Cops will be there. Friends of mine. People I work with. They see those tracks and they're gonna know.'

He looked down at his arms. 'I don't think you'd have to be a cop to know what these are.'

'Don't embarrass me, Hank. It's bad enough I had to tell my boss you're a junkie.'

'I'm sorry about that.'

'Yeah, well,' Lena said, not knowing what else to offer. She was tempted to look him over, to pick at him until he exploded and she got a good fight out of him.

Instead, she turned in her chair, looking away from him. 'I'm not in the mood for a heart-to-heart.'

'Well, I'm sorry to hear that,' Hank said, but he did not get up. 'We need to talk about what to do with your sister's ashes.'

Lena held her hand up to stop him. 'I can't do that right now.'

'I've been talking to Nan –'

She interrupted him. 'I don't care what Nan has to say about this.'

'She was her lover, Lee. They had a life together.'

'So did we,' Lena snapped. 'She was my sister, Han. For God's sake, I'm not going to let Nan Thomas have her.'

'Nan seems like a real nice person.'

'I'm sure she is.'

Hank fiddled with the bottle. 'We can't leave her out of this just because you're uncomfortable with it, Lee.' He paused, then, 'They were in love with each other. I don't know why you have a problem accepting that.'

'Accepting it?' Lena laughed. 'How could I not accept it? They lived together. They took vacations together.' She remembered Gordon's earlier comment. 'Evidently the whole fucking college knew about it,' she said. 'It's not like I had a choice.'

Hank sat back with a sigh. 'I don't know, baby. Were you jealous of her?'

Lena cocked her head. 'Of who?'

'Nan.'

She laughed. 'That's the stupidest thing I've ever heard you say.' She added, 'And we both know I've heard you say some really stupid shit.'

Hank shrugged. 'You had Sibby to yourself for a long time. I can see where her meeting somebody, getting involved with someone, might make it difficult for her to be there for you.'

Lena felt her mouth open in shock. The fight she was hoping for seconds ago was now blowing up in her face. 'You think I was jealous of Nan Thomas because she was fucking my sister?'

He flinched at her words. 'You think that's all they were about?'

'I don't know what they were about, Hank,' Lena said. 'We didn't talk about that part of her life, okay?'

'I know that.'

'Then why did you bring it up?'

He did not answer. 'You're not the only one who lost her.'

'When did you hear me say that I was?' Lena snapped, standing.

'It just seems that way,' Hank said. 'Listen, Lee, maybe you need to talk to somebody about this.'

'I'm talking to you about it right now.'

'Not me.' Hank frowned. 'What about that boy you were seeing? Is he still around?'

She laughed. 'Greg and I split up a year ago, and even if we hadn't, I don't think I'd be crying on his shoulder.'

'I didn't say you would be.'

'Good.'

'I know you better than that.'

'You don't know a goddamn thing about me,' she snapped. Lena left the room, her fists clenching as she took the steps upstairs two at a time, slamming her bedroom door behind her.

Her closet was filled mostly with suits and slacks, but Lena found a black dress tucked in the back. She pulled out the ironing board, stepping back, but not in time to miss the iron slipping off the shelf and smashing into her toe.

'Damnit,' Lena hissed, grabbing her foot. She sat down on the bed, rubbing her toes. This was Hank's fault, getting her worked up this way. He was always doing this kind of thing, always pushing his damn AA philosophies about closure and sharing onto Lena. If he wanted to live his life that way, if he needed to live his life that way so that he did not end up shooting himself full of dope or drinking himself to death, that was fine, but he had no right to try to push that onto Lena.

As for his armchair diagnosis of Lena being jealous of Nan, that was just ridiculous. Her entire life, Lena had worked to help Sibyl become independent. It was Lena who had read reports aloud so that Sibyl did not have to wait for Braille translations. It was Lena who listened to Sibyl practice her oral exams and Lena who helped Sibyl with experiments. All that had been for Sibyl, to help her go out on her own, to get a job, to make a life for herself.

Lena opened the ironing board and placed the dress on it. She smoothed the material, remembering the last time she had worn this dress. Sibyl had asked Lena to take her to a faculty party at the college. Lena was surprised but had agreed to go. There was a clear line between college people and town folks, and she had felt uncomfortable in that crowd, surrounded by people who had completed not only college but also gone on to get higher degrees. Lena was not a country bumpkin, but she remembered feeling like she stuck out like a sore thumb.

Sibyl, on the other hand, had been in her element. Lena could remember seeing her at the center of a crowd, talking to a group of professors who seemed to be really interested in what she was saying. No one was staring at her the way people did when the girls were growing up. No one was making fun of her or making snide comments about the fact that she could not see. For the first time in her life, Lena had realized that Sibyl did not need her.

Nan Thomas had nothing to do with this revelation. Hank was wrong about that. Sibyl had been independent from day one. She knew how to take care of herself. She knew how to get around. She may have been blind, but in some ways she was sighted. In some ways, Sibyl could read people better than someone who could see because she listened to what they were saying. She heard the change of cadence in their voices when they were lying or the tremor when they were upset. She had understood Lena like no one else in her life.

Hank knocked at the door. 'Lee?'

Lena wiped her nose, realizing that she had been crying. She did not open the door. 'What?'

His voice was muffled, but she could hear him loud and clear. He said, 'I'm sorry I said that, honey.'

Lena took a deep breath, then let it go. 'It's okay.'

'I'm just worried about you.'

'I'm okay,' Lena said, turning on the iron. 'Give me ten minutes and I'll be ready to go.'

She watched the door, saw the doorknob turn slightly, then turn back as it was released. She heard his footsteps as he walked down the hall.

The Brock Funeral Home was packed to the gills with Sibyl's friends and colleagues. After ten minutes of shaking hands and accepting condolences from people she had never met in her life, Lena had a tight knot developing in her stomach. She felt like she might explode from standing still for too long. She did not want to be here, sharing her grief with strangers. The room seemed to be closing in on her, and though the air-conditioning was low enough to keep some people in their coats, Lena was sweating.

'Hey,' Frank said, cupping her elbow in his hand.

Lena was surprised at the gesture but did not pull away. She felt overwhelmed with relief to talk to someone familiar.

'You hear what happened?' Frank asked, shooting Hank a sideways look. Lena felt a blush of embarrassment at the look, knowing that Frank had pegged her uncle for a punk. Cops could smell it from a mile away.

'No,' Lena said, escorting Frank to the side of the room.

'Will Harris,' he began in a low tone. 'Somebody threw a rock through his front window.'

'Why?' Lena asked, already guessing the answer.

Frank shrugged. 'I don't know.' He looked over his shoulder. 'I mean, Matt.' Again the shrug came. 'He was with me all day. I don't know.'

Lena pulled him into the hallway so they would not have to whisper. 'You think Matt did something?'

'Matt or Pete Wayne,' he said. 'I mean, they're the only two I can think of.'

'Maybe somebody in the lodge?'

Frank bristled, like she knew he would. She might as well have accused the pope of fiddling with a ten-year-old.

Lena asked, 'What about Brad?'

Frank gave her a look.

'Yeah,' Lena said. 'I know what you mean.' She could not say without a shadow of a doubt that Brad Stephens might not like Will Harris, but she knew that Brad would cut off his own arm before he broke the law. Once Brad had backtracked three miles just to pick up some trash that had accidentally blown out of his car window.

'I was thinking of talking to Pete later on,' Frank said.

Without thinking, Lena checked the time. It was a little after five-thirty. Pete would probably be home.

'Can we take your car?' she asked, thinking she could leave hers for Hank to take home.

Frank looked back into the parlor. 'You wanna leave your sister's wake?' he asked, not hiding his shock.

Lena stared at the floor, knowing she should feel ashamed at the very least. The fact was, she had to get out of this room with these strangers before grief took hold and she became too paralyzed to do anything but sit in her room crying.

Frank said, 'Meet me around the side in ten minutes.'

Lena walked back into the room, looking for Hank. He was standing by Nan Thomas, his arm around her shoulder. She felt herself bristle, seeing them together like that. He certainly had no problem comforting a complete stranger, no matter that his own flesh and blood was not ten feet away from him, alone.

Lena went back into the hallway to get her coat. She was slipping it on when she felt someone helping her. She was surprised to see Richard Carter behind her.

'I wanted to tell you,' he said, his tone hushed, 'that I'm sorry about your sister.'

'Thanks,' she managed. 'I appreciate that.'

'Have you found anything about that other girl?'

'Matthews?' she asked before she could catch herself. Lena had grown up in a small town, but she was still amazed at how quickly word got around.

'That Gordon,' Richard said, giving a dramatic shudder. 'He's not a very nice boy.'

'Yeah,' Lena mumbled, trying to move him along. 'Listen, thanks for coming tonight.'

His smile was slight. He realized she was moving him along, but obviously he did not want to make it easy for her. He said, 'I really enjoyed working with your sister. She was very good to me.'

Lena shifted from one foot to another, not wanting to give him the impression that she was looking for a long conversation. She knew Frank well enough to know he wouldn't wait for very long.

'She enjoyed working with you, too, Richard,' Lena offered.

'Did she say that?' he asked, obviously pleased. 'I mean, I know she respected my work, but did she say that?'

'Yes,' Lena said. 'All the time.' She picked out Hank in the crowd. He still had his arm around Nan. She pointed them out to Richard. 'Ask my uncle. He was just talking about it the other day.'

'Really?' Richard said, putting his hands up to his mouth.

'Yes,' Lena answered, taking her car keys out of her coat pocket. 'Listen, can you give these to my uncle?'

He stared at the keys without taking them. This was one of the reasons Sibyl had gotten along so well with Richard, she wasn't able to see the condescending looks he gave. In fact, Sibyl seemed to have the patience of Job where Richard Carter was concerned. Lena knew for a fact that Sibyl had helped him get out of academic probation on more than one occasion.

'Richard?' she asked, dangling the keys.

'Sure,' he finally said, holding out his hand.

Lena dropped the keys onto his palm. She waited until he had taken a few steps away, then scooted out the side door. Frank was waiting in his car, the lights out.

'Sorry I'm late,' Lena said, getting in. She wrinkled her nose when she smelled smoke. Technically, Frank was not allowed to smoke around her when they were on the job, but she kept her mouth shut since he was doing her a favor letting her ride along.

'Those college people,' Frank said. He took a drag on the cigarette, then chucked it out the window. 'Sorry,' he offered.

'It's okay,' Lena said. She felt odd being dressed up and in Frank's car. For some reason, she was reminded of her first date. Lena was strictly a jeans and T-shirt girl, so putting on a dress was a big deal. She felt awkward wearing heels and hose, and never knew how to sit or where to put her hands. She missed her holster.

'About your sister,' Frank began.

Lena let him off the hook. 'Yeah, thanks,' she said.

Night had fallen while Lena was in the funeral home, and the farther away from town they got, the farther away from streetlights and people, the darker it got in the car.

'This thing at old Will's house,' Frank began, breaking the silence. 'I don't know about that, Lena.'

'You think Pete had a hand in it?'

'I don't know,' Frank repeated. 'Will worked for his daddy, maybe twenty years before Pete came along. That's something you shouldn't forget.' He reached for a cigarette, then stopped himself. 'I just don't know.'

Lena waited, but there was nothing more. She kept her hands in her lap, staring ahead as Frank drove out of town. They crossed the city line and were well into Madison before Frank slowed his car, taking a hard right onto a dead-end street.

Pete Wayne's brick ranch house was modest, much like the man. His car, a 1996 Dodge with red tape where the taillights used to be, was parked in the driveway at an angle.

Frank pulled the car up to the curb and cut the headlights. He gave a nervous laugh. 'You all dressed up like that, I feel like I should get your door for you.'

'Don't you dare,' Lena countered, grabbing the handle in case he was serious.

'Hold on,' Frank said, putting his hand on Lena's arm. She thought he was pushing the joke, but something about his tone made her look up. Pete was coming out of his house, a baseball bat in his hand.

Frank said, 'Stay here.'

'The hell I will,' Lena said, opening her door before he could stop her. The dome light came on in the car, and Pete Wayne looked up.

Frank said, 'Good going, kid.'

Lena bit back her anger over the nickname. She walked up the driveway behind Frank, feeling stupid in the high heels and long dress.

Pete watched them coming, keeping the bat at his side. 'Frank?' he asked. 'What's up?'

'Mind if we come in for a second?' Frank asked, adding, 'Brother.'

Pete gave a nervous sideways look to Lena. She knew these lodge people had their own special code of language. What exactly Frank meant by calling Pete his brother, she had no idea. For all she knew, Frank was telling Pete to hit Lena with the bat.

Pete said, 'I was just going out.'

'I see that,' Frank said, eyeing the bat. 'Little late for practice, ain't it?'

Pete handled the bat nervously. 'I was just putting it into the van. Got a little nervous about what happened at the diner,' he said. 'Thought I'd keep it behind the bar.'

'Let's go inside,' Frank said, not giving Pete a chance to respond. He walked up the front steps and stood at the front door, waiting for Pete to catch up, hovering over the other man as he fumbled with his keys in the lock.

Lena followed them. By the time they reached the kitchen, Pete was noticeably on guard. His hand was wrapped so tightly around the bat that his knuckles had turned white.

'What's the problem here?' Pete asked, directing his question toward Frank.

'Will Harris had a problem this afternoon,' Frank said. 'Somebody threw a rock into his front window.'

'That's too bad,' Pete answered, his voice flat.

'I gotta say, Pete,' Frank said, 'I think you did it.'

Pete laughed uncomfortably. 'You think I got time to run down and toss a brick through that boy's window? I've got a business to run. I don't have time to take a crap most days, let alone take a trip.'

Lena said, 'What makes you think it was a brick?'

Pete swallowed hard. 'Just a guess.'

Frank grabbed the bat out of his hand. 'Will's worked for your family for nearly fifty years.'

'I know that,' Pete said, taking a step back.

'There were times when your daddy had to pay him with food instead of money because he couldn't afford help otherwise.' Frank weighted the bat in his hand. 'You remember that, Pete? You remember when the base closed and y'all almost went under?'

Pete's face flushed. ''Course I remember that.'

'Let me tell you something, boy,' Frank said, putting the tip of the bat squarely against Pete's chest. 'You listen to me good when I tell you this. Will Harris didn't touch that girl.'

'You know that for a fact?' Pete countered.

Lena put her hand on the bat, bringing it down. She stepped in front of Pete, looking him in the eye. She said, 'I do.'

Pete broke eye contact first. His eyes went to the floor, and his posture took on a nervous stance. He shook his head, letting out a heavy breath. When he looked up, it was Frank he spoke to. 'We've gotta talk.'

THIRTEEN

Eddie Linton had purchased acreage around the lake when he first started making money from his plumbing business. He also owned six houses near the college that he rented out to students, as well as an apartment complex over in Madison that he was always threatening to sell. When Sara moved back to Grant from Atlanta, she had refused to live in her parents' house. Something about moving back home, living in her old room, smacked of defeat to Sara, and at the time she was feeling beaten down enough without the constant reminder that she did not even have a space of her own.

She had rented one of her father's houses her first year back, then started working weekends at the hospital in Augusta in order to save up a down payment for her own place. She had fallen in love with her house the first time the realtor showed her through. Built in a shotgun style, the house's front door lined up directly with the back door. Off to the sides of the long hallway were two bedrooms, a bathroom, and a small den on the right, with the living room, dining room, another bathroom and kitchen on the left. Of course, she would have bought the house if it had been a shack, because the view to the lake was phenomenal from the deck off the back. Her bedroom took full advantage of this, a large picture window flanked by three windows that opened out on either side.

On days like today, she could see clear across, nearly to the university. Some days, when the weather was right, Sara took her boat into the school dock and walked to work.

Sara opened the window in her bedroom so she could hear Jeb's boat when he got to the dock. Last night had seen another soft rain, and a cool breeze was coming off the lake. She studied her appearance in the mirror on the back of the door. She had chosen a wraparound skirt with a small floral print and a tight black Lycra shirt that fell just below her navel. Already, she had put her hair up, then let it back down. She was in the process of pinning it back up when she heard a boat at the dock. She slipped on her sandals and grabbed two glasses and a bottle of wine before walking out the back door.

'Ahoy,' Jeb said, tossing her a rope. He tucked his hands into his orange life vest, affecting what Sara supposed he thought was a jaunty sailor look.

'Ahoy yourself,' Sara answered, kneeling by the bollard. She put the wine and glasses down on the dock as she tied off the line. 'Still haven't learned to swim, have you?'

'Both my parents were terrified of the water,' he explained. 'They never got around to it. And it's not like I grew up near water.'

'Good point,' she said. Having grown up on a lake, swimming came second nature to Sara. She could not imagine not knowing how. 'You should learn,' she said. 'Especially since you're boating.'

'Don't need to know how,' Jeb said, patting the boat as he would a dog. 'I can walk on water with this baby.'

She stood up, admiring the boat. 'Nice.'

'Real babe magnet,' he joked, unhooking the vest. She knew he was teasing, but the boat, painted a deep metallic black, was sleek and sexy, with a dangerous look about it. Unlike Jeb McGuire in his bulky orange life jacket.

Jeb said, 'I'll tell you what, Sara, if you ever looked at me the way you're looking at my boat right now, I'd have to marry you.'

She laughed at herself, saying, 'It's a very pretty boat.'

He pulled out a picnic basket and said, 'I'd offer to take you for a ride, but it's a bit nippy on the water.'

'We can sit here,' she said, indicating the chairs and table on the edge of the dock. 'Do I need to get silverware or anything?'

Jeb smiled. 'I know you better than that, Sara Linton.' He opened the picnic basket and took out silverware and napkins. He had also had the foresight to bring plates and glasses. Sara tried not to lick her lips when he pulled out fried chicken, mashed potatoes, peas, corn, and biscuits.

'Are you trying to seduce me?' she asked.

Jeb stopped, his hand on a tub of gravy. 'Is it working?'

The dogs barked, and all Sara could think was Thank God for small favors. She turned back to the house, saying, 'They never bark. I'll just go check.'

'You want me to come, too?'

Sara was about to tell him no but changed her mind. She had not been making that part up about the dogs. Billy and Bob had barked exactly twice since she had rescued them from the racing track in Ebro; once when Sara had accidentally stepped on Bob's tail, and once when a bird had flown down the chimney into the living room.

She felt Jeb's hand at her back as they walked up the yard toward the house. The sun was just dipping down over the roofline, and she shielded her eyes with her hand, recognizing Brad Stephens standing at the edge of the driveway.

'Hey, Brad,' Jeb said.

The patrolman gave a curt nod to Jeb, but his eyes were on Sara.

'Brad?' she asked.

'Ma'am.' Brad took off his hat. 'The chief's been shot.'

Sara had never really pushed the Z3 Roadster. Even when she drove it back from Atlanta, the speedometer had stayed at a steady seventy-five the entire way. She was doing ninety as she drove the back route to the Grant Medical Center. The ten-minute drive seemed to take hours, and by the time Sara made the turn into the hospital, her palms were sweating on the wheel.

She pulled into a handicap space at the side of the building so she would not block the ambulance doors. Sara was running by the time she reached the emergency room.

'What happened?' she asked Lena Adams, who was standing in front of the admitting desk. Lena opened her mouth to answer, but Sara ran past her into the hallway. She checked each room as she went by, finally finding Jeffrey in the third exam room.

Ellen Bray did not seem surprised to see Sara in the room. The nurse was putting a blood pressure cuff around his arm when Sara walked in.

Sara put her hand on Jeffrey's forehead. His eyes opened slightly, but he did not seem to register her presence.

'What happened?' she asked.

Ellen handed Sara the chart, saying, 'Buckshot to his leg. Nothing serious or they would've taken him to Augusta.'

Sara glanced down at the chart. Her eyes wouldn't focus. She couldn't even make out the columns.

'Sara?' Ellen said, her voice filled with compassion. She had worked in the Augusta emergency room most of her career. She was in semiretirement now, supplementing her pension by working nights at the Grant Medical Center. Sara had worked with her years ago, and the two women had a solid professional relationship built on mutual respect.

Ellen said, 'He's fine, really. The Demerol should knock him out soon. Most of his pain is coming from Hare digging around in his leg.'

'Hare?' Sara asked, feeling a little relief for the first time in the last twenty minutes. Her cousin Hareton was a general practitioner who sometimes filled in at the hospital. 'Is he here?'

Ellen nodded, pumping the cuff's bladder. She held up her finger for silence.

Jeffrey stirred, then slowly opened his eyes. When he recognized Sara, a slight smile crept across his lips.

Ellen released the blood pressure cuff, saying, 'One-forty-five over ninety-two.'

Sara frowned, looking back at Jeffrey's chart. The words finally started to make sense.

'I'll go fetch Dr. Earnshaw,' Ellen said.

'Thanks,' Sara said, flipping the chart open. 'When did you start on Coreg?' she asked. 'How long have you had high blood pressure?'

Jeffrey smiled slyly. 'Since you walked into the room.'

Sara skimmed the chart. 'Fifty milligrams a day. You just switched from captopril? Why did you stop?' She got the answer in the chart. ' "Nonproductive cough prompted change," ' she read aloud.

Hare walked into the room, saying, 'That's common with ACE inhibitors.'

Sara ignored her cousin as he put his arm around her shoulders.

She asked Jeffrey, 'Who are you seeing for this?'

'Lindley,' Jeffrey answered.

'Did you tell him about your father?' Sara snapped the chart closed. 'I can't believe he didn't give you an inhaler. What's your cholesterol like?'

'Sara.' Hare snatched the chart from her hands. 'Shut up.'

Jeffrey laughed. 'Thank you.'

Sara crossed her arms, anger welling up. She had been so worried on the drive over, expecting the worst, and now that she was here, Jeffrey was fine. She was inordinately relieved that he was okay, but for some reason she was feeling tricked by her emotions.

'Lookit,' Hare said, popping an X ray into the lightbox mounted on the wall. He gasped audibly, saying, 'Oh my God, that's the worst I've ever seen.'

Sara cut him with a look, turning the X ray right side up.

'Oh, thank God.' Hare sighed dramatically. When he saw she wasn't enjoying his sideshow, he frowned. The thing that made Sara both love and hate her cousin was he seldom took things very seriously.

Hare said, 'Missed his artery, missed his bone. Cut right through here on the inside.' He gave her a reassuring smile. 'Nothing bad at all.'

Sara ignored the evaluation, leaning closer to double-check Hare's findings. Aside from the fact that her relationship with her cousin had always been riddled with fierce competition, she wanted to make sure for herself that nothing had been missed.

'Let's turn you over on your left side,' Hare suggested to Jeffrey, waiting for Sara to help. Sara kept Jeffrey's injured right leg stable as they turned him, offering,

'This should help bring your blood pressure down a little. Are you due for your medication tonight?'

Jeffrey supplied, 'I'm late on a few doses.'

'Late?' Sara felt her own blood pressure rise. 'Are you an idiot?'

'I ran out,' Jeffrey mumbled.

'Ran out? You're within walking distance of the pharmacy.' She leveled a deep frown at Jeffrey. 'What were you thinking?'

'Sara?' Jeffrey interrupted. 'Did you come all the way over here to yell at me?'

She did not have an answer.

Hare suggested, 'Maybe she can give you a second opinion on whether or not you should go home tonight?'

'Ah.' Jeffrey's eyes crinkled with a smile. 'Well, since you're giving a second opinion, Dr. Linton, I've been experiencing some tenderness in my groin. Do you mind taking a look?'

Sara offered a tight smile. 'I could do a rectal exam.'

'It's about time you got your turn.'

'Je-e-sus,' Hare groaned. 'I'm gonna leave you two lovebirds alone.'

'Thanks, Hare,' Jeffrey called. Hare tossed a wave over his shoulder as he left the room.

'So,' Sara began, crossing her arms.

Jeffrey raised an eyebrow. 'So?'

'What happened? Did her husband come home?'

Jeffrey laughed, but there was a strained look in his eyes. 'Close the door.'

Sara did as she was told. 'What happened?' she repeated.

Jeffrey put his hand to his eyes. 'I don't know. It was so fast.'

Sara took a step closer, taking his hand despite her better judgment.

'Will Harris's house was vandalized today.'

'Will from the diner?' Sara asked. 'For God's sake, why?'

He shrugged. 'I guess some people got it into their heads that he was involved with what happened to Sibyl Adams.'

'He wasn't even there when it happened,' Sara answered, not understanding. 'Why would anyone think that?'

'I don't know, Sara.' He sighed, dropping his hand. 'I knew something bad would happen. Too many people are jumping to conclusions. Too many people are pushing this thing out of hand.'

'Like who?'

'I don't know,' he managed. 'I was staying at Will's house to make sure he was safe. We were watching a movie when I heard something outside.' He shook his head, as if he still could not believe what had happened. 'I got up off the couch to see what was going on, and one of the side windows just exploded like that.' He snapped his fingers. 'Next thing I know, I'm on the floor, my leg's on fire. Thank God Will was sitting in his chair or he would've been hit, too.'

'Who did it?'

'I don't know,' he answered, but she could tell from the set of his jaw that he had a good guess.

She was about to question him further when he reached his hand out, resting it on her hip. 'You look beautiful.'

Sara felt a small jolt of electricity as his thumb slipped under her shirt, stroking her side. His fingers slipped under the back of her shirt. They were warm against her skin.

'I had a date,' she said, feeling a rush of guilt for leaving Jeb at her house. He had been very understanding, as usual, but she still felt bad about abandoning him.

Jeffrey watched her through half-closed eyes. He either did not believe her about the date or he would not accept that it could have been anything serious. 'I love it when your hair is down,' he said. 'Did you know that?'

'Yeah,' she said, putting her hand over his, stopping him, breaking the spell. 'Why didn't you tell me you have high blood pressure?'

Jeffrey let his arm drop. 'I didn't want to give you one more fault to add to your list.' His smile was a little forced and incongruous with the glassy look in his eyes. Like Sara, he seldom took anything stronger than aspirin, and the Demerol seemed to be working fast.

'Give me your hand,' Jeffrey said. She shook her head, but he persisted, holding his hand out to her. 'Hold my hand.'

'Why should I?'

'Because you could've seen me at the morgue tonight instead of the hospital.'

Sara bit her lip, fighting back the tears that wanted to come. 'You're okay now,' she said, putting her hand to his cheek. 'Go to sleep.'

He closed his eyes. She could tell that he was fighting to stay awake for her benefit.

'I don't want to go to sleep,' he said, then fell asleep.

Sara stared at him, watching his chest rise and fall with each breath. She reached out, smoothing his hair back off his forehead, leaving her hand there for a few seconds before putting her palm to his cheek. His beard was coming in, a speckled black against his face and neck. She brushed her fingers lightly along the stubble, smiling at the memories that came. Sleeping, he reminded her of the Jeffrey she had fallen in love with: the man who listened to her talk about her day, the man who opened doors for her and killed spiders and changed the batteries in the smoke detectors. Sara finally took his hand and kissed it before leaving the room.

She took her time walking back up the hallway toward the nurses' station, feeling an overwhelming sense of exhaustion. The clock on the wall showed she had been here an hour, and Sara realized with a start that she was back on hospital time, where eight hours went by like eight seconds.

'He asleep?' Ellen asked.

Sara leaned her elbows on the counter of the admitting desk. 'Yeah,' she answered. 'He'll be okay.'

Ellen smiled. 'Sure he will.'

'There you are,' Hare said, rubbing Sara's shoulders. 'How's it feel to be in a real hospital with the big doctors?'

Sara exchanged a look with Ellen. 'You'll have to excuse my cousin, Ellen. What he lacks in hair and height he makes up for by being an asshole.'

'Ow.' Hare winced, pressing his thumbs into Sara's shoulders. 'Want to fill in for me while I run out for a bite to eat?'

'What've we got?' Sara asked, thinking that going home right now probably was not the best thing for her.

Ellen gave a small smile. 'We've got a frequent flier getting fluorescent light therapy in two.'

Sara laughed out loud. In the obscure language of hospital lingo, Ellen had just informed her that the patient in room two was a hypochondriac who had been left to stare at the overhead lights until he felt better.

'Microdeckia,' Hare concluded. The patient was not playing with a full deck.

'What else?'

'Some kid from the college sleeping off a long one,' Ellen said.

Sara turned to Hare. 'I don't know if I can take these complicated cases.'

He chucked her under her chin. 'There's a girl.'

'I guess I should go move my car,' Sara said, remembering she had parked in the handicap spot. As every cop in town knew the car she drove, Sara doubted she was likely to get a ticket. Still, she wanted to walk outside for some fresh air, take some time to collect her thoughts, before she went back in to check on Jeffrey.

'How is he?' Lena asked as soon as Sara walked into the waiting room. Sara looked around, surprised to see the room was empty but for Lena.

'We kept it off the radio,' Lena provided. 'This kind of thing . . . ' She let her voice trail off.

'This kind of thing what?' Sara prompted. 'Am I missing something here, Lena?'

Lena looked away nervously.

'You know who did it, huh?' Sara asked.

Lena shook her head. 'I'm not sure.'

'That's where Frank is? Taking care of business?'

She shrugged. 'I don't know. He dropped me off here.'

'Pretty easy not to know what's going on when you don't bother to ask,' Sara snapped. 'I guess the fact that Jeffrey could've died tonight is lost on you.'

'I know that.'

'Yeah?' Sara demanded. 'Who was watching his back, Lena?'

Lena started to answer, but she turned away before saying anything.

Sara slammed the emergency room doors open with her hands, feeling anger well up. She knew exactly what was going on here. Frank knew who was responsible for shooting Jeffrey, but he was keeping his mouth closed out of some obscure sense of loyalty, probably to Matt Hogan. What was going through Lena's mind, Sara could not begin to guess. After everything Jeffrey had done for her, to have Lena turn her back on him like this was inexcusable.

Sara took a deep breath, trying to calm herself as she walked around to the side of the hospital. Jeffrey could have been killed. The glass could have sliced through his femoral artery and he could have bled to death. For that matter, the original shot could have gone into his chest instead of through the window. Sara wondered what Frank and Lena would be doing now if Jeffrey had died. Probably drawing straws to see who got his desk.

'Oh, God.' Sara stopped short at the sight of her car. Lying on the hood of Sara's car was a nude young woman with her arms spread out. She was on her back, her feet crossed at the ankle in an almost casual pose. Sara's first instinct was to look up to see if the woman had jumped from one of the windows. There were no windows on this side of the two-story building, though, and the hood of the car showed no signs of impact.

Sara took three quick steps to the car, checking the woman's pulse. A fast, hard beat came under Sara's fingers, and she muttered a small prayer before running back into the hospital.

'Lena!'

Lena jumped up, fists clenched, as if she expected Sara to come over and start a fight.

'Get a stretcher,' Sara ordered. When Lena did not move, Sara yelled, 'Now!'

Sara jogged back to the woman, half expecting her to

be gone. Everything was moving in slow time for Sara, even the wind in her hair.

'Ma'am?' Sara called to the woman, raising her voice loud enough to be heard across town. The woman did not respond. 'Ma'am?' Sara tried again. Still nothing.

Sara assessed the body, seeing no immediate signs of trauma. The skin was pink and ruddy, very hot to the touch despite the night cold. With her arms out and feet crossed as they were, the woman could've been sleeping. In the bright light, Sara could make out crusted blood around the palms of the woman's hands. Sara lifted one of the hands to examine it, and the arm moved awkwardly to the side. There was an obvious dislocation at the shoulder.

Sara looked back at the woman's face and was startled to notice that a silver piece of duct tape had been wrapped around her mouth. Sara couldn't remember if the tape had been there before she had gone back into the hospital. Surely she would've noticed it before. Something like a taped mouth wasn't easily overlooked, especially when the tape was at least two inches across by four inches long and dark silver. For just a brief second, Sara felt paralyzed, but Lena Adams's voice brought her back to reality.

'It's Julia Matthews,' Lena said, but her voice sounded far away to Sara.

'Sara?' Hare asked, walking quickly over to the car. His mouth dropped open at the sight of the nude woman.

'Okay, okay,' Sara mumbled, trying to get herself calm. She shot Hare a look of sheer panic, which he returned in kind. Hare was used to an occasional overdose or heart attack, nothing like this.

As if to remind them both of where they were, the woman's body began to convulse.

'She's going to be sick,' Sara said, picking at the edge of the tape. Without pausing, she ripped off the tape. In one swift motion, she rolled the woman onto her side and held her head down as she vomited in fits and starts. A sour smell came, almost like bad cider or beer, and Sara had to turn away to take a breath.

'It's okay,' Sara whispered. She stroked the woman's dirty brown hair back behind her ear, remembering that she had done the same thing for Sibyl just two days ago. The vomiting stopped abruptly, and Sara gently rolled her back over, keeping her head steady.

Hare's tone was urgent. 'She's not breathing.'

Sara cleared the woman's mouth with her finger, surprised to feel some resistance. After a few seconds of digging, she pulled out a folded driver's license, which she handed to a surprised Lena Adams.

'Breathing's back,' Hare said, relief flooding his voice.

Sara rubbed her fingers clean on her skirt, wishing she'd had on a pair of gloves before she had stuck her fingers into the woman's mouth.

Ellen jogged to the car, her jaw set as she angled a long stretcher in front of her. Without words, she stepped to the woman's feet, waiting for Sara's signal.

Sara counted to three, then they both moved the woman onto the bed. Sara felt a sick taste in her mouth as they did this, and for a few seconds she saw herself on the bed instead of the woman. Sara's mouth went dry and she felt a numbness overcome her.

'Ready,' Hare said, strapping the woman to the bed.

Sara trotted beside the gurney, holding on to the young woman's hand. The time it took them to get back into the hospital was interminable. The bed seemed to be rolling through glue as they entered the first trauma room. The woman made small murmurs of pain with each jolt of the bed. Briefly, Sara latched on to the woman's fear.

Twelve years had passed since Sara had practiced emergency medicine and she needed to concentrate on the tasks at hand. In her head, Sara went over what she'd learned her first day in the ER. As if to prompt Sara, the woman started wheezing, then gasping for air. The first priority was to establish an airway.

'Jesus,' Sara hissed as she opened the woman's mouth. Under the bright lights of the exam room, Sara could see that her top front teeth had been knocked out, obviously within the last few days. Again, Sara felt herself freezing up. She tried to shake this off. Sara had to think of this woman as a patient or they would both be in trouble.

In seconds Sara had intubated the woman, careful with the tape so as not to do further damage to the skin around the mouth. Sara fought the urge to cringe as the ventilator kicked in. The sound almost sickened her.

'She's got good sounds,' Hare reported, handing Sara a stethoscope.

'Sara?' Ellen said. 'I can't get a peripheral.'

'She's dehydrated,' Sara reported as she tried to find a vein on the woman's other arm. 'We should drop a central anyway.' Sara held her hand out for the needle, but one was not immediately placed in her hand.

'I'll get it from two,' Ellen said, then left the room.

Sara turned back to the young woman on the bed. There did not seem to be any bruises or cuts on her body other than the marks on her hands and feet. Her skin was warm to the touch, which could point to any number of things. Sara did not want to jump to conclusions, but already the similarities between Sibyl Adams and the woman in front of her were going through her mind. They were both petite women. They both had dark brown hair.

Sara checked the woman's pupils. 'Dilated,' she said, because the last time she'd done something like this, the rule had been to call out your findings. She exhaled slowly, noticing for the first time that Hare and Lena were in the room.

'What's her name?' Sara asked.

'Julia Matthews,' Lena provided. 'We were looking for her at the school. She's been missing for a couple of days.'

Hare glanced at the monitor. 'Pulse ox is falling.'

Sara checked the ventilator. 'FiO2 is thirty percent. Bump it up a little.'

'What's that smell?' Lena interrupted.

Sara sniffed the woman's body. 'Clorox?' she asked.

Lena caught another whiff. 'Bleach,' she confirmed.

Hare nodded as well.

Sara examined the woman's skin carefully. There were lines of superficial scrapes all along the body. Sara noticed for the first time that the woman's pubic hair had been shaved off. From the lack of growth, Sara guessed she had been shaved in the last day or so.

Sara said, 'She's been scrubbed clean.'

She smelled the woman's mouth but did not pick up the strong scent that usually comes from ingesting bleach. Sara had seen some rawness in the back of the throat when she'd tubed the woman, but nothing out of the ordinary. Obviously the woman had been given a drug similar to if not actually belladonna. Her skin was so hot to the touch that Sara could feel it through her gloves.

Ellen entered the room. Sara watched the nurse as she opened the central line kit on one of the trays. Ellen's hands didn't seem as steady as they usually did. This scared Sara more than anything else.

Sara held her breath as she jabbed the three-inch needle into the woman's jugular. The needle, called an introducer, would act as a funnel for three separate IV ports. When they found out what kind of drug the woman had been given, Sara would use one of the extra ports to help counteract the effects.

Ellen stood back from the patient, waiting for Sara's orders.

Sara rattled off the tests as she flushed the ports with heparin solution to keep them from clotting. 'Blood gases, tox screen, LFT, CBC, chem twenty-seven. Go ahead and pull for a coag panel while you're at it.' Sara paused. 'Dip her urine stat. I want to know what's going on before I do anything else. Something's keeping her knocked out. I think I know what it is, but I need to be sure before we start treatment.'

'All right,' Ellen answered.

Sara checked for positive blood return, then flushed the lines again. 'Normal saline, wide open.'

Ellen did as she was told, adjusting the IV.

'Do you have a portable X ray? I'll need to make sure I did this right' Sara said, indicating the internal jugular line. 'Plus I need a chest, a flat of the abdomen, and a look at her shoulder.'

Ellen said, 'I'll get it from down the hall after I draw the blood work.'

'Also, check for GHB, roofies.' Sara spoke as she secured the dressing around the needle. 'We'll need to do a rape kit.'

'Rape?' Lena questioned, stepping forward.

'Yes,' Sara answered, her tone sharp. 'Why else would someone do this to her?'

Lena's mouth worked, but no answer came. She had obviously kept this case separate from her sister's up until that point. Lena's eyes locked on to the young woman, and she stood at the foot of the bed, her body ramrod straight. Sara was reminded of the night Lena had come to the morgue to see Sibyl Adams. The young detective's mouth was set in that same angry line.

'She seems stable,' Ellen offered, more to herself than anyone else.

Sara watched as the nurse used a small syringe to draw blood from the radial artery. Sara rubbed her own wrist, knowing how painful the procedure could be. She leaned against the bed, her hands on Julia Matthews's arm, trying to somehow convey that she was safe now.

Hare brought her back with a gentle 'Sara?'

'Hm?' Sara was startled. They were all looking at her. She turned to Lena. 'Can you help Ellen with the portable?' she asked, trying to use a firm voice.

'Yeah,' Lena returned, giving Sara an odd look.

Ellen filled the last syringe. 'It's down the hall,' she told Lena.

Sara heard them leave, but she kept her eyes on Julia Matthews. Sara's vision tunneled, and for the second time she felt herself on the gurney, saw a doctor leaning over her, taking her pulse, checking her vitals.

'Sara?' Hare was looking at the woman's hands, and Sara was reminded of the marks she had first seen in the parking lot.

Both palms were punctured through the center. Sara glanced down at the woman's feet, noting that they, too, had been punctured in the same way. She bent to examine the wounds, which were clotting rapidly. Specks of rust added color to the dried black blood.

'The palm has been pierced through,' Sara offered. She looked under the woman's fingernails, recognizing thin slivers of wood pressed under the nails. 'Wood,' she reported, wondering why someone would take the time to scrub the victim down with bleach in order to remove physical traces, yet leave slivers of wood under the nails. It did not make sense. And then to leave her arranged on the car in such a way.

Sara worked all of this out in her head, and her stomach responded to the obvious conclusion with a slight pitch. She closed her eyes, picturing the woman as she had been when Sara first found her: legs crossed at the ankles, arms at ninety-degree angles from the body.

The woman had been crucified.

'Those are puncture wounds, right?' Hare said.

Sara nodded, not taking her eyes off the woman. Her body was well nourished and her skin had been taken care of. There were no needle marks to indicate prolonged drug use. Sara stopped in her tracks, realizing she'd assessed the woman as if she was at the morgue rather than the hospital. As if sensing this, the heart monitor went into failure, the shrill scream of the machine putting Sara on alert.

'No,' Sara hissed as she leaned over the woman, starting compressions. 'Hare, bag her.'

He fumbled around in the drawers for the bag. Within seconds, he was squeezing air into the woman's lungs. 'She's in V-tach,' he warned.

'Slow,' Sara said, wincing as she felt one of the patient's ribs crack under her hands. She kept her eyes on Hare, willing him to cooperate. 'One, two, squeeze. Quick and hard. Keep it calm.'

'Okay, okay,' Hare mumbled, concentrating on squeezing the bag.

Despite the great press given CPR, it was merely a stopgap measure. CPR was the act of physically forcing the heart to circulate blood into the brain, and very rarely could this be done manually as efficiently as a healthy heart performing the task on its own. If Sara stopped, so would the heart. It was a time-buying procedure until something else could be done.

Lena, obviously alerted by the shrieking monitor, ran back into the room. 'What happened?'

'She crashed,' Sara said, feeling a slight sense of relief as she spotted Ellen in the hallway. 'Amp of Epi,' she ordered.

Sara watched impatiently as Ellen popped open a box of Epi and put the syringe together.

'Jeesh.' Lena cringed as Sara administered the drug straight into the woman's heart.

Hare's voice rose a few octaves. 'She's in V-fib.'

With one hand Ellen took the paddles off the cart behind her, charging the defibrillator with the other.

'Two hundred,' Sara ordered. The woman's body jumped into the air as Sara electrocuted her. Sara watched the monitor, frowning when there was no corresponding reaction. Sara shocked her two more times with the same response. 'Lidocaine,' she ordered just as Ellen popped another box.

Sara administered the drug, keeping an eye on the monitor.

'Flat line,' Hare reported.

'Again.' Sara reached for the paddles. 'Three hundred,' she ordered.

Again, she shocked the woman. Again, there was no response. Sara felt a cold sweat come over her. 'Epi.'

The sound of the box popping open was like a needle in Sara's ear. She took the syringe, pushing the Adrenalin directly into the woman's heart one more time. They all waited.

'Flat line,' Hare reported.

'Let's go to three-sixty.'

For the fifth time, a charge went through the woman's body with no response.

'Goddamnit, goddamnit,' Sara muttered, resuming compressions. 'Time?' she called.

Hare glanced at the clock. 'Twelve minutes.'

It had seemed like two seconds to Sara.

Lena must have sensed from Hare's tone of voice where he was going with this. She whispered under her breath, 'Don't let her die. Please, don't let her die.'

'She's in prolonged asystole, Sara,' Hare said. He was telling her that it was too late. It was time to stop, time to let go.

Sara narrowed her eyes at him. She turned to Ellen. 'I'm going to crack her chest.'

Hare shook his head, saying, 'Sara, we don't have the capabilities here.'

Sara ignored him. She felt down the woman's ribs, cringing as she made contact with the one she had broken. When Sara's fingers reached the bottom of the diaphragm, she took a scalpel and sliced a six-inch opening into the upper abdomen. She slipped her hand into the incision, reaching under the rib cage and into the woman's chest.

She kept her eyes closed, blocking out the hospital as she massaged the woman's heart. The monitor showed false hope as Sara squeezed, manually circulating the woman's blood. A tingling came to her fingers, and in her ears she could hear a slight piercing tone. Nothing else mattered as she waited for the heart to respond. It was like squeezing a small balloon filled with warm water. Only this balloon was life.

Sara stopped. She counted to five seconds, eight, then up to twelve, before being rewarded with spontaneous beeps from the heart monitor.

Hare asked, 'Is that her or you?'

'Her,' Sara offered, letting her hand slip out. 'Start a lidocaine drip.'

'Jesus Christ,' Lena muttered, hand to her own chest. 'I can't believe you just did that.'

Sara snapped off her gloves, not answering.

The room was quiet but for the beeps of the heart monitor and the in and out of the ventilator.

'So,' Sara said. 'We'll do a darkfield for syphilis and a gram stain for gonorrhea.' Sara felt her face flush over this. 'I'm sure a condom was used, but make a note to follow up in a few days for pregnancy.' Sara was conscious of a waver in her voice that she hoped Ellen and Lena did not pick up. Hare was another matter. She could hear what he was thinking without even looking at him.

He seemed to sense her nervousness and tried to make light of it. 'Good God, Sara. That's the sloppiest incision I've ever seen.'

Sara licked her lips, willing her own heart to calm. 'I was trying not to upstage you.'

'Prima donna,' Hare offered, wiping perspiration from his forehead with a pad of surgical gauze. 'Jesus Christ.' He laughed uncomfortably.

'We don't see much of this around here,' Ellen said as she packed surgical towels into the incision to control the bleeding until it was closed. 'I can call Larry Headley over in Augusta. He lives about fifteen minutes from here.'

'I would appreciate that,' Sara said, taking another pair of gloves from the box on the wall.

'You okay?' Hare asked, his tone casual. His eyes showed his concern.

'Fine,' Sara answered, checking the IV. She told Lena, 'I guess you can find Frank?'

Lena had the decency to look embarrassed. 'I'll go see.' She left the room, her head down.

Sara waited until she was gone, then asked Hare, 'Can you take a look at her hands?'

Hare was silent as he examined the woman's palms, feeling the bone structure. After a few minutes, he said, 'This is interesting.'

Sara asked, 'What's that?'

'Missed all the bones,' Hare answered, rotating the wrist. When he got to the shoulder, he stopped. 'Dislocated,' he said.

Sara crossed her arms, suddenly cold. 'From trying to get away?'

Hare frowned. 'Do you realize how much force it would take to dislocate your shoulder blade?' He shook his head, unable to accept it. 'You'd pass out from the pain before you'd –'

'Do you realize how terrifying it is to be raped?' Sara's gaze bored right into him.

Pain registered in his expression. 'I'm sorry, honey. Are you okay?'

Tears stung the back of her eyes, and Sara had to fight to keep her voice even. 'Check her hips, please. I want you to do a full report.'

He did as he was told, giving Sara a curt nod after the examination. 'I'm thinking there's some ligature damage in the hip, here. I need to do this when she's awake; it's fairly subjective.'

Sara asked, 'Can you tell anything else?'

'All the bones in her hands and feet were missed. Her feet were speared between the second and third cuneiforms and the navicular. That's very precise. Whoever did it knew what he was doing.' He paused, looking down at the floor to regain his composure. 'I don't see why someone would do this.'

'Look at this,' Sara said, pointing to the skin around the woman's ankles. They both had angry black bruises around their circumference. 'Obviously there was a secondary restraint to hold the feet down.' Sara picked up the woman's hand, noticing a fresh scar at the wrist. The other had the same mark. Julia Matthews had attempted suicide at some point during the last month. The scar was a white line slashing vertically across her small wrist. A dark bruise put the old wound in stark relief.

Sara did not bring this to Hare's attention. Instead, she offered, 'It looks to me like a band was used, probably leather.'

'I'm not following.'

'The piercing was symbolic.'

'Of?'

'Crucifixion, I would imagine.' Sara put the woman's hand back by her side.

Sara rubbed her arms, fighting the chill in the room. She walked over, opening drawers, looking for a sheet to cover the young woman. 'If I had to guess, I would say that the hands and feet were nailed back from the body.'

'Crucifixion?' Hare dismissed this. 'That's not how Jesus was crucified. The feet would be together.'

Sara snapped, 'Nobody wanted to rape Jesus, Hare. Of course her legs were spread apart.'

Hare's Adam's apple bobbed as he swallowed this. 'Is this what you do at the morgue?'

She shrugged, looking for a sheet.

'Christ, you've got more balls than I do,' Hare said, breathing heavily.

Sara tucked the sheet around the young woman, trying to comfort her. 'I don't know about that,' she said.

Hare asked, 'What about her mouth?'

'Her front teeth were knocked out, I imagine to facilitate fellatio.'

His voice rose in shock. 'What?'

'It's more common than you think,' Sara told him. 'The Clorox removes trace evidence. I imagine he shaved her so we couldn't do a comb for his pubic hair. Even during normal sex, hairs are torn out. He could have shaved her for the sexual thrill, though. A lot of attackers like to think of their victims as children. Shaving the pubic hair would fuel that fantasy.'

Hare shook his head, overcome with the nastiness of the crime. 'What kind of animal would do this?'

Sara stroked back the woman's hair. 'A methodical one.'

'Do you think she knew him?'

'No,' Sara answered, never more sure of anything in her life. She walked over to the counter where Lena had left the evidence bag. 'Why did he give us her driver's license? He doesn't care if we know who she is.'

Hare's tone was incredulous. 'How can you be so sure?'

'He left –' Sara tried to catch her breath. 'He left her in front of the hospital where anybody could've seen him dump her.' She put her hand over her eyes for just a second, wishing that she could hide. She had to get out of this room. That much she was certain of.

Hare seemed to be trying to read her expression. His face, normally open and kind, took on a stern look. 'She was raped in a hospital.'

'Outside a hospital.'

'Her mouth was taped shut.'

'I know that.'

'By someone who obviously has some kind of religious fixation.'

'Right.'

'Sara –'

She held up her hand for silence as Lena returned. Lena said, 'Frank's on his way.'

THURSDAY

FOURTEEN

Jeffrey blinked his eyes several times, forcing himself not to go back to sleep. For a few seconds, he did not know where he was, but a quick glance around the room reminded him of what had happened last night. He looked over at the window, his eyes taking their time coming into focus. He saw Sara.

He leaned his head back into the pillow, letting out a long sigh. 'Remember when I used to brush your hair?'

'Sir?'

Jeffrey opened his eyes. 'Lena?'

She seemed embarrassed as she walked over to the bed. 'Yeah.'

'I thought you were . . . ' He waved this off. 'Never mind.'

Jeffrey forced himself to sit up in bed, despite the pain shooting through his right leg. He felt stiff and drugged, but he knew if he did not stay upright, the rest of the day would be blown.

'Hand me my pants,' he said.

'They had to throw them away,' she reminded him. 'Remember what happened?'

Jeffrey grumbled an answer as he put his feet on the floor. Standing hurt like a hot knife in his leg, but he could live with the pain. 'Can you find me some pants?' he asked.

Lena left the room and Jeffrey leaned against the wall

so that he wouldn't sit back down. He tried to remember what had happened the night before. Part of him didn't want to deal with it. There was enough on his plate trying to find out who had killed Sibyl Adams.

'How are these?' Lena asked, tossing him a pair of scrubs.

'Great,' Jeffrey said, waiting for her to turn around. He slipped them on, suppressing a groan as he lifted his leg. 'We've got a full day ahead of us,' he said. 'Nick Shelton is coming in at ten with one of his drug guys. We'll get a rundown on the belladonna. We've got that punk, what's his name, Gordon?' He tied the string in the pants. 'I want to go at him again, see if he can remember anything about when he last saw Julia Matthews.' He leaned his hand against the table. 'I don't think he knows where she is, but maybe he saw something.'

Lena turned around without being told. 'We found Julia Matthews.'

'What?' he asked. 'When?'

'She showed up at the hospital last night,' Lena answered. There was something about her voice that sent a sense of dread coursing through his veins.

He sat back down on the bed without even thinking about it.

Lena closed the door and narrated last night's events for him. By the time she was finished, Jeffrey was pacing the room in an awkward gait.

'She just showed up on Sara's car?' he asked.

Lena nodded.

'Where is it now?' he asked. 'The car, I mean?'

'Frank had it impounded,' Lena said, a defensive tone to her voice.

'Where is Frank?' Jeffrey asked, leaning his hand on the bed railing.

Lena was silent, then, 'I don't know.'

He gave her a hard look, thinking she knew exactly where Frank was but wouldn't say.

She said, 'He put Brad on guard upstairs.'

'Gordon's still in jail, right?'

'Yeah, that was the first thing I checked. He was in jail all night. There's no way he could've put her on Sara's car.'

Jeffrey hit the bed with his fist. He knew last night he shouldn't have taken that Demerol. This was the middle of a case, not a holiday.

'Hand me my jacket.' Jeffrey held his hand out, taking the jacket from Lena. He limped out of the room, Lena on his heels. The elevator was slow in coming, but neither of them spoke.

'She's been sleeping all night,' Lena said.

'Right.' Jeffrey jabbed at the button. The elevator bell dinged several seconds later, and they rode up together, still in silence.

Lena began, 'About last night. The shooting.'

Jeffrey waved her off, stepping out of the elevator. 'We'll deal with that later, Lena.'

'It's just –'

He held his hand up. 'You have no idea how little that matters to me right now,' he said, using the railing lining the hallway to work his way toward Brad.

'Hey, Chief,' Brad said, standing up from his chair.

'Nobody in?' Jeffrey asked, motioning for him to sit down.

'Not since Dr. Linton around two this morning,' he answered.

Jeffrey said, 'Good,' leaning his hand on Brad's shoulder as he opened the door.

Julia Matthews was awake. She stared blindly out the window, not moving when they came in.

'Miss Matthews?' he said, leaning his hand against the railing of her bed.

She continued to stare, not answering.

Lena said, 'She hasn't spoken since Sara took the tube out.'

He looked out the window, wondering what held her attention. Dawn had broken about thirty minutes ago, but other than the clouds there wasn't anything remarkable to see out the window.

Jeffrey repeated, 'Miss Matthews?'

Tears streamed down her face, but still she said nothing. He left the room, using Lena's arm to lean on.

As soon as they were outside the room, Lena provided, 'She hasn't said anything all night.'

'Not one word?'

She shook her head. 'We got an emergency number from the college and found an aunt. She's tracking down the parents. They're flying into Atlanta on the first available flight.'

'When's that?' Jeffrey asked, checking his watch.

'Around three today.'

'Frank and I will pick them up,' he said, turning to Brad Stephens. 'Brad, you've been on all night?'

'Yes, sir.'

'Lena will relieve you in a couple of hours.' He looked at Lena, daring her to protest. When nothing came, he said, 'Take me home, then back to the station. You can walk to the hospital from there.'

Jeffrey stared straight ahead as Lena drove to his house, trying to work his mind around what had happened last night. He felt a tension in his neck that even a handful of aspirin couldn't tame. He still could not shake the lethargy from being drugged last night, and his brain was getting sidetracked left and right, even as he came to accept that all this had happened three doors down from where he lay sleeping like a baby. Thank God Sara had been there or he would have two victims instead of one on his hands.

Julia Matthews proved that the killer was escalating. He had gone from a quick assault and murder in the bathroom to keeping a girl for a few days so that he could take his time with her. Jeffrey had seen this kind of behavior over and over again. Serial rapists learned from their mistakes. Their lives were spent figuring out the best way to obtain their objectives, and this rapist, this murderer, was honing his skills even now as Jeffrey and Lena talked about how to catch him.

He had Lena repeat her story about Julia Matthews, trying to see if it was any different in the telling, trying to pull out additional clues. There were none. Lena was very good at reporting things as she saw them, and nothing new came with the second telling.

Jeffrey asked, 'What happened after?'

'After Sara left?'

He nodded.

'Dr. Headley came from Augusta. He closed her up.'

Jeffrey became aware of the fact that throughout Lena's narration of events of the night before, she was using 'her' instead of the woman's name. It was common in law enforcement to look at the criminal rather than the victim, and Jeffrey always felt that this was the quickest way to lose sight of why they did the job in the first place. He didn't want Lena to do this, especially considering what had happened to her sister.

There was something different about Lena today. Whether it was a higher level of tension or anger, he could not say. Her body seemed to vibrate with it, and his main goal was to get her back to the hospital, where she could sit and decompress. He knew Lena would not leave her guard at Julia Matthews's bedside. The hospital was the only place to trust her to stay. There was, of course, the added bonus of knowing that if Lena did finally have some sort of nervous breakdown, she was in the right place. For now, he needed to use her. He needed her to be his eyes and ears for what happened last night.

He said, 'Tell me what Julia looked like.'

Lena tapped the horn, shooing a squirrel out of the road. 'Well, she looked normal.' Lena paused. 'I mean, I thought it was an OD or something from the way she looked. I never would've pegged her for a rape.'

'What convinced you otherwise?'

Lena's jaw worked again. 'Dr. Linton, I suppose. She pointed out the holes in her hands and feet. I must've been blind, I don't know. The bleach smell and all of that gave it away.'

'All of what?'

'Just, you know, physical signs that something wasn't right.' Lena paused again. Her tone took a defensive ring. 'She had her mouth taped shut, with her driver's license shoved down her throat. I suppose she looked raped, but I wasn't seeing it. I don't know why. I would've figured it out; I'm not stupid. It's just that she looked so normal, you know? Not like a rape victim.'

He was surprised by this last part. 'What does a rape victim look like?'

Lena shrugged. 'Like my sister, I guess,' she mumbled. 'Like somebody who can't really take care of themselves.'

Jeffrey had been expecting a physical description, some comment on the state of Julia Matthews's body. He said, 'I don't follow you.'

'Never mind.'

'No,' Jeffrey said. 'Tell me.'

Lena seemed to think over how to phrase her words, then, 'I guess I can understand with Sibyl, because she was blind.' She stopped. 'I mean there's this whole thing about women asking for it and all. I don't think Sibyl was like that, but I know rapists. I've talked to them, I've busted them. I know how they think. They don't pick somebody who they think is going to put up a fight.'

'You think so?'

Lena shrugged. 'I guess you can go into all that feminist bullshit about how women should be able to do whatever they want to do and men should just get used to it, but . . .' Lena paused again. 'It's like this,' she said. 'If I parked my car in the middle of Atlanta with the windows rolled down and the keys in the ignition, whose fault is it when somebody steals it?'

Jeffrey didn't quite get her logic.

'There are sexual predators out there,' Lena continued. 'Everybody knows there are some sick people, usually men, who prey on women. And they're not picking the ones who look like they can take care of themselves. They're picking the ones who won't, or can't, put up a fight. They're picking the quiet ones like Julia Matthews. Or the handicapped ones.' Lena added, 'Like my sister.'

Jeffrey stared at her, not sure he bought her logic. Lena surprised him sometimes, but what she had just said blew him out of the water. He would expect this kind of talk from someone like Matt Hogan, but never from a woman. Not even Lena.

He leaned his head against the headrest, quiet for a few beats. After a while, he asked, 'Run down the case for me. Julia Matthews. Give me the physicals.'

Lena took her time answering. 'Her front teeth were knocked out. Her ankles had been bound. Her pubic hair had been shaved off.' Lena paused. 'Then, you know, he'd cleaned her out on the inside.'

'Bleach?'

Lena nodded. 'Mouth, too.'

Jeffrey watched her closely. 'What else?'

'There was no bruising on her.' Lena indicated her lap. 'No defensive wounds or marks on her hands, other than the holes in her palms and the bruises from the straps.'

Jeffrey considered this. Julia Matthews had probably been drugged the entire time, though that didn't make sense to him either. Rape was a crime of violence, and most rapists got off more from causing women pain, controlling them, than actually having sex with them.

Jeffrey said, 'Tell me what else. What did Julia look like when you found her?'

'She looked like a normal person,' Lena answered. 'I told you that.'

'Naked?'

'Yeah, naked. She was totally naked, and she was laid out like, with her hands straight out. Her feet were crossed at the ankles. Right across the hood of the car.'

'Do you think she was placed like that for a reason?'

Lena answered, 'I dunno. Everybody knows Dr. Linton. Everybody knows what car she drives. It's the only one in town.'

Jeffrey felt his stomach lurch. This was not the response he had been fishing for. He'd meant for Lena to specifically address the positioning of the body, to draw the same conclusion he had, which was that the woman was displayed in a crucifixion pose. He had assumed Sara's car was chosen because it had been parked closest to the hospital where someone would see it. The possibility that this action was directed toward Sara was chilling.

Jeffrey dismissed these thoughts for the moment, quizzing Lena. 'What do we know about our rapist?'

Lena thought out her answer. 'Okay, he's white because rapists tend to rape within their own ethnic group. He's super-retentive, because she was scrubbed thoroughly with bleach; bleach means he's up on his forensics, because that's the best way to dispose of physical evidence. He's probably an older man, has his own house, because he obviously nailed her to some floor or wall or whatever, and it's not like you can do that in an apartment building, so he must be established in town. He's probably not married, because he'd have a lot of explaining to do if his wife came home and found a woman nailed down in the basement.'

'Why do you say basement?'

Lena shrugged again. 'I don't imagine he can keep her out in the open.'

'Even if he lives alone?'

'Not unless he's sure nobody's gonna drop by.'

'So, he's a loner?'

'Well, maybe. But, then, how did he meet her?'

'Good point,' Jeffrey said. 'Did Sara send blood for the tox screen?'

'Yeah,' Lena said. 'She drove it over to Augusta. At least, that's where she said she was going. She said she knew what she was looking for.'

Jeffrey pointed to a side street. 'There.'

Lena made a sharp turn. 'Are we gonna cut Gordon loose today?' she asked.

'I don't think so,' Jeffrey said. 'We can use the drug charge to get his cooperation on who Julia's been hanging around with. From what Jenny Price said, he kept her on a tight leash. He'd be the most likely person to notice who was new in her life.'

'Yeah,' Lena agreed.

'Up here on the right,' he instructed, sitting up. 'You want to come in?'

Lena sat behind the wheel. 'I'll stay here, thanks.'

Jeffrey sat back in his seat. 'There's something else you're not telling me, isn't there?'

She took a deep breath, then let it go. 'I feel like I let you down.'

'About last night?' he asked, then: 'Me getting shot?'

She said, 'There's things you don't know.'

Jeffrey put his hand on the door handle. 'Is Frank taking care of it?'

She nodded.

'Could you have stopped what happened?'

She shrugged, her shoulders going up to her ears. 'I don't know if I can stop anything anymore.'

'Good thing that's not your job,' he said. He wanted to say more to her, to take some of her load, but Jeffrey knew from experience that Lena would have to work this out for herself. She had spent the last thirty-three years building a fortress around herself. He wasn't about to break through it in three days.

Instead, he said, 'Lena, my number one focus right now is to find out who killed your sister and who raped Julia Matthews. This' – he indicated his leg — 'I can deal with when it's over. I think we both know where to start looking. It's not like they're all gonna leave town.'

He pushed the door open and physically lifted his injured leg out with his hand. 'Jesus Christ,' he groaned, feeling an intense protest from his knee. His leg had gotten stiff from sitting in the car for so long. By the time Jeffrey stood up from the car, a line of perspiration beaded over his lip.

Pain shot through his leg as he walked toward his house. His house keys were on the same ring as the car keys, so he walked to the back of the house, entering through the kitchen. For the last two years, Jeffrey had been remodeling the house himself. His latest project was the kitchen, and he had gutted the back wall of the house one three-day weekend, planning to have it built back in time to return to work. A shooting had cut his plans short, and he had ended up buying plastic strips from a freezer supply house in Birmingham and nailing them up over the naked two-by-fours. The plastic kept the rain and wind out, but meanwhile he still had a big hole at the back of his house.

In the living room, Jeffrey picked up the phone and dialed Sara's number, hoping he could catch her before she left for work. Her machine picked up, so he dialed the Linton house.

Eddie Linton answered the phone on the third ring. 'Linton and Daughters.'

Jeffrey tried to remain pleasant. 'Hey, Eddie, it's Jeffrey.'

The phone clattered as it was dropped onto the floor. Jeffrey could hear dishes and pans in the background, then muffled conversation. A few seconds later Sara picked up the phone.

'Jeff?'

'Yeah,' he answered. He could hear her opening the door onto the deck. The Lintons were the only people he knew who didn't have a cordless phone in their house. There was an extension in the bedroom and one in the kitchen. If not for the ten-foot cord the girls had put on the kitchen phone when they were back in high school, privacy would not have been possible.

He heard the door close, then Sara said, 'Sorry.'

'How're you doing?'

She skipped an answer, saying, 'I'm not the one who got shot last night.'

Jeffrey paused, wondering about the sharp tone to her

voice. 'I heard about what happened with Julia Matthews.'

'Right,' Sara said. 'I ran the blood in Augusta. Belladonna has two specific markers.'

He cut short a chemistry lesson. 'You found both of them?'

'Yes,' she answered.

'So, we're looking for the same guy on both.'

Her voice was clipped. 'Looks that way.'

A few seconds passed, then Jeffrey said, 'Nick has this guy who's kind of a specialist on belladonna poisoning. He's bringing him by at ten. Can you make it?'

'I can pop over between patients, but I can't stay long,' Sara offered. There was a change in her voice, something softer, when she said, 'I need to go now, okay?'

'I want to go over what happened last night.'

'Later, okay?' She didn't give him time to answer. The phone clicked in his ear.

Jeffrey let out a sigh as he limped toward the bathroom. On the way, he looked out the window, checking on Lena. She was still in the car, both hands gripping the wheel. It seemed like every woman in his life had something they were hiding today.

After a hot shower and shave, Jeffrey felt considerably better. His leg was still stiff, but the more he moved it the less it hurt. There was something to be said for staying mobile. The drive to the station was tense and quiet, the only noise in the car being the sound of Lena's teeth gritting. Jeffrey was glad to see the back of her as she walked toward the hospital.

Marla met him at the front door, her hands clasped in front of her chest. 'I'm so glad you're okay,' she said, taking his arm, leading him back toward his office. He put a stop to her fussing when she opened the door for him.

'I've got it,' Jeffrey said. 'Where's Frank?'

Marla's face fell. If Grant was a small place, its police force was even smaller. Rumors traveled faster within the ranks than a bolt of lightning through a steel rod.

Marla said, 'I think he's in the back.'

'Go fetch him for me, will you?' Jeffrey asked, making his way toward his office.

Jeffrey sat in his chair with a groan. He knew he was tempting fate with his leg, keeping it still for a while, but he did not have a choice. His men needed to know he was back on the job, ready to work.

Frank rapped his knuckles on the door and Jeffrey nodded him in.

Frank asked, 'How you doing?'

Jeffrey made sure he had the other man's attention. 'I'm not gonna get shot at anymore, am I?'

Frank had the decency to look down at his shoes. 'No, sir.'

'What about Will Harris?'

Frank rubbed his chin. 'I hear he's going to Savannah.'

'That right?'

'Yeah,' Frank answered. 'Pete gave him a bonus. Will bought himself a bus ticket.' Frank shrugged. 'Said he was gonna spend a couple of weeks with his daughter.'

'What about his house?'

'Some fellas at the lodge volunteered to take care of the window.'

'Good,' Jeffrey said. 'Sara's gonna want her car back. Did you find anything?'

Frank took a plastic evidence bag out of his pocket and set it down on the desk.

'What's this?' Jeffrey asked, but it was a stupid question. There was a Ruger .357 Magnum in the bag.

'It was under her seat,' Frank said.

'Sara's seat?' he asked, still not getting it. The gun was a man stopper, the caliber enough to blow a hole into someone's chest. 'In her car? This is hers?'

Frank shrugged. 'She doesn't have a permit for it.'

Jeffrey stared at the gun as if it could talk to him. Sara certainly wasn't against private citizens having weapons, but he knew for a fact that she wasn't exactly comfortable around guns, especially the kind that could shoot the lock off a barn door. He slipped the gun out of the bag, checking it.

'Serial numbers were filed off,' Frank said.

'Yeah,' Jeffrey answered. He could see that. 'Was it loaded?'

'Yep.' Frank was obviously impressed with the weapon. 'Ruger security six, stainless steel. That's a custom handle, too.'

Jeffrey dropped the gun into his desk drawer, then looked back at Frank. 'Anything on the sex offender lists yet?'

Frank seemed disappointed that the discussion about Sara's gun was over. He answered, 'Not really. Most of 'em have some kind of alibi. The ones who don't aren't really what we're looking for.'

'We've got a meeting at ten with Nick Shelton. He's got a specialist on belladonna. Maybe we can give the guys something more to look for after that.'

Frank took a seat. 'I got that nightshade in my own backyard.'

'Me, too,' Jeffrey said, then, 'I want to head over to the hospital after the meeting, see if Julia Matthews feels like talking.' He paused, thinking about the young girl. 'Her parents will be in around three. I want to be at the airport to meet them. You're riding shotgun with me today.' If Frank found Jeffrey's word choice funny, he did not comment.

FIFTEEN

Sara left the clinic at quarter till ten so that she could go by the pharmacy before she saw Jeffrey. There was a chill in the air and the clouds promised more rain. She tucked her hands into her pockets as she walked down the street, keeping her eyes on the sidewalk in front of her, hoping her posture and her pace would make her seem unapproachable. She needn't have bothered, though. Since Sibyl's death downtown had taken on an eerie quiet. It was as if the whole town had died with her. Sara knew how they felt.

All night, Sara had lain awake in bed, going over each step she had taken with Julia Matthews. No matter what she did, Sara kept seeing the girl laid out on her car, her hands and feet pierced, her eyes glazed as she stared without seeing the night sky. Sara never wanted to go through anything like that again.

The bell over the pharmacy door jingled as Sara walked in, breaking her out of her solitude.

'Hey, Dr. Linton,' Marty Ringo called from behind the checkout counter. Her head was bent down, reading a magazine. Marty was a plump woman with an unfortunate mole growing just above her right eyebrow. Black hairs shot out from it like bristles on a brush. Working in the pharmacy, she knew the latest gossip about anyone and everyone in town. Marty would be certain to mention to whoever wandered into the store next that Sara Linton made a special trip to see Jeb today.

Marty smiled slyly. 'You looking for Jeb?'

'Yes,' Sara answered.

'Heard about last night,' Marty said, obviously fishing for information. 'That's a college girl, huh?'

Sara nodded, because that much could be found from the paper.

Marty's voice lowered. 'Heard she was messed with.'

'Mmm,' Sara answered, looking around the store. 'Is he here?' she asked.

'They both looked alike, too.'

'What's that?' Sara asked, suddenly paying attention.

'Both them girls,' Marty said. 'You think there's some kind of connection?'

Sara cut the conversation short. 'I really need to talk to Jeb.'

'He's out back.' Marty pointed toward the pharmacy, a hurt expression on her face.

Sara thanked Marty with a forced smile as she made her way toward the back of the store. Sara had always liked being in the pharmacy. She had bought her first tube of mascara here. On weekends, her father used to drive them to the store for candy. Not much had changed since Jeb bought the place. The soda counter, which was more for show than for serving drinks, still shone from polish. Contraceptives were still kept behind the counter. The narrow aisles up and down the length of the store were still labeled with signs made from marker and poster board.

Sara peered over the pharmacy counter but didn't see Jeb. She noticed the back door was open, and with a look over her shoulder, she walked behind the counter.

'Jeb?' she called. There was no response, and Sara walked to the open door. Jeb was standing to the side, his back to Sara. She tapped him on the shoulder and he jumped.

'God,' he yelled, turning around quickly. The fear on his face was replaced by pleasure when he saw Sara.

He laughed. 'You scared the crap out of me.'

'I'm sorry,' Sara apologized, but the truth was she was glad he could get worked up over something. 'What were you doing?'

He pointed to a row of bushes lining the long parking lot behind the buildings. 'See in that bush?'

Sara shook her head, not seeing anything but bushes. Then, 'Oh,' as she saw a small bird nest.

'Finches,' Jeb said. 'I put a feeder out there last year, but some kids from the school took it away.'

Sara turned toward him. 'About last night,' she began.

He waved her off. 'Please, Sara, believe me, I understand. You were with Jeffrey a long time.'

'Thank you,' she said, meaning it.

Jeb looked back into the pharmacy, lowering his voice. 'I'm sorry about what happened, too. You know, with the girl.' He shook his head slowly side to side. 'It's just hard to think about things like that happening in your own town.'

'I know,' Sara answered, not really wanting to get into it.

'I guess I can forgive you, skipping out on our date to save somebody's life.' He put his hand over the right side of his chest. 'Did you really put your hand on her heart?'

Sara moved his hand to the left side. 'Yes.'

'Good Lord,' Jeb breathed. 'How did it feel?'

Sara gave him the truth. 'Scary,' she said. 'Very scary.'

His voice was filled with admiration when he said,

'You are a remarkable woman, Sara. Do you know that?'

She felt silly being praised. 'I'll give you a rain check if you want,' she offered, trying to move him off the topic of Julia Matthews. 'For our date, I mean.'

He smiled, genuinely pleased. 'That'd be great.'

A breeze came and Sara rubbed her arms. 'It's getting cold again.'

'Here.' He led her back inside, shutting the door behind them. 'You doing anything this weekend?'

'I don't know,' Sara said. Then, 'Listen, I came to see if Jeffrey picked up his medication.'

'Well.' Jeb clasped his hands together. 'I guess that means you're busy this weekend.'

'No, it doesn't.' Sara paused, then said, 'It's just complicated.'

'Yeah.' He forced a smile. 'No problem. I'll check his script.'

She couldn't stand to see the disappointment on his face. She turned the Medic Alert display to give herself something to do. Bookmarks with religious sayings were alongside diabetes bracelets.

Jeb opened a large drawer under the counter and pulled out an orange pill bottle. He double-checked the label, then said, 'He called it in but didn't pick it up yet.'

'Thanks,' Sara managed, taking the bottle. She held it in her hand, staring at Jeb. She spoke before she could back out of it. 'Why don't you call me?' she asked. 'About this weekend.'

'Yeah, I will.'

She reached out with her free hand, smoothing the lapel of his lab coat. 'I mean it, Jeb. Call me.'

He was quiet for a few seconds, then suddenly he

leaned down, kissing her lightly on the lips. 'I'll call you tomorrow.'

'Great,' Sara said. She realized she was gripping the pill bottle so tightly that the top was about to pop off. She had kissed Jeb before. It was really no big deal. Something in the back of her mind was scared that Marty would see, though. Something in her mind was scared that news of the kiss would get back to Jeffrey.

'I can give you a bag for that,' Jeb offered, pointing to the bottle.

'No,' Sara mumbled, tucking the bottle into her jacket pocket.

She murmured a thanks and was out the door before Marty could look up from her magazine.

Jeffrey and Nick Shelton were out in the hall when Sara got to the station. Nick stood with his hands tucked into the back pockets of his jeans, his regulation GBI dark blue dress shirt tight across his chest. His nonregulation beard and mustache were trimmed neatly to his face, and his equally forbidden gold rope chain was hanging from his neck. At just under five feet six inches, he was short enough for Sara to rest her chin on the top of his head. This had not prevented him from asking her out a number of times.

'Hey, girl,' Nick said, putting his arm around her waist.

Jeffrey had about as much to worry about competition-wise from Nick Shelton as he did from a reindeer, but he still seemed to bristle at the familiar way Nick held her. Sara thought Nick was overly solicitous for this very reason.

'Why don't we start the meeting?' Jeffrey grumbled. 'Sara has to get back to work.'

Sara caught up with Jeffrey as they walked down the

hallway toward the back. She tucked the pill bottle into his coat pocket.

'What's this?' he asked, taking it out. Then, 'Oh.'

'Oh,' Sara repeated, opening the door.

Frank Wallace and a reedy-looking young man in khakis and a shirt like Nick's were sitting in the briefing room when they entered. Frank stood, shaking Nick's hand. He gave Sara a firm nod, which she did not return. Something told Sara that Frank had a hand in what happened last night, and she did not like it.

'This is Mark Webster,' Nick said, indicating the other man. He was a boy, really, hardly older than twenty-one. He had that still-wet-behind-the-ears look about him, and a piece of his hair stuck out in the back in a classic cowlick.

'Nice to meet you,' Sara said, shaking his hand. It was like squeezing a fish, but if Nick had brought Mark Webster all the way down here from Macon, he couldn't be as goofy as he looked.

Frank said, 'Why don't you tell them what you were telling me?'

The boy cleared his throat and actually tugged at his collar. He addressed his words toward Sara. 'I was saying it's interesting your twist picked belladonna for his drug of choice. It's very unusual. I've only seen three cases in my work, and most of those were rule-outs, stupid kids who thought they'd have some fun.'

Sara nodded her head, knowing that 'rule-outs' meant ruling out foul play in a death. As a coroner as well as a pediatrician, she was especially careful when young children came into the morgue with cause of death unknown.

Mark leaned against the table, addressing his remarks to the rest of the group. 'Belladonna is in the deadly nightshade family. During the Middle Ages, women chewed small quantities of the seeds in order to dilate their pupils. A woman with dilated eyes was considered more attractive, and that's where they got the name "belladonna." It means "beautiful woman." '

Sara supplied, 'Both victims had extremely dilated pupils.'

'Even a slight dose would cause this,' Mark answered. He picked up a white Tyvek envelope and pulled out some photographs, which he handed to Jeffrey to circulate.

Mark said, 'Belladonna is bell shaped, usually purple, and smells kind of funny. It's not something you'd keep around in your yard if you had kids or small animals. Whoever is growing it probably has a fence around it, maybe three feet tall at the least, in order to keep from poisoning everybody around.'

'Does it need any specific kind of soil or feed?' Jeffrey asked, passing the photo to Frank.

'It's a weed. It can grow practically anywhere. That's what makes it so popular. The only thing is, it's a bad drug.' Mark paused at this. 'The high is prolonged, lasts about three to four hours, depending on how much you take. Users report very real hallucinations. A lot of times they'll actually think it happened, if they can remember it.'

Sara asked, 'It causes amnesia?'

'Oh yes, ma'am, selective amnesia, which means they only remember bits and pieces. Like she might remember it was a man that took her, but she won't remember what he looked like even if she was staring him in the face. Or she might say he was purple with green eyes.' He paused. 'It's a hallucinogen, but not like your typical PCP or LSD. Users report that there's no discerning between the hallucination and the real thing. With, say, angel dust, ecstasy, what have you, you know you're hallucinating. Belladonna makes everything seem real. If I gave you a cup of Datura, when you came around you might swear to me you had a conversation with a coatrack. I could hook you up to a lie detector and you'd come out as telling the truth. It takes things that are there in reality and puts a twist on them.'

'Tea?' Jeffrey ased, giving Sara a look.

'Yes, sir. Kids've been boiling it in tea to drink.' He clasped his hands behind him. 'I've got to tell you, though, it's dangerous stuff. Real easy to OD on.'

Sara asked, 'How else can you ingest it?

'If you've got the patience,' Mark answered, 'you can soak the leaves in alcohol for a couple of days, then evaporate it. It's still a crapshoot, though, because the consistency isn't guaranteed, even with people who grow it for medical purposes.'

'What medical purposes?' Jeffrey asked.

'Well, you know when you go to the eye doctor and he dilates your eyes? It's a belladonna compound. Very diluted, but it's belladonna. You couldn't take a couple of bottles of the eyedrops and kill somebody, for instance. At this low level of concentration, the worst you could do is give them a really bad headache and killer constipation. It's at the pure level that you have to be careful.'

Frank bumped her arm, handing her the photograph. Sara looked down at the plant. It looked pretty much like every plant she had ever seen. Sara was a doctor, not a horticulturist. She couldn't even grow a Chia Pet.

Without warning, her mind was racing again, thinking back to when she first found Julia Matthews on her car. She was trying to remember if the duct tape had been there. With sudden clarity, Sara remembered that it had. She could see the tape on the woman's mouth.

She could see Julia Matthews's body crucified on the hood of the car.

'Sara?' Jeffrey asked.

'Hm?' Sara looked up. Everyone was staring at her, as if they were anticipating a response to something. 'I'm sorry,' she apologized. 'What was it you asked?'

Mark answered, 'I asked if you noticed anything strange about the victims. Were they unable to speak? Did they have a blank stare?'

Sara handed back the photo. 'Sibyl Adams was blind,' she provided. 'So of course her stare was blank. Julia Matthews . . . ' She paused, trying to force the image from her mind. 'Her eyes were glazed. I imagine it was from being gorked out on this drug more than anything else.'

Jeffrey gave her a funny look. 'Mark mentioned something about belladonna interfering with vision.'

'There's a sort of blindsightedness,' Mark said in a tone that implied he was repeating himself. 'According to user reports, you can see, but your mind can't make out what it is you're seeing. Like I could show you an apple or an orange, and you would be aware that you were seeing something round, maybe textured, but your brain wouldn't recognize what it is.'

'I know what blindsightedness is,' Sara returned, realizing too late that her tone was condescending. She tried to cover for this by saying, 'Do you think Sibyl Adams experienced this? Maybe that's why she didn't scream out?'

Mark looked at the other men. Obviously, this was another thing he had covered while Sara was zoning out. 'There's been reported loss of voice from the drug. Nothing physically happens in the voice box. There's no physical restraint or damage caused by the drug. I think it's more to do with something happening in the language center of the brain. It has to be similar to whatever causes the sight recognition problems.'

'Makes sense,' Sara agreed.

Mark continued. 'Some signs that it's been ingested would be cotton mouth, dilated pupils, high body temperature, elevated heart rate, and difficulty breathing.'

'Both victims experienced all of those symptoms,' Sara provided. 'What kind of dose would bring this about?'

'It's pretty potent stuff. Just one bag of tea can send somebody loopy, especially if they're not recreational drug users. The berries aren't that bad on a scale of things, but anything from the root or the leaf is going to be dangerous, unless you know exactly what you're doing. And then there's no guarantee.'

'The first victim was a vegetarian,' Sara said.

'She was a chemist, too, right?' Mark asked. 'I can think of a million different drugs to fool around with other than belladonna. I don't think anybody who took the time to research it would take that kind of risk. It's Russian roulette, especially if you're dealing with the root. That's the deadliest part. Just a little bit too much from the root and you're gone. There's no known antidote.'

'I didn't see any signs of drug use in Julia Matthews.' She said to Jeffrey, 'I suppose you're going to interview her after this?'

He nodded, then asked Mark, 'Anything else?'

Mark brushed his fingers through his hair. 'After the drug, there's noted constipation, still the cotton mouth, sometimes hallucinations. It's interesting to know that the drug was used in a sex crime, ironic even.'

'How's that?' Jeffrey asked.

'During the Middle Ages, the drug was sometimes

inserted with a vaginal applicator so that the rush would come sooner. There are even some people who think the whole myth of witches flying on broomsticks comes from the image of a woman inserting the drug with a wooden applicator.' He smiled. 'But then we'd have to get into a protracted discussion on deity worshipping and the rise of Christianity in European cultures.'

Mark seemed to sense he had lost his audience. 'People in drug communities who know about belladonna tend to stay away from it.' He looked at Sara. 'If you'll excuse the language, ma'am?'

Sara shrugged. Between the clinic and her father, she had pretty much heard it all.

Mark still blushed when he said, 'It's a total mind fuck.' He offered Sara a smile in apology. 'The number one memory, even among users with amnesia, is flying. They really believe they're flying, and they can't understand, even after they come down, that they haven't actually flown.'

Jeffrey crossed his arms. 'That might explain why she keeps staring out the window.'

'Has she said anything yet?' Sara asked.

He shook his head. 'Nothing.' Then, 'We're going to the hospital next if you want to see her.'

Sara looked at her watch, pretending to consider this. There was no way in hell she was going to see Julia Matthews again. It was too much to even think about. 'I've got patients,' she said.

Jeffrey indicated his office. 'Sara, mind if I talk to you for a second?'

Sara felt the urge to bolt, but she fought it. 'Is this about my car?'

'No.' Jeffrey waited until she was in his office, then shut the door. Sara sat on the edge of his desk, trying for a casual pose. 'I had to take my boat in to work this morning,' Sara said. 'Do you know how cold it is on the lake?'

He ignored this, getting straight to the point. 'Found your gun.'

'Oh,' Sara answered, trying to think of what to say. Of all the things she had been expecting him to say, this was the last one. The Ruger had been in her car for so long that she had forgotten about it. 'Am I under arrest?'

'Where did you get it?'

'It was a gift.'

Jeffrey gave her a hard look. 'What, somebody gave you a three-fifty-seven with the serial numbers filed off for your birthday?'

Sara shrugged this off. 'I've had it for years, Jeffrey.'

'When did you buy that car, Sara? Couple of years ago?'

'I moved it from the old one when I bought it.'

He stared at her, not speaking. Sara could tell that he was mad, but she did not know what to say. She tried, 'I've never used it.'

'That makes me feel good, Sara,' he snapped. 'You've got a gun in your car capable of literally taking somebody's head off and you don't know how to use it?' He paused, obviously trying to understand. 'What're you gonna do if someone comes after you, huh?'

Sara knew the answer to this, but she did not say.

Jeffrey asked, 'Why do you have it in the first place?'

Sara studied her ex-husband, trying to figure out the best way to get out of this office without having another fight. She was tired and she was upset. This wasn't the time to go a few rounds with Jeffrey. Sara just did not have the fight in her at the moment.

'I just had it,' she answered.

'You don't just have this kind of gun,' he said.

'I need to get back to the clinic.' She stood, but he was blocking her exit.

'Sara, what the hell is going on?'

'What do you mean?'

His eyes narrowed, but he did not answer. He moved aside, opening the door for her.

Sara thought for a second that it was a trick. 'That's it?' she asked.

He stepped aside. 'It's not like I can beat it out of you.'

She put her hand to his chest, feeling guilty. 'Jeffrey.'

He looked out into the squad room, 'I need to go over to the hospital,' he said, obviously dismissing her.

SIXTEEN

Lena leaned her head into her hand, trying to close her eyes for just a minute of rest. She had been sitting in a chair outside Julia Matthews's room for over an hour, and the last few days were finally catching up with her. She was tired and about to start her period. Despite this, her pants were loose on her hips from not eating. When she snapped her paddle holster on over her belt this morning, it was loose against her hip. As the day wore on, it started to rub, chafing her side.

Lena knew she needed to eat, needed to get back to living her life instead of just dragging along through every day like she was living on borrowed time. For now, she could not imagine doing that. She didn't want to get up in the morning and go for a run, like she had every morning for the last fifteen years. She did not want to go down to the Krispy Kreme and get coffee with Frank and the other detectives. She did not want to go to pack her lunch or go out to dinner. Every time she looked at food, she felt sick. All she could think was that Sibyl would never eat again. Lena was walking around while Sibyl was dead. Lena was breathing while Sibyl was not. Nothing made sense. Nothing would ever be the same again.

Lena took a deep breath and let it go, looking up and down the hallway. Julia Matthews was the only patient in the hospital today, which made Lena's job easy.

Except for a nurse who had been floated down on loan from Augusta, it was just Lena and Julia on this floor.

She stood, trying to walk some sense into her brain. She was feeling punch-drunk, and Lena could not think of anything to fight this other than to remain in motion. Her body ached from restless sleep, and she was still unable to get the image of Sibyl in the morgue out of her mind. Part of Lena was glad that there was another victim, though. Part of Lena wanted to go into Julia Matthews's room and shake her, to beg her to speak, to tell them who had done this to her, who had killed Sibyl, but Lena knew this would get them nowhere.

The few times Lena had gone into the room to check on the girl, she had been silent, not answering even the most innocuous questions from Lena. Did she want another pillow? Was there anyone she wanted Lena to call for her?

Thirsty, the girl had pointed to the pitcher on the hospital table rather than asked for water. Her eyes still had a haunted look about them, too, caused by the fact that the drug was still in her system. Her pupils were wide open, and she had the look of someone who was blind – blind like Sibyl had been. Only Julia Matthews would recover from this. Julia Matthews would see again. She would get better. She would go back to school and make friends, maybe meet a husband one day and have kids. Memories of what had happened would always be in the back of Julia Matthews's mind, but at least she would have a life. At least she would have a future. Lena knew that part of her resented Matthews for this. Lena knew, too, that she would trade Julia Matthews's life for Sibyl's on a second's notice.

The elevator dinged open, and Lena put her hand to her gun without thinking. Jeffrey and Nick Shelton walked into the hallway, followed by Frank and a skinny-looking kid who looked like he had just come from his high school graduation. She dropped her hand, walking to meet them, thinking she'd be damned if all those men were going to go into the small hospital room containing a woman who had just been raped. Especially Opie.

'How's she doing?' Jeffrey asked.

Lena skipped the question. 'You're not all going in there, are you?'

The look on Jeffrey's face said he had planned just this.

'She's still not talking,' Lena said, trying to help him save face. 'She hasn't said anything.'

'Maybe just you and I should go in,' he finally decided. 'Sorry, Mark.'

The young man did not seem to mind. 'Hey, I'm just glad this got me out of the office for a day.'

Lena thought it was pretty shitty of him to say this within walking distance of a woman who had arguably been to hell and back, but Jeffrey caught her arm before she could say anything. He led her up the hallway, talking as they walked.

'She's stable?' he asked. 'Her medical condition?'

'Yeah.'

Jeffrey stopped at the door to the room, his hand on the handle but not opening it. 'How about you? You're doing okay?'

'Sure.'

'I have a feeling her parents are going to want to move her to Augusta. How do you feel about going with her?'

Lena's first impulse was to protest, but she nodded an uncharacteristic acquiescence. It might do her some good to get out of town. Hank would be going back to

Reece in a day or two. Maybe she would feel differently when she had the house back to herself.

'I'll let you start,' Jeffrey said. 'If she looks like she'll be more comfortable with just you, then I'll step out.'

'Right,' Lena said, knowing this was standard procedure. Generally, the last thing a woman who had been raped wanted to do was talk to a man about it. As the only female detective on the squad, this job had fallen to Lena a couple of times before. She had even gone to Macon once to help interview a young girl there who had been brutally beaten and raped by her next-door neighbor. Still, even though Lena had been at the hospital all day with Julia, something about actually talking to the girl, interviewing her, made Lena feel sick to her stomach. It was too close to home.

'You ready?' Jeffrey asked, his hand on the door.

'Yeah.'

Jeffrey opened the door, letting Lena go in ahead of him. Julia Matthews was asleep, but she woke at the noise. Lena didn't imagine the young girl would have a good night's sleep for a long while, if ever.

'Want some water?' Lena asked, walking to the far side of the bed, picking up the pitcher. She filled the girl's glass, then turned the straw so she could drink.

Jeffrey stood with his back close to the door, obviously wanting to give the young girl space. He said, 'I'm Chief Tolliver, Julia. Do you remember me from this morning?'

She gave a slow nod.

'You've ingested a drug called belladonna. Do you know what that is?'

She shook her head side to side.

'It causes you to lose your voice sometimes. Do you think you can speak?'

The girl opened her mouth, and a scratchy sound

came out. She moved her lips, obviously trying to form words.

Jeffrey gave an encouraging smile. 'Want to try to tell me your name?'

She opened her mouth again, her voice raspy and small. 'Julia.'

'Good,' Jeffrey said. 'This is Lena Adams. You know her, right?'

Julia nodded, her eyes finding Lena.

'She's going to ask you some questions, okay?'

Lena tried not to hide her surprise. She wasn't sure she could tell Julia Matthews the time of day, let alone question the young woman. Lena fell back on her training, starting with what she knew.

'Julia?' Lena pulled a chair up to the young woman's bed. 'We need to know if you can tell us anything about what was done to you.'

Julia closed her eyes. Her lips quivered, but she did not answer.

'Did you know him, sweetie?'

She shook her head.

'Was it someone from one of your classes? Had you seen him around school?'

Julia's eyes closed. Tears came a few seconds later. She finally said, 'No.'

Lena put her hand on the girl's arm. It was thin and frail, much as Sibyl's had seemed in the morgue. She tried not to think about her sister when she said, 'Let's talk about his hair. Can you tell me what color it was?'

Again she shook her head.

'Any tattoos or marks that might help us identify him?'

'No.'

Lena said, 'I know this is hard, honey, but we have to

find out what happened. We need to get this guy off the street so he can't hurt anyone else.'

Julia kept her eyes closed. The room was intolerably quiet, so much so that Lena felt the urge to do something loud. The silence was making her nervous for some reason.

Without warning, Julia finally spoke. Her voice was husky. 'He tricked me.'

Lena pressed her lips together, letting the girl have her time.

'He tricked me,' Julia repeated, squeezing her eyes shut even tighter. 'I was at the library.'

Lena thought about Ryan Gordon. Her heart thumped in her chest. Had she been wrong about him? Was he capable of doing something like this? Maybe Julia had escaped while he was in jail.

'I had a test,' Julia continued, 'and I stayed late to study.' Her breathing became labored at the memory.

'Let's take some deep breaths,' Lena said, then she breathed in and out, in and out, with Julia. 'That's good, honey. Just keep calm.'

She started to cry in earnest now. 'Ryan was there,' she said.

Lena allowed herself to look at Jeffrey. He was focused on Matthews, his brow furrowed. She could almost read his thoughts.

'At the library?' Lena asked, trying not to sound too pushy.

Julia nodded, then reached out for her glass of water.

'Here,' Lena said, helping her lean up so that she could drink.

The girl took several swallows, then let her head drop back down. She stared out the window again, her mind obviously taking time to recover. Lena tried not to tap her foot. She wanted to reach over the bed and force the girl to talk. She could not understand how Julia Matthews could be so passive in her interrogation. If Lena were in that bed, she would be spitting out every detail she had. Lena would be pushing whoever would listen to find the man who did this. Her hands would be itching to rip his heart out of his chest. How Julia Matthews could just lie there, she did not know.

Lena counted to twenty, forcing herself to give the woman some time. She had counted in the Ryan Gordon interview; it was an old trick of hers and the only way she could make herself at least appear patient. When she reached fifty, Lena asked, 'Ryan was there?'

Julia nodded.

'In the library?'

She nodded again.

Lena reached over, putting her hand on Julia's arm again. She would have held her hand if it had not been wrapped in tight bandages. She kept her tone even, putting in just a little bit of pressure, as she said, 'You saw Ryan at the library. Then what happened?'

Julia responded to the pressure. 'We talked a little while, then I had to go back to the dorm.'

'Were you mad at him?'

Julia's eyes found Lena's. Something passed between them, an unvoiced message. Lena knew then that Ryan had some kind of control over Julia, but that she wanted to break it. Lena also knew that as much of a bastard as Ryan Gordon was, he had not been the man to do this to his girlfriend.

Lena asked, 'Did you argue?'

'We kind of made up, though.'

'Kind of, but not really?' Lena clarified, sensing what had happened in the library that night. She could see Ryan Gordon trying to push Julia into making some kind of commitment to him. She could also see that

Julia's eyes had finally been opened as to what kind of person her ex-boyfriend was. Julia had finally seen him for what he was. But someone else more evil than Ryan Gordon could ever hope to be had been waiting for her.

Lena asked, 'So you left the library, then what?'

'There was a man,' she said. 'On the way to the dorm.'

'Which way did you walk?'

'The back way, around the agri-building.'

'By the lake?'

She shook her head. 'The other side.'

Lena waited for her to continue.

'I ran into him, and he dropped his books, and I dropped mine.' Her voice trailed off, but her breathing became loud in the small room. She was nearly panting.

'Did you see his face then?'

'I don't remember. He gave me a shot.'

Lena felt her eyebrows furrow. 'Like a shot with a syringe?'

'I felt it. I didn't see it.'

'Where did you feel it?'

She put her hand to her left hip.

'He was behind you when you felt it?' Lena asked, thinking this would make the killer left-handed, just like Sibyl's attacker.

'Yeah.'

'So he took you then?' Lena asked. 'He ran into you, then you felt the shot, then he took you somewhere?'

'Yes.'

'In his car?'

'I don't remember,' she said. 'The next thing I knew, I was in a basement.' She put her hands over her face, crying in earnest. Her body started to shake with grief.

'It's okay,' Lena said, putting her hand over the other

woman's. 'Do you want to stop now? You're in charge of this.'

The room was quiet again but for Julia's breathing. When she did speak again, her voice was a hoarse, almost imperceptible whisper. 'He raped me.'

Lena felt a lump in her throat. She knew this already, of course, but the way Julia said the word stripped Lena of every defense she had. Lena felt raw and exposed. She did not want Jeffrey in the room. For some reason, he seemed to sense this. When she looked up at him, he nodded toward the door. Lena mouthed a yes, and he left without a sound.

'Do you know what happened next?' Lena asked.

Julia moved her head, trying to find Jeffrey.

'He's gone,' Lena said, giving her voice an assured tone that she did not feel. 'It's just us, Julia. It's just you and me, and we've got all day if you need it. All week, all year.' She paused, lest the girl take that as encouragement to stop the interview. 'Just keep in mind that the sooner we get the details, the sooner we can stop him. You don't want him to do this to another girl, do you?'

She took the question hard, as Lena expected she would. Lena knew she had to be a little tough or the girl would simply shut up, keeping the details to herself.

Julia sobbed, the noise filling the room, ringing in Lena's ears.

Julia said, 'I don't want this to happen to anyone else.'

'Me, either,' Lena answered. 'You have to tell me what he did to you.' She paused, then, 'Did you see his face at any time?'

'No,' she answered. 'I mean, I did, but I couldn't tell. I couldn't make the connection. It was so dark all the time. There was no light at all.'

'Are you sure it was a basement?'

'It smelled,' she said. 'Musty, and I could hear water dripping.'

'Water?' Lena asked. 'Like dripping from a faucet, or maybe from the lake?'

'A faucet,' Julia said. 'More like a faucet. It sounded . . . ' She closed her eyes, and for a few seconds she seemed to let herself go back to that place. 'Like a metallic clinking.' She mimicked the sound, 'Clink, clink, clink, over and over. It never stopped.' She put her hands over her ears, as if to stop the noise.

'Let's go back to the college,' Lena said. 'You felt the shot in your hip, then what? Do you know what kind of car he was driving?'

Julia shook her head again in an exaggerated sweep left to right. 'I don't remember. I was picking up my books, and then the next thing I knew, I was, I was . . . ' Her voice trailed off.

'In the basement?' Lena provided. 'Do you remember anything about where you were?'

'It was dark.'

'You couldn't make anything out?'

'I couldn't open my eyes. They wouldn't open.' Her voice so soft that Lena had to strain to hear. 'I was flying.'

'Flying?'

'I kept floating up, like I was on water. I could hear the waves from the ocean.'

Lena took a deep breath, then let it out slowly. 'Did he have you on your back?'

Julia's face crumpled at this, and she shook with sobs.

'Honey,' Lena prompted. 'Was he white? Black? Could you tell?'

She shook her head again. 'I couldn't open my eyes. He talked to me. His voice.' Her lips were trembling, and her face had turned an alarming shade of red. The tears came in earnest now, marking a continual stream down her face. 'He said he loved me.' She gasped for air as the panic took hold. 'He kept kissing me. His tongue.' She stopped, sobbing.

Lena took a deep breath, trying to calm herself down. She was pushing too hard. Lena counted to a slow one hundred, then said, 'The holes in your hands. We know he put something in your hands and feet.'

Julia looked at the bandages, as if seeing them for the first time. 'Yes,' she said. 'I woke up, and my hands were nailed down. I could see the nail go through, but it didn't hurt.'

'You were on the floor?'

'I think so. I felt' – she seemed to look for a word – 'I felt suspended. I was flying. How did he make me fly? Was I flying?'

Lena cleared her throat. 'No,' she answered. Then began, 'Julia, can you think of anybody new in your life, maybe someone on campus or in town, who was making you uncomfortable? Maybe you felt like you were being watched?'

'I'm still being watched,' she said, looking out the window.

'I'm watching you,' Lena said, turning the girl's face back toward her. 'I'm watching you, Julia. Nobody is going to hurt you again. Do you understand that? Nobody.'

'I don't feel safe,' she said, her face crumpling as she started to cry again. 'He can see me. I know he can see me.'

'It's just you and me here,' Lena assured her. When she spoke, it was like talking to Sibyl, assuring Sibyl that she would be taken care of. 'When you go to

Augusta, I'll be with you. I'm not going to let you out of my sight. Do you understand that?'

Julia seemed to be more frightened despite Lena's words. Her voice was raspy when she asked, 'Why am I going to Augusta?'

'I don't know that for sure,' Lena answered, reaching for the water pitcher. 'Don't worry about that right now.'

'Who's going to send me to Augusta?' Julia asked, her lips trembling.

'Drink some more water,' Lena told her, holding the cup up to her lips. 'Your parents are going to be here soon. Don't worry about anything but taking care of yourself and getting better.'

The girl choked, and water spilled down her neck and onto the bed. Her eyes opened wide in panic. 'Why are you moving me?' she asked. 'What's going to happen?'

'We won't move you if you don't want,' Lena said. 'I'll talk to your parents.'

'My parents?'

'They should be here soon,' Lena assured her. 'It's okay.'

'Do they know?' Julia asked, her voice raised. 'Did you tell them what happened to me?'

'I don't know,' Lena answered. 'I'm not sure if they know any of the details.'

'You can't tell my daddy,' the girl sobbed. 'Nobody can tell my father, okay? He can't know what happened.'

'You didn't do anything,' Lena said. 'Julia, your dad's not going to blame you for this.'

Julia was quiet. After a while, she looked back out the window, tears streaming down her cheeks.

'It's okay,' Lena soothed, taking a tissue out of the box on the table. She reached over the girl, blotting the water off the pillow. The last thing this girl needed to think about was how her father would react to what had happened to her. Lena had worked with rape victims before. She knew how the blame worked. Very seldom did a victim blame anyone but herself.

There was a strange noise Lena found vaguely familiar. Too late she realized it was her gun.

'Move away,' Julia whispered. She held the gun awkwardly in her bandaged hands. It tilted toward Lena, then back toward Julia as she tried to get a better grip on the weapon. Lena looked toward the door, thinking to call for Jeffrey, but Julia warned her, 'Don't.'

Lena held her hands out to her sides, but did not back up.

Lena said, 'Give me the gun.'

'You don't understand,' the girl said, tears welling into her eyes. 'You don't understand what he did to me, how he –' She stopped, choking on a sob. She did not have a good grip on the gun, but the barrel was pointed toward Lena and her finger was on the trigger. Lena felt a cold sweat overcome her, and she honestly could not recall if the safety was on or off. What she did know was that a round was already chambered. Once the safety was off, a tap on the trigger would fire the weapon.

Lena tried to keep her voice calm. 'What, sweetheart? What don't I understand?'

Julia tilted the gun back toward her own head. She fumbled, almost dropping it, before letting the barrel rest on her chin.

'Don't do that,' Lena begged. 'Please give me the gun. There's a bullet in the chamber.'

'I know about guns.'

'Julia, please,' Lena said, knowing she needed to keep the girl talking. 'Listen to me.'

A slight smile came to her lips. 'My daddy used to take me hunting with him. He used to let me help him clean the rifles.'

'Julia –'

'When I was there.' She choked back a sob. 'When I was with him.'

'The man? The man who abducted you?'

'You don't know what he did,' she said, her voice tight in her throat. 'The things he did to me. I can't tell you.'

'I'm so sorry,' Lena said. She wanted to move forward, but there was a look to Julia Matthews's eyes that kept her rooted to the floor. Charging the girl was not an option.

Lena said, 'I won't let him hurt you again, Julia. I promise.'

'You don't understand,' the girl sobbed, sliding the gun up to the cleft of her chin. She could barely grip the weapon, but Lena knew this wouldn't matter at such a close range.

'Honey, please don't,' Lena said, her eyes going to the door. Jeffrey was on the other side, maybe she could alert him somehow without letting Julia know.

'Don't,' Julia said, as if reading Lena's mind.

'You don't have to do this,' Lena said. She tried to make her voice firmer, but the truth was Lena had only read about this kind of situation in procedural manuals. She had never talked someone out of suicide.

Julia said, 'The way he touched me. The way he kissed me.' Her voice broke. 'You just don't know.'

'What?' Lena asked, slowly moving her hand toward the gun. 'What don't I know?'

'He –' She stopped, a guttural sound coming from her throat. 'He made love to me.'

'He –'

'He made love to me,' she repeated, a whisper that echoed in the room. 'Do you know what that means?' she asked. 'He kept saying he didn't want to hurt me. He wanted to make love to me. He did.'

Lena felt her mouth open, but there was nothing she could say. She couldn't be hearing what she thought she was hearing. 'What are you saying?' she asked, aware of the sharpness in her tone. 'What do you mean?'

'He made love to me,' Julia repeated. 'The way he touched me.'

Lena shook her head, as if to rid this from her mind. She could not keep the incredulity out of her tone when she asked, 'Are you saying you enjoyed it?'

A snapping sound came as Julia disengaged the safety. Lena felt too stunned to move but somehow managed to reach Julia seconds before the girl pulled the trigger. Lena looked down in time to see Julia Matthews's head explode beneath her.

The water from the shower came like needles against Lena's skin. She was aware of the burning, but it was not uncomfortable. She was numb to all sensations, numb from the inside out. Her knees gave, and Lena let herself slide down into the tub. She pulled her knees to her chest, closing her eyes as the water beat down on her breasts and face. She bent her head forward, feeling like a rag doll. The water pummeled the top of her head, bruised the back of her neck, but she did not care. Her body did not belong to her anymore. She was empty. She could not think of one thing that had meaning in her life, not her job, not Jeffrey, not Hank Norton, and certainly not herself.

Julia Matthews was dead, just like Sibyl. Lena had failed them both.

The water started to run cold, the spray pricking against her skin. Lena turned off the shower and dried herself with a towel, feeling as if she was just going through the motions. Her body still felt dirty despite the fact that this was her second shower in the last five hours. There was a strange taste in her mouth, too. Lena wasn't sure if it was her imagination or if something had gone into her mouth when Julia had pulled the trigger.

She shuddered thinking about this.

'Lee?' Hank called from outside the bathroom door.

'I'll be down in a minute,' Lena answered, putting paste on her toothbrush. She looked at herself in the mirror as she tried to scrub the taste out of her mouth. The resemblance to Sibyl was gone today. There was nothing left of her sister.

Lena went down to the kitchen in her robe and bedroom slippers. Outside the kitchen door, she put her hand to the wall, feeling lightheaded and sick to her stomach. She was forcing her body to move, otherwise she would go to sleep and never wake up. Her body ached to give in to that, ached to cut off, but Lena knew that as soon as her head hit the pillow she would be wide awake, her mind playing back the sight of Julia Matthews just before she killed herself. The girl had been looking at Lena when she pulled the trigger. Their eyes had locked, and Lena did not need to see the gun to know that death was on the younger woman's mind.

Hank was at the kitchen table, drinking a Coke. He stood when she entered the room. Lena felt a flush of shame and couldn't look him in the eye. She had been strong in the car as Frank drove her back to the house. She had not said a word to her partner, or commented on the fact that despite her efforts to clean herself at the hospital, she had grey matter and blood sticking to her like hot wax. There were pieces of bone in her breast pocket, and she could feel blood dripping down her face and neck, even though she had wiped it all off at the hospital. It was not until she had the front door closed behind her that Lena let herself go. That Hank had been there, that she had let him hold her in his arms while she sobbed, was something that still brought a sense of shame to her. She did not know herself anymore. She did not know who this weak person was.

Lena glanced out the window, noting, 'It's dark out.'

'You slept awhile,' Hank said, going to the stove. 'You want some tea?'

'Yeah,' Lena said, though she had not slept at all. Closing her eyes only brought her closer to what had happened. If she never slept again, Lena would be fine.

'Your boss called to check on you,' Hank said.

'Oh,' Lena answered, sitting at the table, her leg tucked underneath her. She wondered what was going through Jeffrey's mind. He had been out in the hallway, waiting for Lena to call him in, when the gun went off. Lena remembered the expression of absolute shock on his face when he burst through the doorway. Lena had stood there, still leaning over Julia, flesh and bone dripping from her chest and face. Jeffrey had forced her out of this position, patting his hands down Lena's body, checking to make sure she had not been shot in the process.

Lena had stood mute while he did this, unable to take her eyes off what was left of Julia Matthews's face. The young girl had put the gun under her chin, blowing out the back of her head. The wall behind and over the bed was splattered. A bullet hole was three feet down from the ceiling. Jeffrey had forced Lena to stay in that room, drilling her for every bit of information she had gotten from Julia Matthews, questioning every detail of Lena's narrative as Lena stood there, her lip trembling uncontrollably, unable to follow the words coming out of her own mouth.

Lena put her head in her hands. She listened as Hank filled the kettle, heard the click as the electric starter on the gas stove kicked in.

Hank sat in front of her, his hands crossed in front of him. 'You okay?' he asked.

'I don't know,' she answered, her own voice sounding far away. The gun had gone off close to her ear. The ringing had stopped a while ago, but sounds still came like a dull ache.

'You know what I was thinking?' Hank asked, sitting back in his chair. 'Remember that time you fell off the front porch?'

Lena stared at him, not understanding where he was going with this. 'Yeah?'

'Well.' He shrugged, smiling for some reason. 'Sibyl pushed you.'

Lena wasn't sure she had heard him right. 'What?'

He assured Lena, 'She pushed you. I saw her.'

'She pushed me off the porch?' Lena shook her head. 'She was trying to keep me from falling.'

'She was blind, Lee, how did she know you were falling?'

Lena's mouth worked. He had a point. 'I had to get sixteen stitches in my leg.'

'I know.'

'She pushed me?' Lena questioned, her voice raised a few octaves. 'Why did she push me?'

'I don't know. Maybe she was just kidding.' Hank chuckled. 'You let out such a holler I thought the neighbors were gonna come.'

'I doubt the neighbors would've come if they'd heard a twenty-one gun salute,' Lena commented. Hank Norton's neighbors had learned early on to expect all kinds of commotion coming from his house night and day.

'Remember that time at the beach?' Hank began.

Lena stared at him, trying to figure out why he was bringing this up. 'What time?'

'When you couldn't find your kickboard?'

'The red one?' Lena asked. Then, 'Don't tell me, she pushed it off the balcony.'

He chuckled. 'Nope. She lost it in the pool.'

'How can you lose a kickboard in the pool?'

He waved this off. 'I guess some kid took it. The point was, it was yours. You told her not to take it and she did, and she lost it.'

Despite herself, Lena felt some of the weight on her shoulders lifting. 'Why are you telling me this?' she asked.

Again, he gave a small shrug. 'I don't know. I was just thinking about her this morning. Remember that shirt she used to wear? The one with the green stripes?'

Lena nodded.

'She still had it.'

'No,' Lena said, surprised. They had fought over that shirt during high school until Hank had settled it with a coin toss. 'Why did she keep it?'

'It was hers,' Hank said.

Lena stared at her uncle, not sure what to say.

He stood up, taking a mug from the cabinet. 'You want some time to yourself, or do you want me around?'

Lena considered his question. She needed to be alone, to get some sense of herself back, and she could not do that around Hank of all people. 'Are you going back to Reece?'

'I thought I'd stay at Nan's tonight and help her sort through some things.'

Lena felt a slight panic. 'She's not throwing things away, is she?'

'No, of course not. She's just going through things, getting her clothes together.' Hank leaned against the counter, his arms crossed. 'She shouldn't have to do that alone.'

Lena stared at her hands. There was something under her fingernails. She couldn't tell if it was dirt or blood. She put her finger in her mouth, using her bottom teeth to clean it.

Hank watched this. He said, 'You could come by later if you felt like it.' Lena shook her head, biting the nail. She would tear it off to the quick before she let the blood stay there. 'I have to get up early for work tomorrow,' she lied.

'But if you change your mind?'

'Maybe,' she mumbled around her finger. She tasted blood, surprised to see that it was her own. The cuticle had come away on the nail. A bright red dot radiated from the spot.

Hank stood, staring, then grabbed his coat off the back of his chair. They had been through this kind of thing before, though admittedly never on this scale. It was an old, familiar dance, and they both knew the moves. Hank took one step forward, Lena took two steps back. Now wasn't the time to change any of this.

He said, 'You can call me if you need me. You know that, right?'

'Mm-hm,' she mumbled, pressing her lips together. She was going to cry again, and Lena thought that a part of her would die if she broke down in front of Hank again.

He seemed to sense this because he put his hand on her shoulder, then kissed the top of her head.

Lena kept her head down, waiting for the click as the front door closed. She gave a long sigh as Hank's car backed out of the driveway.

The kettle was steaming, but the whistle had not started yet. Lena did not particularly like tea, but she rummaged around in the cabinets anyway, looking for the bags. She found a box of Tummy Mint just as a knock came at the back door.

She expected to see Hank, so Lena was surprised when she opened the door.

'Oh, hi,' she said, rubbing her ear as a shrill noise came. She realized the teakettle was whistling and said, 'Hold on a second.'

She was turning off the burner when she felt a presence behind her, then a sharp sting came to her left thigh.

SEVENTEEN

Sara stood in front of the body of Julia Matthews with her arms crossed over her chest. She stared at the girl, trying to assess her with a clinical eye, trying to separate the girl whose life Sara had saved from the dead woman on the table. The incision Sara had made to access Julia's heart was not yet healed, the black sutures still thick with dried blood. A small hole was at the base of the woman's chin. Burns around the entrance wound revealed the barrel of the gun was pressed into the chin when it was fired. A gaping hole at the back of the girl's head revealed the exit wound. Bone hung from the open skull, like macabre ornaments on a bloody Christmas tree. The smell of gunpowder was in the air.

Julia Matthews's body lay on the porcelain autopsy table much as Sibyl Adams's had a few days ago. At the head of the table was a faucet with a black rubber hose attached. Hanging over this was an organ scale much like the scales grocers use to weigh fruit and vegetables. Beside the table were the tools of autopsy: a scalpel, a sixteen-inch-long surgically sharpened bread knife, a pair of equally sharpened scissors, a pair of forceps, or 'pickups,' a Stryker saw to cut bone, and a set of longhandled pruning shears one would normally find in a garage by the lawn mower. Cathy Linton had a similar set for herself, and whenever Sara saw her mother pruning azaleas she always thought about using the shears at the morgue to cut away the rib cage.

Sara mindlessly followed the various steps for preparing the body of Julia Matthews for autopsy. Her thoughts were elsewhere, back to the night before, when Julia Matthews was on Sara's car; back to when the girl was alive and had a chance.

Sara had never minded performing autopsies before, never been disturbed by death. Opening a body was like opening a book; there were many things which could be learned from tissue and organ. In death, the body was available for thorough evaluation. Part of the reason Sara had taken the job as medical examiner for Grant County was that she had become bored with her practice at the clinic. The coroner's job presented a challenge, an opportunity to learn a new skill and to help people. Though the thought of cutting up Julia Matthews, exposing her body to more abuse, cut through Sara like a knife.

Again, Sara looked at what was left of Julia Matthews's head. Gunshots to the head were notoriously unpredictable. Most times the victim ended up comatose, a vegetable who, through the miracles of modern science, quietly lived out the rest of the life they did not want in the first place. Julia Matthews had done a better job than most when she put the gun under her chin and pulled the trigger. The bullet had entered her skull at an upward trajectory, breaking the spheroid, plowing along the lateral cerebral fissure, then busting out through the occipital bone. The back of the head was gone, affording a straight view into the brain case. Unlike in her earlier suicide attempt witnessed by the scarring on her wrists, Julia Matthews had meant to end her life. Unquestionably, the girl had known what she was doing.

Sara felt sick to her stomach. She wanted to shake the girl back to life, to demand she go on living, to ask her how she could have gone through everything that had happened to her in the last few days only to end up taking her life. It seemed that the very horrors Julia Matthews had survived had also ended up killing her.

'You okay?' Jeffrey asked, giving her a concerned look.

'Yeah,' Sara managed, wondering if she really was. She felt raw, like a wound that would not scab. Sara knew that if Jeffrey made a pass at her, she would take him up on the offer. All she could think of was how good it would feel to let him take her into his arms, to feel his lips kissing hers, his tongue in her mouth. Her body ached for him now in a way she had not ached for him in years. She did not particularly want sex, she just wanted the assurance of his presence. She wanted to feel protected. She wanted to belong to him. Sara had learned a long time ago that sex was the only way Jeffrey knew how to give her these things.

From across the table, Jeffrey asked, 'Sara?'

She opened her mouth, thinking to proposition him, but stopped herself. So much had happened in the last few years. So much had changed. The man she wanted did not really exist anymore. Sara wasn't sure if he ever had.

She cleared her throat. 'Yeah?'

'You want to hold off on this?' he asked.

'No,' Sara answered in a clipped tone, inwardly berating herself for thinking she needed Jeffrey. The truth was she didn't. She had gotten this far without him. She could certainly go further.

She tapped her foot on the remote for the Dicta-phone, stating, 'This is the unembalmed body of a thin but well-built, well-nourished young adult white female weighing' – Sara looked at the chalkboard over Jeffrey's shoulder where she had made notations – 'one hundred and twelve pounds and having a length of sixty-four inches.' She tapped the recorder off, taking a deep breath to clear her mind. Sara was having trouble breathing.

'Sara?'

She tapped the recorder back on, shaking her head at him. The sympathy she had so wanted a few minutes ago now irritated her. She felt exposed.

She dictated, 'The appearance of the decedent is consistent with the stated age of twenty-two. The body has been refrigerated for a period of no less than three hours and is cool to the touch.' Sara stopped, clearing her throat. 'Rigor mortis is formed and fixed in the upper and lower extremities, and patches of livor mortis are seen posteriorly on the trunk and extremities, except in areas of pressure.'

And on it went, this clinical description of a woman who only hours ago had been battered but alive, who weeks ago had been content if not happy. Sara cataloged the exterior appearance of Julia Matthews, imagining in her mind what the woman must have gone through. Was she awake when her teeth were pulled out so that her attacker could rape her face? Was she conscious when her rectum was being ripped open? Did the drugs block the sensations when she was nailed to the floor? An autopsy could only reveal the physical damage; the girl's state of mind, her level of consciousness, would remain a mystery. No one would know what was going through her mind as she was assaulted. No one would ever see exactly what this girl had seen. Sara could only guess, and she did not like the images such guessing brought to mind. Again, she saw herself on the hospital gurney. Again, she saw herself being examined.

Sara forced herself to look up from the body, feeling shaky and out of place. Jeffrey was staring at her, a strange look on his face. 'What?' she asked.

He shook his head, still keeping his eyes on her.

'I wish,' Sara began, then stopped, clearing the lump in her throat. 'I wish you wouldn't look at me like that, okay?' She waited, but he did not acknowledge her request.

He asked, 'How am I looking at you?'

'Predatorily,' she answered, but that wasn't quite right. He was looking at her the way she wanted him to look at her. There was a sense of responsibility to his expression, like he wanted nothing more than to take charge of things, to make things better. She hated herself for wanting this.

'It's unintentional,' he said.

She snapped off her gloves. 'Okay.'

'I'm worried about you, Sara. I want you to talk to me about what's going on.'

Sara walked toward the supply cabinet, not wanting to have this conversation over the body of Julia Matthews. 'You don't get to do that anymore. Remember why?'

If she had slapped him, his expression would have been the same. 'I never stopped caring about you.'

She swallowed hard, trying not to let this get to her. 'Thanks.'

'Sometimes,' he began, 'when I wake up in the morning, I forget that you're not there. I forget that I lost you.'

'Kind of like when you forgot you were married to me?'

He walked toward her, but she stepped back until she

was a few inches from the cabinet. He stood in front of her, his hands on her arms. 'I still love you.'

'That's not enough.'

He stepped closer to her. 'What is?'

'Jeffrey,' she said. 'Please.'

He finally backed away, his tone sharp as he asked, 'What do you think?' He was referring to the body. 'Do you think you'll find anything?'

Sara crossed her arms, feeling the need to protect herself. 'I think she died with her secrets.'

Jeffrey gave her a strange look, probably because Sara wasn't one to buy into melodrama. She made a conscious effort to act more like herself, to be more clinical about the situation, but even the thought of doing this was too emotionally taxing.

Sara kept her hand steady as she made the standard Y-incision across the chest. The sound as she skinned back the flesh cut through her thoughts. She tried to talk over them. 'How are her parents holding up?'

Jeffrey said, 'You can't imagine how horrible it was telling them she'd been raped. And then, this.' He indicated the body. 'You can't imagine.'

Sara's mind wandered again. She saw her own father standing over a hospital bed, her mother embracing him from behind. She closed her eyes for a few seconds, willing this image from her mind. She would not be able to do this if she kept putting herself in Julia Matthews's place.

'Sara?' Jeffrey asked.

Sara looked up, surprised to realize that she had stopped the autopsy. She was standing in front of the body, arms crossed in front of her. Jeffrey waited patiently, not asking her the obvious question.

Sara picked up the scalpel and went to work, dictating, 'The body is opened with the usual Y-incision and the organs of the thoracic and abdominal cavities are in their normal anatomic positions.'

Jeffrey started talking again as soon as she stopped. Thankfully, he chose a different topic this time. He said, 'I don't know what I'm going to do about Lena.'

'What's that?' Sara asked, glad for the sound of his voice.

'She's not holding up well,' he said. 'I told her to take a couple of days off.'

'Do you think she will?'

'I think she actually might.'

Sara picked up the scissors, cutting the pericardial sac with quick snips. 'So, then, what's the problem?'

'She's at the edge. I can sense that. I just don't know what to do.' He indicated Julia Matthews. 'I don't want her to end up doing something like this.'

Sara scrutinized him over the rim of her glasses. She did not know whether or not he was using dime store psychology, hiding his concern for Sara by pretending a concern for Lena, or if he really was looking for advice on how to handle Lena.

She gave him an answer that would suit either scenario. 'Lena Adams?' She shook her head no, certain of this one thing. 'She's a fighter. People like Lena don't kill themselves. They kill other people, but they don't kill themselves.'

'I know,' Jeffrey answered. He was quiet then as Sara clamped off and removed the stomach.

'This won't be pleasant,' she warned, placing the stomach in a stainless steel bowl. Jeffrey had been through plenty of autopsies before, but there was nothing so pungent as the odors of the digestive tract.

'Hey.' Sara stopped, surprised at what she saw. 'Look at this.'

'What is it?'

She stood to the side so that he could see the contents of the stomach. The digestive juices were black and soupy, so she used a strainer to scoop out the contents.

'What is it?' he repeated.

'I don't know. Maybe seeds of some sort,' Sara told him, using a pair of pickups to remove one. 'I think we should call Mark Webster.'

'Here,' he offered, holding out an evidence bag.

She dropped the seed into the bag, asking, 'You think he wants to get caught?'

'They all want to get caught, don't they?' he countered. 'Look at where he left them. Both in semipublic places, both displayed. He's getting off on the risk as much as anything else.'

'Yeah,' she agreed, willing herself not to say more. She did not want to go into the gritty details of the case. She wanted to do her job and get out of here, away from Jeffrey.

Jeffrey didn't seem to want to comply. He asked, 'The seeds are potent, right?'

Sara nodded.

'So, you think he kept her out of it while he was raping her?'

'I couldn't begin to guess,' she answered truthfully.

He paused, as if he did not know how to phrase his next sentence.

'What?' she prompted.

'Lena,' he said. 'I mean, Julia told Lena that she enjoyed it.'

Sara felt her brow furrow. 'What?'

'Not exactly that she enjoyed it, but that he made love to her.'

'He pulled her teeth out and ripped her rectum open. How could anyone call what he did to her making love?'

He shrugged, as if the answer was lost on him, but said, 'Maybe he kept her so drugged up that she didn't feel it. Maybe she didn't know what was going on until after.'

Sara considered this. 'It's possible,' she said, uncomfortable with the scenario.

'It's what she said, anyway,' he answered.

The room was quiet but for the compressor on the freezer cycling down. Sara went back to the autopsy, using clamps to section off the small and large intestines. They were limp in her hands, like wet spaghetti, as she lifted them out of the body. Julia Matthews had not eaten anything of substance during the last few days of her life. Her digestive system was relatively empty.

'Let's see,' Sara said, placing the intestines on the grocer's scale to weigh them. A metallic clink came, like a penny being dropped into a tin cup.

'What's that?' Jeffrey asked.

Sara did not answer him. She picked the intestines back up, then dropped them again. The same noise came, a tinny vibration through the scale. 'Something's in there,' Sara mumbled, walking over to the light box mounted on the wall. She used her elbow to turn on the light, illuminating Julia Matthews's X rays. Her pelvic series was in the center.

'See anything?' Jeffrey asked.

'Whatever it is, it's in the large intestines,' Sara answered, staring at what looked like a splinter in the bottom half of the rectum. She had not noticed the sliver before or had assumed it was a problem with the film. The portable X ray in the morgue was old and not known for its reliability.

Sara studied the film for another few seconds, then walked back to the scale. She separated the terminal ileum at the ileocecal valve and carried the large intestines to the foot of the table. After using the faucet to clean off the blood, she squeezed her fingers down from the base of the sigmoid colon, searching for the object that had made the noise. She found a hard lump about five inches into the rectum.

'Hand me the scalpel,' she ordered, holding out her hand. Jeffrey did as he was told, watching her work.

Sara made a small incision, releasing a foul odor into the room. Jeffrey stepped back, but Sara did not have that luxury. She used the pickups to remove an object that was approximately a half inch long. A rinse under the faucet revealed that it was a small key.

'A handcuff key?' Jeffrey asked, leaning over for a better look.

'Yes,' Sara answered, feeling a little light-headed. 'It was forced up into the rectum from the anus.'

'Why?'

'I guess so that we would find it,' Sara answered. 'Could you get an evidence bag?'

Jeffrey did as he was told, opening the bag so that she could drop the key in. 'Do you think we'll find anything on it?'

'Bacteria,' she answered. 'If you mean fingerprints, I seriously doubt it.' She pressed her lips together, thinking this through. 'Turn the lights off for a second.'

'What are you thinking?'

Sara walked toward the light box, using her elbow to turn it off. 'I'm thinking he put the key up there relatively early in the game. I'm thinking the edge is sharp. Maybe it tore the condom.'

Jeffrey walked over to the light switch as Sara peeled off her gloves. She picked up the black light, which would highlight traces of seminal fluid.

'Ready?' he asked.

'Yeah,' she said, and the lights went out.

Sara blinked several times, letting her eyes adjust to the unnatural light. Slowly, she cast the black light along the incision she had made in the rectum. 'Hold this,' she said, giving Jeffrey the light. She slipped on a fresh pair of gloves and with the scalpel opened the incision farther. A small pocket of purple showed in the opening.

Jeffrey gave a small sigh, as if he had been holding his breath. 'Is it enough for a DNA comparison?'

Sara stared at the purplish glowing matter. 'I think so.'

Sara tiptoed through her sister's apartment, peeking around the bedroom door to make sure Tessa was still alone.

'Tessie?' she whispered, shaking her slightly.

'What?' Tessa grumbled, rolling over. 'What time is it?'

Sara looked at the clock on the bedside table. 'About two in the morning.'

'What?' Tessa repeated, rubbing her eyes. 'What's wrong?'

Sara said, 'Scoot over.'

Tessa did as she was told, holding up the sheet for Sara. 'What's wrong?'

Sara did not answer. She pulled the comforter up under her chin.

'Is something wrong?' Tessa repeated.

'Nothing's wrong.'

'Is that girl really dead?'

Sara closed her eyes. 'Yes.'

Tessa sat up in bed, turning on the light. 'We've got to talk, Sara.'

Sara rolled over, her back to her sister. 'I don't want to talk.'

'I don't care,' Tessa answered, pulling the covers away from Sara. 'Sit up.'

'Don't order me around,' Sara countered, feeling annoyed. She had come here to feel safe so that she could sleep, not to be pushed around by her kid sister.

'Sara,' Tessa began. 'You have got to tell Jeffrey what happened.'

Sara sat up, angry that this was starting again. 'No,' she answered, her lips a tight line.

'Sara,' Tessa said, her voice firm. 'Hare told me about that girl. He told me about the tape on her mouth and about the way she was put on your car.'

'He shouldn't talk about that kind of stuff with you.'

'He wasn't telling it as a point of interest,' Tessa said. She got out of bed, obviously angry.

'What are you so pissed at me about?' Sara demanded, standing, too. They faced each other on opposite sides of the room, the bed between them.

Sara put her hands on her hips. 'It's not my fault, okay? I did everything I could do to help that girl, and if she couldn't live with it, then that's her choice.'

'Great choice, huh? I guess it's better to put a bullet in your brain than to keep it in all the time.'

'What the fuck does that mean?'

'You know what it means,' Tessa snapped back. 'You need to tell Jeffrey, Sara.'

'I won't.'

Tessa seemed to size her up. She crossed her arms over her chest, threatening, 'If you don't, I will.'

'What?' Sara gasped. If Tessa had punched her, Sara would have felt less shock. Her mouth opened in surprise. 'You wouldn't.'

'Yes, I would,' Tessa answered, her mind obviously made up. 'If I don't, then Mom will.'

'You and Mom hatched this little plan together?' Sara

gave a humorless laugh. 'I suppose Dad's in on it, too?' She threw her hands up into the air. 'My whole family's ganging up on me.'

'We're not ganging up on you,' Tessa countered. 'We're trying to help you.'

'What happened to me,' Sara began, her words clipped and precise, 'has nothing to do with what happened to Sibyl Adams and Julia Matthews.' She leaned across the bed, giving Tessa a look of warning. They could both play at this game.

'That's not your decision to make,' Tessa countered.

Sara felt her anger boiling over at the threat. 'You want me to tell you how they're different, Tessie? You want to know the things I know about these cases?' She did not give her sister time to answer. 'For one, nobody carved a cross on my chest and left me to bleed out in the toilet.' She paused, knowing the impact her words would have. If Tessa wanted to push Sara, Sara knew how to push back.

Sara continued, 'For another, no one knocked out my front teeth so they could sodomize my face.'

Tessa's hand went to her mouth. 'Oh, God.'

'Nobody nailed my hands and feet to the floor so he could fuck me.'

'No,' Tessa breathed, tears coming to her eyes.

Sara could not stop herself, even though her words were obviously acid in Tessa's ears. 'Nobody scrubbed out my mouth with Clorox. Nobody shaved my pubic hair so there wouldn't be any trace evidence.' She paused for breath. 'Nobody stabbed a hole in my gut so he could –' Sara forced herself to stop, knowing she was going too far. Still, a small sob escaped from Tessa's mouth as she made the connection. Her eyes had been on Sara's the entire time, and the look of horror on her face sent waves of guilt through Sara.

Sara whispered, 'I'm sorry, Tessie. I'm so sorry.'

Tessa's hand slowly fell from her mouth. She said, 'Jeffrey is a policeman.'

Sara put her hand to her chest. 'I know that.'

'You're so beautiful,' Tessa said. 'And you're smart and you're funny and you're tall.'

Sara laughed so that she wouldn't cry.

'And this time twelve years ago, you were raped,' Tessa finished.

'I know that.'

'He sends you postcards every year, Sara. He knows where you live.'

'I know that.'

'Sara,' Tessa began, a begging quality to her voice. 'You have to tell Jeffrey.'

'I can't.'

Tessa stood firm. 'You don't have a choice.'

FRIDAY

EIGHTEEN

Jeffrey slipped on a pair of underwear and limped toward the kitchen. His knee was still stiff from the buckshot, and his stomach had been upset since he walked into Julia Matthews's room. He was worried about Lena. He was worried about Sara. He was worried about his town.

Brad Stephens had taken the DNA sample to Macon a few hours ago. It would take at least a week to get something back, perhaps another week to get time on the FBI DNA database to cross-check for known offenders. As with most police work, this was a waiting game. Meanwhile, there was no telling what the perpetrator was up to. For all Jeffrey knew, he could be stalking his next victim at this very moment. He could be raping his next victim at this very moment, doing things to her that only an animal would think to do.

Jeffrey opened the refrigerator, taking out the milk. On the way to get a glass, he flicked the overhead light switch, but nothing happened. He mumbled a curse toward himself as he took a glass out of the cabinet. He had disconnected the kitchen lights a couple of weeks ago when a new fixture he had ordered arrived in the mail. A call had come from the station just as he was stripping the wires, and the chandelier sat upended in its box, waiting for Jeffrey to find the time to hang it. At this rate, Jeffrey would be eating by the light from the refrigerator for the next few years.

He finished his milk and limped over to the sink to rinse the glass. He wanted to call Sara, to check on her, but knew better than that. She was blocking him out for her own reasons. He didn't really have a leg to stand on since the divorce. Maybe she was with Jeb tonight. He had heard through Marla who had been talking to Marty Ringo that Sara and Jeb were seeing each other again. He vaguely remembered Sara saying something about a date at the hospital the other night, but his mind could not connect her words. Since the memory had come after Marla had deigned to mention the gossip to him, he could not rely on it.

Jeffrey groaned as he sat back down on the bar stool in front of the kitchen island. He had built the island months ago. He had actually built it twice, because he had not been pleased with the way it had looked the first time. Jeffrey was above all things a perfectionist, and he hated when things weren't symmetrical. Since he lived in an old house, this meant that he was constantly having to adjust and readjust, because there wasn't a wall in the house that was straight.

A slight breeze stirred the thick plastic strips lining the back wall of the kitchen. He was vacillating between French doors and a wall of windows, or extending the kitchen out about ten feet into the backyard. Some kind of breakfast nook would be nice, a place to sit in the mornings and look out at the birds in the backyard. What he really wanted was to put a large deck out there with a hot tub or maybe one of those fancy outdoor barbecues. Whatever he did, he wanted to keep the house open. Jeffrey liked the way the light came in during the day through the semitransparent strips. He liked being able to see into the backyard, especially at times like right now, when he saw someone walking back there.

Jeffrey stood, grabbing a bat out of the laundry room. He slid through a crack in the plastic strips, tiptoeing across the lawn. The grass was wet from a slight mist in the night air, and Jeffrey shivered from the chill, hoping to God he did not get shot again, especially since he was dressed only in a pair of underwear. The thought occurred to him that whoever was lurking in the backyard might collapse from laughter rather than fear at seeing Jeffrey standing in the yard, naked but for his green boxers, holding a bat over his head.

He heard a familiar noise. It was a lapping, licking sound, the kind a dog made while grooming. He squinted in the moonlight, making out three figures by the side of the house. Two of them were short enough to be dogs. One of them was tall enough to only be Sara. She was looking into his bedroom window.

Jeffrey let the bat hang down as he tiptoed up behind her. He wasn't worried about Billy or Bob, as the two greyhounds were the laziest animals he had ever seen. True to form, they barely moved as he sneaked up behind her.

'Sara?'

'Oh, Jesus.' Sara jumped, tripping over the nearest dog. Jeffrey reached forward, catching her before she fell on her backside.

Jeffrey laughed, giving Bob a pat on the head. 'Peeping Tom?' he asked.

'You asshole,' Sara hissed, slapping her hands into his chest. 'You scared the shit out of me.'

'What?' Jeffrey asked innocently. 'I'm not the one sneaking around your house.'

'Like you haven't before.'

'That's me,' Jeffrey pointed out. 'Not you.' He leaned

against the bat. Now that his adrenaline had stopped pumping, the dull ache had come back to his leg. 'You want to explain why you're looking in my window in the middle of the night?'

'I didn't want to wake you up if you were asleep.'

'I was in the kitchen.'

'In the dark?' Sara crossed her arms, levering him with a nasty look. 'Alone?'

'Come on in,' Jeffrey offered, not waiting for her to respond. He kept his pace slow as he walked back toward the kitchen, glad when he heard Sara's footsteps behind him. She was wearing a pair of faded blue jeans with an equally old white button-down shirt.

'You walk the dogs over here?'

'I borrowed Tessa's car,' Sara said, scratching Bob on the head.

'Good thinking, bringing your attack dogs.'

'I'm glad you weren't looking to kill me.'

'What makes you think I wasn't?' Jeffrey asked, using the bat to hold the plastic aside so that she could get into the house.

Sara looked at the plastic, then at him. 'I love what you've done to the place.'

'It needs a woman's touch,' Jeffrey suggested.

'I'm sure there are plenty of volunteers.'

He suppressed a groan as he headed back into the kitchen. 'Power's out in here,' he offered, lighting a candle by the stove.

'Ha-ha,' Sara said, trying the light switch nearest her. She walked across the room, trying the other switch as Jeffrey lit another candle. 'What's the deal?'

'Old house.' He shrugged, not wanting to confess his laziness. 'Brad took the sample to Macon.'

'A couple of weeks, huh?'

'Yeah,' he nodded. 'Do you think he's a cop?'

'Brad?'

'No, the perpetrator. Do you think he's a cop? Maybe that's why he left the handcuff key in . . . there.' He paused. 'You know, as a clue.'

'Maybe he uses handcuffs to restrain them,' Sara said. 'Maybe he's into S&M. Maybe his mama used to cuff him to the bed when he was a little boy.'

He was puzzled by her flippant tone but knew better than to comment on it.

Out of the blue, Sara said, 'I want a screwdriver.'

Jeffrey frowned at this, but he walked over to his toolbox and rummaged around. 'Phillips?'

'No, a drink,' Sara answered. She opened the freezer door, taking out the vodka.

'I don't think I've got orange juice,' he said as she opened the other door.

'This'll do,' she said, holding out the cranberry juice. She rummaged in the cabinets for a glass, then poured what looked like a very stiff drink.

Jeffrey watched all this, concerned. Sara seldom drank, and when she did a glass of wine could turn her tipsy. He had never seen her drink anything stronger than a margarita their entire marriage.

Sara shuddered as she swallowed the drink. 'How much was I supposed to put?' she asked.

'Probably a third of what you poured,' he answered, taking the drink from her. He took a small sip, nearly gagging from the taste. 'Jesus Christ,' he managed around a cough. 'Are you trying to kill yourself?'

'Me and Julia Matthews,' she tossed back. 'Do you have anything sweet?'

Jeffrey opened his mouth to ask her what the hell she meant by that comment, but Sara was already rummaging through the cabinets.

He offered, 'There's some pudding in the fridge. Bottom shelf in the back.'

'Fat free?' she asked.

'Nope.'

'Good,' Sara said, bending at the waist to find the pudding.

Jeffrey crossed his arms, watching her. He wanted to ask her what she was doing in his kitchen in the middle of the morning. He wanted to ask her what had been going on lately, why she was acting so odd.

'Jeff?' Sara asked, rooting through the fridge.

'Hmm?'

'Are you looking at my ass?'

Jeffrey smiled. He hadn't been, but he answered, 'Yeah.'

Sara stood, holding the pudding cup in the air like a trophy. 'Last one.'

'Yep.'

Sara pulled the top off the pudding as she scooted onto the counter. 'This is getting to be a bad thing.'

'You think?'

'Well.' She shrugged, licking the pudding off the top. 'College girls being raped, killing themselves. That's not what we're all about, is it?'

Again, Jeffrey was surprised by her cavalier attitude. This wasn't like Sara, but lately he wasn't sure exactly how she was.

'I guess not,' he said.

'You tell her parents?'

Jeffrey answered, 'Frank picked them up at the airport.' He paused, then said, 'Her father.' He stopped again. The sight of Jon Matthews's anguished face was not something Jeffrey would soon forget.

'Father took it hard, huh?' Sara said. 'Daddies don't like to know their little girls have been messed with.'

'I guess not,' Jeffrey answered, wondering at her choice of words.

'You would guess right.'

'Yeah,' Jeffrey said. 'He took it really hard.'

Something flashed in Sara's eyes, but she looked down before he could tell what was going on. She took a long drink from her glass, spilling some down the front of her shirt. She actually giggled.

Despite his better judgment, Jeffrey asked, 'What's wrong with you, Sara?'

She pointed at his waist. 'When'd you start wearing those?' she asked.

Jeffrey looked down. Since the only thing he was wearing were his green boxers, he assumed that's what she meant. He looked back at her, shrugging. 'A while ago.'

'Less than two years,' she noted, licking more pudding.

'Yeah,' he offered, walking over to her, arms out from his sides, showing off his underwear. 'You like 'em?'

She clapped her hands.

'What're you doing here, Sara?'

She stared at him for a few seconds, then put the pudding down beside her. She leaned back, her heels lightly hitting the bottom cabinets. 'I was thinking the other day about that time I was on the dock. Do you remember?'

He shook his head, because they had spent practically every free second of every summer on the dock.

'I had just gone for a swim, and I was sitting on the dock, brushing my hair. And you came up and you took the brush and you started to brush it for me.'

He nodded, remembering that was the very thing he

had been thinking about when he woke up in the hospital this morning. 'I remember.'

'You brushed my hair for at least an hour. Do you remember that?'

He smiled.

'You just brushed my hair, and then we got ready for dinner. Remember?'

He nodded again.

'What did I do wrong?' she asked, and the look in her eyes almost killed him. 'Was it sex?'

He shook his head. Sex with Sara had been the most fulfilling experience of his adult life. 'Of course not,' he said.

'Did you want me to cook you dinner? Or be there more when you got home?'

He tried to laugh. 'You did cook me dinner, remember? I was sick for three days.'

'I'm being serious, Jeff. I want to know what I did wrong.'

'It wasn't you,' he answered, knowing the excuse was trite even as he finished the sentence. 'It was me.'

Sara sighed heavily. She reached for the glass, finishing the drink in one gulp.

'I was stupid,' he continued, knowing he should just shut up. 'I was scared because I loved you so much.' He paused, wanting to say this the right way. 'I didn't think you needed me as much as I needed you.'

She levered him with a gaze. 'Do you still want me to need you?'

He was surprised to feel her hand on his chest, her fingers lightly stroking his hair. He closed his eyes as she traced her fingers up to his lips.

She said, 'Right now, I really need you.'

He opened his eyes. For just a split second, he thought she was joking. 'What did you say?'

'You don't want it now that you have it?' Sara asked, still touching his lips.

He licked the tip of her finger with his tongue.

Sara smiled, her eyes narrowing, as if to read his mind. 'Are you going to answer me?'

'Yeah,' he said, not even remembering the question. Then, 'Yes. Yes, I still want you.'

She started kissing his neck, her tongue making light strokes along his skin. He put his hands around her waist, pulling her closer to the edge of the counter. She wrapped her legs around his waist.

'Sara.' He sighed, trying to kiss her mouth, but she pulled away, instead letting her lips travel down his chest. 'Sara,' he repeated. 'Let me make love to you.'

She looked back at him, a sly smile on her face. 'I don't want to make love.'

His mouth opened, but he did not know how to respond. Finally he managed, 'What does that mean?'

'It means . . . ' she began, then took his hand and held it up to her mouth. He watched as she traced the tip of his index finger with her tongue. Slowly, she took his finger into her mouth and sucked it. After what seemed not nearly enough time, she took it out, smiling playfully. 'Well?'

Jeffrey leaned in to kiss her, but she slid off the counter before he could. He moaned as Sara took her time kissing her way down his chest, nipping the band of his underwear with her teeth. With difficulty, he knelt on the floor in front of her, again trying to kiss her mouth. Again, she pulled away.

'I want to kiss you,' he said, surprised at the begging tone to his voice.

She shook her head, unbuttoning her shirt. 'I can think of some other things you can do with your mouth.'

'Sara –'

She shook her head. 'Don't talk, Jeffrey.'

He thought it was odd that she had said this, because the best part of sex with Sara was the talking. He put his hands to either side of her face. 'Come here,' he said.

'What?'

'What's wrong with you?'

'Nothing.'

'I don't believe you.' He waited for her to answer his question, but she just stared at him.

He asked, 'Why won't you let me kiss you?'

'I just don't feel like kissing.' Her smile was not as sly. 'On the mouth.'

'What's wrong?' he repeated.

She narrowed her eyes at him as a warning.

'Answer me,' he repeated.

Sara kept her eyes on him as she let her hand travel down past the waist of his shorts. She pressed her hand against him, as if to make sure he got her meaning. 'I don't want to talk to you.'

He stopped her hand with his own. 'Look at me.'

She shook her head, and when he made her look up she closed her eyes.

He whispered, 'What's wrong with you?'

Sara didn't answer. She kissed him full on the mouth, her tongue forcing its way past his teeth. It was a sloppy kiss, far from what he was used to with Sara, but there was an underlying passion that would have buckled his knees had he been standing.

She stopped suddenly, dropping her head to his chest. He tried to make her look back up at him, but she wouldn't.

He asked, 'Sara?'

He felt her arms go around him again, but in a very

different way from before. There was a desperate quality to her tightening hold, as if she were drowning.

'Just hold me,' she begged. 'Please just hold me.'

Jeffrey woke with a start. He reached out, knowing even as he did that Sara would not be there beside him. He vaguely recalled her sneaking out some time ago, but Jeffrey had been too tired to move, let alone stop her. He turned over, pressing his face into the pillow she had used. He could smell lavender from her shampoo and a slight trace of the perfume she wore. Jeffrey held the pillow, rolling over onto his back. He stared at the ceiling, trying to remember what had happened last night. He still could not get his head around it. He had carried Sara to bed. She had cried softly on his shoulder. He had been so afraid of what was behind her tears that he had not questioned her anymore.

Jeffrey sat up, scratching his chest. He could not stay in bed all day. There was still the list of convicted sexual offenders to complete. He still needed to interview Ryan Gordon and whoever had been at the library with Julia Matthews the last night she had been seen before the abduction. He also needed to see Sara, to make sure she was okay.

He stretched, touching the top of the door jamb as he walked into the bathroom. He stopped in front of the toilet. There was a stack of papers on the sink basin. A silver sliding clip was across the top pages, binding together what looked to be about two hundred sheets of paper. The pages looked dog-eared and yellowed, as if someone had paged through them a number of times. It was, Jeffrey recognized, a trial transcript.

He looked around the bathroom, as if the transcript fairy who had left it might still be around. The only person who had been in the house was Sara, and he could not think why she would leave something like this. He read the title page, noting the date was from twelve years ago. The case was the *State of Georgia v. Jack Allen Wright*.

A yellow Post-it note was sticking out from one of the pages. He flipped the transcript open, stopping at what he saw. Sara's name was listed at the top of the page. Another name, Ruth Jones, probably the district attorney who had prosecuted the case, was listed as the questioner.

Jeffrey sat on the toilet and began to read Ruth Jones's examination of Sara Linton.

Q. Dr. Linton, could you please tell us in your own words the events which took place on the twenty-third day of April, this time last year?

A. I was working at Grady Hospital where I was a pediatric resident. I had a difficult day and decided to go for a drive in my car between shifts.

Q. Was there anything unusual you noticed at this time?

A. When I got to my car, the word cunt had been scraped into the passenger's side door. I thought perhaps this was the work of a vandal, so I used some duct tape I kept in the trunk to cover it.

Q. Then what did you do?

A. I went back into the hospital for my shift.

Q. Would you like a drink of water?

A. No, thank you. I went to the rest room, and while I was washing my hands at the sink, Jack Wright came in.

Q. The defendant?

A. That's correct. He came in. He was carrying a mop and wearing grey coveralls. I knew he was the janitor. He apologized for not knocking, said he'd come back later to clean, then left the bathroom.

Q. Then what happened?

A. I went into the stall to use the bathroom. The defendant, Jack Wright, jumped down from the ceiling. It was a drop ceiling. He handcuffed my hands to the handicapped railing, then taped my mouth shut with silver duct tape.

Q. Are you sure this was the defendant?

A. Yes. He had on a red ski mask, but I recognized his eyes. He has very distinctive blue eyes. I remember thinking before that with his long blond hair, beard, and blue eyes he looked like Bible pictures of Jesus. I am certain that it was Jack Wright who attacked me.

Q. Is there any other distinguishing mark that leads you to believe it was the defendant who raped you?

A. I saw a tattoo on his arm of Jesus nailed to the cross with the words JESUS above it and SAVES below it. I recognized this tattoo as belonging to Jack Wright, a janitor at the hospital. I had seen him several times before in the hallway, but we had never spoken to each other.

Q. What happened next, Dr. Linton?

A. Jack Wright pulled me down off the toilet. My ankles were pinned by my pants. They were on the floor. My pants. Around my ankles.

Q. Please, take your time, Dr. Linton.

A. I was pulled forward, but my arms were back behind me like this. He kept me pulled forward by putting one arm around my waist. He held a long knife, approximately six inches, to my face. He cut my lip to warn me, I suppose.

Q. Then what did the defendant do?

A. He put his penis in me and raped me.

Q. Dr. Linton, could you tell us what, if anything, the defendant said during the time he raped you?

A. He kept referring to me as 'cunt.'

Q. Could you tell us what happened next?

A. He tried several times to bring himself to ejaculation, but was unsuccessful. He pulled his penis out of me and brought himself to climax [mumbled]

Q. Could you repeat that?

A. He brought himself to climax on my face and chest.

Q. Could you tell us what happened then?

A. He cursed me again, then stabbed me with his knife. In the left side, here.

Q. Then what happened?

A. I tasted something in my mouth. I choked. It was vinegar.

Q. He poured vinegar into your mouth?

A. Yes, he had a small vial, like a perfume sample would come in. He tilted it into my mouth and said, 'It is finished.'

Q. Does this phrase have any particular significance to you, Dr. Linton?

A. It's from John, in the King James version of the Bible. 'It is finished.' According to John, these are the last words Jesus says as he's dying on the cross. He calls for something to drink, and they give him vinegar. He drinks the vinegar, then, to quote the verse, he gives up the ghost. He dies.

Q. This is from the crucifixion?

A. Yes.

Q. Jesus says, 'It is finished.'

A. Yes.

Q. His arms pinned back like this?

A. Yes.

Q. A sword is stabbed into his side?

A. Yes.

Q. Was anything else said?

A. No. Jack Wright said this, then left the bathroom.

Q. Dr. Linton, do you have any idea how long you were left in the bathroom?

A. No.

Q. Were you still handcuffed?

A. Yes. I was still handcuffed and I was on my knees looking down at the floor. I was unable to right myself, to sit back.

Q. Then what happened?

A. One of the nurses came in. She saw the blood on the floor and started to scream. A few seconds later, Dr. Lange, my supervisor, came into the room. I'd lost a great deal of blood, and I was still handcuffed. They started to help me, but they couldn't do much with the cuffs on. Jack Wright had rigged the lock so that they would not open. He had shoved something into the lock, a toothpick or something. A locksmith had to be called to cut them off. I passed out during this time. The position of my body was such that blood continued to pool from the stab wound. I lost a great deal of blood during this time from the stab wound.

Q. Dr. Linton, take your time. Would you like to take a short break?

A. No, I want to continue.

Q. Could you tell me what happened subsequent to the rape?

A. I became pregnant from this contact, and subsequently developed an ectopic pregnancy, which is to say that an egg was implanted in my fallopian

275

tube. There was a rupture which caused bleeding into my abdomen.

Q. What effect, if any, has this had on you?

A. A partial hysterectomy was performed wherein my reproductive organs were removed. I can no longer have children.

Q. Dr. Linton?

A. I would like to take a recess.

Jeffrey sat in his bathroom, staring at the pages of the transcript. He read through them again, then once more, sobs echoing in the bathroom as he cried for the Sara he had never known.

NINETEEN

Lena lifted her head slowly, trying to get some sense of where she was. All she saw was darkness. She held her hand inches from her face, unable to make out her palm and fingers. The last thing she remembered was sitting in her kitchen talking to Hank. After that, she drew a complete blank. It was as if she blinked one second and the next was transported to this spot. Wherever this spot was.

She groaned, moving to her side so that she could sit up. With sudden clarity, she realized that she was naked. The floor underneath her was rough against her skin. She could feel the grain in the wooden planks. Her heart started pounding for some reason, but her mind would not tell her why. Lena reached in front of her, feeling more rough wood, but it was vertical, a wall.

Pressing her hands into the wall, she managed to stand. In the back of her mind, she could make out a noise, but it was unfamiliar to her. Everything seemed disjointed and out of place. She felt physically as if she did not belong here. Lena found she was leaning her head against the wall, the wood pressing into the skin of her forehead. The noise was a staccato in her periphery, pounding, then nothing, pounding, then nothing, like a hammer on a piece of steel. Like a blacksmith fashioning a horseshoe.

Clink, clink, clink.

Where had she heard that before?

Lena's heart stopped as she finally made the connection. In the darkness, she could see Julia Matthews's lips moving, voicing the noise.

Clink, clink, clink.

The sound was dripping water.

TWENTY

Jeffrey stood behind the one-way glass, looking into the interview room. Ryan Gordon sat at the table, his skinny arms crossed over his concave chest. Buddy Conford sat beside him, his hands clasped in front of him on the table. Buddy was a fighter. At the age of seventeen, he had lost his right leg from the knee down in a car accident. At the age of twenty-six, he had lost his left eye from cancer. At thirty-nine, a dissatisfied client had attempted to pay Buddy off with two bullets. Buddy had lost a kidney and suffered a collapsed lung, but was back in the courtroom two weeks later. Jeffrey was hoping Buddy's sense of right and wrong would help move things along today. Jeffrey had downloaded a picture of Jack Allen Wright from the state database this morning. Jeffrey would have a lot stronger leg to stand on in Atlanta if he had a positive ID.

Jeffrey had never considered himself an emotional man, but there was an ache in his chest that would not go away. He wanted to talk to Sara so badly, but he was terrified that he would say the wrong thing. Driving in to work, he had gone over and over in his mind what he would say to her, even talking out loud to see how his words sounded. Nothing would come out right, and Jeffrey ended up sitting in his office for ten minutes with his hand on the phone before he could coax up enough courage to dial Sara's number at the clinic.

After telling Nelly Morgan that it wasn't an emergency but he would like to talk to Sara anyway, he got a snippy 'She's with a patient,' followed by a slam of the phone. This brought Jeffrey an enormous sense of relief, then a feeling of disgust at his own cowardice.

He knew that he needed to be strong for her, but Jeffrey felt too blindsided to be capable of anything but sobbing like a child every time he thought about what had happened to Sara. Part of him was hurt that she had not trusted him enough to tell him what had happened to her in Atlanta. Another part of him was angry that she had flat out lied to him about everything. The scar on her side had been explained away as the result of an appendectomy, though, in retrospect, Jeffrey remembered the scar was jagged and vertical, nothing like a surgeon's clean incision.

That she could not have children was something he had never pushed her on, because obviously it was a sensitive topic. He was comfortable leaving her at peace with that, assuming that it was some medical condition or that perhaps, like some women, she just was not meant to carry a child. He was supposed to be a cop, a detective, and he had taken everything she said at face value because Sara was the type of woman who told the truth about things. Or at least he had thought she was.

'Chief?' Marla said, knocking on the door. 'Guy called from Atlanta and said to tell you everything's set up. Wouldn't leave a name. That mean anything to you?'

'Yes,' Jeffrey said, checking the folder he held in his hand to make sure the printout was still there. He stared at the picture again, even though he had practically memorized the blurred photo. He brushed past Marla into the hallway. 'I'm leaving for Atlanta after this. I don't know when I'll be back. Frank will be in charge.'

Jeffrey didn't give her time to respond. He opened the door to the interview room and walked in.

Buddy took on a righteous tone. 'We've been here ten minutes.'

'And we're only going to be here another ten more if your client decides to cooperate,' Jeffrey said, taking the chair across from Buddy.

The only thing Jeffrey knew with any certainty was that he wanted to kill Jack Allen Wright. He had never been a violent man off the football field, but Jeffrey wanted so badly to kill the man who had raped Sara that his teeth ached.

'We ready to start?' Buddy asked, tapping his hand on the table.

Jeffrey glanced out the small window in the door. 'We need to wait for Frank,' he said, wondering where the man was. Jeffrey hoped he was checking on Lena.

The door opened and Frank entered the room. He looked as if he hadn't slept all night. His shirt was untucked at the side, and a coffee stain was on his tie. Jeffrey gave a pointed glance at his watch.

'Sorry,' Frank said, taking the chair beside Jeffrey.

'Right,' Jeffrey said. 'We've got some questions we need to ask Gordon. In exchange for his being forthcoming, we'll drop the pending charges on the drug bust.'

'Fuck that,' Gordon snarled. 'I told you those weren't my pants.'

Jeffrey exchanged a look with Buddy. 'I don't have time for this. We'll just send him up to the Atlanta pen and cut our losses.'

'What kind of questions?' Buddy asked.

Jeffrey dropped the bomb. Buddy had been expecting a simple plead on yet another drug charge against one of the kids from the college. Jeffrey kept his tone even when he said, 'About the death of Sibyl Adams and the rape of Julia Matthews.'

Buddy seemed to register a little shock. His face turned white, making his black eye patch stand out even more against his pale face. He asked Gordon, 'Do you know anything about this?'

Frank answered for him. 'He was the last person to see Julia Matthews in the library. He was her boyfriend.'

Gordon piped up, 'I told you, they weren't my pants. Get me the fuck out of here.'

Buddy gave Gordon the eye. 'You'd best be telling them what happened or you're gonna be writing your mama letters from jail.'

Gordon crossed his arms, obviously angry. 'You're supposed to be my lawyer.

'You're supposed to be a human being,' Buddy countered, picking up his briefcase. 'Those girls were beaten and killed, son. You're looking at walking on a felony possession by simply doing what you should be doing in the first place. If you got a problem with that, you need to get yourself another lawyer.'

Buddy stood, but Gordon stopped him. 'She was in the library, okay?' Buddy sat back down, but he kept his briefcase in his lap.

'On campus?' Frank asked.

'Yeah, on campus,' Gordon snapped. 'I just ran into her, okay?'

'Okay,' Jeffrey answered.

'So, I started talking to her, you know. She wanted me back. I could tell that.'

Jeffrey nodded, though he imagined Julia Matthews had been very upset to see Gordon in the library.

'Anyway, we talked, got a little lip action going, if

you know what I mean.' He nudged Buddy, who moved away. 'Made some plans to see each other later on.'

'Then what?' Jeffrey asked.

'Then, you know, she left. That's what I'm saying, she just left. Got her books and all, said she would meet me later, then she was out of there.'

Frank asked, 'Did you see anyone following her? Anyone suspicious?'

'Naw,' he answered. 'She was alone. I would've noticed if anyone was watching her, you know? She was my girl. I kept an eye on her.'

Jeffrey said, 'You can't think of anyone she might know, not just a stranger, who was making her uncomfortable? Maybe she was dating somebody after y'all broke up?'

Gordon gave him the same look he would give a stupid dog. 'She wasn't seeing anybody. She was in love with me.'

'You don't remember seeing any strange cars on campus?' Jeffrey asked. 'Or vans?'

Gordon shook his head. 'I didn't see anything, okay?'

Frank asked, 'Let's go back to the meeting. You were supposed to see her later on?'

Gordon supplied, 'She was supposed to meet me behind the agri-building at ten.'

'She didn't show up?' Frank said.

'No,' Gordon answered. 'I waited around, you know. Then, I got kind of pissed off and I went to find her. I went to her room to see what was up, and she wasn't there.'

Jeffrey cleared his throat. 'Was Jenny Price there?'

'That whore?' Gordon waved this off. 'She was probably out fucking half the science team.'

Jeffrey felt himself bristle over this. He had a problem with men who saw all women as whores, not least because this attitude usually went hand in hand with violence toward women. 'So, Jenny wasn't there,' Jeffrey summarized. 'Then what did you do?'

'I went back to my dorm.' He shrugged. 'I went to bed.'

Jeffrey sat back in his seat, crossing his arms over his chest. 'What aren't you telling us, Ryan?' he asked. 'Because the way I'm looking at it, the "forthcoming" part of our deal isn't being met here. The way I'm looking at it, that orange jumper you're wearing is gonna be on your back for the next ten years.'

Gordon stared at Jeffrey with what Jeffrey assumed the young punk thought was a menacing look. 'I told you everything.'

'No,' Jeffrey said. 'You didn't. You're leaving something out that's pretty important, and I swear to God we're not gonna leave this room until you tell me what you know.'

Gordon turned shifty-eyed. 'I don't know anything.'

Buddy leaned over and whispered something that made Gordon's eyes go as round as two walnuts. Whatever the attorney had said to his client, it worked.

Gordon said, 'I followed her out of the library.'

'Yeah?' Jeffrey encouraged.

'She met up with this guy, okay?' Gordon fiddled with his hands in front of him. Jeffrey wanted to reach over and throttle the punk. 'I tried to catch up with them, but they were fast.'

'Fast meaning how?' Jeffrey asked. 'Was she walking with him?'

'No,' Gordon said. 'He was carrying her.'

Jeffrey felt a knot in the pit of his stomach. 'And you didn't think this was suspicious, her being carried off by a guy?'

Gordon's shoulders went up to his ears. 'I was mad, okay? I was mad at her.'

'You knew she wouldn't meet you later on,' Jeffrey began, 'so you followed her.'

He gave a slight shrug that could have been a yes or no.

'And you saw this guy carrying her off?' Jeffrey continued.

'Yeah.'

Frank asked, 'What did he look like?'

'Tall, I guess,' Gordon said. 'I couldn't see his face, if that's what you mean.'

'White? Black?' Jeffrey quizzed.

'Yeah, white,' Gordon supplied. 'White and tall. He was wearing dark clothes, all black. I couldn't really see them except that she was wearing this white shirt, right? It kind of caught the light, so she showed up, but not him.'

Frank said, 'Did you follow them?'

Gordon shook his head.

Frank was silent, his jaw taut with anger. 'You know she's dead now, don't you?'

Gordon looked down at the table. 'Yeah, I know that.'

Jeffrey opened the file and showed Gordon the printout. He had used a black marker to cross out Wright's name, but the rest of the statistics were left uncovered. 'This the guy?'

Gordon glanced down. 'No.'

'Look at the fucking photograph,' Jeffrey ordered, his tone so loud that Frank started beside him.

Gordon did as he was told, putting his face so close to the printout that his nose almost touched it. 'I don't know, man,' he said. 'It was dark. I couldn't see his face.' His eyes scanned down the vitals on Wright. 'He was tall like this. About this build. It could've been him, I guess.' He gave a casual shrug. 'I mean, Jesus, I wasn't paying attention to him. I was watching her.'

The drive to Atlanta was long and tedious, with nothing but the occasional patch of trees with the requisite kudzu to break the monotony. He tried twice to call Sara at home and leave some kind of message, but her machine wouldn't pick up, even after twenty rings. Jeffrey felt a rush of relief followed by an overwhelming shame. The closer he got to the city, the more he convinced himself that he was doing the right thing. He could call Sara when he knew something. Maybe he could call her with the news that Jack Allen Wright had met with an unfortunate accident involving Jeffrey's gun and Wright's chest.

Even going eighty, it took Jeffrey four hours before he got off 20 and onto the downtown connector. He passed Grady Hospital a little ways past the split, and felt tears wanting to come again. The building was a monster looming over the interstate in what Atlanta traffic reporters called the Grady Curve. Grady was one of the largest hospitals in the world. Sara had told him that during any given year the emergency clinics saw over two hundred thousand patients. A recent four-hundred million-dollar renovation made the hospital look like part of the set for a Batman movie. In typical City of Atlanta politics, the renovation had been the subject of an explosive investigation, kickbacks and payoffs reaching as far up as city hall.

Jeffrey took the downtown exit, then drove by the capitol. His friend on the Atlanta force had been shot on the job and taken a guard's position at the court-house rather than early retirement. A call back in Grant had scheduled a meeting for one o'clock. It was quarter till by the time Jeffrey found a parking space in the crowded capitol section of downtown.

Keith Ross was waiting outside the courts building when Jeffrey walked up. In one hand, he held a large file folder; in the other, a plain white mailing envelope.

'Ain't seen you in a coon's age,' Keith said, giving Jeffrey's hand a firm shake.

'Good to see you, too, Keith,' Jeffrey returned, trying to force a lightness into his voice that he did not feel. The ride up to Atlanta had done nothing but get Jeffrey more wound up. Even the brisk walk from the parking garage to the courts building had not alleviated his tension.

'I can only let you have these for a second,' Keith said, obviously sensing Jeffrey's need to move this along. 'I got it from a buddy of mine over at records.'

Jeffrey took the folder, but he did not open it. He knew what he would find inside: pictures of Sara, witness testimony, detailed descriptions of exactly what had happened in that bathroom.

'Let's go inside,' Keith said, ushering Jeffrey into the building.

Jeffrey flashed his badge at the door, bypassing the security check. Keith led him into a small office to the side of the entrance. A desk surrounded by television monitors filled the room. A kid wearing thick glasses and a police uniform looked up with surprise as they entered.

Keith took a twenty-dollar bill out of his pocket. 'Go buy yourself some candy,' he said.

The kid took the money and left without another word.

'Devotion to the job,' Keith commented wryly. 'You gotta wonder what they're doing on the force.'

'Yeah,' Jeffrey mumbled, not wanting to have a

protracted conversation about the quality of police recruits.

'I'll leave you to it,' Keith said. 'Ten minutes, okay?'

'Okay,' Jeffrey answered, waiting for the door to close.

The file was coded and dated with some obscure notations that only a city employee could figure out. Jeffrey rubbed his hand down the front of the folder, as if he could absorb the information without actually having to see it. When that did not work, he took a deep breath and opened the folder.

Pictures of Sara after the rape greeted him. Close-ups of her hands and feet, the stab wound in her side, and her battered female parts spilled out onto the desk in full color. He actually gasped at the sight of them. His chest felt tight and a stabbing pain ran down his arm. Jeffrey thought for just a second that he was having a heart attack, but a few deep breaths helped clear his mind. He realized that his eyes had been closed, and he opened them, not looking at the pictures of Sara as he turned them facedown.

Jeffrey loosened his tie, trying to push the images from his mind. He thumbed through the other photographs, finding a picture of Sara's car. It was a silver BMW 320 with black bumpers and a blue stripe down the sides. Carved into the door, probably with a key, was the word CUNT just as Sara had said in her trial testimony. Pictures showed a before and after of the door, with and without the silver duct tape. Jeffrey got a flash of Sara kneeling in front of the door, taping over the damage, probably thinking in her mind that she would get her uncle Al to repair the damage when she was back in Grant next.

Jeffrey checked his watch, noting five minutes had passed. He found Keith in one of the security cameras, his hands tucked into his pockets as he shot the shit with the guards at the door.

Thumbing through the back of the file, he found the arrest report on Jack Allen Wright. Wright had been arrested twice before on suspicion but never charged. In the first incident, a young woman about the age Sara had been when she was attacked had dropped the charges and moved out of town. In the other case, the young woman had taken her own life. Jeffrey rubbed his eyes, thinking about Julia Matthews.

A knock came at the door, then Keith said, 'I gotta call time, Jeffrey.'

'Yeah,' Jeffrey said, closing the file. He didn't want to hold it in his hands anymore. He held it out to Keith without looking at the other man.

'This help you any?'

Jeffrey gave a nod, straightening his tie. 'Some,' he said. 'Were you able to find out where this guy is?'

'Just down the street,' Keith answered. 'Working at the Bank Building.'

'That's what, ten minutes from the university? Another five from Grady?'

'You got it.'

'What's he do?'

'He's a janitor, like he was at Grady,' Keith said. He had obviously looked at the file before giving it to Jeffrey. 'All those college girls, and he's ten minutes from them.'

'Do the campus police know?'

'They do now,' Keith provided, giving Jeffrey a knowing look. 'Not that he's much of a threat anymore.'

'What does that mean?' Jeffrey asked.

'Part of his parole,' Keith said, indicating the file. 'You didn't get to that? He's taking Depo.'

Jeffrey felt an uneasiness spread over him like warm water. Depoprovera was the latest trend in treating sexual offenders. Normally used in women as part of a hormone replacement therapy, a high enough dosage could curb a man's sexual appetite. When the drug was used on sexual predators, it was referred to as chemical castration. Jeffrey knew the drug only worked as long as the perpetrator took it. It was more like a tranquilizer than a cure.

Jeffrey indicated the folder. He could not say Sara's name in this room. 'He raped someone else after this?'

'He raped two someone elses after this,' Keith answered. 'There was this Linton girl. He stabbed her, right? Attempted murder, six years. Got early parole for good behavior, went on the Depo, went off the Depo, went out and raped three more women. They caught him on one, other girl wouldn't testify, put him back in jail for three years, now he's out on parole with the Depo administered under close supervision.'

'He's raped six girls and he's only served ten years?'

'They only nailed him on three, and except for her' – he indicated Sara's file – 'the other IDs were pretty shaky. He wore a mask. You know how it gets with those girls on the stand. They get all nervous and before you know it opposing counsel has them wondering if they were even raped in the first place, let alone who did it.'

Jeffrey held his tongue, but Keith seemed to read his mind.

'Hey,' Keith said, 'I'd been working those cases, the bastard would've been sent to the chair. Know what I mean?'

'Yeah,' Jeffrey said, thinking this boasting wasn't getting them anywhere. 'Is he ready for his third strike?' he asked. Georgia, like many states, had enacted a 'third strike' law some time ago, meaning that a convict's third felony offence, no matter how innocuous, would send him or her back to jail, conceivably for the rest of his or her life.

'Sounds like it,' Keith answered.

'Who's his PO?'

'Already took care of that one,' Keith said. 'Wright's on a bracelet. PO says he's clean going back the last two years. Also says he'd pretty much cut off his head before going back to jail.'

Jeffrey nodded at this. Jack Wright was forced to wear a monitoring bracelet as a condition of his parole. If he left his designated roaming area or missed his curfew, an alarm would go off at the monitoring station. In the City of Atlanta, most parole officers were stationed at police precincts around town so they could snatch up violators on a moment's notice. It was a good system, and despite the fact that Atlanta was such a large city, not many parolees slipped through the cracks.

'Also,' Keith said, 'I walked on down to the Bank Building.' He shrugged apologetically, recognizing he had overstepped the line. This was Jeffrey's case, but Keith was probably bored out of his mind from checking purses for handguns all day.

'No,' Jeffrey said. 'That's fine. What'd you get?'

'Got a peek at his time cards. He was punched in every morning at seven, then out to lunch at noon, back at noon-thirty, then out at five.'

'Somebody could've punched it for him.'

Keith shrugged. 'Supervisor didn't eyeball him, but she says there would've been complaints from the offices if he hadn't been on the job. Evidently, those professional types like to have their cans taken care of bright and early.'

Jeffrey pointed to the white mailing envelope Keith held in his hand. 'What's that?'

'Registration,' Keith said, handing him the envelope. 'He drives a blue Chevy Nova.'

Jeffrey slit the envelope open with his thumb. Inside was a photocopy of Jack Allen Wright's vehicle registration. An address was under his name. 'Current?' Jeffrey asked.

'Yeah,' Keith answered. 'Only, you understand you didn't get it from me.'

Jeffrey knew what he meant. Atlanta's chief of police ran her department by its short hairs. Jeffrey knew her reputation and admired her work, but he also knew that if she thought some hick cop from Grant County was stepping on her toes, the next thing Jeffrey would feel would be a three-inch stiletto parked firmly on the back of his neck.

'You get what you need from Wright,' Keith said, 'then call in APD.' He handed Jeffrey a business card with Atlanta's rising phoenix in the center of it. Jeffrey turned it over, seeing a name and number scribbled on the back.

Keith said, 'This is his PO. She's a good gal, but she'll want something solid to explain why you just happen to be in Wright's face.'

'You know her?'

'Know of her,' Keith said. 'Real ball breaker, so watch yourself. You call her in to snatch up her boy and she thinks you're looking at her funny, she'll make sure you never see him again.'

Jeffrey said, 'I'll try to be a gentleman.'

Keith offered, 'Ashton is just off the interstate. Let me give you directions.'

TWENTY-ONE

Nick Shelton's voice boomed across the telephone line. 'Hey, lady.'

'Hey, Nick,' Sara returned, closing a chart on her desk. She had been at the clinic since eight that morning and seen patients right up until four o'clock. Sara felt as if she had been running in quicksand all day. There was a slight ache in her head and her stomach was queasy from drinking a little too much the night before, not to mention her uneasiness over the emotional drama that had unfolded. As the day wore on, Sara began to feel more drained. At lunch, Molly had commented that Sara looked as if she should be the patient today instead of the doctor.

'I showed Mark those seeds,' Nick said. 'He says they're belladonna all right, only it's the berries, not the seeds.'

'I guess that's good to know,' Sara managed. 'He's certain?'

'One hundred percent,' Nick returned. 'He says it's kind of funny they ate the berries. Remember, those are the least poisonous. Maybe your guy down there gives them the berries to keep them a little jazzed, then doesn't give them the final dose until he turns 'em loose.'

'That makes sense,' Sara said, not even wanting to think about it. She did not want to be a doctor today.

She did not want to be a coroner. She wanted to be in bed with some tea and mindless television. As a matter of fact, that was exactly what she was going to do as soon as she finished updating the last chart from today. Thankfully, Nelly had booked tomorrow for Sara's day off. She would take the weekend to decompress. Monday, Sara would be back to her old self.

Sara asked, 'Anything on the semen sample?'

'We're having some problems with that, considering where you found it. I think we'll be able to get something out of it, though.'

'That's good news, I guess.'

Nick said, 'You gonna tell Jeffrey about the berries, or should I call him?'

Sara felt her stomach drop at the mention of Jeffrey's name.

'Sara?' Nick asked.

'Yeah,' Sara answered. 'I'll talk to him about it as soon as I get off work.'

Sara hung up the phone after the appropriate good-byes, then sat in her office, rubbing the small of her back. She reviewed the next chart at a glance, updating a change in medication as well as a follow-up visit for lab results. By the time she had finished with the last chart, it was five-thirty.

Sara crammed a couple of files into her briefcase, knowing she would have some time over the weekend where guilt would set in and she would want to do some work. Dictation was something she could do at home with a small tape recorder. There was a transcription place in Macon that would type up the notes for her and have them back in a couple of days.

She buttoned her jacket as she crossed the street, heading downtown. She took the sidewalk opposite the pharmacy, not wanting to run into Jeb. Sara kept her head down, passing the hardware store and the dress shop, not wanting to invite conversation. That she stopped in front of the police station was something of a surprise. Her mind was working without her knowing, and with each step she got more and more angry with Jeffrey for not calling. She had arguably left her soul laid out on his bathroom sink, and he had not even had the decency to call her.

Sara walked into the station house, managing a smile for Marla. 'Is Jeffrey in?'

Marla frowned. 'I don't think so,' she said. 'He checked out about noon or so. You might ask Frank.'

'He's in the back?' Sara indicated the door with her briefcase.

'I think,' Marla answered, returning to the task before her.

Sara glanced down as she passed the older woman. Marla was working on a crossword puzzle.

The back room was empty, the ten or so desks normally occupied by the senior detective vacant for the time being. Sara assumed they were out working down Jeffrey's list or grabbing dinner. She kept her head up, strolling into Jeffrey's office. Of course he wasn't there.

Sara stood in the small office, resting her briefcase on his desk. She had been in this room so many times she couldn't begin to count them. Always, she had felt safe here. Even after the divorce, Sara had felt that in this one area, Jeffrey was trustworthy. As a policeman, he had always done the right thing. He had done everything in his power to make sure the people he served were protected.

When Sara first moved back to Grant twelve years ago, no amount of reassurances from her father and her family could convince her that she was safe. Sara had known that as soon as she walked into the pawnshop, news would spread that she had purchased a weapon. What's more, she knew that in order to register a gun, she would have to go to the police station. Ben Walker, the chief of police before Jeffrey, played poker with Eddie Linton every Friday night. There had been no way for Sara to buy it without alerting everyone who knew her.

Around that time, a gang banger had come into the Augusta hospital with his arm nearly torn off by a bullet. Sara had worked on the kid and saved his arm. He was only fourteen, and when his mother came in, she had started beating him on his head with her purse. Sara had left the room, but a few moments later, the mother had found her. The woman had given Sara her son's weapon and asked Sara to take care of it. If Sara had been a Christian woman, she would have called the event a miracle.

The gun, Sara knew, was now in Jeffrey's desk drawer. She checked over her shoulder before sliding it open, taking out the bag with the Ruger in it. She tucked it in her briefcase and was out the door within a few minutes.

Sara kept her head up as she walked toward the college. Her boat was docked in front of the boathouse, and she tossed her briefcase in with one hand while untying the line with another. Her parents had given her the boat as a housewarming present, and it was an old but sturdy vessel.

The engine was strong, and Sara had skied behind it many times, her father at the wheel, holding back on the throttle for fear of jerking her arms off.

After checking that she was not being watched, Sara slipped the gun out of her briefcase and locked it in the watertight glove box in front of the passenger's seat, plastic bag and all. She stepped her leg outside the boat, using her foot to push away from the dock. The engine sputtered when she turned the key. Technically, she should have had the motor checked before using the boat again after not using it all winter, but she did not really have a choice, since the techs would not be finished with her car until Monday. Asking her father for a lift would have invited too much conversation, and Jeffrey was not an option.

After emitting a cloud of nasty-looking blue smoke, the engine caught, and Sara pulled away from the dock, allowing a small smile. She had felt like a criminal leaving with the gun in her briefcase, but she was feeling safer. Whatever Jeffrey thought when he saw the gun was gone was not really Sara's concern.

By the time she reached the center of the lake, the boat was skipping across the water. Cold wind cut through her face, and she put her glasses on to protect her eyes. Though the sun was beating down, the water was cool from the recent rains that had fallen on Grant County. It looked ready to storm again tonight, but probably well after the sun went down.

Sara zipped her jacket closed to fight the cold. Still, by the time she could see the back of her house, her nose was running and her cheeks felt as if she had put her face into a bucket of cold ice water. Cutting a hard left, she steered away from a group of rocks under the water. There had been a sign marking the spot at one time, but it had rotted away years ago. With the recent rains, the lake was high, but Sara did not want to risk it.

She had docked into the boathouse and was using the electric winch to pull the boat out of the water when her mother appeared from the back of the house.

'Shit,' Sara mumbled, pressing the red button to stop the winch.

'I called the clinic,' Cathy said. 'Nelly said you were taking tomorrow off.'

'That's right,' Sara answered, pulling the chains to lower the door behind the boat.

'Your sister told me about your argument last night.'

Sara jerked the chain tight, sending a clattering through the metal structure. 'If you're here to threaten me, the damage has been done.'

'Meaning?'

Sara walked past her mother, stepping off the dock. 'Meaning he knows,' she said, tucking her hands into her hips, waiting for her mother to follow.

'What did he say?'

'I can't talk about it,' Sara answered, turning toward the house. Her mother followed her up the lawn but was thankfully silent.

Sara unlocked the back door, leaving it open for her mother as she went into the kitchen. She realized too late that the house was a mess.

Cathy said, 'Really, Sara, you can make time to clean.'

'I've been very busy at work.'

'That's not an excuse,' Cathy lectured. 'Just say to yourself, "I'm going to do one load of laundry every other day. I'm going to make sure I put things back where I found them." Pretty soon you're organized.'

Sara ignored the familiar advice as she walked into the living room. She pressed the scroll on the caller ID unit, but no calls had been logged.

'Power went off,' her mother said, pressing the buttons on the stove to set the time. 'These storms are playing havoc with the cable. Your father almost had a heart attack last night when he turned on *Jeopardy!* and got nothing but fuzz.'

Sara felt some relief from this. Maybe Jeffrey had

called. Stranger things had happened. She walked over to the sink, filling the teakettle with water. 'Do you want some tea?'

Cathy shook her head.

'Me, either,' Sara mumbled, leaving the kettle in the sink. She walked to the back of the house, taking off her shirt, then her skirt as she walked into the bedroom. Cathy followed her, keeping a trained mother's eye on her daughter.

'Are you fighting with Jeffrey again?'

Sara slipped a T-shirt over her head. 'I'm always fighting with Jeffrey, Mother. It's what we do.'

'When you're not busy squirming in your seat over him in church.'

Sara bit her lip, feeling her cheeks turn red.

Cathy asked, 'What happened this time?'

'God, Mama, I really don't want to talk about it.'

'Then tell me about this thing with Jeb McGuire.'

'There's no "thing." Really.' Sara slipped on a pair of sweatpants.

Cathy sat on the bed, smoothing the sheet out with the flat of her hand. 'That's good. He's not really your type.'

Sara laughed. 'What's my type?'

'Someone who can stand up to you.'

'Maybe I like Jeb,' Sara countered, aware there was a petulant tone to her voice. 'Maybe I like the fact that he's predictable and nice and calm. God knows he's waited long enough to go out with me. Maybe I should start seeing him.'

Cathy said, 'You're not as angry with Jeffrey as you think.'

'Oh, really?'

'You're just hurt, and that's making you feel angry. You so seldom open yourself up to other people,' Cathy continued. Sara noticed that her mother's voice was soothing yet firm, as if she were coaxing a dangerous animal out of its hole. 'I remember when you were little. You were always so careful about who you let be your friend.'

Sara sat on the bed so she could put on her socks. She said, 'I had lots of friends.'

'Oh, you were popular, but you only let a few people in.' She stroked Sara's hair back behind her ear. 'And after what happened in Atlanta –'

Sara put her hand over her eyes. Tears came, and she mumbled, 'Mama, I really can't talk about that right now. Okay? Please, not now.'

'All right,' Cathy relented, putting her arm around Sara's shoulder. She pulled Sara's head to her chest. 'Shh,' Cathy hushed, stroking Sara's hair. 'It's okay.'

'I just . . .' Sara shook her head, unable to continue. She had forgotten how good it felt to be comforted by her mother. The last few days she had been so intent upon pushing Jeffrey away that she had managed to distance herself from her family as well.

Cathy pressed her lips to the crown of Sara's head, saying, 'There was an indiscretion between your father and me.'

Sara was so surprised that she stopped crying. 'Daddy cheated on you?'

'Of course not.' Cathy frowned. A few seconds passed before she provided, 'It was the other way around.'

Sara felt like an echo. 'You cheated on Daddy?'

'It was never consummated, but in my heart I felt that it was.'

'What does that mean?' Sara shook her head, thinking this sounded like one of Jeffrey's excuses: flimsy. 'No, never mind.' She wiped her eyes with the back of her hands, thinking she did not really want to hear this. Her parents' marriage was the pedestal upon which Sara had placed all her ideas about relationships and love.

Cathy seemed intent on telling her story. 'I told your father that I wanted to leave him for another man.'

Sara felt silly with her mouth hanging open, but there wasn't much she could do about it. She finally managed, 'Who?'

'Just a man. He was stable, had a job over at one of the plants. Very calm. Very serious. Very different from your father.'

'What happened?'

'I told your father that I wanted to leave him.'

'And?'

'He cried and I cried. We were separated for about six months. In the end we decided to stay together.'

'Who was the other man?'

'It doesn't matter now.'

'Is he still in town?'

Cathy shook her head. 'Doesn't matter. He's not in my life anymore, and I'm with your father.'

Sara concentrated on her breathing for a while. She finally managed to ask, 'When did this happen?'

'Before you and Tessie were born.'

Sara swallowed past the lump in her throat. 'What happened?'

'What's that?'

Sara slipped a sock on. It was like pulling teeth getting the story from her mother. She prompted, 'To change your mind? What made you want to stay with Daddy?'

'Oh, about a million things,' Cathy answered, a sly smile at her lips. 'I think I just got a little distracted by this other man and I didn't realize how important your father was to me.' She sighed heavily. 'I remember waking up one morning in my old room at Mama's and all I could think was that Eddie should've been there with me. I wanted him so badly.' Cathy frowned at Sara's reaction to this. 'Don't go getting your color up, there are other ways to want someone.'

Sara cringed at the scolding, slipping on her other sock. 'So you called him up?'

'I went over to the house and I sat on the front porch and practically begged him to take me back. No, on second thought, I did beg. I told him that if we were both going to be miserable without each other, we might as well be miserable together and that I was so sorry and I'd never take him for granted again as long as I lived.'

'Take him for granted?'

Cathy put her hand on Sara's arm. 'That's the part that hurts, isn't it? The part where you feel like you don't matter to him as much as you used to.'

Sara nodded, trying to remember to breathe. Her mother had hit the nail on the head. She prompted, 'What did Daddy do when you said this?'

'Told me to get up off the porch and come in for some breakfast.' Cathy put her hand to her chest, patting it. 'I don't know how Eddie found it in his heart to forgive me, he's such a proud man, but I'm thankful he did. It made me love him even more to know that he could forgive me for something so horrible like that; that I could hurt him to the core and he could still love me. I think starting out like that made the marriage stronger.' The smile intensified. 'Of course, then, I did have a secret weapon.'

'What's that?'

'You.'

'Me?'

Cathy stroked Sara's cheek. 'I was seeing your father again, but it was so strained. Nothing was like it was before. Then I got pregnant with you, and life just took over. I think having you between us made your father see the big picture. Next thing Tessie was here, then you were both in school, then you were both grown and off to college.' She smiled. 'It just takes time. Love and time. And having a little redheaded hellion to chase after is a good distraction.'

'Well, I'm not going to get pregnant,' Sara countered, conscious of the edge to her tone.

Cathy seemed to think out her answer. 'Sometimes it takes thinking you've lost something to realize the real value of it,' she said. 'Don't tell Tessie.'

Sara nodded her agreement. She stood, tucking her T-shirt into her pants. 'I told him, Mama,' she said. 'I left the transcript for him.'

Cathy asked, 'The trial transcript?'

'Yeah,' Sara said, leaning against the chest of drawers. 'I know he's read it. I left it in the bathroom for him.'

'And?'

'And,' Sara said, 'he hasn't even called. He hasn't said anything to me all day.'

'Well,' Cathy said, her mind obviously made up. 'Fuck him, then. He's trash.'

TWENTY-TWO

Jeffrey found 633 Ashton Street easily enough. The house was dilapidated, no more than a square made of cinder blocks. The windows seemed to be an afterthought, none of them the same size. A ceramic fireplace was on the front porch, stacks of papers and magazines piled to the side of it, probably to use for kindling.

He took a look around the house, trying to act casually. Wearing a suit and tie, driving the white Town Car, it wasn't like Jeffrey fit in with the surroundings. Ashton Street, at least the part Jack Wright lived on, was run-down and seedy. Most of the houses in the vicinity were boarded up, yellow posters warning they were condemned. Kids played in the packed dirt yards of these houses, their parents nowhere to be seen. There was a smell to the place, not exactly sewage but something in that same family. Jeffrey was reminded of driving past the city dump on the outskirts of Madison. On a good day, even when you were downwind, the smell of decomposing trash still reached your nose. Even with the windows up and the air on.

Jeffrey took a few breaths, trying to get used to the smell as he approached the house. The door had a heavy mesh screen over it with a padlock securing it to the frame. The actual door had three dead bolts and one lock that looked like it required a puzzle piece to open it rather than a key. Jack Wright had been in prison a great deal of his life. This was obviously a man who wanted his privacy. Jeffrey took a look around before walking over to one of the windows. It, too, had a wire mesh and a heavy lock, but the casing was old and easily broken. A couple of firm pushes dislodged the entire frame. Jeffrey glanced around before removing the window, casing and all, and slipping into the house.

The living room was dark and dingy, with trash and papers stacked around the room. There was an orange couch on the floor with dark stains dripping down. Jeffrey could not tell if it was from tobacco juice or some kind of body fluid. What he did know was an overpowering odor of sweat mixed with Lysol permeated the room.

Edging the top of the living room walls like a decorative border were all kinds of crucifixes. They varied in size from something you would get out of a candy vending machine to some that were at least ten inches long. They were nailed into the wall, edge to edge, tight up against one another in one continuous band. Continuing the Jesus theme, posters on the wall that looked like they had been taken from a Sunday school room showed Jesus and the disciples. In one, He was holding a lamb. In another, He was holding out his hands, showing the wounds in His palms.

Jeffrey felt his heart rate quicken at the sight of this. He reached to his gun, taking the strap off his holster as he walked toward the front of the house to make sure no one was coming up the drive.

In the kitchen, plates were stacked in the sink, crusted and foul-looking. The floor was sticky, and the whole room felt wet from something other than water. The bedroom was the same way, a musky odor clinging like a wet washrag against Jeffrey's face. On the wall over the stained mattress was a large poster of Jesus Christ, a halo behind His head. Like the poster in the living room, Jesus held His palms out to show the wounds on His hands. The crucifixion motif continued around the periphery of the bedroom, but these were larger crosses. Standing on the bed, Jeffrey could see that someone, probably Wright, had used red paint to exaggerate Jesus' wounds, dripping the blood down the torso, enhancing the crown of thorns resting on his head. Black Xs were across the eyes on every Jesus Jeffrey could see. It was as if Wright had wanted to stop His eyes from watching him. What Wright was doing that he felt needed to be hidden was the question Jeffrey needed to answer.

Jeffrey stepped off the bed. He looked through some of the magazines, taking the time to put on a pair of latex gloves from his pockets before touching anything. The magazines were mostly older editions of *People* and *Life*. The bedroom closet was stacked floor to ceiling with pornography. *Busty Babes* sat beside *Righteous Redheads*. Jeffrey thought of Sara and a lump came to his throat.

Using his foot, Jeffrey kicked the mattress up. A Sig Sauer nine millimeter was resting on the boxspring. The weapon looked new and well cared for. In a neighborhood like this one, only an idiot would go to sleep without a gun handy. Jeffrey smiled as he pushed the mattress back. This could help him out later on.

Opening the dresser, Jeffrey did not know what he expected to find. More porn, maybe. Another gun, or some kind of makeshift weapon. Instead, the top two drawers were filled with women's underwear. Not just underwear, the silky, sexy kind that Jeffrey liked to see Sara in. There were teddies and thongs, French-cut panties with bows at the hips. And they were all extremely large; large enough to fit a man.

Jeffrey resisted the urge to shudder. He took out a pen to go through the contents of the drawers, not wanting to get stuck with a needle or anything sharp, not wanting to get a venereal disease. Jeffrey was about to close one of the drawers when something changed his mind. He was missing something. Moving aside a pair of dark green lace panties, he saw what he was looking for. The newspaper lining the bottom of the drawers was from the special Sunday section of the *Grant County Observer*. He had recognized the masthead.

Pushing aside the clothes, Jeffrey took out the sheet of newspaper. The front page showed a slow news day. A picture of the mayor holding a pig in his arms beamed back at Jeffrey. The date put the paper at more than a year old. He opened the other drawers, looking for more *Observers*. He found a few, but most of them carried innocuous stories. Jeffrey found it interesting that Jack Wright subscribed to the *Grant County Observer*.

He went back into the living room, checking out the stacks of papers on the floor with renewed interest. Brenda Collins, one of Wright's other victims after Sara, had been from Tennessee, Jeffrey remembered. A copy of the *Monthly Vols,* a newsletter for University of Tennessee graduates, was tucked in with some newspapers from Alexander City, Alabama. In the next stack, Jeffrey found more out-of-state papers, all from small towns. Beside these were postcards, all from Atlanta, all showing different scenes around town. The backs were blank, waiting to be filled in. Jeffrey could not imagine what a man like Wright would be doing with the postcards. He did not strike Jeffrey as the type of person to have friends.

Jeffrey turned around, making sure he had not missed anything in the cramped room. There was a television set tucked into the old fireplace. It looked fairly new, the kind you could buy on the street for fifty bucks if you did not ask too many questions about where it had come from. On top of the set was a cable converter box.

He walked back toward the front window to leave but stopped when he saw something under the couch. He used his foot to tilt the couch over, sending cockroaches scurrying across the floor. A small black keyboard was on the floor.

The converter box was actually a receiver for the keyboard. Jeffrey turned the set on, pressing the buttons on the keyboard until the receiver logged on to the Internet. He sat on the edge of the upturned couch as he waited for the system to make a connection. At the station, Brad Stephens was the computer person, but Jeffrey had learned enough from watching the young patrolman to know how to navigate his way around.

Wright's E-mail was easy enough to access. Aside from an offer from a Chevy parts dealership and the requisite hot young teens looking for college money, the kind of E-mail that everyone in the world got, there was a long letter from a woman who appeared to be Wright's mother. Another E-mail had a photo attachment of a young woman posed with her legs wide open. The sender's E-mail address was a series of random numbers. Probably, he was a prison buddy of Wright's. Still, Jeffrey wrote down the address on a scrap piece of paper he had in his pocket.

Using the arrow keys, Jeffrey went to the bookmarks section. In addition to various porn and violence sites, Jeffrey found a link for the *Grant Observer* on-line. He could not have been more shocked. There, on the television screen, was today's front page announcing the suicide of Julia Matthews last night. Jeffrey punched the down arrow, skimming the article again. He went into the archives and performed a search for Sibyl Adams. Seconds later, an article on career day from last year came on-screen. A search for Julia Matthews brought up today's front page, but nothing else. Over sixty articles came up when he typed in Sara's name.

Jeffrey logged off and turned the couch right side up. Outside, he pressed the window back into the hole he had made. It did not want to stay, so he was forced to drag one of the chairs over to prop it in. From his car, it didn't look like the window had been tampered with, but Jack Wright would know as soon as he walked on his front porch that someone had been in his house. As security conscious as the man seemed to be, this would probably be a good way to push his buttons.

The streetlight over Jeffrey's car came on as he got in. Even on this hellhole of a street, the sunset dipping into the Atlanta skyline was something to behold. Jeffrey imagined but for the sun setting and rising, the people on this block wouldn't feel human.

He waited for three and a half hours before the blue Chevy Nova pulled into the driveway. The car was old and dirty, flakes of rust showing through at the trunk and taillights. Wright had obviously tried to make a few repairs. Silver duct tape crisscrossed the tail end, and on one side of the bumper was a decal that said GOD IS MY COPILOT. On the other side was a zebra-striped sticker that said I'M GOING WILD AT THE ATLANTA ZOO.

Jack Wright had been in the system long enough to know what a cop looks like. He gave Jeffrey a wary glance as he stepped out of the Nova. Wright was a pudgy man with a receding hairline. His shirt was off, and Jeffrey could see he had what could only be described as breasts. Jeffrey guessed this was from the Depo. One of the main reasons rapists and pedophiles tended to go off the drug was the nasty side effect that caused some of them to put on weight and take on womanly attributes.

Wright nodded to Jeffrey as Jeffrey made his way up the driveway. As neglected as this area of town was, all the streetlights were in working order. The house was lit like it was broad daylight.

When Wright spoke, his voice was high-pitched, another side effect of the Depo. He asked, 'You looking for me?'

'That's right,' Jeffrey answered, stopping in front of the man who had raped and stabbed Sara Linton.

'Well, damn,' Wright said, pursing his lips. 'I guess some girl done got snatched up, huh? Y'all always come knocking on my door when some young thing goes missing.'

'Let's go into the house,' Jeffrey said.

'I don't think so,' Wright countered, leaning back against the car. 'She a pretty girl, the one missing?' He paused, as if he expected an answer. He licked his tongue slowly along his lips. 'I only pick the pretty ones.'

'It's an older case,' Jeffrey said, trying not to let himself get baited.

'Amy? Is it my sweet little Amy?'

Jeffrey stared. He recognized the name from the case file. Amy Baxter had taken her life after being raped by Jack Wright. She was a nurse who had moved to Atlanta from Alexander City.

'No, not Amy,' Wright said, putting his hand to his chin as if in thought. 'Was it that sweet little –' He stopped himself, looking over at Jeffrey's car. 'Grant County, huh? Why didn't you say so?' He smiled, showing one of his chipped front teeth. 'How's my little Sara doing?'

Jeffrey took a step toward the man, but Wright did not take the intimidation.

Wright said, 'Go on and hit me. I like it rough.'

Jeffrey stepped back, willing himself not to punch the man.

Suddenly, Wright scooped his breasts into his hands. 'You like these, daddy?' He smiled at the look of disgust that must have been on Jeffrey's face. 'I take the Depo, but you know that already, don't you, honey? You know what it does to me, too, don't you?' He lowered his voice. 'Makes me like a girl. Gives the boys the best of both worlds.'

'Stop it,' Jeffrey said, glancing around. Wright's neighbors had come out to see the show.

'I got balls the size of marbles,' Wright said, putting his hands to the waist of his blue jeans. 'You wanna see 'em?'

Jeffrey lowered his voice to a grumble. 'Not unless you want to take the word "chemical" out of your castration.'

Wright chuckled. 'You're a big, strong man, you know that?' he asked. 'You supposed to be taking care of my Sara?'

Jeffrey could do nothing but swallow.

'They all wanna know why I picked 'em. Why me? Why me?" he trilled, his voice higher. 'Her, I wanted to see was she a real redhead.'

Jeffrey stood there, unable to move.

'I guess you know she is, huh? I can tell by looking in your eyes.' Wright crossed his arms over his chest, his eyes on Jeffrey's. 'Now, she's got some great tits. I loved sucking them.' He licked his lips. 'I wish you could've seen the fear on her face. I could tell she wasn't used to it. Hadn't had herself a real man yet, know what I mean?'

Jeffrey put his hand around the man's neck, backing him into the car. The action was so fast Jeffrey wasn't even sure what he was doing until he felt Jack Wright's long fingernails digging into the skin on the back of his hand.

Jeffrey forced himself to take his hand away. Wright sputtered, coughing, trying to catch his breath. Jeffrey walked a tight circle, checking on the neighbors. None of them had moved. They all seemed entranced by the show.

'You think you can scare me?' Wright said, his voice raspy. 'I had bigger than you, two at a time, in prison.'

'Where were you last Monday?' Jeffrey asked.

'I was at work, brother. Check with my PO.'

'Maybe I will.'

'She made a spot check on me around' – Wright pretended to think this through – 'I'd say around two, two-thirty. That the time you looking for?'

Jeffrey did not answer. Sibyl Adams's time of death had been printed in the *Observer*.

'I was sweeping and mopping and taking out the trash,' Wright continued.

Jeffrey indicated the tattoo. 'I see you're a religious man.'

Wright looked at his arm. 'That's what caught me up with Sara.'

'You like to keep up with your girls, huh?' Jeffrey asked. 'Maybe look through the newspapers? Maybe keep up with them on the Internet?'

Wright looked nervous for the first time. 'You been in my house?'

'I like what you did with the walls,' he said. 'All those little Jesuses. Their eyes just follow you when you walk around the room.'

Wright's face changed. He showed Jeffrey the side

that only a handful of unfortunate women had ever seen as he screamed, 'That is my personal property. You don't belong in there.'

'I was in there,' Jeffrey said, able to be calm now that Wright was not. 'I went through everything.'

'You bastard,' Wright yelled, throwing a punch. Jeffrey sidestepped, twisting the man's arm behind him. Wright pitched forward, falling face first into the ground. Jeffrey was on top of him, his knee pressed into the man's back.

'What do you know?' Jeffrey demanded.

'Let me go,' Wright begged. 'Please, let me go.'

Jeffrey took out his handcuffs and forced Wright into them. The clicking sound of the locks sent the man into hyperventilation.

'I just read about it,' Wright said. 'Please, please, let me go.'

Jeffrey leaned down, whispering in the man's ear. 'You're going back to jail.'

'Don't send me back,' Wright begged. 'Please.'

Jeffrey reached down, tugging the ankle bracelet. Knowing how the City of Atlanta worked, this would be faster than dialing 911. When the bracelet would not budge, Jeffrey used the heel of his shoe to bust it.

'You can't do that,' Wright screamed. 'You can't do that. They saw you.'

Jeffrey looked up, remembering the neighbors. He watched wordlessly as they all turned their backs, disappearing into their houses.

'Oh, God, please don't send me back,' Wright begged. 'Please, I'll do anything.'

'They're not going to like that nine mill under your mattress, either, Jack.'

'Oh, God,' the man sobbed, shaking.

Jeffrey leaned against the Nova, taking out the

business card Keith had given him earlier. The name on the card was Mary Ann Moon. Jeffrey glanced at his watch. At ten till eight on a Friday night, he doubted very seriously that she would be happy to see him.

TWENTY-THREE

Lena closed her eyes as the sun beat down on her face. The water was warm and inviting, a slight breeze crossing her body as each wave gently rolled under her. She could not remember the last time she had been to the ocean, but the vacation was well earned to say the least.

'Look,' Sibyl said, pointing above them.

Lena followed her sister's finger, spotting a seagull in the ocean sky. She found herself concentrating on the clouds instead. They looked like cotton balls against a baby blue backdrop.

'Did you want this back?' Sibyl asked, handing Lena a red kickboard. Lena laughed. 'Hank told me you lost it.'

Sibyl smiled. 'I put it where he couldn't see it.'

With sudden clarity, Lena realized it was Hank and not Sibyl who had been blinded. She could not understand how she had gotten the two confused, but there was Hank on the beach, dark glasses covering his eyes. He sat back, propped up on his hands, letting the sun hit him square on the chest. He looked more tan than Lena had ever seen him. As a matter of fact, all the times they had gone to the beach before, Hank had stayed in the hotel room instead of going out on the beach with the girls. What he did in there all day, Lena did not know. Sometimes Sibyl would join him to take some time out from the sun, but Lena loved being on the beach. She loved playing in the water or looking for impromptu volleyball games she could flirt her way into.

That was how Lena had met Greg Mitchell, her last boyfriend of any consequence. Greg was playing volleyball with a group of his friends. He was about twenty-eight years old, but his friends were much younger and more interested in looking at girls than actually playing the game. Lena had walked over, knowing she was being sized up, rated like a side of meat, by the young men, and asked to join the game. Greg had thrown the ball at her straight from his chest and Lena had caught it the same way.

After a while, the younger men trailed off in search of alcohol or women or both. Lena and Greg played for what seemed like hours. If he had been expecting Lena to throw the games in honor of his masculinity, he had another thing coming. She had beaten him so badly that by the end of the third game, he had forfeited, offering to buy her dinner as her prize.

He took her to some cheap Mexican place that would have made Lena's grandfather keel over had he not already been dead. They drank sugary sweet margaritas, then they danced, then Lena gave Greg a sly smile instead of a good night kiss. The next day he was back in front of her hotel, this time with a surfboard. She had always wanted to learn how to surf, and she took up his offer for lessons without having to be asked twice.

Now, she could feel the surfboard underneath her, the waves sending her body up into the air, then down. Greg's hand was at the small of her back, then lower, then lower, until he was cupping her ass in his hand. She turned over slowly, letting him see and feel her naked body. The sun beat down, making her skin feel warm and alive.

He poured suntan oil in his hands, then started rubbing her feet. His hands encircled her ankles, pushing her legs far apart. They were still floating on the ocean but the water was somehow firm, holding her body up for Greg. His hands worked their way up her thighs, stroking, touching, moving past her intimate parts until his palms were cupping her breasts. He used his tongue, kissing then biting her nipples, her breasts, working his way up to her mouth. Greg's kisses were forceful and rough, like Lena had never known from him. She felt herself responding to him in ways she could not have imagined.

The pressure of his body on top of hers was alarmingly sensual. His hands were calloused, his touch rough, as he did with her what he wanted. For the first time in her life, Lena was not in control. For the first time in her life, Lena was completely helpless under this one man. She felt an emptiness that could only be filled by him. Anything he wanted, she would do. Any wish he uttered, she would fulfill.

His mouth moved down her body, his tongue exploring between her legs, his teeth rough against her. She tried to reach her hands to him, to pull him closer, but she found herself immobilized. Suddenly, he was on top of her, pushing her hands away from her body, out to the side as if to pin her back as he entered her. There was a wave of pleasure that seemed to last for hours, then sudden, excruciating release. Her whole body opened to him, her back arching, wanting to weld her flesh into his.

Then, it was over. Lena felt her body letting go, her mind coming back into focus. She rolled her head side to side, revering in the aftermath. She licked her lips, opening her eyes to just a slit as she looked into the dark room. A clinking sound came from far away. Another more immediate sound came from all around, an irregular ticktock, like a clock, only with water. She found that she could no longer remember the word for water pouring out of the clouds.

Lena tried to move, but her hands seemed unwilling. She glanced out, seeing the tips of her fingers, even though there was no light to show them. Something was around her wrists, something tight and unrelenting. Her mind made the connection to move her fingers, and she felt the rough surface of wood against the back of her hand. Likewise, something encircled her ankles, holding her feet to the floor. She could not move her legs or arms. She was literally splayed to the floor. Her body seemed to come alive with this one realization: she was trapped.

Lena was back in the dark room, back where she had been taken hours ago; or was it days? Weeks? The clinking was there, the slow beat of water torture pounding into her brain. The room had no windows and no light. There was only Lena and whatever was holding her to the floor.

A light came suddenly, a blinding light that burned her eyes. Lena tried to pull away from the restraints again, but she was helpless. Someone was there; someone she knew who should be helping her but was not. She writhed against the bonds, twisting her body, trying to free herself, to no avail. Her mouth opened, but no words would come. She forced the words through her mind – Help me, please – but was not rewarded with the sound of her own voice.

She turned her head to the side, blinking her eyes, trying to look past the light, just as a minute pressure came against the palm of her hand. The sensation was dull, but Lena could see from the light that the tip of a long nail was pressed into the palm of her hand. Also in the light, a hammer was raised.

Lena closed her eyes, not feeling the pain.

She was back at the beach, only not in the water. This time she was flying.

TWENTY-FOUR

Mary Ann Moon was not a pleasant woman. There was a set to her mouth that said 'don't fuck with me' before Jeffrey even had the opportunity to introduce himself. She had taken one look at Wright's broken monitoring bracelet and directed her comments to Jeffrey.

'Do you know how much those things cost?'

It had gone downhill from there.

Jeffrey's biggest problem with Moon, as she liked to be called, was the language barrier. Moon was from somewhere up east, the kind of place where consonants took on a life of their own. In addition to this, she spoke loudly and abruptly, two things that were considered very rude to southern ears. On the elevator ride up from central processing to the interview rooms, she stood too close to him, her mouth set in a fixed line of disapproval, her arms crossed low over her waist. Moon was about forty years old, but it was the hard kind of forty that too much smoking and drinking can do to a person. She had dark blond hair with light strands of grey mixed in. Her lips had wrinkles spreading out from them in deep rays.

Her nasal tone and the fact that she spoke sixty miles an hour gave Jeffrey the impression that he was talking to a French horn. Every response Jeffrey gave her was slow in coming because he had to wait for his brain to translate her words. He could tell early on that Moon took this slowness for stupidity, but there really wasn't anything he could do about it.

She said something to him over her shoulder as they walked through the precinct. He slowed it down, realizing she had said, 'Tell me about your case, Chief.'

He gave her a quick rundown of what had happened since Sibyl Adams had been found, leaving out his connection to Sara. He could tell the story wasn't progressing quickly enough, because Moon kept interrupting him with questions he was about to answer if she would give him a second to finish his sentence.

'I take it you went into my boy's house?' she said. 'You see all that Jesus shit?' She rolled her eyes. 'That nine mill didn't walk in under your pant leg, did it, Sheriff Taylor?'

Jeffrey gave her what he hoped was a threatening look. She responded with an outburst of laughter that pierced his eardrum. 'That name sounds familiar.'

'What's that?'

'Lipton. Tolliver, too.' She put her tiny hands on her slim hips. 'I'm very good about notification, Chief. I've called Sara maybe a handful of times to let her know where Jack Allen Wright is. It's my job to do victim notification on an annual basis. Her case was ten years ago?'

'Twelve.'

'So, that's at least twelve times I've talked to her.'

He came clean, knowing he was busted. 'Sara is my ex-wife. She was one of Wright's first victims.'

'They let you work the case knowing your connection?'

'I'm in charge of the case, Ms. Moon,' he answered.

She gave him a steady look that probably worked on her parolees, but did nothing but irritate Jeffrey. He was about two feet taller than Mary Ann Moon and not about to be intimidated by this little ball of Yankee hate.

'Wright's a Depo freak. You know what I mean by that?'

'He obviously likes taking it.'

'This goes way back to his early days, right after Sara. You've seen pictures of him?'

Jeffrey shook his head.

'Follow me,' Moon said.

He did as he was told, trying not to step on her heels. She was fast about everything but walking, and his stride was more than double hers. She stopped in front of a small office that was jam-packed with file storage boxes. She stepped over a pile of manuals, pulling a file off her desk.

'This place is a mess,' she said, as if the fact had nothing to do with her. 'Here.'

Jeffrey opened the file, seeing a younger, slimmer, less womanly photograph of Jack Allen Wright clipped to the top page. He had more hair on his head, and his face was lean. His body was cut the way men who spend three hours a day lifting weights get, and his eyes were a piercing blue. Jeffrey remembered Wright's rheumy eyes from before. He also remembered that part of Sara's ID had come from his clear blue eyes. Every aspect of Wright's appearance had been altered since he had assaulted Sara. This was the man Jeffrey had been expecting when he searched Wright's house. This was the man who had raped Sara, who had robbed her of her ability to give Jeffrey a child.

Moon shuffled through the file. 'This is his release photo,' she said, sliding out another photograph.

Jeffrey nodded, seeing the man he knew as Wright.

'He served hard time, you know that?'

Jeffrey nodded again.

'Lots of men try to fight. Some of them just give in.'

'You're breaking my heart,' Jeffrey mumbled. 'He have many visitors in prison?'

'Just his mother.'

Jeffrey closed the file and handed it back to her. 'What about when he got out of jail? He obviously went off the Depo, right? He raped again.'

'He says he didn't, but there's no way in hell he'd be able to get it up on the dosage he was supposed to be taking.'

'Who was supervising it?'

'He was under his own supervision.' She stopped him before he could say anything. 'Listen, I know it's not perfect, but we have to trust them sometimes. Sometimes we're wrong. We were wrong with Wright.' She threw the folder back on her desk. 'He goes to the clinic now and gets his Depo injected once a week. It's all nice and clean. The bracelet you were kind enough to destroy kept him under close supervision. He was in line.'

'He hasn't left the city?'

'No,' she answered. 'I did a spot check on him last Monday at work. He was at the Bank Building.'

'Nice of you to put him near all those college girls.'

'You're crossing a line,' she warned.

He held up his hands, palms out.

'Write down whatever questions you want asked,' she said. 'I'll talk to Wright.'

'I need to work off his answers.'

'Technically, I don't even have to let you in here. You should be glad I'm not kicking your ass all the way back to Mayberry.'

He literally bit his tongue so he would not snap back at her. She was right. He could call some friends of his on the APD tomorrow morning so he would get better treatment, but for right now, Mary Ann Moon was in charge.

Jeffrey said, 'Can you give me a minute?' He indicated the desk. 'I need to check in with my people.'

'I can't make long-distance calls.'

He held up his cell phone. 'It's more privacy that I was looking for.'

She nodded, turning around.

'Thanks,' Jeffrey offered, but she did not answer in kind. He waited until she was down the hallway, then closed the door. After stepping over a group of boxes, he sat at her desk. The chair was low to the ground, and his knees felt like they were about to touch his ears. Jeffrey looked at his watch before dialing Sara's number. She was an early-to-bed kind of person, but he needed to talk to her. He felt a wave of excitement wash over him as the phone rang.

She answered the phone on the fourth ring, her voice heavy with sleep. 'Hello?'

He realized he had been holding his breath. 'Sara?'

She was silent, and for a moment he thought she had hung up the phone. He heard her moving, sheets rustling; she was in bed. He could hear rain falling outside, and a distant thunder rumbled over the phone. Jeffrey had a flash of a night they had shared a long time ago. Sara never liked storms, and she had awakened him, wanting Jeffrey to take her mind off the thunder and lightning.

'What do you want?' she asked.

He searched for something to say, knowing suddenly that he had waited too long to get in touch with her. He could tell from the tone of her voice that something had changed in their relationship. He was not altogether sure how or why.

'I tried to call before,' he said, feeling like he was lying even though he was not. 'At the clinic,' he said.

'That so?'

'I talked to Nelly,' he said.

'Did you tell her it was important?'

Jeffrey felt his stomach drop. He didn't answer.

Sara gave what he thought was a laugh.

He said, 'I didn't want to talk to you until I had something.'

'Something on what?'

'I'm in Atlanta.'

She was silent, then, 'Let me guess, 633 Ashton Street.'

'Earlier,' he answered. 'I'm at APD headquarters now. We've got him in an interview room.'

'Jack?' she asked.

Something about her familiar use of his name set Jeffrey's teeth on edge.

'Moon called me when his monitor went off,' Sara provided in a dull tone. 'I had a feeling that's where you were.'

'I wanted to talk to him about what's going on before I called in the cavalry.'

She sighed heavily. 'Good for you.'

The line was quiet again, and Jeffrey was again lost for words. Sara interrupted the silence.

She asked, 'Is that why you called me? To tell me that you arrested him?'

'To see if you were okay.'

She gave a small laugh. 'Oh, yeah. I'm just peachy, Jeff. Thanks for calling.'

'Sara?' he asked, scared she would hang up. 'I tried to call before.'

'Evidently not that hard,' she said.

Jeffrey could feel her anger coming across the phone.

'I wanted to have something to tell you when I called. Something concrete.'

She stopped him, her tone terse and low. 'You didn't know what to say, so instead of walking two blocks to the clinic or making sure you got through to me, you scooted off to Atlanta to see Jack face-to-face.' She paused. 'Tell me how it felt to see him, Jeff.'

He could not answer her.

'What'd you do, beat him up?' Her tone turned accusatory. 'Twelve years ago, I could've used that. Right now I just wanted you to be there for me. To support me.'

'I'm trying to support you, Sara,' Jeffrey countered, feeling blindsided. 'What do you think I'm doing up here? I'm trying to find out if this guy is still out there raping women.'

'Moon says he hasn't left town in the last two years.'

'Maybe Wright's involved in what's going on in Grant. Did you think of that?'

'No, actually,' she answered glibly. 'All I could think was I showed you that transcript this morning, I bared my soul to you, and your response was to get out of town.'

'I wanted –'

'You wanted to get away from me. You didn't know how to deal with it, so you left. I guess it's not as tricky as letting me come home and catch you with another woman in our bed, but it sends the same kind of message, doesn't it?'

He shook his head, not understanding how it had come to this. 'How is it the same? I'm trying to help you.'

Her voice changed then, and she didn't seem angry so much as deeply hurt. She had talked to him like this only once before, right after she had caught him cheating. He had felt then as he felt now, like a selfish asshole.

She said, 'How are you helping me in Atlanta? How does it help me having you four hours away? Do you know how I felt all day, jumping every time the phone rang, hoping it was you?' She answered for him. 'I felt like an idiot. Do you know how hard it was for me to show you that? To let you know what had happened to me?'

'I didn't –'

'I'm nearly forty years old, Jeffrey. I choose to be a good daughter to my parents and a supportive sister to Tessa. I chose to push myself so I could graduate at the top of my class from one of the finest universities in America. I chose to be a pediatrician so I could help kids. I chose to move back to Grant so I could be close to my family. I chose to be your wife for six years because I loved you so much, Jeffrey. I loved you so much.' She stopped, and he could tell that she was crying. 'I didn't choose to be raped.'

He tried to speak, but she wouldn't let him.

'What happened to me took fifteen minutes. Fifteen minutes and all of that was wiped out. None of it matters when you take those fifteen minutes into account.'

'That's not true.'

'It's not?' she asked. 'Then why didn't you call me this morning?'

'I tried to –'

'You didn't call me because you see me as a victim now. You see me the same way you see Julia Matthews and Sibyl Adams.'

'I don't, Sara,' he countered, shocked that she would accuse him of such a thing. 'I don't see –'

'I sat there in that hospital bathroom on my knees for

327

two hours before they cut me loose. I nearly bled to death,' she said. 'When he was done with me, there was nothing left. Nothing at all. I had to rebuild my life. I had to accept that because of that bastard I would never have children. Not that I ever wanted to think about having sex again. Not that I thought any man would want to touch me after what he did to me.' She stopped, and he wanted so badly to say something to her, but the words would not come.

Her voice was low when she said, 'You said I never opened up to you? Well, this is why. I tell you my deepest, darkest secret and what do you do? You run off to Atlanta to confront the man who did it instead of talking to me. Instead of comforting me.'

'I thought you'd want me to do something.'

'I did want you to do something,' she answered, her tone filled with sadness. 'I did.'

The phone clicked in his ear as she hung up. He dialed her number again, but the line was busy. He kept hitting 'send' on the phone, trying the line five more times, but Sara had taken her phone off the hook.

Jeffrey stood behind the one-way glass in the observation room, playing back his conversation with Sara in his mind. An overwhelming sadness enveloped him. He knew that she was right about calling. He should have insisted Nelly put him through. He should have gone to the clinic and told her that he still loved her, that she was still the most important woman in his life. He should have gotten on his knees and begged her to come back to him. He shouldn't have left her. Again.

Jeffrey thought of how Lena had used the term victim a few days ago, describing targets of sexual predators. She had put a spin on the word, saying it the same way she would say 'weak' or 'stupid.' Jeffrey had not liked that classification from Lena, and he certainly did not like hearing it from Sara. He probably knew Sara better than any other man in her life, and Jeffrey knew that Sara was not a victim of anything but her own damning self-judgment. He did not see her as a victim in that context. If anything, he saw her as a survivor. Jeffrey was hurt to his very core that Sara would think so little of him.

Moon interrupted his thoughts, asking, 'About ready to start?'

'Yeah,' Jeffrey answered, blocking Sara from his mind. No matter what she had said, Wright was still a viable lead to what was going on in Grant County. Jeffrey was already in Atlanta. There was no reason to go back until he had gotten everything he needed from the man. Jeffrey clenched his jaw, forcing himself to concentrate on the task at hand as he stared through the glass.

Moon entered the room loudly, banging the door closed behind her, raking a chair out from the table, the legs screeching against the tiled floor. For all the APD's money and special funding, the city's interview rooms were not nearly as clean as the ones in Grant County. The room Jack Allen Wright sat in was dingy and dirty. The cement walls were unpainted and gray. There was a gloominess to the room that would encourage anyone to confess just to get out of the place. Jeffrey took this all in as he watched Mary Ann Moon work Wright. She was not nearly as good as Lena Adams, but there was no denying Moon had a rapport with the rapist. She talked to him like a big sister.

She asked, 'That old redneck didn't fool with you, did he?'

Jeffrey knew she was trying to bridge some trust with Wright, but he did not appreciate the characterization, mostly because he guessed Mary Ann Moon thought it was an accurate one.

'He busted my bracelet,' Wright said. 'I didn't do that.'

'Jack.' Moon sighed, sitting across from him at the table. 'I know that, okay? We need to find out how that gun got under your mattress. That's a clear violation and you're on your third strike. Right?'

Wright glanced at the mirror, probably knowing full well that Jeffrey was behind it. 'I don't know how it got there.'

'Guess he put your fingerprints on it, too?' Moon asked, crossing her arms.

Wright seemed to think this over. Jeffrey knew that gun belonged to Wright, but he also knew that there was no way in hell Moon would have been able to run the gun through forensics this quickly and get any kind of ID on the prints.

'I was scared,' Wright finally answered. 'My neighbors know, all right? They know what I am.'

'What are you?'

'They know about my girls.'

Moon stood from the chair. She turned her back to Wright, looking out the window. A mesh just like the ones at Wright's house covered the frame. Jeffrey was startled to realize that the man had made his own home resemble a prison.

'Tell me about your girls,' Moon said. 'I'm talking about Sara.'

Jeffrey felt his hands clench at Sara's name.

Wright sat back, licking his lips. 'There was a tight pussy.' He smirked. 'She was good to me.'

Moon's voice was bored. She had been doing this long enough not to be shocked. She asked, 'She was?'

'She was so sweet.'

Moon turned around, leaning her back against the mesh. 'You know what's going on where she lives. I take it you know what's been happening to the girls.'

'I only know what I read in the papers,' Wright said, offering a shrug. 'You ain't gonna send me up on that gun, are you, boss? I had to protect myself. I was scared for my life.'

'Let's talk about Grant County,' Moon offered. 'Then we'll talk about the gun.'

Wright picked at his face, gauging her. 'You're being straight with me?'

'Of course I am, Jack. When have I not been straight with you?'

Wright seemed to weigh his options. As far as Jeffrey could see, it was a no-brainer: jail or cooperation. Still, he imagined Wright wanted some semblance of control in his life.

'That thing that was done to her car,' Wright said.

'What's that?' Moon asked.

'That word on her car,' Wright clarified. 'I didn't do that.'

'You didn't?'

'I told my lawyer, but he said it didn't matter.'

'It matters now, Jack,' Moon said, just the right amount of insistence in her voice.

'I wouldn't write that on somebody's car.'

'Cunt?' she asked. 'That's what you called her in the bathroom.'

'That was different,' he said. 'That was the heat of the moment.'

Moon did not respond to this. 'Who wrote it?'

'That, I don't know,' Wright answered. 'I was in the hospital all day, working. I didn't know what kind of car she drove. Could've guessed it, though. She had that attitude, you know? Like she was better than everybody else.'

'We're not going to get into that, Jack.'

'I know,' he said, looking down. 'I'm sorry.'

'Who do you think wrote that on her car?' Moon asked. 'Somebody at the hospital?'

'Somebody who knew her, knew what she drove.'

'Maybe a doctor?'

'I don't know.' He shrugged. 'Maybe.'

'You being straight with me?'

He seemed startled by her question. 'Hell, yeah, I am.'

'So, you think somebody at the hospital might have written that on her car. Why?'

'Maybe she pissed them off?'

'She piss a lot of people off?'

'No.' He shook his head vehemently. 'Sara was good to people. She always talked to everybody.' He seemed to not remember his earlier comments about how conceited Sara was. Wright continued, 'She always said hey to me in the hall. You know, not like "How you doing" or anything like that but, "Hey, I know you're there." Most people, they see you but they don't. Know what I mean?'

'Sara's a nice girl,' Moon said, keeping him on track. 'Who would do that to her car?'

'Maybe somebody was pissed at her about something?'

Jeffrey put his hand to the glass, feeling the hair on the back of his neck rise. Moon picked up on this as well.

She asked, 'About what?'

'I don't know,' Wright answered. 'I'm just saying I never wrote that on her car.'

'You're sure about that.'

Wright swallowed hard. 'You said you'd trade the gun for this, right?'

Moon gave him a nasty look. 'Don't question me, Jack. I told you up front that was the deal. What have you got for us?'

Wright glanced toward the mirror. 'That's all I have, that I didn't do that to her car.'

'Who did, then?'

Wright shrugged. 'I told you I don't know.'

'You think the same guy who scratched her car is doing this stuff in Grant County?'

He shrugged again. 'I'm not a detective. I'm just telling you what I know.'

Moon crossed her arms over her chest. 'We're gonna keep you in lockup over the weekend. When we talk on Monday, you see if you've got an idea who this person might be.'

Tears came to Wright's eyes. 'I'm telling you the truth.'

'We'll see if it's the same truth on Monday morning.'

'Don't send me back in there, please.'

'It's just holding, Jack,' Moon offered. 'I'll make sure you get your own cell.'

'Just let me go home.'

'I don't think so,' Moon countered. 'We'll let you stew for a day. Give you some time to get your priorities straight.'

'They are straight. I promise.'

Moon did not wait for more. She left Wright in the room, his head in his hands, crying.

SATURDAY

TWENTY-FIVE

Sara woke with a start, not certain where she was for a brief, panicked second. She looked around her bedroom, keeping her eyes on solid things, comforting things. The old chest of drawers that had belonged to her grandmother, the mirror she had found in a yard sale, the armoire that had been so wide her father had helped her take the hinges off the bedroom door so they could squeeze it in.

She sat up in bed, looking out the bank of windows at the lake. The water was rough from last night's storm, and choppy waves rode across the surface. Outside, the sky was a warm gray, blocking the sun, keeping the fog down low to the ground. The house was cold, and Sara imagined that outside was even colder. She took the quilt from the bed with her as she walked to the bathroom, wrinkling her nose as her feet padded across the cold floor.

In the kitchen, she started the coffeemaker, standing in front of the unit as she waited for enough to fill a cup. She went back to the bedroom, slipping on a pair of spandex running shorts, then an old pair of sweatpants. The phone was still off the hook from Jeffrey's call last night, and Sara replaced the receiver. The phone rang almost immediately.

Sara took a deep breath, then answered, 'Hello?'

'Hey, baby,' Eddie Linton said. 'Where you been?'

'I accidentally knocked the phone off the hook,' Sara lied.

Her father either did not catch the lie or was letting it pass. He said, 'We've got breakfast cooking here. Wanna come?'

'No, thanks,' Sara answered, her stomach protesting even as she did. 'I'm about to go for a run.'

'Maybe come by after?'

'Maybe,' Sara answered, walking toward the desk in the hallway. She opened the top drawer and pulled out twelve postcards. Twelve years since the rape, one postcard for every year. There was always a Bible verse along with her address typed across the back.

'Baby?' Eddie said.

'Yeah, Pop,' Sara answered, keying into what he was saying. She slid the cards back into the drawer, using her hip to shut it.

They made small talk about the storm, Eddie telling her that a tree limb had missed the Linton house by a couple of yards, and Sara offering to come by later and help clean up. As he talked, Sara flashed back to the time just after she was raped. She was in the hospital bed, the ventilator hissing in and out, the heart monitor assuring her that she had not died, though Sara remembered that she had not found that reminder in the least bit comforting.

She had been asleep, and when she woke, Eddie was there, holding her hand in both of his. She had never seen her father cry before, but he was then, small, pathetic sobs escaping from his lips. Cathy was behind him, her arms around his waist, her head resting on his back. Sara had felt out of place there and she had briefly wondered what had upset them until she remembered what had happened to her.

After a week in the hospital, Eddie had driven her

back to Grant. Sara had kept her head on his shoulder the entire way, sitting in the front seat of his old truck, tucked between her mother and father, much as she had been before Tessa was born. Her mother sang an off-key hymn Sara had never heard before. Something about salvation. Something about redemption. Something about love.

'Baby?'

'Yeah, Daddy,' Sara answered, wiping a tear from her eye. 'I'll drop by later, okay?' She blew a kiss to the phone. 'I love you.'

He answered in kind, but she could hear the concern in his voice. Sara kept her hand on the receiver, willing him not to be upset. The hardest part about recovering from what Jack Allen Wright had done to her was knowing that her father knew every single detail of the rape. She had felt so exposed to him for such a long time that the nature of their relationship had changed. Gone was the Sara he played pickup games with. Gone were the jokes about Eddie wishing she had become a gynecologist, at least, so that he could say both his girls were in plumbing. He did not see her as his invulnerable Sara anymore. He saw her as someone he needed to protect. As a matter of fact, he saw her the same way Jeffrey did now.

Sara tugged the laces on her tennis shoes, tightening them too much and not caring. She had heard pity in Jeffrey's voice last night. Instantly, she had known that things had irrevocably changed. He would only see her as a victim from now on. Sara had fought too hard to overcome that feeling only to let herself give in to it now.

Slipping on a light jacket, Sara left the house. She jogged down the driveway to the street, taking a left away from her parents' house. Sara did not like to jog on the street; she had seen too many injured knees blown from the constant impact. When she worked out, she used the treadmills at the Grant YMCA or swam in the pool there. In the summertime, she took early morning swims in the lake to clear her mind and get her focus back for the day ahead. Today, she wanted to push herself to the limit, damn the consequences to her joints. Sara had always been a physical person, and sweating brought her center back.

About two miles from her house, she took a side trail off the main road so that she could run along the lake. The terrain was rough in spots, but the view was spectacular. The sun was finally winning its battle with the dark clouds overhead when she realized she was at Jeb McGuire's house. She had stopped to look at the sleek black boat moored at his dock before she made the connection as to where she was. Sara cupped her hand over her eyes, staring at the back of Jeb's house.

He lived in the old Tanner place, which had just recently come on the market. Lake people were hesitant to give up their land, but the Tanner children, who had moved away from Grant years ago, were more than happy to take the money and run when their father finally succumbed to emphysema. Russell Tanner had been a nice man, but he had his quirks, like most old people. Jeb had delivered Russell's medications to him personally, something that probably helped Jeb get into the house cheap after the old man died.

Sara walked up the steep lawn toward the house. Jeb had gutted the place a week after moving in, replacing the old crank windows with double-paned ones, having the asbestos shingles removed from the roof and sideboards. The house had been a dark grey for as long as Sara remembered, but Jeb had painted over this in a cheery yellow. The color was too bright for Sara, but it suited Jeb.

'Sara?' Jeb asked, coming out of the house. He had a tool belt on with a shingle hammer hanging from the strap on the side.

'Hey,' she called, walking toward him. The closer she got to the house, the more aware she became of a dripping sound. 'What's that noise?' she asked.

Jeb pointed to a gutter hanging off the roofline. 'I'm just now getting to it,' he explained, walking toward her. He rested his hand on the hammer. 'I've been so busy at work, I haven't had time to breathe.'

She nodded, understanding the dilemma. 'Can I give you a hand?'

'That's okay,' Jeb returned, picking up a six-foot ladder. He carried it over to the hanging gutter as he talked. 'Hear that thumping? Damn thing's draining so slow, it hits the base of the downspout like a jackhammer.'

She heard the noise more clearly as she followed him toward the house. It was an annoying, constant thump, like a faucet dripping into a cast-iron sink. She asked, 'What happened?'

'Old wood, I guess,' he said, turning the ladder right side up. 'This house is a money pit, I hate to say. I get the roof fixed and the gutters fall off. I seal the deck and the footings start to sink.'

Sara looked under the deck, noting the standing water. 'Is your basement flooded?'

'Thank God I don't have one or it'd be high tide down there,' Jeb said, reaching into one of the leather pouches on his belt. He took out a gutter nail with one hand and fumbled for the hammer with the other.

Sara stared at the nail, making a connection. 'Can I see that?'

He gave her a funny look, then answered, 'Sure.'

She took the nail, testing its weight in her hand. At twelve inches, it was certainly long enough for the job of tacking up a gutter, but could someone have also used this type of nail to secure Julia Matthews to the floor?

'Sara?' Jeb asked. His hand was out for the nail. 'I've got some more in the storage shed,' he said, indicating the metal shed. 'If you want to keep one.'

'No,' she answered, handing him the nail. She needed to get back to her house and call Frank Wallace about this. Jeffrey was probably still in Atlanta, but certainly someone would need to track down who had bought this type of nail recently. It was a good lead.

She asked, 'Did you get this at the hardware store?'

'Yeah,' he answered, giving her a curious look. 'Why?'

Sara smiled, trying to put his mind at ease. He probably thought it was odd that she was so interested in the gutter nail. It wasn't like she could tell him why. Sara's dating pool was small enough without taking Jeb McGuire out of the picture by suggesting his gutter nails would be a good way to pin a woman to the floor so she could be raped.

She watched him secure the drooping gutter to the house. Sara found herself thinking about Jeffrey and Jack Wright in the same room together. Moon had said that Wright had let himself go in prison, that the chiseled threat to his body had been replaced by soft fat, but Sara still saw him as she had that day twelve years ago. His skin was tight to his bones, his veins sticking out along his arms. His expression was a carved study in hatred, his teeth gritting in a menacing smile as he raped her.

Sara gave an involuntary shudder. Her life for the last

twelve years had been spent blocking Wright out of her mind, and having him back now, in whatever form, be it through Jeffrey or a stupid postcard, was making her feel violated all over again. She hated Jeffrey for that, mostly because he was the only one who could suffer any impact from her hatred.

'Hold on,' Jeb said, snapping her out of her reflection. Jeb cupped his hand to his ear, listening. The thumping noise was still there as water dripped into the downspout.

'This is going to drive me crazy,' he said, over the thump, thump, thump of the water.

'I can see that,' she said, thinking that five minutes of the dripping sound was already giving her a headache.

Jeb came down off the ladder, tucking the hammer back into his belt. 'Is something wrong?'

'No,' she answered. 'Just thinking.'

'About what?'

She took a deep breath, then said, 'About our rain check.' She looked up at the sky. 'Why don't you come over to the house around two for a late lunch? I'll get some takeout from the deli in Madison.'

He smiled, an unexpected nervous edge to his voice. 'Yeah,' he answered. 'That sounds great.'

TWENTY-SIX

Jeffrey tried to keep his focus on driving, but there was too much going on in his mind to concentrate. He had not slept all night, and exhaustion was taking over his body. Even after pulling over to the side of the road for a thirty-minute nap, he still did not feel like his head was on straight. Too much was happening. Too many things were pulling him in different directions at the same time.

Mary Ann Moon had promised to subpoena the employment records from Grady Hospital dating back to the time Sara had worked there. Jeffrey prayed that the woman was as good as her word. She had estimated that the records would be available for Jeffrey's perusal sometime Sunday afternoon. Jeffrey's only hope was that a name from the hospital would sound familiar. Sara had never mentioned anyone from Grant working with her back in those days, but he still needed to ask her. Three calls to her house had gotten him her machine. He knew better than to leave a message for her to call. The tone of her voice last night had been enough to convince him that she would probably never talk to him again.

Jeffrey pulled the Town Car into the station parking lot. He needed to go home to shower and change, but he also had to show his face at work.

His trip to Atlanta had taken more time than

planned, and Jeffrey had missed the early morning briefing.

Frank Wallace was walking out the front door as Jeffrey put the car in park. Frank tossed a wave before walking around the car and getting in.

Frank said, 'The kid's missing.'

'Lena?'

Frank gave a nod as Jeffrey put the car in gear.

Jeffrey asked, 'What happened?'

'Her uncle Hank called at the station looking for her. He said the last he saw of her she was in the kitchen right after that Matthews went south.'

'That was two days ago,' Jeffrey countered. 'How the hell did this happen?'

'I left a message on her machine. I figured she was lying low. Didn't you give her time off ?'

'Yeah,' Jeffrey answered, feeling guilt wash over him. 'Hank's at her house?'

Frank gave another nod, slipping on his seat belt as Jeffrey pushed the car past eighty. Tension filled the car as they drove toward Lena's house. When they got there, Hank Norton was sitting on the front porch waiting.

Hank jogged to the car. 'Her bed hasn't been slept in,' he said as a greeting. 'I was at Nan Thomas's house. Neither one of us had heard from her. We assumed she was with you.'

'She wasn't,' Jeffrey said, offering the obvious. He walked into Lena's house, scanning the front room for clues. The house had two stories, like most homes in the neighborhood. The kitchen, dining room, and living room were on the main level with two bedrooms and a bath upstairs.

Jeffrey took the steps two at a time, his leg protesting at the movement. He walked into what he assumed was

Lena's bedroom, searching for anything that might make sense of all of this. A hot pain was at the back of his eyes and everything he looked at had a tinge of red to it. Going through her drawers, moving clothes around in her closet, he had no idea what he expected to find. He found nothing.

Downstairs in the kitchen, Hank Norton was talking to Frank, his words a hot staccato of blame and denial. 'She was supposed to be working with you,' Hank said. 'You're her partner.'

Jeffrey got a brief flash of Lena in her uncle's voice. He was angry, accusatory. There was the same underlying hostility he had always heard in Lena's tone.

Jeffrey took the heat off of Frank, saying, 'I gave her time off, Mr. Norton. We assumed she would be at home.'

'Girl blows her head off right under my niece and you just assume she's gonna be okay?' he hissed. 'Jesus Christ, that's the end of your responsibility, giving her the day off?'

'That's not what I meant, Mr. Norton.'

'For fuck sakes, stop calling me Mr. Norton,' he screamed, throwing his hands into the air.

Jeffrey waited for the man to say more, but he turned suddenly, walking out of the kitchen. He slammed the back door behind him.

Frank spoke slowly, visibly upset. 'I should've checked on her.'

'I should have,' Jeffrey said. 'She's my responsibility.'

'She's everybody's responsibility,' Frank countered. He started searching the kitchen, opening and closing drawers, going through cabinets. Frank obviously wasn't really paying attention to what he was doing. He slammed the cabinet doors, more to work out his anger than to look for anything concrete. Jeffrey watched this for a while, then walked toward the window. He saw Lena's black Celica in the driveway.

Jeffrey said, 'Car's still here.'

Frank slammed a drawer closed. 'I saw that.'

'I'll go check it out,' Jeffrey offered. He walked out the back door, passing Hank Norton, who was sitting on the steps leading into the backyard. He was smoking a cigarette, his movements awkward and angry.

Jeffrey asked him, 'Has the car been here all the time you were gone?'

'How the fuck would I know that?' Norton snapped.

Jeffrey let this slide. He walked to the car, noting the lock was down on both doors. The tires on the passenger's side looked fine and the hood of the car felt cool as he walked around it.

'Chief?' Frank called from the kitchen door. Hank Norton stood as Jeffrey walked back toward the house.

'What is it?' Norton asked. 'Did you find something?'

Jeffrey walked back into the kitchen, spotting instantly what Frank had found. The word CUNT had been carved on the inside door of the cabinet over the stove.

'I don't give a good goddamn about subpoenas,' Jeffrey told Mary Ann Moon as he sped toward the college. He held the phone in one hand and drove with the other.

'One of my detectives is missing right now, and the only lead I've got is this list.' He took a breath, trying to calm himself. 'I have got to get access to those employment records.'

Moon was diplomatic. 'Chief, we have to go through protocol here. This isn't Grant County. We step on somebody's toes and it's not like we can make nice at the next church social.'

'Do you know what this guy's been doing to women

here?' he asked. 'Are you willing to take responsibility for my detective being raped right now? Because I guarantee you that's what's happening to her.' He held his breath for a moment, trying not to let that image sink in.

When she did not respond, he said, 'Someone carved something on a cabinet in her kitchen.' He paused, letting her absorb that. 'Do you want to take a guess as to what that word is, Ms. Moon?'

Moon was silent, obviously thinking. 'I can probably talk to a girl I know in records over there. Twelve years is a long time. I can't make guarantees they'll keep something like that handy. It's probably on microfiche at the state records building.'

He gave her his cell phone number before ringing off.

'What's the dorm number?' Frank asked as they drove through the gates of the college.

Jeffrey took out his notepad, flipping back a few pages. 'Twelve,' he said. 'She's in Jefferson Hall.'

The Town Car fishtailed as he stopped in front of the dormitory. Jeffrey was out the door and up the steps in a flash. He pounded his fist on the door to number twelve, throwing it open when there was no answer.

'Oh, Jesus,' Jenny Price said, grabbing a sheet to cover herself. A boy Jeffrey had never seen before jumped up from the bed, slipping on his pants in one practiced movement.

'Get out,' Jeffrey told him, walking toward Julia Matthews's side of the room. Nothing had been moved since he had been here last time. Jeffrey did not imagine Matthews's parents felt much like going through their dead daughter's things.

Jenny Price was dressed, more bold than she had been the day before. 'What are you doing here?' she demanded.

Jeffrey ignored her question, searching through clothes and books.

Jenny repeated the question, this time to Frank.

'Police business,' he mumbled from the hallway.

Jeffrey turned the room upside down in seconds. There had not been much to begin with, and as with the search before, nothing new turned up. He stopped, looking around the room, trying to find what he was missing. He was turning to search the closet again when he noticed a stack of books by the door. A thin film of mud covered the spines. They had not been there the first time Jeffrey had searched the room. He would have remembered them.

He asked, 'What are those?'

Jenny followed his gaze. 'The campus police brought those by,' she explained. 'They were Julia's.'

Jeffrey clenched his fist, wanting to pound something. 'They brought them by here?' he asked, wondering why he was surprised. Grant Tech's campus security force was comprised of mostly middle-aged deputy dogs who hadn't a brain between them.

The girl explained, 'They found them outside the library.'

Jeffrey forced his hands to unclench, bending at the knee to examine the books. He thought about putting gloves on before touching them, but it was not as if a chain of custody had been maintained.

The Biology of Microorganisms was on top of the stack, flecks of mud scattered along the front cover. Jeffrey picked up the book, thumbing through the pages. On page twenty-three, he found what he was looking for. The word CUNT was printed in bold red marker across the page.

'Oh my God,' Jenny breathed, hand to her mouth.

Jeffrey left Frank to seal off the room. Instead of

driving to the science lab where Sibyl worked, he jogged across the campus, going the opposite direction he had gone with Lena just a few days ago. Again, he took the stairs two at a time; again, he did not bother to wait for an answer to his knock outside Sibyl Adams's lab.

'Oh,' Richard Carter said, looking up from a note-book. 'What can I do for you?'

Jeffrey leaned his hand on the closest desk, trying to catch his breath. 'Was there anything,' he began, 'unusual the day Sibyl Adams was killed?'

Carter's face took on an exasperated expression. Jeffrey wanted to smack it off him, but he refrained.

Carter said in a self-righteous tone, 'I told you before, there was nothing out of the ordinary. She's dead, Chief Tolliver, don't you think that I'd mention something unusual?'

'Maybe a word was written on something,' Jeffrey suggested, not wanting to give too much away. It was amazing what people thought they remembered if you asked them the right way. 'Did you see something written on one of her notebooks? Maybe she had something she kept close by that someone tampered with?'

Carter's face fell. Obviously, he remembered something. 'Now that you mention it,' he began, 'just before her early class on Monday, I saw something written on the chalkboard.' He crossed his arms over his large chest. 'Kids think it's funny to pull those kinds of pranks. She was blind, so she couldn't really see what they were doing.'

'What did they do?'

'Well, someone, I don't know who, wrote the word cunt on the blackboard.'

'This was Monday morning?'

'Yes.'

'Before she died?'

He had the decency to look away before answering, 'Yes.'

Jeffrey stared at the top of Richard's head for a moment, fighting the urge to pummel him. He said, 'If you had told me this last Monday, do you realize Julia Matthews might be alive?'

Richard Carter did not have an answer for that.

Jeffrey left, slamming the door behind him. He was making his way down the steps when his cell phone rang. He answered on the first ring. 'Tolliver.'

Mary Ann Moon got right to the point. 'I'm in the records department right now, looking at the list. It's everybody who worked on the first-floor emergency department, from the doctors to the custodians.'

'Go ahead,' Jeffrey said, closing his eyes, blocking out her Yankee twang as she called out the first, middle, and last names of the men who had worked with Sara. It took her a full five minutes to read them all. After the last one, Jeffrey was silent.

Moon asked, 'Anybody on there sound familiar?'

'No,' Jeffrey responded. 'Fax the list to my office if you don't mind.' He gave her the number, feeling as if he had been punched in the stomach. His mind conjured the image of Lena again, nailed to a basement floor, terrified.

Moon prompted, 'Chief?'

'I'll have some of my guys cross-reference it with voter polls and the phone book.' He paused, debating whether or not to go on. Finally, good breeding won out. 'Thank you,' he said. 'For looking that list up.'

Moon did not give him her customary abrupt goodbye. She said, 'I'm sorry the names didn't ring any bells.'

'Yeah,' he answered, checking his watch. 'Listen, I

can be back in Atlanta in around four hours. Do you think I can get some time alone with Wright?'

There was another hesitation, then, 'He was attacked this morning.'

'What?'

'Seems the guards at the lockup didn't think he deserved his own cell.'

'You promised to keep him out of the general population.'

'I know that,' she snapped. 'It's not like I can control what happens when he goes back inside. You of all people should know those good old boys operate by their own rules.'

Considering Jeffrey's behavior yesterday with Jack Wright, he was in no position to defend himself.

'He'll be out of it for a while,' Moon said. 'They cut him up pretty bad.'

He muttered a curse under his breath. 'He didn't give you anything after I left?'

'No.'

'Is he sure it's somebody who worked in the hospital?'

'No, as a matter of fact.'

'It's somebody who saw her at the hospital,' Jeffrey said. 'Who would see her at the hospital without working there?' He put his free hand over his eyes, trying to think. 'Can you pull patient files from there?'

'Like charts?' She sounded dubious. 'That's probably pushing it.'

'Just names,' he said. 'Just that day. April twenty-third.'

'I know the day.'

'Can you?'

She obviously had covered the mouthpiece on the phone, but he could still hear her talking to someone.

After a few beats, she was back on the line. 'Give me an hour, hour and a half.'

Jeffrey suppressed the groan that wanted to come. An hour was a lifetime. Instead, he said, 'I'll be here.'

TWENTY-SEVEN

Lena heard a door open somewhere. She lay there on the floor, waiting for him, because that's all she could do. When Jeffrey had told her Sibyl was dead, Lena's main focus had been on finding out who had killed Sibyl, on bringing him to justice. She had wanted nothing more than to find the bastard and send him to the chair. Those thoughts had so obsessed her from day one that she had not had time to stop and grieve. Not one day had been spent mourning the loss of her sister. Not one hour had gone by where she had stopped and taken the time to reflect on her loss.

Now, trapped in this house, nailed to the floor, Lena had no choice but to think about it. All of her time was devoted to memories of Sibyl. Even when she was drugged, a sponge held over her mouth, bittertasting water hitting the back of her throat until she was forced to swallow, Lena mourned Sibyl. There were days at school that were so real Lena could feel the grain of the pencil she held in her hand. Sitting with Sibyl in the back of classrooms, she could smell the ink from the ditto machine. There were car rides and vacations, senior pictures and field trips. She was reliving them all, Sibyl by her side, every one of them as if she was actually there in the moment.

The light came again as he entered the room. Her eyes were so dilated she could not see anything but shadows, but he still used the light to block her vision. The pain was so intense she was forced to close her eyes. Why he did this, she couldn't guess. Lena knew who her captor was. Even if she had not recognized his voice, the things he said could only come from the town's pharmacist.

Jeb sat at her feet, resting the light on the floor. The room was completely dark except for this small ray of light. Lena found it somewhat comforting to be able to see something after being in darkness for so long.

Jeb asked, 'Are you feeling better?'

'Yes,' Lena answered, not remembering if she had felt worse before. He was injecting her with something every four hours or so. She guessed from the way her muscles relaxed shortly after that it was some kind of pain medication. The drug was potent enough to keep her from hurting, but not enough to knock her out. He only knocked her out at night, then with whatever he was putting in the water. He held a wet sponge over her mouth, forcing her to swallow the bitter-tasting water. She prayed to God it was not belladonna she was ingesting. Lena had seen Julia Matthews with her own eyes. She knew how lethal the drug was. What's more, Lena doubted Sara Linton would be around to save her. Not that Lena was sure she wanted to be saved. In the back of her mind, Lena was coming to the conclusion that the best thing that could happen to her was for her to die here.

'I've tried to stop that dripping,' Jeb said, as if to apologize. 'I don't know what the problem is.'

Lena licked her lips, holding her tongue.

'Sara came by,' he said. 'You know, she really has no idea who I am.'

Again, Lena was silent. There was a lonely quality to his voice that she did not want to respond to. It was as if he wanted comfort.

'Do you want to know what I did to your sister?' he asked.

'Yes,' Lena answered before she could stop herself.

'She had a sore throat,' he began, taking off his shirt. Out of the corner of her eye, Lena watched him as he continued to undress himself. His tone was casual, the same one he used when recommending an over-the-counter cough medicine or a particular brand of vitamin.

He said, 'She didn't like to take any medication, even aspirin. She asked me if I knew of a good herbal cough remedy.' He was completely naked now, and he moved closer to Lena. She tried to jerk away as he lay down beside her, but it was useless. Her hands and feet were securely nailed to the floor. The secondary restraints all but paralyzed her.

Jeb continued, 'Sara told me she would be going to the diner at two. I knew Sibyl would be there. I used to watch her walk by every Monday on her way to eat lunch. She was very pretty, Lena. But not like you. She didn't have your spirit.'

Lena jerked as his hand came out to stroke her stomach. His fingers played lightly on her skin, sending a tremor of fear through her body.

He rested his head on her shoulder, watching his hand as he spoke. 'I knew Sara was going to be there, that Sara could save her, but of course that's not how it worked out, was it? Sara was late. She was late, and she let your sister die.'

Lena's body shook uncontrollably. He had kept her drugged during the past assaults, making them somewhat bearable. If he raped her now, like this, she wouldn't survive it. Lena remembered Julia Matthews's last words. She had said that Jeb made love to her; that was what had killed Julia. Lena knew if he made it gentle, if he was soft with her rather than savage, if he kissed her and caressed her as a lover, she would never be able to go back from this point. No matter what he did to her, if she lived beyond tomorrow, if she survived this ordeal, part of her would already be dead.

Jeb leaned over, tracing his tongue along her lower abdomen, into her navel. He gave a pleased laugh. 'You're so sweet, Lena,' he whispered, tracing his tongue up to her nipple. He sucked her breast gently, using his palm to attend to her other breast. His body was pressed into hers, and she could feel the hardness of him against her leg.

Lena's mouth trembled as she asked, 'Tell me about Sibyl.'

He used his fingers to gently squeeze her nipple. In another setting, under different circumstances, it would be almost playful. There was a hushed lover's tone to his voice that sent a wave of repulsion screaming down her spine.

Jeb said, 'I walked around the back of the buildings and hid in the toilet. I knew the tea would make her have to use the bathroom, so . . .' He ran his fingers down her stomach, stopping just above her pubic area. 'I locked myself in the other stall. It happened very fast. I should have guessed she was a virgin.' He gave the kind of satisfied sigh a dog would give after a large meal. 'She was so warm and wet when I was inside of her.'

Lena shuddered as his finger probed between her legs. He massaged her, his eyes locked onto hers to see her reaction. The direct stimulation caused her body to react in ways contrary to the terror she was feeling. He leaned over, kissing the side of her breasts. 'God, you've got a beautiful body,' he moaned, holding his finger up to her lips, pressing her mouth open. She tasted herself as he slid his finger deeper; in and out, in and out.

He said, 'Julia was pretty, too, but not like you.' He put his hand back between her legs, pressing his finger deep inside her. She felt herself being stretched as he slipped in another finger.

'I could give you something,' he said. 'Something to dilate you. I could get my whole fist inside of you.'

A sob filled the room: Lena's. She had never heard such grief in her life. The sound itself was more frightening than what Jeb was doing to her. Her entire body moved up and down as he fucked her, the chains from her restraints raking against the floor, the back of her head rubbing against the hard wood.

He slipped his fingers out and lay beside her, his body pressed into her side. She could feel every part of him, tell how excited this was making him. There was a sexual odor in the room that made it difficult for her to breathe. He was doing something, she could not tell what.

He put his lips close to her ear, whispering, ' "Behold, I give unto you power to tread on serpents and scorpions, and over all the power of the enemy; and nothing shall by any means hurt you." '

Lena's teeth started to chatter. She felt a pinch at her thigh and knew he had given her another injection.

' "For a small moment have I forsaken thee; but with great mercies I shall gather thee." '

'Please,' Lena cried, 'please don't do this.'

'Julia, Sara could save. Not your sister,' Jeb said. He sat up, crossing his legs again. He stroked himself as he spoke, his tone almost conversational. 'I don't know if she'll be able to save you, Lena. Do you?'

Lena could not look away from him. Even as he picked his pants off the floor and pulled something from the back pocket, her eyes stayed on his. He held up a pair of pliers in her line of vision. They were large, about ten inches long, and the stainless steel gleamed in the light.

'I've got a late lunch,' he said, 'then I've got to run into town and take care of some paperwork. The bleeding should be stopped by then. I've mixed a blood-clotting compound with the Percodan. I also added a little something for the nausea. It's going to hurt a little. I won't lie to you.'

Lena rolled her head side to side, not understanding. She felt the drugs kicking in. Her body felt like it was melting to the floor.

'Blood is a great lubricant. Did you know that?'

Lena held her breath, not knowing what was coming, but sensing the danger.

His penis brushed against her chest as he straddled her body. He steadied her head with a strong hand, forcing her mouth open by pressing his fingers into her jaw. Her vision blurred, then doubled as he reached the pliers into her mouth.

TWENTY-EIGHT

Sara pulled back on the throttle as she neared the dock. Jeb was already there, taking off his orange life vest, looking just as goofy as he had before. Like Sara, he was wearing a heavy sweater and a pair of jeans. Last night's storm had dropped the temperature considerably, and she could not guess why anyone would get out on the lake today unless they absolutely had to.

'Let me help you,' he offered, reaching out toward her boat. He grabbed one of the lines and walked along the deck, pulling the boat toward the winch.

'Just tie it here,' Sara said, stepping out of the boat. 'I've got to go back over to my parents' house later.'

'Nothing wrong, I hope?'

'No,' Sara answered, tying the other line. She glanced at Jeb's rope, noting the girlie knot he had used looping it around the bollard. The boat would probably be loose inside of ten minutes, but Sara did not have the heart to give him a rope-tying lesson.

She reached into the boat, taking out two plastic grocery bags. 'I had to borrow my sister's car to go to the store,' she explained. 'My car's still impounded.'

'From the –' He stopped, looking somewhere over Sara's shoulder.

'Yeah,' she answered, walking along the dock. 'Did you get your gutter fixed?'

He was shaking his head as he caught up with her, taking the bags. 'I don't know what the problem is.'

'Have you thought about putting a sponge or something in the bottom of the spout?' she suggested. 'Maybe that'll help dampen the noise.'

'That's a great idea,' he said. They had reached the house, and she opened the back door for him.

He gave her a concerned look as he placed the bags on the counter alongside his boat keys. 'You really should lock your door, Sara.'

'I was just gone for a few minutes.'

'I know,' Jeb said. 'But, you never know. Especially with what's been going on lately. You know, with those girls.'

Sara sighed. He had a point. She just could not reconcile what was happening in town with her own home. It was as if Sara was somehow protected by the old 'lightning never strikes twice' rule. Of course, Jeb was right. She would need to be more careful.

She asked, 'How's the boat doing?' as she walked toward the answering machine. The message light was not blinking, but a scroll through the caller ID showed that Jeffrey had called three times in the last hour. Whatever he wanted to say, Sara wasn't listening. She was actually thinking about quitting at the coroner's office. There had to be a better way to get Jeffrey out of her life. She needed to focus on the present instead of wishing for the past. Truth be told, the past was not as great as she had made it out to be.

'Sara?' Jeb asked, holding out a glass of wine.

'Oh.' Sara took the glass, thinking it was a little early for her to be drinking alcohol.

Jeb held up his glass. 'Cheers.'

'Cheers,' Sara returned, tilting the glass. She gagged

at the taste. 'Oh, God,' she said, putting her hand to her mouth. The sharp taste sat on her tongue like a wet rag.

'What's wrong?'

'Ugh,' Sara groaned, holding her head under the kitchen faucet. She washed her mouth out several times before turning back to Jeb. 'It turned. The wine turned.'

He waved the glass under his nose, frowning. 'It smells like vinegar.'

'Yes,' she said, taking another swig of water.

'Gosh, I'm sorry. I guess I kept it a little too long.'

The phone rang as she turned off the faucet. Sara gave an apologetic smile to Jeb as she crossed the room, checking the caller ID. It was Jeffrey again. She did not pick up the phone.

'This is Sara,' her voice said from the answering machine. She was trying to remember which button to press when the beep came, then Jeffrey.

'Sara,' Jeffrey said, 'I'm getting patient records to go over from Grady so we –'

Sara pulled the power cord out of the back of the machine, cutting Jeffrey off in midsentence. She turned back to Jeb with what she hoped was an apologetic smile. 'Sorry,' she said.

'Is something wrong?' he asked. 'Didn't you use to work at Grady?'

'In another lifetime,' she answered, taking the phone off the hook. She listened for the dial tone, then rested the receiver on the table.

'Oh,' Jeb said.

She smiled at the quizzical look he gave her, fighting the urge to spit out the taste in her mouth. She walked over to the counter and started unpacking the bags. 'I got deli meats at the grocery store instead,' she offered. 'Roast beef, chicken, turkey, potato salad.' She stopped at the look he was giving her. 'What?'

He shook his head. 'You're so pretty.'

Sara felt herself blush at the compliment. 'Thanks,' she managed, taking out a loaf of bread. 'Do you want mayonnaise?'

He gave her a nod, still smiling. His expression was almost worshipful. It was making her uncomfortable.

To interrupt the moment, she suggested, 'Why don't you put on some music?'

Following her directions he turned toward the stereo. Sara finished making the sandwiches as he trailed his finger down her CD collection.

Jeb said, 'We've got the same taste in music.'

Sara suppressed a 'Great' as she took plates out of the cabinet. She was halving the sandwiches when the music came on. It was an old Robert Palmer CD she had not heard in ages.

'Great sound system,' Jeb said. 'Is that surround sound?'

'Yeah,' Sara answered. The speaker system was something Jeffrey had installed so that music could be heard throughout the house. There was even a speaker in the bathroom. They had taken baths at night sometimes, candles around the tub, something soft playing on the stereo.

'Sara?'

'Sorry,' she said, realizing she had zoned out.

Sara put down the plates on the kitchen table, setting them across from each other. She waited for Jeb to come back, then sat down, her leg tucked underneath her. 'I haven't heard this in a long time.'

'It's pretty old,' he said, taking a bite of his sandwich. 'My sister used to listen to this all the time.' He smiled. '*Sneakin' Sally Through the Alley*. That was her name, Sally.'

Sara licked some mayonnaise off her finger, hoping

the taste would mask the wine. 'I didn't know you had a sister.'

He sat up in his chair, taking his wallet out of his back pocket. 'She died a while ago,' he said, thumbing through the pictures in the front. He slid a photo from one of the plastic sleeves, holding it out to Sara. 'Just one of those things.'

Sara thought that was an odd thing to say about the death of his sister. Still, she took the picture, which showed a young girl in a cheerleading outfit. She held her pom-poms out from her sides. A smile was on her face. The girl looked just like Jeb. 'She was very pretty,' Sara said, handing him back the photograph. 'How old was she?'

'She had just turned thirteen,' he answered, looking at the picture for a few beats. He slipped it into its plastic sleeve, then tucked the wallet in his back pocket. 'She was a surprise baby for my parents. I was fifteen when she was born. My father had just gotten his first church.'

'He was a minister?' Sara asked, wondering how she could have dated Jeb before and not known this. She could have sworn he had once told her that his father was an electrician.

'He was a Baptist preacher,' Jeb clarified. 'He was a firm believer in the power of the Lord to heal what ails you. I'm glad he had his faith to get him through, but . . .' Jeb shrugged. 'Some things you just can't let go of. Some things you can't forget.'

'I'm sorry for your loss,' Sara answered, knowing what he meant about not being able to let go. She looked down at her sandwich, thinking it was probably not appropriate to take a bite at this moment. Her stomach growled to spur her on, but she ignored it.

'It was a long time ago,' Jeb finally answered. 'I was

just thinking about her today, with all that's been going on.'

Sara did not know what to say. She was tired of death. She did not want to comfort him. This date had been made to take her mind off what had been happening lately, not remind her of it.

She stood from the table, offering, 'Did you want something else to drink?' Sara walked over to the refrigerator as she talked. 'I've got Cokes, some Kool-Aid, orange juice.' She opened the door and the sucking sound reminded her of something. She just could not put her finger on it. Suddenly it hit her. Rubber stripping on the doors to the ER at Grady had made the exact same sucking noise when they opened. She had never made the connection before, but there it was.

Jeb said, 'Coke's fine.'

Sara reached into the fridge, shuffling around for the sodas. She stopped, her hand resting on the trademark red can. She felt a lightheadedness, as if she had too much air in her lungs. She closed her eyes, trying to keep her sense of balance. Sara was back in the ER. The doors opened with that sucking sound. A young girl was wheeled in on a gurney. Stats were called out by the EMT, IVs were started, the girl was intubated. She was in shock, her pupils blown, her body warm to the touch. Her temperature was called out, one hundred three. Her blood pressure was through the roof. She was bleeding profusely from between her legs.

Sara ran the case, trying to stop the bleeding. The girl started to convulse, jerking out the IVs, kicking over the supply tray at her feet. Sara leaned over her, trying to stop the girl from doing any further damage. The seizing stopped abruptly, and Sara thought she might have died. Her pulse was strong. Her reflexes were weak but registering.

A pelvic examination revealed the girl had recently had an abortion, though not one that had been given by a qualified physician. Her uterus was a mess, the walls of her vagina scraped and shredded. Sara repaired what she could, but the damage was done. Whatever healing she would do was left up to the girl.

Sara went to her car to change her shirt before talking to the girl's parents. She found them in the waiting area and told them the prognosis. She used the right phrases, like 'guarded optimism' and 'critical, but stable.' Only the girl did not make it through the next three hours. She had another seizure, effectively frying her brain.

At that point in her career, the thirteen-year-old girl was the youngest patient Sara had ever lost. The other patients who had died under Sara's care had been older, or sicker, and it was sad to lose them, but their deaths had not been so unexpected. Sara was shocked by the tragedy as she made her way toward the waiting area. The girl's parents seemed just as shocked. They had no idea their daughter had been pregnant. To their knowledge, she had never had a boyfriend. They couldn't understand how their daughter could be pregnant, let alone dead.

'My baby,' the father whispered. He repeated the phrase over and over, his voice quiet with grief. 'She was my baby.'

'You must be wrong,' the mother said. Rummaging around in her purse, she pulled out a wallet. Before Sara could stop her, a photograph was found, a school picture of the young girl in a cheerleading uniform. Sara did not want to look at the picture, but there was no consoling the woman until she did. Sara glanced down quickly, then looked a second, more careful time. The photograph showed a young girl in a cheerleading outfit. She held her pom-poms out from her sides. A smile was on her face. The expression was a sharp contrast to the one on the lifeless girl lying on the gurney, waiting to be moved to the morgue.

The father had reached out, taking Sara's hands. He bent his head down and mumbled a prayer that seemed to last a long time, asking for forgiveness, restating his belief in God. Sara was by no means a religious person, but there was something about his prayer that moved her. To be able to find such comfort in the face of such a horrible loss was amazing to her.

After the prayer, Sara had gone to her car to collect her thoughts, to maybe take a drive around the block and work her mind around this tragic, unnecessary death. That was when she had found the damage done to her car. That was when she had gone back into the bathroom. That was when Jack Allen Wright had raped her.

The picture Jeb had just shown her was the same picture she had seen twelve years ago in the waiting room.

'Sara?'

The song changed on the stereo. Sara felt her stomach drop as the words 'Hey, hey, Julia' came from the speakers.

'Something wrong?' Jeb asked, then quoted the words from the song. ' "You're acting so peculiar." '

Sara stood, holding up a can as she closed the refrigerator. 'This is the last Coke,' she said, edging toward the garage door. 'I've got some outside.'

'That's okay.' He shrugged. 'I'm fine with just water.' He had put his sandwich down and was staring at her.

Sara popped the top on the Coke. Her hands were shaking slightly, but she didn't think Jeb noticed. She brought the can to her mouth, sipping enough to let some of the Coke spill onto her sweater.

'Oh,' she said, trying to act surprised. 'Let me go change. I'll be right back.'

Sara returned the smile he gave her, her lips trembling as she did so. She forced herself to move, walking down the hall slowly so as not to raise the alarm. Inside her room, she snatched up the phone, glancing out the bank of windows, surprised to see the bright sunlight pouring in. It was so incongruous with the terror she felt. Sara dialed Jeffrey's number, but there were no corresponding beeps when she pressed the buttons. She stared at the phone, willing it to work.

'You took it off the hook,' Jeb said. 'Remember?'

Sara jumped up from her bed. 'I was just calling my dad. He's coming by in a few minutes.'

Jeb stood in the doorway, leaning against the jamb. 'I thought you said you were going by their house later.'

'That's right,' Sara answered, backing toward the other side of the room. This put the bed between them, but Sara was trapped, her back to the window. 'He's coming to get me.'

'You think so?' Jeb asked. He was smiling the same way he always did, a lopsided half grin that you would find on a child. There was something so casual about him, something so nonthreatening, that Sara wondered for half a second if she had drawn the wrong conclusion. A glance down at his hand snapped her out of it. He was holding a long boning knife at his side.

'What gave it away?' he asked. 'The vinegar, wasn't it? I had a bear of a time getting it in through the cork. Thank God for cardiac syringes.'

Sara put her hand behind her, feeling the cold glass of the window under her palm. 'You left them for me,' she said, going through the last few days in her mind. Jeb had known about her lunch with Tessa. Jeb had known she was at the hospital the night Jeffrey was shot.

'That's why Sibyl was in the bathroom. That's why Julia was on my car. You wanted me to save them.'

He smiled, nodding slowly. There was a sadness around his eyes, as if he regretted that the game was over. 'I wanted to give you that opportunity.'

'Is that why you showed me her picture?' she asked. 'To see if I would remember her?'

'I'm surprised you did.'

'Why?' Sara asked. 'Do you think I could forget something like that? She was a baby.'

He shrugged.

'Did you do that to her?' Sara asked, recalling the brutality of the home abortion. Derrick Lange, her supervisor, had guessed a clothes hanger had been used.

She said, 'Were you the one who did it?'

'How did you know?' Jeb asked, a defensive edge to his tone. 'Did she tell you?'

There was something more to what he was saying, a more sinister secret behind his words. When Sara spoke, she knew the answer before she even finished her sentence. Taking into account what she had seen Jeb was capable of, it made perfect sense.

She asked, 'You raped your sister, didn't you?'

'I loved my sister,' he countered, the defensive tone still there.

'She was just a child.'

'She came to me,' he said, as if this was some kind of excuse. 'She wanted to be with me.'

'She was thirteen years old.'

' "If a man shall take his sister, his father's daughter, and see her nakedness and she see his nakedness, it is a wicked thing." ' His smile seemed to say he was pleased with himself. 'Just call me wicked.'

'She was your sister.'

'We are all God's children, are we not? We share the same parents.'

'Can you quote a verse to justify rape? Can you quote a verse to justify murder?'

'The good thing about the Bible, Sara, is that it's open to interpretation. God gives us signs, opportunities, and we either follow them or we don't. We can choose what happens to us that way. We don't like to think about it, but we are the captains of our own destinies. We make the decisions that direct the course of our lives.' He stared at her, not speaking for a few beats. 'I would have thought you learned that lesson twelve years ago.'

Sara felt the earth shift under her feet as a thought came to her. 'Was it you? In the bathroom?'

'Lord, no,' Jeb said, waving this off. 'That was Jack Wright. He beat me to it, I guess. Gave me a good idea, though.' Jeb leaned against the door jamb, the same pleased smile twisting his lips. 'We're both men of faith, you see. We both let the Spirit guide us.'

'The only thing you both are is animals.'

'I guess I owe him for bringing us together,' Jeb said. 'What he did for you has served as an example for me, Sara. I want to thank you for that. On behalf of the many women who have come since then, and I do mean come in the biblical sense, I offer a sincere thank-you.'

'Oh, God,' Sara breathed, putting her hand to her mouth. She had seen what he had done to his sister, to Sibyl Adams, and to Julia Matthews. To think that this had all started when Jack Wright had attacked her made Sara's stomach turn. 'You monster,' she hissed. 'You murderer.'

He straightened, his expression suddenly changed by rage. Jeb went from being a quiet, unassuming pharmacist to the man who had raped and killed at least two

370

women. Anger radiated from his posture. 'You let her die. You killed her.'

'She was dead before she got to me,' Sara countered, trying to keep her voice steady. 'She lost too much blood.'

'That's not true.'

'You didn't get it all out,' she said. 'She was rotting from the inside.'

'You're lying.'

Sara shook her head. She moved her hand behind her, looking for the lock on the window. 'You killed her.'

'That's not true,' he repeated, though she could tell from the change in his voice that part of him believed her.

Sara found the lock, tried to twist it open. It wouldn't budge. 'Sibyl died because of you, too.'

'She was fine when I left her.'

'She had a heart attack,' Sara told him, pressing against the lock. 'She died from an overdose. She had a seizure, just like your sister.'

His voice was frighteningly loud in the bedroom, and the glass behind Sara shook when he yelled, 'That is not true.'

Sara gave up on the lock as he took a step toward her. He still held the knife down at his side, but the threat was there. 'I wonder if your cunt's still as sweet as it was for Jack,' he mumbled. 'I remember sitting through your trial, listening to the details. I wanted to take notes, but I found after the first day that I didn't need to.' He reached into his back pocket, taking out a pair of handcuffs. 'You still got that key I left for you?'

She stopped him with her words. 'I won't go through this again,' she said with conviction. 'You'll have to kill me first.'

He looked down at the floor, his shoulders relaxed.

She felt a brief moment of relief until he looked back up at her. There was a smile at his lips when he said, 'What makes you think it matters to me if you're dead or not?'

'You gonna cut a hole in my belly?'

He was so shocked that he dropped the handcuffs on the floor. 'What?' he whispered.

'You didn't sodomize her.'

She could see a bead of sweat roll down the side of his head as he asked, 'Who?'

'Sibyl,' Sara provided. 'How else could shit get inside her vagina?'

'That's disgusting.'

'Is it?' Sara asked. 'Did you bite her while you fucked the hole in her belly?'

He shook his head vehemently side to side. 'I didn't do that.'

'Your teeth marks are on her shoulder, Jeb.'

'They are not.'

'I saw them,' Sara countered. 'I saw everything you did to them. I saw how you hurt all of them.'

'They weren't hurting,' he insisted. 'They didn't hurt at all.'

Sara walked toward him until she was standing with her knees against the bed. He stood on the other side, watching her, a stricken look on his face. 'They suffered, Jeb. Both of them suffered, just like your sister. Just like Sally.'

'I never hurt them like that,' he whispered. 'I never hurt them. You're the one who let them die.'

'You raped a thirteen-year-old child, a blind woman, and an emotionally unstable twenty-two-year-old. Is that what gets you off, Jeb? Attacking helpless women? Controlling them?'

His jaw clenched. 'You're just going to make it harder for yourself.'

'Fuck you, you sick bastard.'

'No,' he said. 'It'll be the other way around.'

'Come on,' Sara taunted, clenching her fists. 'I dare you to try.'

Jeb lunged toward her, but Sara was already moving. She ran full force toward the picture window, tucking her head as she broke out the glass. Pain flooded her senses, shards of glass cutting into her body. She landed in the backyard, tucking as she rolled a few feet down the hill.

Sara stood quickly, not looking over her shoulder as she ran toward the lake. Her arm was cut across the bicep and a gash was in her forehead, but these were the least of her concerns. By the time she got to the dock, Jeb was close behind her. She dove into the cold water without thinking, swimming under the water until she could no longer breathe. Finally, she surfaced ten yards from the dock. Sara saw Jeb jump into her boat, too late remembering she had left the key in the ignition.

Sara dove under the water, pushing herself, swimming as far as she could before surfacing. When she looked back around, she could see the boat coming toward her. She dove down, touching the bottom of the lake as the boat sped over her. Sara turned underwater, heading toward the rock field lining the far side of the lake. The area was no more than twenty feet away, but Sara felt her arms tiring as she swam. The coldness of the water hit her like a slap in the face, and she realized that the low temperature would slow her down.

She surfaced, looking around for the boat. Again, Jeb came at her full throttle. Again, she ducked under the water. She came up just in time to see the boat skimming toward the submerged rocks. The nose of the boat hit the first one head-on, popping up, flipping the boat over. Sara watched as Jeb was thrown from the boat. He flew through the air, splashing into the water. His hands clawed helplessly as he tried to keep himself from drowning. Mouth open, eyes wide with terror, he flailed as he was pulled down below the surface. She waited, holding her breath, but he did not come back up.

Jeb had been thrown about ten feet from the boat, away from the rock field. Sara knew the only way she would make it to the shore was to swim through the rocks. She could tread water for only so long before the cold enveloped her. The distance to the dock was too great. She would never make it. The safest route to the shore would take Sara past the overturned boat.

What she really wanted to do was stay where she was, but Sara knew the cold water was luring her into a sense of complacency. The lake's temperature wasn't down to freezing, but it was cold enough to bring on moderate hypothermia if she stayed in too long.

She swam a slow crawl to conserve body heat, her head just above the water as she made her way through the field. Her breath was a cloud in front of her, but she tried to think of something warm; sitting in front of a fire, roasting marshmallows. The hot tub at the YMCA. The steam room. The warm quilt on her bed.

Altering her course, she went around the far side of the boat, away from where Jeb had gone down. She had seen too many movies. She was terrified he would come from the deep, grabbing her leg, pulling her down. As she passed the boat, she could see a large hole in the front where the rock had torn through the bow. It was overturned, the belly up to the sky. Jeb was on the other side, holding on to the torn bow. His lips were dark blue, a stark contrast against his white face. He was shivering uncontrollably, his breath coming out in sharp puffs of white. He had been struggling, wasting his energy trying to keep his head above water. The cold was probably lowering his core temperature with every passing minute.

Sara kept swimming, moving more slowly. Jeb's breathing and her hands pushing through the water were the only sounds on the still lake.

'I c-c-can't swim,' he said.

'That's too bad,' Sara answered, her voice tight in her throat. She felt as if she was circling a wounded but dangerous animal.

'You can't leave me here,' he managed around chattering teeth.

She started to sidestroke, turning in the water so as not to put her back to him. 'Yes, I can.'

'You're a doctor.'

'Yes, I am,' she said, continuing to move away from him.

'You'll never find Lena.'

Sara felt a weight drop onto her. She treaded water, keeping her eyes on Jeb. 'What about Lena?'

'I tot-took her,' he said. 'She's somewhere safe.'

'I don't believe you.'

He gave what she assumed was a shrug.

'Where's somewhere safe?' Sara demanded. 'What did you do to her?'

'I left her for you, Sara,' he said, his voice catching as his body started shaking. From the recesses of her mind, Sara recalled that the second stage of hypothermia was marked by uncontrollable shaking and irrational thought.

He said, 'I left her somewhere.'

Sara moved slightly closer, not trusting him. 'Where did you leave her?'

'You non-need to save her,' he mumbled, closing his eyes. His face dipped down, his mouth dropping below the waterline. He snorted as water went up his nose, his grip on the boat tightening. There was a cracking sound as the boat moved against the rock.

Sara felt a sudden rush of heat through her body. 'Where is she, Jeb?' When he didn't answer, she told him, 'You can die out here. The water's cold enough. Your heart will slow down until it stops. I'd give you twenty minutes, tops,' she said, knowing it would be more like a few hours. 'I'll let you die,' Sara warned, never more certain of anything in her life. 'Tell me where she is.'

'I'll tell you on th-th-the shore,' he mumbled.

'Tell me now,' she said. 'I know you wouldn't leave her somewhere to die alone.'

'I wouldn't,' he said, a spark of understanding in his eyes. 'I wouldn't leave her alone, Sara. I wouldn't let her die alone.'

Sara moved her arms out to her side, trying to keep her body moving so that she would not freeze. 'Where is she, Jeb?'

He shook so hard the boat shuddered in the water, sending small wakes toward Sara. He whispered, 'You need to save her, Sara. You need to save her.'

'Tell me or I'll let you die, Jeb, I swear to God, I'll let you drown out here.'

His eyes seemed to cloud and a slight smile came to his blue lips. He whispered, '"It is finished,"' as his head dropped again, but this time he didn't stop it. Sara watched as he let go of the boat, his head slipping under water.

'No,' Sara screamed, lunging toward him. She grabbed the back of his shirt, trying to pull him up. Instinctively, he started to fight her, pulling her down instead of letting her pull him up. They struggled this way, Jeb grabbing her pants, her sweater, trying to use her as a ladder to climb back up for air. His fingernails raked across the cut in her arm, and Sara reflexively pulled away. Jeb was pushed back from her, the tips of his fingers brushing across the front of her sweater as he tried to find purchase.

Sara was pulled down as he climbed up. There was a solid thud as his head slammed against the boat. His mouth opened in surprise, then he slipped soundlessly back under the water. Behind him, a streak of bright red blood marked the bow of the boat. Sara tried to ignore the pressure in her lungs as she reached toward him, trying to pull him back up. There was just enough sunlight for her to see him sinking to the bottom. His mouth was open, his hands stretched out to her.

She surfaced, gasping for air, then ducked her head back underwater. She did this several times, searching for Jeb. When she finally found him, he was resting against a large boulder, his arms held out in front of him, eyes open as he stared at her. Sara put her hand to his wrist, checking to see if he was alive. She went up for air, treading water, her arms out to the side. Her teeth were chattering, but she counted out loud.

'One-one thousand,' she said through clicking teeth. 'Two-one thousand.' Sara continued counting, furiously treading water. She was reminded of old games of Marco Polo, where either she or Tessa would tread water, their eyes closed, as they counted out the requisite number before searching each other out.

At fifty, she took a deep breath, then dove back down. Jeb was still there, his head back. She closed his eyes, then scooped him up under his arms. On the surface, she crooked her arm around his neck, using her other arm to swim. Holding him this way, she started toward the shore.

After what seemed like hours but was only a minute

at most, Sara stopped, treading water so that she could catch her breath. The shore seemed farther away than it had before. Her legs felt disconnected from her body, even as she willed them to tread water. Jeb was literally deadweight, pulling her down. Her head dipped just below the surface, but she stopped herself, coughing out the lake, trying to clear her mind. It was so cold, and she felt so sleepy. She blinked her eyes, trying not to keep them closed too long. A small period of rest would be good. She would rest here, then drag him back to the shore.

Sara leaned her head back, trying to float on her back. Jeb made this impossible, and again she started to dip below the water. She would have to let Jeb go. Sara realized that. She just could not force herself to do it. Even as the weight of his body started to pull her down again, Sara could not let go.

A hand grabbed her, then an arm was around her waist. Sara was too weak to struggle, her brain too frozen to make sense of what was happening. For a split second she thought it was Jeb, but the force pulling her up to the surface was too strong. Her grip around Jeb loosened, and she opened her eyes, watching his body float back down to the bottom of the lake.

Her head broke the surface and her mouth opened wide as she gasped for air. Her lungs ached with each breath, her nose ran. Sara started to cough the kind of wracking coughs that could stop the heart. Water came out of her mouth, then bile, as she choked on the fresh air. She felt someone beating on her back, knocking the water out of her. Her head tilted down into the water again, but she was jerked back by her hair.

'Sara,' Jeffrey said, one hand around her jaw, the other holding her up by the arm. 'Look at me,' he demanded. 'Sara.'

Her body went limp, and she was conscious of the fact that Jeffrey was pulling her back toward the shore. His arm was hooked across her body, under her arms, as he did an awkward one-handed backstroke.

Sara put her hands over Jeffrey's arm, leaned her head against his chest, and let him take her home.

TWENTY-NINE

Lena wanted Jeb. She wanted him to take the pain away from her. She wanted him to send her back to that place where Sibyl and their mother and father were. She wanted to be with her family. She did not care what price she had to pay; she wanted to be with them.

Blood trickled down the back of her throat in a steady stream, causing her to cough occasionally. He had been right about the throbbing pain in her mouth, but the Percodan made it bearable. She trusted Jeb that the bleeding would stop soon. She knew he was not finished with her yet. He would not let her choke to death on her own blood after all the trouble he had gone through to keep her here. Lena knew he had something more spectacular in mind for her.

When her mind wandered, she imagined herself being left in front of Nan Thomas's house. For some reason, this pleased her. Hank would see what had been done to Lena. He would know what had been done to Sibyl. He would see what Sibyl had not been able to see. It seemed fitting.

A familiar noise came from downstairs, footsteps across the hard wooden floor. The steps were muffled as he walked across the carpet. Lena assumed this was in the living room. She did not know the layout of the house, but by listening to the distinct noises, making the connection between the hollow taps of his shoes on the floor as he walked around the house and the dull thud as he took off his shoes to come see her, she could generally tell where he was.

Only, this time there seemed to be a second set of footsteps.

'Lena?' She could barely make out his voice, but she knew instinctively that it was Jeffrey Tolliver. For just a second, she wondered what he was doing there.

Her mouth opened, but she did not say anything. She was upstairs in the attic. Maybe he would not think to look here. Maybe he would leave her alone. She could die here and no one would ever know what had been done to her.

'Lena?' another voice called. It was Sara Linton.

Her mouth was still open, but she could not speak.

For what seemed like hours, they walked around downstairs. She heard the heavy scrapes and bangs as furniture was moved around, closets searched. The muffled sounds of their voices sounded like a disjointed harmony to her ears. She actually smiled, thinking they sounded like they were banging pots and pans together. It wasn't like Jeb could have hid her in the kitchen.

This thought struck her as funny. She started to laugh, an uncontrollable reaction that shook her chest, making her cough. Soon, she was laughing so hard that tears came to her eyes. Then, she was sobbing, her chest tightening with pain as her mind let her see everything that had happened to her in the last week. She saw Sibyl on the slab in the morgue. She saw Hank mourning the loss of his niece. She saw Nan Thomas, eyes red-rimmed and stricken. She saw Jeb on top of her, making love to her.

Her fingers curled in around the long nails securing her to the floor, her entire body seizing up at the knowledge of the physical assaults against her.

'Lena?' Jeffrey called, his voice stronger than it had been before. 'Lena?'

She heard him moving closer, heard knocking in quick staccato, then a pause, then more knocking.

Sara said, 'It's a false panel.'

More knocking came, then the sound of their footsteps on the attic stairs. The door burst open, light cutting through the darkness. Lena squeezed her eyes shut, feeling like needles were pressing into her eyeballs.

'Oh my God,' Sara gasped. Then, 'Get some towels. Sheets. Anything.'

Lena slit her eyes open as Sara knelt in front of her. There was a coldness coming off Sara's body, and she was wet.

'It's okay,' Sara whispered, her hand on Lena's forehead. 'You're going to be okay.'

Lena opened her eyes more, letting her pupils adjust to the light. She looked back at the door, searching for Jeb.

'He's dead,' Sara said. 'He can't hurt you –' She stopped, but Lena knew what she was going to say. She heard the last word to Sara's sentence in her mind if not her ears. He can't hurt you anymore, she had started to say.

Lena allowed herself to look up at Sara. Something flashed in Sara's eyes, and Lena knew that Sara somehow understood. Jeb was part of Lena now. He would be hurting her every day for the rest of her life.

SUNDAY

THIRTY

Jeffrey drove back from the hospital in Augusta feeling like a soldier returning from war. Lena would physically recover from her wounds, but he had no idea if she would ever recover from the emotional damage Jeb McGuire had wrought. Like Julia Matthews, Lena was not talking to anybody, not even her uncle Hank. Jeffrey did not know what to do for her, other than give her time.

Mary Ann Moon had called him exactly an hour and twenty minutes after they had talked. Sara's patient's name had been Sally Lee McGuire. Moon had taken the time to key the surname into a general search of the hospital staff. With a specific name, it only took a few seconds for Jeremy 'Jeb' McGuire's name to come up. He was doing his internship at the pharmacy on Grady's third floor when Sara worked there. Sara would have no cause to meet him, but Jeb could have certainly made it a point to meet her.

Jeffrey would never forget the look on Lena's face when he busted down the attic door. In his mind, he recalled the photographs of Sara whenever he thought of Lena lying there, nailed to Jeb's attic floor. The room had been designed to be a dark box. Dull black paint covered everything, including the panels of plywood nailed over the windows. Chains through eye hooks had been screwed to the floor, and two sets of nail holes at both the top and bottom of the restraints showed where the victims had been crucified.

In the car, Jeffrey rubbed his eyes, trying not to think about everything he had seen since Sibyl Adams had been murdered. As he crossed the Grant County line, all he could think was that everything was different now. He would never look at the people in town, the people who were his friends and neighbors, with the same trusting eyes as he had this time last Sunday. He felt shell-shocked.

Turning into Sara's driveway, Jeffrey was aware that her house, too, looked different to him. This was where Sara had fought Jeb. This was where Jeb had drowned. They had pulled his body out of the lake, but the memory of him would never be gone.

Jeffrey sat in his car, staring at the house. Sara had told him she needed time, but he wasn't about to give it to her. He needed to explain what had been going through his mind. He needed to reassure himself as well as her that there was no way in hell he was going to stay out of her life.

The front door was open, but Jeffrey gave a knock before walking in. He could hear Paul Simon singing 'Have a Good Time' on the stereo. The house was turned upside down. Boxes lined the hallway and books were off the shelves. He found Sara in the kitchen, holding a wrench. Dressed in a white sleeveless T-shirt and a pair of ratty grey sweatpants, he thought that she had never looked more beautiful in her life. She was looking down the drain when he knocked on the door jamb.

She turned, obviously not surprised to see him. 'Is this your idea of giving me some time?' she asked.

He shrugged, tucking his hands into his pockets. She had a bright green Band-Aid covering the cut on her forehead and a white bandage around her arm where the glass had gone deep enough for sutures. How she had managed to survive what she did was a miracle to Jeffrey. Her strength of spirit amazed him.

The next song came on the stereo, 'Fifty Ways to Leave Your Lover.' Jeffrey tried to joke with her, saying, 'It's our song.'

Sara gave him a wary look before fumbling for the remote. Abruptly, the music stopped, the silence replacing the song filling the house. They both seemed to take a few seconds to adjust to the change.

She said, 'What're you doing here?'

Jeffrey opened his mouth, thinking that he should say something romantic, something to sweep her off her feet. He wanted to tell her that she was the most beautiful woman he had ever known, that he had never really known what it meant to be in love until he had met her. None of these things came, though, so he offered her information instead.

'I found the transcripts from your trial, Wright's trial, in Jeb's house.'

She crossed her arms. 'That so?'

'He had newspaper clippings, photographs. That kind of thing.' He stopped, then, 'I guess Jeb moved here to be close to you.'

She gave a condescending, 'You think?'

He ignored the warning behind her tone. 'There are some other attacks over in Pike County,' Jeffrey continued. He couldn't stop himself, even though he could tell from her expression that he should just shut the hell up, that she did not want to know these things. The problem was that it was much easier to tell Sara the facts than for Jeffrey to come up with something on his own.

He continued. 'The sheriff over there has four cases

he's trying to tie to Jeb. We'll need to get some samples for the lab so he can do a crosscheck with the DNA samples they took at the scene. Plus what we have from Julia Matthews.' He cleared his throat. 'His body's over at the morgue.'

'I'm not doing it,' Sara answered.

'We can get somebody from Augusta.'

'No,' Sara corrected. 'You don't understand. I'm going to hand in my resignation tomorrow.'

He could not think of anything to say but 'Why?'

'Because I can't do this anymore,' she said, indicating the space between them. 'I can't keep this up, Jeffrey. This is why we divorced.'

'We divorced because I made a stupid mistake.'

'No,' she said, stopping him. 'We're not going to have this same argument over and over again. This is why I'm resigning. I can't keep putting myself through this. I can't let you hang around the periphery of my life. I have to get on with it.'

'I love you,' he said, as if that made any difference. 'I know I'm not good enough for you. I know I can't begin to understand you and I do the wrong things and I say the wrong things and I should've been here with you instead of going to Atlanta after you told me about – after I read about – what happened.' He paused, then, 'I know all that. And I still can't stop loving you.' She did not answer, so he said, 'Sara, I can't not be with you. I need you.'

'Which me do you need?' she asked. 'The one from before or the one who was raped?'

'They're both the same person,' he countered. 'I need them both. I love them both.' He stared at her, trying to find the right thing to say. 'I don't want to be without you.'

'You don't have a choice.'

'Yes, I do,' he answered. 'I don't care what you say, Sara. I don't care if you resign or you move out of town or you change your name, I'm still going to find you.'

'Like Jeb?'

Her words cut deep. Of all the things she could have said, this was the cruelest. She seemed to realize this, because she apologized quickly. 'That wasn't fair,' she said. 'I'm sorry.'

'Is that what you think? That I'm like him?'

'No.' She shook her head side to side. 'I know you're not like him.'

He looked at the floor, still feeling wounded by her words. She could have screamed that she hated him and caused less pain.

'Jeff,' she said, walking toward him. She put her hand to his cheek and he took it, kissing the palm.

He said, 'I don't want to lose you, Sara.'

'You already have.'

'No,' he said, not accepting this. 'I haven't. I know I haven't because you wouldn't be standing here right now. You would be back over there, telling me to leave.'

Sara did not contradict him, but she walked away, back toward the sink. 'I've got work to do,' she mumbled, picking up the wrench.

'Are you moving?'

'Cleaning,' she said. 'I started last night. I don't know where anything is. I had to sleep on the sofa because so much shit's on my bed.'

He tried to lighten things up. 'At the very least, you'll make your mama happy.'

She gave a humorless laugh, kneeling down in front of the sink. She covered the drain pipe with a towel, then locked the wrench over it. Putting her shoulder into it, she pushed the wrench. Jeffrey could tell it wouldn't budge.

'Let me help,' he offered, taking off his coat. Before she could stop him, he was kneeling beside her, pushing the wrench. The pipe was old, and the fitting would not budge. He gave up, saying, 'You'll probably have to cut it off.'

'No I won't,' she countered, gently pushing him out of the way. She braced her foot on the cabinet behind her and pushed with all of her might. The wrench turned slowly, Sara moving forward with it.

She flashed a smile of accomplishment. 'See?'

'You're amazing,' Jeffrey said, meaning it. He sat back on his heels, watching her take the pipe apart. 'Is there anything you can't do?'

'A long list of things,' she mumbled.

He ignored this, asking, 'Was it clogged?'

'I dropped something down it,' she answered, digging around the P trap with her finger. She pulled something out, cupping it in her palm before he could see it.

'What?' he asked, reaching toward her hand.

She shook her head, keeping her hand fisted.

He smiled, more curious than ever. 'What is it?' he repeated.

She sat up on her knees, holding her hands behind her back. Her brow furrowed in concentration for a moment, then she held her hands in front of her, fisted.

She said, 'Pick one.'

He did as he was told, tapping her right hand.

She said, 'Pick another one.'

He laughed, tapping her left hand.

Sara rolled her wrist, opening her fingers. A small gold band was in the palm of her hand. The last time he had seen the ring, Sara had been tugging it off her finger so she could throw it in his face.

Jeffrey was so surprised to see the ring he did not know what to say. 'You told me you threw that away.'

'I'm a better liar than you think.'

He gave her a knowing look, taking the wedding band from her. 'What are you still doing with it?'

'It's like a bad penny,' she said. 'Keeps turning up.'

He took this as an invitation, asking, 'What are you doing tomorrow night?'

She sat back on her heels, sighing. 'I don't know. Probably catching up at work.'

'Then what?'

'Home, I guess. Why?'

He slipped the ring in his pocket. 'I could bring dinner by.'

She shook her head. 'Jeffrey –'

'The Tasty Pig,' he tempted, knowing this was one of Sara's favorite places to eat. He took her hands in his, offering, 'Brunswick stew, barbecued ribs, pork sandwiches, beer baked beans.'

She stared at him, not answering. Finally she said, 'You know this won't work.'

'What have we got to lose?'

She seemed to think this over. He waited, trying to be patient. Sara let go of his hands, then used his shoulder to help her stand.

Jeffrey stood as well, watching her sort through one of many junk drawers. He opened his mouth to speak to her but knew there was nothing he could say. The one thing he knew about Sara Linton was that when she had made up her mind, there was no going back.

He stood behind her, kissing her bare shoulder. There should be a better way to say good-bye, but he could not think of one. Jeffrey had never been good at words. He was better at action. Most of the time, anyway.

He was walking down the hall when Sara called to him.

'Bring silverware,' she said.

He turned around, sure he had not heard right.

Her head was still bent down as she rummaged through the drawer. 'Tomorrow night,' she clarified. 'I can't remember where I put the forks.'

ACKNOWLEDGMENTS

Victoria Sanders, my agent, served as my anchor throughout this entire process. I do not know how I could have done any of this without her. My editor, Meaghan Dowling, was instrumental in helping me define this book and has my heartfelt gratitude for making me rise to the challenge. Captain Jo Ann Cain, chief of detectives for the city of Forest Park, Georgia, kindly shared her war stories. The Mitchell Cary family answered all of my plumbing questions and gave me some interesting ideas. Michael A. Rolnick, M.D., and Carol Barbier Rolnick lent Sara some credibility. Tamara Kennedy gave great advice early on. Any mistakes made in the above areas of expertise are entirely my own.

Fellow authors Ellen Conford, Jane Haddam, Eileen Moushey, and Katy Munger have my thanks; they each know why. Steve Hogan waded through my neuroses on a daily basis, and for that he should get some kind of medal. Readers Chris Cash, Cecile Dozier, Melanie Hammet, Judy Jordan, and Leigh Vanderels were invaluable. Greg Pappas, patron saint of signage, made things very easy. B.A. offered good advice and a quiet place to write. S.S. was my rock in a hard place. Lastly, thanks to D.A. – you are more myself than I am.

ALSO AVAILABLE IN ARROW

Kisscut

Karin Slaughter

When a teenage quarrel in the small town of Heartsdale explodes into a deadly shoot-out, Sara Linton – paediatrician and medical examiner – finds herself entangled in a horrific tragedy. And what seems at first to be a terrible but individual catastrophe proves to have wider implications when the autopsy reveals evidence of long-term abuse and ritualistic self-mutilation.

Sara and police chief Jeffrey Tolliver start to investigate, but the children surrounding the victim close ranks. The families turn their backs. Then a young girl is abducted, and it becomes clear that the first death is linked to an even more brutal crime. And unless Sara and Jeffrey can uncover the deadly secrets the children hide, it's going to happen again . . .

Praise for Karin Slaughter

'A complex and confident thriller in which character goes deep'
Daily Mirror

'With *Blindsighted*, Karin Slaughter left a great many thriller writers looking anxiously over their shoulders. With *Kisscut*, she leaves most of them behind'
John Connolly

'A fast-paced and unsettling story . . . A compelling and fluid read'
Daily Telegraph

a r r o w b o o k s

A Faint Cold Fear

Karin Slaughter

Sara Linton, medical examiner in the small town of Heartsdale, is called out to an apparent suicide on the local college campus. The mutilated body provides little in the way of clues – and the college authorities are keen to avoid a scandal – but for Sara and police chief Jeffrey Tolliver, things don't add up.

Two more suspicious suicides follow, and a young woman is brutally attacked. For Sara, the violence strikes far too close to home. And as Jeffrey pursues the sadistic killer, he discovers that ex-police detective Lena Adams, now a security guard on campus, may be in possession of crucial information. But, bruised and angered by her expulsion from the force, Lena seems to be barely capable of protecting herself, let alone saving the next victim . . .

Praise for Karin Slaughter

'A good read that should come with a psychological health warning' *Guardian*

'She's excellent at portraying the undertones and claustrophobia of communities where everyone knows everyone else's business, and even better at creating an atmosphere of lurking evil' *The Times*

arrow books

Indelible

Karin Slaughter

When medical examiner Sara Linton and police chief Jeffrey Tolliver take a trip away from the small town of Heartsdale, it should be a straightforward weekend at the beach. But they decide to take a detour via Jeffrey's hometown and things go violently wrong when Jeffrey's best friend Robert shoots dead an intruder who breaks into his home. Jeffrey and Sara are first on the scene and Jeffrey's keen to clear his friend's name, but for Sara things aren't so simple. And when Jeffrey appears to change the crime scene, Sara no longer knows who to trust.

Twelve years later, Sara and Jeffrey are caught up in a shockingly brutal attack which threatens to destroy both their lives. But they're not random victims. They've been targeted. And it seems the past is catching up with both of them . . .

Praise for Karin Slaughter

'*Indelible* is a salutary reminder that Slaughter is one of the most riveting writers in the field today'
Sunday Express

'A great read . . . crime fiction at its finest'
Michael Connelly

'Brilliantly chilling'
heat

arrow books

Faithless

Karin Slaughter

There are many ways to die. But some are more terrifying than others . . .

A walk in the woods takes a sinister turn for police chief Jeffrey Tolliver and medical examiner Sara Linton when they stumble across the body of a young girl. Incarcerated in the ground, all the initial evidence indicates that she has, quite literally, been scared to death.

But as Sara embarks on the autopsy, something even more horrifying comes to light. Something which shocks even Sara. Detective Lena Adams, talented but increasingly troubled, is called in from vacation to help with the investigation – and the trail soon leads to a neighbouring county, an isolated community and a terrible secret . . .

'Brutal and chilling' *Daily Mirror*

'*Faithless* confirms her at the summit of the school of writers specialising in forensic medicine and terror' *The Times*

arrow books

Triptych

Karin Slaughter

Three people with something to hide. One killer with nothing to lose.

When Atlanta police detective Michael Ormewood is called out to a murder scene at the notorious Grady Homes, he finds himself faced with one of the most brutal killings of his career: Aleesha Monroe is found in the stairwell in a pool of her own blood, her body horribly mutilated.

As a one-off killing it's shocking, but when it becomes clear that it's just the latest in a series of similar attacks, the Georgia Bureau of Investigation are called in, and Michael is forced into working with Special Agent Will Trent of the Criminal Apprehension Team – a man he instinctively dislikes.

Twenty-four hours later, the violence Michael sees around him every day explodes in his own back yard. And it seems the mystery behind Monroe's death is inextricably entangled with a past that refuses to stay buried . . .

'This is without doubt an accomplished, compelling and complex tale, with page-turning power aplenty' *Daily Express*

'Criminally spectacular' *OK!*

arrow books

Skin Privilege

Karin Slaughter

It's no simple case of murder.

Lena Adams has spent her life struggling to forget her childhood in Reece, the small town which nearly destroyed her. She's made a new life for herself as a police detective in Heartsdale, a hundred miles away – but nothing could prepare her for the violence which explodes when she is forced to return. A vicious murder leaves a young woman incinerated beyond recognition. And Lena is the only suspect.

When Heartsdale police chief Jeffrey Tolliver, Lena's boss, receives word that his detective has been arrested, he has no choice but to go to Lena's aid – taking with him his wife, medical examiner Sara Linton. But soon after their arrival, a second victim is found. The town closes ranks. And both Jeffrey and Sara find themselves entangled in a horrifying underground world of bigotry and rage – a violent world which shocks even them. But can they discover the truth before the killer strikes again?

'No one does American small-town evil more chillingly . . . Slaughter tells a dark story that grips and doesn't let go' *The Times*

'Thoroughly gripping' *Daily Mirror*

'Beautifully paced, appropriately grisly, and terrifyingly plausible' *Time Out*

arrow books

Fractured

Karin Slaughter

A broken window. A bloody footprint. A murder hunt begins . . .

When Atlanta housewife Abigail Campano comes home unexpectedly one afternoon, she walks into a nightmare. A broken window, a bloody footprint on the stairs and, most devastating of all, the horrifying sight of her teenage daughter lying dead on the landing, a man standing over her with a bloody knife. The struggle which follows changes Abigail's life forever.

When the local police make a misjudgement which not only threatens the investigation but places a young girl's life in danger, the case is handed over to Special Agent Will Trent of the Criminal Apprehension Team – paired with detective Faith Mitchell, a woman who resents him from their first meeting.

But in the relentless heat of a Georgia summer, Will and Faith realise that they must work together to find the brutal killer who has targeted one of Atlanta's wealthiest, most privileged communities – before it's too late . . .

'Heart-pounding . . . Slaughter brings the same raw energy and brutal violence that distinguishes her Grant County Series . . . to this new series with chilling results, while Trent and Mitchell, a pair of complex and deeply flawed heroes, will leave fans clamouring for the next instalment' *Publishers Weekly*, starred review

arrow books

Genesis

Karin Slaughter

Someone had spent time with her – someone well-practised in the art of pain . . .

Three and a half years ago former Grant County medical examiner Sara Linton moved to Atlanta hoping to leave her tragic past behind her. Now working as a doctor in Atlanta's Grady Hospital, she is starting to piece her life together. But when a severely wounded young woman is brought in to the emergency room, she finds herself drawn back into a world of violence and terror. The woman has been hit by a car but, naked and brutalised, it's clear that she has been the prey of a twisted mind.

When Special Agent Will Trent of the Criminal Investigation Team returns to the scene of the accident, he stumbles on a torture chamber buried deep beneath the earth. And this hidden house of horror reveals a ghastly truth – Sara's patient is just the first victim of a sick, sadistic killer. Wrestling the case away from the local police chief, Will and his partner Faith Mitchell find themselves at the centre of a grisly murder hunt. And Sara, Will and Faith – each with their own wounds and their own secrets – are all that stand between a madman and his next crime.

arrow books

Broken

Karin Slaughter

The cruellest of deaths. The worst of betrayals. The deadliest of cases . . .

When the body of a young woman is discovered deep beneath the icy waters of Lake Grant, a note left under a rock by the shore points to suicide. But within minutes, it becomes clear that this is no suicide. It's a brutal, cold-blooded murder.

All too soon, former Grant County medical examiner Sara Linton – home for Thanksgiving after a long absence – finds herself unwittingly drawn into the case. The chief suspect is desperate to see her, but when she arrives at the local police station she is met with a horrifying sight – he lies dead in his cell, the words 'Not me' scrawled across the walls.

Something about his confession doesn't add up and, deeply suspicious of Lena Adams, the detective in charge, Sara immediately calls in the Georgia Bureau of Investigation. Shortly afterwards, Special Agent Will Trent is brought in from his vacation to investigate. But he is immediately confronted with a wall of silence. Grant County is a close-knit community with loyalties and ties that run deep. And the only person who can tell the truth about what really happened is dead . . .

arrow books

Martin Misunderstood

Karin Slaughter

A darkly comic tale about Mr Less-Than-Average in an average world.

Crime fiction obsessive Martin Reed is the proverbial butt of everyone's jokes. Working as a glorified accountant at Southern Toilet Supply and still living with his mother, he has become resigned to the world in which he lives – the school bullies now pick on him in the workplace, women still spurn him and his arch enemy is now his supervisor.

But then he arrives at work one morning to find the police on site. A co-worker has been brutally murdered and her body abandoned in a ditch. And the overwhelming evidence points to Martin – especially when he can't or won't admit that he has an alibi.

When a second victim is found in the company bathroom, things really conspire against Martin. The one bright star on his otherwise bleak horizon is the beautiful and sympathetic Detective Anther Albada, but even she's beginning to have her doubts about his innocence. Could Martin be guilty? Or is he just misunderstood?

arrow books

Like a Charm

Ed. by Karin Slaughter

One bracelet, sixteen charms . . .

Desire leaves a man destroyed . . . a young girl's curiosity reveals secrets better left hidden . . . jealousy drives a woman insane . . . ambition leads to a curious exchange . . . an uncanny likeness changes two lives forever . . . the hand of fate lies buried in the past . . .

From nineteenth-century Georgia, where the bracelet is forged in fire, to wartime Leeds, the seedy underside of London's Soho, a Manhattan taxi, the frozen cliffs of Nova Scotia and back to Georgia, each writer weaves a gripping story of murder, betrayal and intrigue.

Karin Slaughter, Emma Donoghue, Peter Robinson, Fidelis Morgan, Lynda La Plante, Lee Child, Mark Billingham, Denise Mina, John Harvey, Kelley Armstrong, John Connolly, Jane Haddam, Laura Lippman, Peter Moore Smith, Jerrilyn Farmer

'It's fascinating to see some of my favourite crime novelists coming together to create a taut, tense thriller; each chapter stands alone as a powerful story, yet they also combine seamlessly into a great read. Genuinely gripping'
Harlan Coben

arrow books

THE POWER OF READING